THE EDEN [INHERITANCE]

The Eden Inheritance is [...]
novel (she also wrote t[... under the name of]
Jade Shannon). Her more recent novels include
Daughter of Riches and *Deception and Desire*. Janet
Tanner lives near Bath with her husband and their
German shepherd dog, Charlie. She has two
daughters.

THE EDEN INHERITANCE

Janet Tanner

ARROW

Published by Arrow Books in 1995

1 3 5 7 9 10 8 6 4 2

© Janet Tanner 1994

First published in the United Kingdom by Century in 1994

Arrow Books Limited
20 Vauxhall Bridge Road, London, SW1V 2SA

Random House Australia (Pty) Limited
20 Alfred Street, Milsons Point, Sydney,
New South Wales 2061, Australia

Random House New Zealand Limited
18 Poland Road, Glenfield
Auckland 10, New Zealand

Random House, South Africa (Pty) Limited
PO Box 337, Bergvlei, South Africa

A CIP catalogue record for this book is available from the
British Library

Random House UK Limited Reg. No. 954009

Papers used by Random House UK are natural, recyclable
products made from wood grown in sustainable forests. The
manufacturing processes conform to the environmental
regulations of the country of origin.

ISBN 0 09 919121 0

Printed and bound in Great Britain by
Bookmarque Ltd, Croydon, Surrey

And the Lord God planted a garden eastward in Eden.

Genesis

Damnosa hereditas.
Ruinous inheritance.

Gaius (2nd century AD)

These two
Imparadised in one another's arms,
The happier Eden, shall enjoy their fill
Of bliss on bliss.

John Milton

ACKNOWLEDGMENTS

My grateful thanks to Elizabeth Buchan, who shared with me her knowledge of the Resistance; and to Kay Crooke, who helped me with research into the Charente region – and tasted some cognac at the same time!

But most especially to Gerry Gowan, whose experiences whilst flying as a professional pilot in the Caribbean gave me the original idea, and who not only helped me think of the book's title, answered my constant flow of questions without a word of complaint, and read the finished manuscript for me, but also risked life and limb to teach me to fly!

PROLOGUE

'LILLI! LILLI — COME here a moment! I want to speak to you.'
The little girl, who had been trying to sneak unnoticed into
the villa, paused like a gazelle in flight, long dark hair inherited
from her South American mother flying in the stiff afternoon
breeze blowing in off the Caribbean, black-brown eyes huge and
round in her small olive-skinned face. The breeze was scented now
by frangipani and pineapple, bougainvillaea and nutmeg, all the
exotic perfumes of the island mixed together into one intoxicating
cocktail, but Lilli scarcely noticed. It was, to her, simply the way
things were, a small part of her world. She had known nothing else
and though in years to come those perfumes would always evoke
for her, more powerfully than any photograph ever could, a
bittersweet nostalgic memory of the island where she had been
born and raised, for the moment she simply took them for granted.

Besides, Lilli had more important things on her mind. Mainly,
how she would explain herself to her father; why she had been
playing with Josie again when he had strictly forbidden it. Josie
was her friend, at eight just a year older than Lilli herself. When
they were little, Josie's mother, Martha, had been a maid at the villa
and she had brought Josie with her so that the two little girls could
amuse one another while she worked. But that had been in the
days before Lilli's own mother had gone away.

Lilli's small face clouded as the memories came rushing in:
Mama, with her long dark hair, so very like Lilli's own, her
jangling bracelets and her scarlet-tipped nails; Mama with her
irrepressible gaiety and the aura of glamour which gave her a
quality of elusive desirability as if she were a film star or a royal
princess, not an ordinary mortal at all. Lilli had adored her just as

she had adored Jorge, her father's business partner, who had often been on the island in those days and with whom, in memory, her mother was inextricably linked; and she knew without question that her father had adored her too. When Mama had said it was permissible for her to play with Josie, it had been.

'Lilli needs company of her own age,' she had said, and Daddy had smiled and concurred.

But now things were different. One terrible night Lilli's safe little world had turned upside down in a scarlet-tainted maelstrom of horror and grief which she tried never to think about but which returned in nightmares to haunt her.

Mama was dead, Patsy, Lilli's nurse, had told her, and even though she had glimpsed Mama that night lying on the floor, she could scarcely take in the finality of it. Lilli had once seen the corpse of a turtle on the beach and its horrible sprawled stillness and the foul smell that emanated from it had frightened and disgusted her. Mama couldn't be like the turtle, surely? But Patsy would say little by way of explanation and Daddy said nothing at all. He had shut himself away for weeks, only to emerge gaunter, greyer and more morose.

Jorge had disappeared from her life too – he was looking after their business enterprises elsewhere, Daddy had said, but he seemed as reluctant to talk about Jorge as he was to talk about Mama.

From that day on, it seemed to Lilli, Daddy had changed. There was a remoteness about him now that made him quite unapproachable and a sternness which, although it was not new, was now not tempered by Mama's softness and sense of fun.

'It's not right for you to play with the locals now, Lilli,' he had informed her one day. 'You are too big for that sort of nonsense.'

'But Daddy . . .'

'Josie is the daughter of one of the maids. I don't want you having any more to do with her.'

'Then who will I play with?'

'You have your dolls, you have your books, you have everything you need to keep you entertained. Far more than Josie or any of the other locals have.'

But not so much fun, Lilli had thought, though even she had not dared to say it.

'Soon you will be at school in Caracas. Then you will meet other girls like yourself. You will make plenty of friends then – suitable ones.'

But Lilli was not quite the obedient child her father thought her. Within her sunny nature was a streak of rebelliousness and a liking for getting her own way. Whenever she could escape without being noticed, and sometimes, it has to be said, with Patsy's connivance, she would run away across the beautifully manicured lawns which surrounded the villa to the far side of the island where Josie lived in the shanty town of tin huts and corrugated-iron shacks which housed the black servants – the maids, the cooks and the labourers. There she whiled away the long hot days of summer playing all the games that a child could not play alone. When the rains came and the river flowed down its narrow bed they would chase one another from stepping stone to stepping stone; when it was hot and dry they hid in the thick croton hedges, spying on those who passed by and giggling at their own daring. They built their own little tree house with some old curtains Lilli had begged from the housekeeper, they scavenged for bits of broken pottery to serve as plates, and then pretended to entertain Lilli's favourite doll, Rosita, with her china face and go-to-sleep eyes, and Josie's home-made rag doll, Maisie. They searched for eggs which the scraggly hens laid in the hedges around the dusty compound when they got broody, they drank milk, warm from the goats, and ate fresh pineapple and mango and bananas. Sometimes Lilli was missing from the villa for hours but Daddy did not seem to notice. He was always engrossed in his business concerns and occupied with the strangers who came and went. Lilli did not know what Daddy's business was and she did not ask. She simply accepted that he was very rich and very busy: the trappngs of wealth she took as much for granted as she did the delights of the island, the busyness simply meant she was free to do as she liked.

Usually Lilli could creep back into the villa without Daddy ever knowing she had been gone at all. Today was the exception. As Lilli skirted the big salon she heard him calling to her in the cultured yet guttural accents of the German homeland he had not seen for more than a decade, and she stopped guiltily, knowing that now he had seen her there was no escape.

The salon, which ran the full depth of the villa, was totally open along the side which fronted the lawns. At this point room became veranda, floor became patio, though a trellis over which bougainvillaea twined and rioted formed a roof of sorts to provide shelter from the sun. Lilli walked in between the slatted wooden panels which could, if so desired, be closed to divide the inside of the villa from the outside, a long-legged child in vermilion shorts and a vermilion-and-white spotted suntop, bare feet thrust into chunky-soled flipflops.

'Where have you been, Lilli? Patsy has been looking everywhere for you.'

Lilli bit her lip, though she suspected Patsy had only *pretended* to look for her — a really thorough search and she would have known very well where Lilli could be found.

'I'm sorry, Daddy . . .' She paused, expecting him to question her further and wondering how she could avoid telling him the whole truth. But instead he only sighed, a strange dry explosion that was halfway to being a laugh, except that Daddy never really laughed.

'Oh Lilli, Lilli, what shall I do with you?'

But he did not sound angry, merely regretful.

Lilli scuffed the toe of her flipflop into the rim of one of the marble tiles which covered the floor.

'I don't know, Daddy.'

'No, neither do I. Still, never mind that now. Come over here.'

He held out his hand to her, a tall man in a royal-blue shirt and cream slacks, his bearing aristocratic and erect in spite of the slight limp which was apparent when he walked. Otto Brandt was fifty- six years old but it would have been difficult to put an age to him. His hair was prematurely snow white, his skin tanned to a rich brown by the Caribbean sun, his eyes the startling clear blue of the true Aryan. If one noticed only that well-toned body Otto could have passed for a man twenty years younger; look into the eyes and the wealth of experience and life lived made him much older.

Lilli, of course, cared nothing for her father's age. He was, quite simply, Daddy, stern, sometimes unapproachable, yet with a surprising capacity for tenderness where she was concerned. In the last resort Lilli knew, without acknowledging it, that she could wind him around her little finger.

This, however, she judged, was not the time to try. Obediently she went into the salon.

'What is it, Daddy?'

'I want to talk to you.'

After the brightness of the sunshine outside it was dim in the salon; Lilli, her eyes not yet accustomed to the change in the light, could not read the expression on his face. But even if she had been able to see his features clearly it did not necessarily mean she could have guessed at his mood. Otto Brandt was nothing if not enigmatic.

He put an arm around her shoulders now, leading her to a chaise, covered in soft green velvet, which might have been more at home in the drawing room of a French château or an English castle than here in this luxurious but undeniably alfresco salon.

'I have to go away for a little while, Lilli.'

'Oh?' She was sorry, but not surprised. For as long as she could remember Daddy had gone away on business trips at fairly regular intervals. 'Where are you going?'

He smiled and tapped her small straight nose.

'That's not something you need to know. I should only be gone for a few weeks, but one never knows. It might be longer. Whichever, I want you to promise to be a good girl for me while I am away.'

'Of course, Daddy!' But already she was thinking of the glorious days she would be able to enjoy with Josie. 'You'll be back before I have to go away to school, though, won't you?'

'Of course. Yes, I am sure I shall. I just wanted to tell you, Lilli, that . . . your daddy loves you very much.'

Something in the way he said it frightened her suddenly; a prickle of intense cold ran down her sun-warmed spine.

'I know that, Daddy.'

'Of course you do. And something else. Supposing, just supposing, something should happen to me, you know that you are well provided for.'

The prickle became worse, fingers of burning ice.

'What do you mean, Daddy? If something should happen to you?'

He took her hand, his long fingers closing over her small brown ones.

'I'm not planning on leaving you for a long time yet, Lilli, but one never knows. This is a very uncertain world. It is best to be prepared.'

Lilli had begun to tremble violently. Mama had gone away. Jorge had gone away. She could not bear it if Daddy went away too. Oh please! I'll never again wish I could be free to play with Josie all the time just as long as Daddy doesn't go away too! Lilli prayed.

'Daddy . . .'

Daddy smiled, the wide curve of his well-shaped mouth making him look young and handsome again.

'Don't look so frightened, little one. I didn't mean to scare you. But I want you to understand that this will one day all be yours. You will want for nothing.'

With a wide sweep of his hand he indicated the salon and its contents. Lilli's face puckered.

'I don't understand.'

'No, I don't suppose you do. You take it all for granted, don't you? You have no idea of the value of the treasures in this room. You see the silver candlesticks and the bronze statuette of Ceres, goddess of the harvest, and the pretty little Louis XIV clock? Together they are probably worth a king's ransom. I know they mean nothing to you now but one day you will love them as I do. And if hard times should ever come . . .'

His voice tailed away. Now, with her eyes growing more accustomed to the dim light, Lilli could see just how serious was the expression on his handsome face, marred only by a long silver scar which ran from the corner of one eye down his cheek and which now seemed to stand out more vividly than ever.

'I do like them, Daddy,' she said, eager suddenly to please him. She looked around, trying to see the treasures through his eyes but aware only of items she had grown up with but never been allowed to touch. Then her glance lighted on just one of them and she brightened. 'I like the picture – you know I do.'

'The picture . . .' He followed her gaze. 'Ah, you mean the triptych. Yes, it's beautiful, isn't it?'

He got up, taking her hand and leading her across the marble-tiled floor to where the triptych hung. Intricately painted, the three panels arranged so that the softly diffused light caught the rich colours and made them glow, the triptych portrayed the life and death at the stake of Joan of Arc, the Maid of Orleans. Lilli looked up at it. She did like the picture – or triptych as Daddy called it. It fascinated her, although it also frightened her a little.

'Supposing I say that it is yours *now*, Lilli – would that make you feel better?'

'Mine!'

'Yes. It must stay where it is, of course, but it can be Lilli's triptych. Not many little girls of your age own something so beautiful or so precious. Doesn't that make you feel special?'

Lilli gazed up at the triptych, awed, and suddenly yes, she did feel better.

Not because she was concerned with its value or even with its artistic worth, for such things were beyond her, but because somehow she knew in that moment that the triptych was going to play a very important part in her life. Mysteriously it was almost as if the future had reached out and touched her with a teasing finger, bestowing on her all the glory and the suffering portrayed in the picture. It did not occur to her then, or for many years to come, to wonder where the treasures had come from or what story they might have to tell. Lilli's fingers curled trustingly into her father's.

'Thank you, Daddy,' she said.

PART ONE
Holocaust

I

Bristol, 1971

THE TWIN-ENGINED Piper Navajo touched down smoothly,
wheels kissing runway with scarcely a judder, and slowed to
turn on to the taxiway.

In the pilot's seat Guy de Savigny let go the controls, steering
with the rudder pedals as he attended to the shut-down pre-
liminaries whilst the aircraft was still rolling. The hour was late;
the runway markers and the lights blazing out of the control tower
and airport buildings, to which he was heading, were the only
sparks of illumination in the velvet darkness now that the rolling
hills hid the neon glow of the city from his view. Guy manoeuvred
the aircraft on to the apron and parked in one of the unloading
bays. Now that he had landed he felt suddenly tired. Whilst flying
the need for complete concentration kept him on his toes, and with
no first officer in the co-pilot's seat the workload was high enough
to necessitate his remaining alert throughout the whole flight.
There had been times when Guy, who suffered from occasional
migraines, had brought the plane in and not even noticed the
needles of white-hot fire in his temples until the shut-down checks
were completed, so total was the concentration demanded of him.
But that was the way he liked it. It was the reason he had remained
a freelance commercial pilot instead of moving on, as many of his
friends had done, to the big airlines. There might be prestige in
being a captain or first officer with BOAC or British Caledonian.
The logbooks of those who chose to go with the big boys might
read like a world gazetteer. But how much did they see of their
exotic destinations? One hotel room is very like another, however
luxurious, and Guy felt, with a slight edge of scorn, that the way
they earned their fat salaries could hardly be described as flying –

not flying as he knew it. He would go crazy, he thought, if he had to rely on a computer to do all his work for him, and the very idea of sitting in a cockpit for up to eight hours with nothing more stimulating than the *Telegraph* crossword to occupy his mind made him shudder. As for the money, that was scarcely a consideration. Guy was not exactly wealthy yet, but he would be one day. As heir to the de Savigny estates in Charente, and all that entailed, a nest egg and a pension were the last things on his mind.

Not, of course, that flying the mail from Aberdeen to Bristol five nights a week exactly consituted a dream job. To begin with it had not been so bad; the Navajo was an aeroplane Guy had been itching to get his hands on and there had been other routes to vary the monotony – to Oslo and Antwerp, St Malo and Amsterdam. But things had changed; the company he worked for on a freelance basis had arranged their schedules so that he now found himself regularly on the Aberdeen–Bristol route and he was beginning to tire of it.

What the hell is the matter with me? he sometimes wondered when the familiar restlessness prickled beneath his skin. Why do I always have to be looking for something different, some new avenue to explore or mountain to climb? Why can't I, for once, be satisfied and stay satisfied? But he couldn't. He was thirty-one years old and he still felt as eager to go out and conquer the world as he had been at nineteen, with not the slightest desire to put down roots anywhere.

Perhaps, he thought, it was because he knew he had the de Savigny inheritance hanging over him. When his grandfather died he would be the next Baron de Savigny. It was an awesome prospect and not one he relished, but it was a destiny from which it was impossible to escape.

Then again perhaps it was because he was the product of two cultures, two countries, with both French and English blood running in his veins. Guy had been brought up in England but he had always spent a good portion of each summer at the Château de Savigny with his grandparents. Kathryn, his mother, had insisted on it. But the division of his time between England and France had unsettled him. Far from feeling as much at home in Charente as in England, as Kathryn had intended, he had actually felt at home in neither. In both countries he was something of a foreigner, he thought wryly, his English upbringing marking him out as different in Charente in spite of the respect accorded him as the future Baron, his heritage a constant pinprick of discomfort when he was amongst his English friends. As a child at public school in England he had been ragged mercilessly once his peers had ferreted out the reason for his foreign name – until he had learned to stand up for himself. Guy had learned early to use his fists; it had landed him in all kinds of trouble but the word had soon got around amongst the other boys that to jeer at Guy de Savigny was to get a bloody nose, and they had come to respect him for it. But there was still the odd remark, the odd occasion when Guy was only too well aware of his divided loyalties, and that strange sense of lack of belonging had followed him into adulthood.

Being half French had its advantages too, of course. The fluently bilingual Guy had found French lessons so totally unncessary that he had been able to spend them reading his favourite space-travel novels under the desk. In adult life as a pilot he had few communication problems when he flew abroad – by using one or the other language he could usually make himself understood.

Then again his mixed blood and his French name seemed to make him attractive to women – at least, that was what Guy put his success with them down to. He was always faintly surprised by the attention they paid to him, underestimating the effect his dark good looks and slim but powerful frame could have on the most sophisticated and experienced of them. He was too used to the startlingly blue eyes that stared back at him from the shaving mirror each morning, and the aquiline nose and firm jaw did not, in his opinion, constitute conventional male beauty. He had no idea of how well the white shirt and black uniform jacket with the captain's insignia suited him, and the easy-going confidence of his manner was totally unconscious.

But Guy seldom took advantage of the opportunities that presented themselves to him in this direction. He liked the company of women well enough and was a good and generous lover. What he did not like was the way they invariably tried to tie him down. To Guy, freedom was the most important considera-tion. Perhaps, he thought – when he did think about it, which was seldom – perhaps it was knowing that the baronage, with all its inherent responsibilities and restrictions, was lying in wait for him that made him so averse to any other ties. But for whatever reason, whenever a woman began to show signs of possessiveness his instinctive reaction was to back away – fast.

Tonight, however, the problems that involvement with a woman could cause were the last thing on his mind. The only consideration looming large was getting back to his bachelor flat on the other side of town, pouring himself a large whisky, running a bath and then falling into bed – alone.

He parked the Navajo, watched the post office workers unload and then locked up the plane and went into the airport building.

At this time of night, two-thirty a.m., in the middle of winter, the concourse was as deserted as the runway had been, the airline pigeonholes shuttered like sleeping eyes, the small shop and bureau de change locked up for the night. Guy's footsteps echoed hollowly on the tiled floor. A security guard was standing in the doorway smoking and looking out at the stars. Guy said good night to him and walked across to the staff car park where a few vehicles glimmered with a light dusting of frost.

As he neared the car park Guy heard the hollow rasp and dying whine of an engine that someone was trying, unsuccessfully, to start up. Some poor sod has got trouble, he thought – it didn't sound good.

His path took him close to the car in question and as he approached, the driver gave up the struggle and got out, closing the door with a slam.

'Having problems?' Guy called.

'Yes – damned thing won't start. Hey – Guy – is that you?'

'Yes,' Guy said, faintly surprised. 'Who's that?' The car park was badly lit and his tired eyes had not yet fully accustomed themselves to the dark.

'Bill Walker, you dozy bugger!'

'Bill!'

They had trained together in their early flying days, racing one another for their private pilot's licences, then both instructing with the same club as they strove to accumulate the hours they needed to progress to the next stage and the next. Their paths had diverged when they began professional commercial flying but occasionally they would bump into one another on an airport concourse, in the briefing room, or in a bar.

6

'What are you doing here?' Guy asked. 'The last I heard you were in exotic climes – the Caribbean, wasn't it?'

'The Windward Islands, yes.'

'Beats England in the middle of January, I'd have thought.'

'Yep. Especially a bloody car park at two in the morning when the car won't start. You haven't got jump leads by any chance, have you?'

'Sorry, no. I used to have but I think I must have left my boot unlocked and somebody helped themselves. I've never replaced them.'

'Well, with motors like you drive, I don't suppose you have much need of them. We can't all afford E-types, though.'

Guy ignored the gibe.

'So what's the problem? Flat battery?'

'I think so. I left the car here while I went for a session with some of the boys and I must have left my lights on. They dropped me off out on the road so they'd gone before I realised I had problems. I don't think I'll get her going tonight. You couldn't give me a lift, I suppose?'

'I was just going to offer. Where are you headed?'

'I was intending to drive up to Gloucester – I've got a cottage there. But don't worry, I'm not asking you to take me home, just into town so I can get myself a room for what's left of the night. You go through town, don't you?'

'Yes – well, the outskirts, anyway. But there's no need for you to go booking into hotels. Why don't you come home with me?'

'Are you sure?' Bill managed to sound surprised and in the dark Guy smiled to himself – he was fairly sure a bed for the night was exactly what Bill had been angling for. He didn't mind, though. It was good to see the old son of a bitch. He'd always liked Bill.

'Come on. Lock up that heap of junk, as you call it. Let's get going. I've had a long flight and I'm tired if you're not.'

'You're a pal,' Bill replied with alacrity.

'So – you haven't told me what you're doing back in this country,' Guy said, pouring whisky into two tumblers and handing one to Bill.

'I'm getting married. In a fortnight's time, as a matter of fact.'

'Are you? Well, congratulations, I suppose. Diane, is it?'

7

'Yep. I reckon it's time I made an honest woman of her.'

'But why come home?' Guy threw himself down on the low sofa and levered his feet up on to the coffee table. 'Why not take Diane out to the Caribbean with you?'

'She won't come. Her mother hasn't been too well and she doesn't want her only daughter on the other side of the world.'

'Mother-in-law trouble already! Watch it, Bill!'

'It's not only that.' Bill took a drink of his whisky, his good-natured face, tanned from the Caribbean sunshine, serious for once. 'The Caribbean is a lovely spot, I grant you, but the pay's not that fantastic. I was hard put to it to keep myself in the manner to which I like to be accustomed. Supporting a wife as well would stretch things to the limits.'

'Pity.'

'Yes, but there you are. All good things come to an end, as you'll find out one day.'

'Not too soon, I hope.'

'How is the lovely Wendy?'

Guy grimaced slightly at the mention of his girlfriend in the context of marriage. He was fond of Wendy, she was attractive, she was intelligent, and he enjoyed her company. But of late she had been dropping a few too many hints that she would like to put their relationship on a more permanent basis, and her thinly veiled desire to get a ring on her finger was frankly scaring the hell out of him. At his age he should be ready to settle down, he sometimes thought, but it did not make the proposition any more attractive. He didn't want to settle down. At least, not with Wendy. The very thought made a hand grip his insides like a steel vice.

'She's fine,' he said noncommittally. 'She works pretty hard – being the secretary to the managing director of an up-and-coming company like Arden Electrical makes her a fairly high-powered lady.'

'I thought secretary was just a word for glorified typist.'

'Not as far as Arden is concerned. And Wendy is very ambitious.'

'You hope. Just so long as she doesn't turn her ambition to hooking you. You're a confirmed bachelor, aren't you, Guy?'

'You could say that. I like my freedom, certainly.'

'And what are you doing now – workwise, that is?'

'Flying the mail five nights a week. And getting a bit fed up with it.'

'So why don't you go after the job I'm jacking in – especially if you want to escape from Wendy's clutches? It would suit you down to the ground. All the sunshine you could wish for, and the money wouldn't bother you, would it?' Bill was glancing enviously around the flat, noticing that whilst it was rather untidy and certainly not the height of luxury, Guy certainly managed to live in a style way above that which most freelance commercial pilots could afford. The wherewithal for that did not come entirely from flying the mail, he knew.

'I was thinking about going to the States, I have to admit. Or maybe Australia.'

'The Caribbean is better. St Lucia, St Vincent, Mustique, Union Island ... need I go on? I was based on an island called Madrepora. The work is mainly island-hopping, a sort of glorified taxi service from one tiny little airstrip to another, and all surrounded by sea so blue you wouldn't believe it. Sometimes you get to fly celebrities, too. They like their holiday homes in the sun, do the beautiful people.'

Guy drained his glass and reached for the bottle to refuel it.

'I'm not interested in celebrities, Bill. They bore me. And right now, if you don't mind, I think I'm ready for bed.'

Bill, however, full of the *bonhomie* that came not only from Guy's whisky but from all the others he had drunk earlier in the evening, was not ready to take the hint.

'There are some amazing characters out there, you know. Nobs and snobs and pop stars, all with their own little hideaways. And they're not the only ones taking advantage of the seclusion, either. I reckon there's a few international criminals living in luxury on their ill-gotten gains, and some still operating. It's a haven for them.'

'Sure, but ... another time, eh, Bill?' Guy stood up. His back was aching and a dull throb of tiredness had started in his temples. He hoped he was not going to have a migraine.

'There was one I thought was particularly odd,' Bill continued, unabashed. 'A German geezer who owns Madrepora, I think. There's nothing much there except his mansion and a hotel. I used to have to fly the guests in sometimes. They were all Germans too, and highly suspicious, if you ask me. Of a certain age, if you get my meaning.'

'No, I don't.' Guy was beginning to be irritated by Bill's persistent garrulousness and regretting his own impulse to offer him a bed for the night. 'What are you getting at?'

Bill stretched comfortably.

'War criminals, my son. At least, that's what I think. A lot of them escaped to South America, didn't they, and I reckon that's where these hotel guests come from. Even war criminals living in exile need a holiday sometimes and where better than a hotel on a remote island owned by one of their own? If some of them didn't have a previous existence as high-ranking Nazis then I'm a Dutchman. They all have new identities now, of course, but they still like to keep a low profile. The last thing they want is to be recognised and brought back to face trial. The bastards.'

'Well, if the job includes playing chauffeur to a load of Nazis I certainly don't want it,' Guy said shortly. 'I'm half French, remember? A lot of my countrymen – not to mention my own family – suffered too much at their hands for me ever to be able to forgive them.'

'Christ, yes. I had forgotten. Didn't they kill your father?'

'They did. My father and my uncle were both shot for resisting. And not content with that, the bastards turned my grandparents out of their home, lived there themselves, and then looted the place when they saw the war was going against them. God knows what happened to the treasures – things that had been in the family for generations just disappeared. They got them out of the country, I suppose.'

'To places like South America and the Caribbean.' Bill shifted himself to an even more comfortable position. 'I went to this German geezer's place once – he invited me for drinks. Just drinks, mind you. I thought I'd be getting dinner as well and didn't bother to eat, but no, at seven-thirty sharp I was thrown out – still hungry. That's the form over there, I've since learned. But at least I got a good insight into how the other half live. I've never forgotten that villa. Beautiful place – and stacked to the eaves with treasures I wouldn't mind betting were looted from France. Silverware, porcelain, a bronze, a triptych . . .'

'A triptych?' Guy repeated, his tiredness forgotten. 'What kind of triptych?'

'Is there more than one kind? Very old, glowing colours, religious pictures highlighted with gold leaf . . . you know the sort of thing.'

'Yes,' Guy said. 'I know.' He was experiencing a strange prickling sensation, as if an electric force field had come into action on his skin. 'It couldn't have been scenes from the life of the Maid of Orleans, could it?'

'Could have been, I suppose. I didn't study it that closely. But now you come to mention it, I think I do remember a bonfire.'

Guy ignored the irreligious reference to St Joan's burning at the stake.

'What did you say this German's name was?'

'Brandt. Otto Brandt. But I don't suppose that's his real name.'

'What did he look like?'

'Tall, white hair, scar on his left cheek, a limp. Why?'

'You don't happen to have a photograph, I suppose?'

'God no! I only met him two or three times – him and his wife. I did hear he had a daughter – very beddable by all accounts – but I never got to meet her at all, more's the pity. She's in the States, I understand, but I thought it was a bit peculiar she never came home for holidays. And there were rumours that there was something funny going on on the island.'

'Funny? What do you mean – funny?'

'Couldn't really say. Just the suggestion that there was more going on there than met the eye – something not quite as above board as they'd have you believe.'

'The German visitors, you mean?'

'No, no, nothing to do with them. Something else entirely . . .'

'Well it's the Germans I'm interested in,' Guy said. 'And your Herr Otto Brandt, with his triptych, in particular.'

'What are you getting at?'

Guy drank savagely at his whisky.

'I am probably going quite mad. But for one moment there I wondered if you might actually have stumbled on the Nazi who was responsible for my father's death.'

Bill whistled softly.

'Bit of a long shot, surely? I mean – there must be hundreds of them scattered around the globe.'

'True. But from the sound of it your Nazi was probably a high-ranking officer, which narrows the field a bit – the one I'd like to get my hands on was responsible for the whole district where my family live. And when you mentioned the triptych – well, that certainly rings bells.'

'Your family lost one?'

'Yes. Very old, very valuable. Depicting scenes from the life of the Maid of Orleans. If the one you saw showed a bonfire, as you called it, I should think there is a pretty fair chance that it was St Joan burning at the stake, wouldn't you say? Most triptychs depict the crucifixion or the Blessed Virgin Mary, not bonfires.'

'Hmm. Well, fate does play some pretty odd tricks sometimes. If something is meant to be . . . And in any case, even if Brandt isn't your man, there are a fair few coming in and out from South America, as I told you. Any one of them could be.'

'Or then again, might not be.' Guy drained his glass and set it down. 'I'm going to bed. Some of us have to work tomorrow. I'll show you your room.'

This time Bill, too, rose.

'Yeah. Sorry to have kept you up, Guy. Kick me out as early as you like in the morning. I have to see about getting that car of mine going and Diane will be wondering what the hell has happened to me.' He stretched with the slight clumsiness of a man who has had a little too much to drink. 'Don't forget, if you change your mind about wanting my job I'll put in a word for you. But don't leave it too long. There will be plenty of others who will find the prospect appealing, even if you don't.'

Guy nodded. 'Thanks. I'll think about it. But not tonight. All I want at the moment is to get my head down and catch up on some sleep.'

But he could not sleep. Tired as he was, his mind was racing now in wild erratic circles and he lay, staring at a patch of light on the ceiling thrown by the streetlamp outside the window and slanting in through the imperfectly drawn curtains, thinking about what Bill said.

It was crazy, of course. The probability that the German whose island Bill had visited in the Caribbean should be one and the same as the man who had devastated the lives of his own family was so remote as to be almost nonexistent. Yet Guy could not dismiss the possibility, however unlikely. For all the prosaic outer layers of his personality, deep inside a small insistent part of him believed in fate. The bastard had to be somewhere. He had never been caught. Somewhere on God's earth he was living out his life – a life he had denied to Charles, Guy's father. Why not this remote Caribbean island? Why not this – what had Bill called it? – Madrepora?

Guy rucked the pillow up under his neck and closed his eyes. Otto von Rheinhardt. That was the name of the Nazi who had ordered his father's death. It was a name that had haunted him ever since he was a little boy, a name that his grandfather always spat out with hatred. Otto von Rheinhardt. Guy had often thought that if he could find him he would like to kill him. But Otto had disappeared, back into the sewers from which he had come, and Guy had never expected to be given the opportunity.

Was it possible now that fate had presented him with Otto von Rheinhardt on a plate? In the silent dark he seemed to hear his grandfather's voice, deep, resonant, cultured French, relating as he so often did the horror and the atrocities and sufferings his countrymen had endured at the hands of the German oppressors.

'They were devils, *mon petit*,' he would say, and Guy, curled up at his grandfather's feet, would listen with a breathlessness that was part fascination, part revulsion. He didn't like the stories, they gave him nightmares, but in some strange way they brought the father he had never known a little closer.

Guy had been only three years old when his father had died, and Kathryn, his English mother, had always been curiously reluctant to talk about him. She had told him of course that Charles had died a hero and explained that she had allowed Guillaume, his father, to keep the Croix de Guerre which he had been awarded posthumously because she knew how much it would mean to him. Even as a very small boy Guy had realised instinctively that remembering caused her pain, and because he loved her he had not pressed her, though sometimes his curiosity and the need to know had been almost more than he could bear.

In the pretty cottage where they lived on the edge of the New Forest there was not one picture of his father, not one single memento of the years in France before Guy's birth and the early part of his life, though the photographs and keepsakes that marked his growing-up in England abounded.

Guy had thought it very odd and once he had asked her about it.

'I couldn't bring anything with me,' she had said, her voice, in contrast to her usual vivaciousness, flat and curiously emotionless. 'I left in a great hurry.'

'Too much of a hurry to bring *anything*?'

'Yes. I'm afraid so. It was wartime, Guy. The Germans were everywhere. One didn't have time to worry about possessions. I brought you. That was all that mattered.'

'What about Papa? Why didn't he come too?'

'He couldn't. There wasn't room in the plane. And in any case he wouldn't have wanted to leave Savigny.'

'Not even to be with us?'

'Your father loved you very much. But he had a duty to stay at Savigny to try to look after it and all the people who depended on him. Your father always believed Savigny to be . . . well, a sacred trust. You'll understand that one day.'

'Does it have to be a sacred trust for me too?' Guy already knew that one day he would be the next Baron.

'It will be whatever you choose to make it, Guy, though I hope you won't do so at the expense of your happiness.'

He hadn't known then what she meant and even now, with the insight of a grown man, he was not that much the wiser, though he could guess.

'Well, if you couldn't bring your things with you then, couldn't you have gone back for them after the Germans had gone?' he had asked with the reasonableness of a seven-year-old. 'I would have if I'd left things like . . . well, my toy cars and my petrol pumps and things.' Guy had a collection of tin vehicles, Belisha beacons and other road signs, which he added to obsessively whenever his pocket money allowed.

Kathryn had smiled briefly before her face had grown serious again.

'There was really nothing I wanted that much,' she had said. 'And even if there had been I doubt any of it would have been left after the Germans had finished with the château.'

Guy's small olive-skinned brow had furrowed.

'But there *are* photographs at the château. I know. I've seen them.'

'That's all right then. You can look at them when you're there, can't you? Grandpapa will let you have one if you ask him, I expect.'

And he had to be content with that. But it still bothered him that Kathryn had never been back, wouldn't go, though she packed him off religiously every summer for at least six weeks.

'Why don't you come with me, Mummy?' he had asked once – he missed her dreadfully, though he always had a wonderful time in Charente, with his French grandparents, his Aunt Celestine and Uncle Henri and all the servants and estate workers making a great fuss of him.

'I wouldn't be welcome, Guy,' was all she would say, and he felt, yet again, that he was banging his head against a brick wall.

So every summer he allowed himself to be put in the care of an air hostess and flown to Bordeaux, where one of the members of his French family would be waiting with the car to meet him, a small boy exchanging one world for another, completely, utterly different.

Whenever he arrived in Savigny the château seemed vast, with its enormous vaulted rooms and echoing passageways; when he returned to the New Forest the cottage, two up, two down, appeared even more tiny and cramped than he remembered it. Everything in Savigny was on a grand scale – the château, the grounds, the cars, even the dining table, yards long, around which the whole family gathered for meals – whilst the cottage with its small sunny kitchen, tiny cluttered living room and his bedroom under the eaves, which looked out on a garden bright with roses and delphiniums and bounded by laurel hedges, reminded him a little of his cousin Lise's dolls' house. Except that Lise's dolls' house was much grander and more elaborate.

The way of life was different too. There were servants at Savigny, cooks and maids and gardeners and a chauffeur, not to mention all the workers on the estate, whilst at home in England his mother did everything herself, with the single exception of the laundry, which was done by a woman in the village whose son collected it each Monday and brought it back, clean and neatly ironed, on a Wednesday – or maybe a Thursday if the weather was too wet for easy drying. There were three cars at Savigny, big cars with foreign names, whilst at home his mother had only her little

Austin. Extended meals, several courses of elaborate dishes, pungent with garlic and rich with cream, took the place of the more familiar chops and rissoles and milk puddings, and the days were longer and sunnier, though Guy wondered if that was simply because he was always there in July and August when the English summer, too, was at its height.

But the best difference of all was that he could talk about his father. Here there was no reticence, no anxiety to change the subject. Guy was always given the room that had been his father's when *he* had been a boy, and looking out of the window at the fountains playing in the courtyard and the rooks nesting in the tall poplars that hid the château from the world outside he liked to imagine his father doing just the same.

'Tell me about when you and my father were children,' he would press his Aunt Celestine and she would relate to him the familiar favourite stories of picnics in the woods and swimming parties in the lake, of pony rides and parties, of Monsieur Lacroix, the fussy tutor, and Anne-Marie, the cook, who had allowed them to lick out the bowls when she had finished making her delicious cakes. These were the stories he loved best, painting a picture of a happy time, long ago, before all their lives had been darkened by the shadow of the Nazi invasion.

But he was ready, too, to hear about that, since it went some way to explaining the mystery of what had happened to his father. The story was incomplete, he knew, there were things his grandfather left out just as his mother did because they were too painful, but as he grew older he was able to piece together what his grandfather told him with history as it was written and make at least some sense of the mystery. His father and his Uncle Christian had been engaged in Resistance activities and as a result of this they had been arrested, tortured and shot. Of the three de Savigny children only his Tante Celestine had survived the war, which was why Guy was now heir to the Baronage de Savigny. Knowing that his father had been a hero of the Resistance made Guy glow with pride; he could not understand why his mother was so reluctant to talk about it.

That same childish passion that made his delight in the heroism of his father, even if it had cost his life, also made him burn with fervent hatred of the Nazis. Not only had they robbed him of his father, leaving him with only the fuzziest of memories and the faded photographs which Grandpapa gave him when he asked for them, but they had also stolen a good part of his inheritance, treasures that had graced the château for generations.

'*Cochons*! We should never have trusted their word, even for a moment. They weren't satisfied with the lifeblood of our noble Frenchmen. They had to steal from us too,' Grandpapa would say. 'That pig von Rheinhardt always liked the château, being an animal didn't stop him from having an eye for what is beautiful and he wanted it for himself. He turned us out after your father and uncle were arrested and moved his staff in. And if that wasn't bad enough, when he saw Germany was losing the war he spirited out all the most precious and priceless pieces. God knows how he did it or where they went, he must have had a route planned, perhaps to Switzerland, I don't know. He shouldn't have done it, of course. Anything of value would have become the property of the Third Reich if Germany had won the war. But von Rheinhardt wasn't going to let something like that worry him. He was an arrogant swine – and he was the officer commanding. In the absence of higher authority he did as he liked. And then of course when he realised it was all over and there was no way Hitler was going to end up ruling the whole of the western world as he had planned, von Rheinhardt went the same way as the treasures. By the time the Allies arrived he had long gone. He wasn't going to stay and risk arrest and trial for the terrible things he had done, oh no, not him. He was too clever and too lacking in scruples for that. I expect now he is living somewhere enjoying being surrounded by our heirlooms – the heirlooms that belong in the Château de Savigny, the heirlooms that should, by rights, be yours one day, *mon petit*.'

'What were the heirlooms, Grandpapa?' Guy had asked solemnly.

And Grandpapa had told him – silverware, paintings, cut from their frames, porcelain, miniatures, a bronze statuette of Ceres – and a triptych.

'What is a triptych?' Guy asked. He had never heard the word before.

Grandpapa explained.

'A picture in three parts, Guy. That's why it is called a triptych, from the Greek for threefold, do you understand? The tablets are hinged, like the shutters on the windows. Originally they were used as altar pieces so they depict religious scenes in glowing colours and gold flake. This particular triptych was very special – it showed scenes from the life of the Maid of Orleans. Now I suppose it is giving pleasure to von Reinhardt, wherever he may be. Well, all I can say is I hope it brings him ill-fortune. I'd like to think it was the death of him.'

'How could that be, Grandpapa?'

'There is a story about our triptych that my father used to tell. It had been blessed with holy water by the Pope himself and consecrated for the use of the de Savignys in the private chapel. Twice it was stolen, twice the perpetrators of the crime met a violent end and the triptych was returned to us. The first time it was stolen by a vagrant who had been given shelter; he was found two days later in the woods where he had fallen into a trap set for the animals. The second was at the time of the Revolution. A band of marauding peasants stole it, trying, no doubt, to emulate what was going on in Paris. But they were overcome by troops loyal to the Baron. They were all killed. The man who actually had the triptych in his possession had his throat cut, and the triptych was returned to the château. So you see I'd like to think that history might repeat itself and the triptych bring down a curse on the man who stole it just as it did twice before.' He had smiled sadly. 'I'm just a fanciful old man. I expect that's what you think, isn't it, Guy?'

'No, sir.' Guy had shaken his head, his thick dark hair bouncing around his narrow olive face. 'I think . . . I think . . .'

'Yes?'

'I think it's a wonderful story.'

And that was no more than the truth; the romance of what his grandfather had told him had excited his imagination; it ran through his veins like prickling fire and that night when he was alone in his room, tucked up beneath the soft feather eiderdown, he had thought about it again. A triptych that belonged on the altar in the de Savigny private chapel and which could bring down a curse on whoever possessed it unlawfully; a triptych which would, one day, find its way back to the château where it belonged.

After a while, of course, the magic and excitement of the story had worn off. The triptych did not return to the château and although Grandpapa still told his gruesome stories and bemoaned the loss of both his sons and his heirlooms – the one just as much as the other, Guy thought – he never again mentioned the curse.

Guy had not given it a thought now for years. Von Reinhardt had disappeared and the treasures with him, that was all there was to it. Occasionally, when a bounty-hunter claimed to have found yet another Nazi war criminal in some remote part of the world, Guy thought of von Reinhardt and wondered if he too would one day be tracked down, but for the most part he allowed the war, the Nazi occupation and all it had meant for his family, to slip to the back of his mind.

Now, however, lying sleepless and staring at that little patch of neon light on the ceiling of his bedroom, he found himself thinking of it once more.

Was there a possibility that the German Bill had met might be von Reinhardt, living under an assumed name? Could the triptych he had described be the very one looted with the other treasures from the Château de Savigny?

Perhaps because he was light-headed from tiredness, perhaps because of two large whiskies on an empty stomach, Guy was half inclined to think that it might just be.

2

KATHRYN DE SAVIGNY looked at her son, sitting in her favourite winged Parker Knoll on the opposite side of her fireplace, and found herself wondering yet again why he had come to see her today.

It wasn't that his visits were all that infrequent – irregular, yes, his work as a professional pilot precluded any sort of regularity, but he managed to come about ten times a year, sometimes staying over in the bedroom under the eaves that had been his since early childhood. He often telephoned without any prior arrangement to say he would be in the area, or that he had a couple of days between jobs and would come over if she didn't have other plans. Kathryn was happy with that – she liked to think that Guy still looked on Rose Cottage as his home, and enjoyed the hectic scurrying around to get things ready for him which made a total change from the predictability of her everyday life – planning his favourite meals, making sure there was a bottle of his favourite single malt whisky in the chiffonier and clean sheets on his bed. Even if it meant closing early at the small antique shop she ran in the village she never attempted to put him off. The shop would still be there tomorrow, Guy might not be. Quite apart from the fact that his job could take him anywhere in the world, there was always the shadow of Savigny hanging over her. The Baron, Guy's grandfather, was in his mid-eighties now, and though he was a remarkable man for his age, not even he could last forever. One day in the not-too-distant future he would die, and when he did Guy would become the next Baron, with all that entailed. He would give up his career and go to France, she was certain of it – Guy had the same sense of duty to his heritage that his father had had, and she had done nothing to discourage it. Quite the opposite. She had been careful always to ensure that Guy had as much contact as possible with his paternal grandparents and grew up knowing exactly what would be expected of him when the time came.

Handing so much of her son over to them had not been easy – he had been, after all, all she had left and there had been times when she had wished with all her heart that she could metaphorically pull up the drawbridge and keep him in England, all to herself. But she had known that she must not do that. The de Savignys had suffered enough, it would be wicked to deprive them of their grandson too. And besides, she owed it to Charles to see that the title and heritage that should have been his passed smoothly to his son.

Dear God, he was so like him! Kathryn thought now, looking at Guy – physically like him, at any rate. With only the soft light of the table lamp and the flickering firelight to illuminate the room, it might almost have been Charles sitting there in the chair opposite her. The dark hair, the olive skin, the aquiline nose that was so unmistakably de Savigny, even the build, taut and wiry beneath the baggy jumper and twill trousers, were so like Charles as to almost constitute a reincarnation.

Guy was not so like Charles in character, though. He was stronger, less intense, much more his own man. Though she was not so vain as to take credit for it, there was a great deal of Kathryn in Guy. His inner confidence and ease with himself came from her, as did his stubbornness and refusal to accept defeat. And she had taught him, she hoped, not to be afraid to give and receive love – though so far she had to admit there had been little sign of him finding the lasting happiness with a woman that was her dearest wish for him.

Perhaps that was why he had come today, she thought, hope sparking briefly. Perhaps he was going to tell her he had finally decided to ask Wendy to marry him, but in all honesty she didn't think so. There was a slight edge of wary defensiveness about him that was more in keeping with a confession than the bearing of good news, and surely if there had been someone important in his life she would have had some inkling of it before now.

There was something, though, she was certain of it – had been from the moment he telephoned to tell her he was coming. One aspect of Guy that was very like his father was his transparency –

to her, at any rate. She knew, had always known, when he was keeping something from her, and he was doing it now.

She rose from her chair, a still-slim woman in a nut-brown polo skinny-rib jumper and full-length tweed skirt that nipped her waist and fell smoothly over her hips to make her appear taller than her five feet four inches. She liked to wear long skirts in the evenings and was glad they were all the fashion; there was something very cosy about the feel of the wool swirling gracefully about her legs, and the cottage, for all her efforts, could be draughty in the depths of winter. She crossed to the basket of logs, lifted one out and tossed it on to the fire, pressing it down with the poker until a shower of sparks flew. Firelight flickered on her face, almost unlined in spite of her fifty-three years, and lit the golden lights in her close-cropped hair. Then she straightened, rested one wool-clad elbow against the mantelpiece, and looked directly at her son.

'Don't you think, Guy, that it's time you told me whatever it is you came to say?'

She saw the slight narrowing of his eyes – so slight as to have been virtually unnoticeable to anyone who knew him less well – and knew without question that she had been right.

'You're not in some kind of trouble, are you?' she asked.

'Oh no, nothing like that. I just wanted to talk to you and I don't know quite where to begin.'

'Whyever not? I'm not some kind of ogre, am I? And I'm not easily shocked, either. I've been around too long and seen too much of life for that.'

He smiled briefly. His mother's life here in a sleepy village in Hampshire, with her antique shop and her garden her main interests, scarcely constituted life in the fast lane and it was difficult for him to imagine that it had ever been much different. She had, he thought, been protected from harsh reality for most of her life, born the child of doting, reasonably well-off parents, married briefly into a wealthy respected family with a history that stretched back for hundreds of years, cushioned by the soft cocoon of country life. She had brought him up virtually unaided, it was true, and that, he supposed, could not always have been easy, but still it was hardly the sort of existence to describe as 'seeing life'. Whatever Kathryn had experienced, it seemed to have left scarcely a mark on her, and apart from her occasional explosions of fiery anger, soon over, he could not remember ever seeing her composure dented.

Except when it came to this one subject.

'Because it's something you never want to talk about,' he said.

She stiffened. He saw it in the sudden straightness of her back, the way her hand with its perfectly manicured but unvarnished nails gripped the edge of the mantelpiece.

'I want to talk about the war,' he said, hating the fact that he was distressing her but having to go on anyway.

'Why?' There was a slight tremor, but also the stubbornness he knew so well in her voice. 'The war was over and done with a very long time ago, Guy. Why should you want to talk about it now?'

'Because it's not over and done with as far as I'm concerned. Something has happened, something I want to follow up, but knowing how you feel about all that I didn't want to do it without telling you. And besides, I need your help.'

'What are you talking about, Guy?'

He hesitated. There was no easy way to do this.

'I think it's possible I might have found Otto von Rheinhardt.'

He heard the quick intake of her breath and went on swiftly: 'Look – I know this upsets you, but as I said, I think it's just possible that I might know where he is. He's never been caught, has he? He's never had to answer for his crimes. If he's still alive, then I think it's time he was made to, don't you?'

Her hand was at her throat now, playing nervously with the slender gold chain that hung over the brown wool polo-neck. He did not think he could ever remember having seen her so agitated.

'I've heard about a German living in exile,' he went on. 'A German with a houseful of treasures that sound suspiciously like the ones that went missing from the château. Grandpapa used to tell me about them, all the things that were looted. In particular, there was a triptych . . .'

'The world is full of triptychs. Why on earth should you suppose it's the same one?'

'I don't know. It might not be, of course.' He didn't feel like going into details. 'You're right, it's a very long shot. But all the same, a German of about the right age, living in luxury on a remote Caribbean island with a houseful of what appears to be very

French treasure . . . I want to check it out. This man may not be von Rheinhardt. The triptych and the treasures might not be the ones stolen from Savigny. But I wouldn't mind betting they were stolen from someone. If I don't get our stuff back, then perhaps someone, at least, will get theirs.'

There was a prolonged silence. In it the crackling of the fire and the ticking of the antique clock on the mantelpiece sounded very loud. Guy looked away uncomfortably, looked back again. Kathryn was, he thought, very pale.

'The thing is,' he said, 'I need some pointers. You knew von Rheinhardt. To start with I need to know what he looked like.'

'My dear Guy, it's thirty years since I last saw him. He'll have changed now, even if he didn't have plastic surgery, which I understand many of them did. Haven't you any idea how thirty years can change someone?'

'Thirty years haven't changed you. I've seen photographs of you when you got married and when I was a baby, and I don't think you've altered at all.'

Kathryn laughed shortly.

'That's rubbish! Of course I have.'

'Well, you're older, yes. But there's no mistaking you really.'

'You say that because you see me regularly – have done through all those years. The changes take place gradually, little by little, and you simply assimilate them. Your French grandparents and Tante Celestine would think I had changed, I am sure. As would anyone who has not seen me from that day to this. It would be the same with von Rheinhardt. I expect I could pass him in the street and not know him.'

But the tiny tremor was back in her voice, telling Guy that was not the truth. The arrogance of the man would not have changed, those cold eyes in the handsome Aryan face . . . she was seeing them now. Thirty years or three hundred, she would never forget.

'Don't you think he deserves to be brought to justice?' Guy said harshly. 'Why should someone who commits the sort of crimes he committed get away with it? And live with the proceeds of his wickedness? Surely if he was so evil you want to see him punished?'

'I'm sure he will be punished,' Kathryn said quietly. 'If not in this life, then the next. I think I am content to leave it at that.'

Guy prickled with frustation.

'How can you say that?'

'Von Rheinhardt had a way of contaminating everything and everyone around him, spreading evil. He'd do it again.'

'He wouldn't have much chance of getting away with it in a prison cell.'

'Don't be so sure. There are people who manage to spread mayhem whatever the circumstances. Von Rheinhardt is one of those. I don't just mean tangible disasters, Guy. He somehow manages to bring out the worst in people. No, I honestly believe the past is best left alone now. I have managed to put it behind me. Why can't you do the same?'

'Because unlike you, it seems, I want the man who is responsible for my father's death brought to justice, if that is at all possible, and I want the family treasures back where they belong. I don't want to hurt you, Mum. I don't want to drag up memories that are painful to you. But I owe it to my father, don't you see? I owe it to my heritage.'

'The Savigny inheritance.' She said it wearily, looking, he thought, suddenly older than her fifty-three years, though such a short time ago she had looked much younger. 'Oh Guy, what a lot *that* has to answer for!'

'What do you mean by that?'

She was silent for a moment, then she shrugged.

'Family pride and duty. You sound just like your father. I'm sure your grandpapa has instilled it in you just as it was instilled in him. I know it's up to you to carry on the Savigny line. I've done my best to make it easy for you, though God knows, it isn't what I'd have chosen for you. We've lived in England but I have tried to ensure you were as much at home in France as you were here, that you understood their ways, that you would be worthy of the title and your family name. I've accepted that one day I will lose you to them . . .'

'That's rubbish!' he interrupted. 'You don't have to lose me at all!'

'I've accepted that your place will be there, just as it would have been if your father had lived,' she went on as if she had not heard him speak. 'But this one thing I ask you, Guy. Don't go after vengeance for the sake of vengeance. It won't do anyone any good and it may do a great deal of harm.'

'Then you won't help me?'

She looked at him long and steadily. He thought he saw a flash of that old familiar fire in her eyes, then her mouth set in a determined line.

'That's right. I won't help you. I'd go further. I have very rarely asked anything of you. I want you to have your own life and I've avoided making any demands of you. But I am asking you now. If you have any respect for my feelings, forget this whole thing. Please. Leave the past where it belongs.'

He looked at her, feeling her pain, wanting to alleviate it and knowing he could not. This was something he had to do, for his father, for his family.

'I'm sorry. I'm truly sorry if it upsets you. But I have to find out if this man is von Rheinhardt.'

'I see.' Her breath came out on a sigh. 'Well, I wish you wouldn't do it, Guy, but I think I understand.' She paused, regaining control of herself. 'Would you like a drink? I've got a bottle of Glenfiddich in the chiffonier.'

'Yes, please.'

'To be honest,' Kathryn said, 'I think we could both do with one.'

After he had gone she sat staring into the fire until the last embers glowed and died.

She had thought it was over, but it was not. No, correction, she had known it would never be over but she had learned to live with it. Now it was all going to begin again. Thirty years had gone by and she had a new life now, the life she had built for herself and for Guy in this quiet Hampshire village. A life that had revolved first around him and then around the pursuits that were all she wanted now – her little shop, her home, her garden. A life that had been spared to her in spite of all the odds. It was not the life she had envisaged for herself. But it had not been so bad. In the curiously acquiescent way of those who have lived through hell, lived more in a few brief years than some people live in a whole lifetime, she had accepted it and been grateful. She had Guy. She had seen him grow up, which was more than she had expected during those dark days. She had her independence, which she prized above all else. She had her memories, precious ones as well as the distressing ones which she had chosen to close her mind to.

Now, suddenly, the chasm was threatening to open beneath her once more, the bolts on the dark door to the past that she had closed so firmly were scraping in their rusty housings.

This man, this German of whom Guy had spoken, might not of course be von Rheinhardt. The odds must surely be stacked against it being him. Yet Kathryn had the most dreadful feeling that it was.

The ogre had not been dead at all but merely sleeping. If Guy found him and managed to bring him to trial it would all come out, all the secrets she had fought to keep hidden. Well, there was nothing she could do about it now, except hope and pray.

The last of the fire fizzed and died. Kathryn shivered slightly as she moved out of the aura of warmth it had thrown, collecting the empty glasses and taking them into her little kitchen for washing. But she wouldn't do it tonight.

As she passed the mirror in the tiny hall, wood-framed, slightly crazed, bought at one of her beloved auction sales because it suited the cottage, her reflection leaped up to meet her and for a moment it seemed she was looking not at her fifty-three-year-old self but at the girl she had once been, just as if what Guy had said was true and she had not changed at all. The soft light in the hall miraculously removed every trace of crow's-foot and wrinkle, camouflaged the sprinkling of grey that was beginning to dull the bright golden brown of her hair at the temples, and she saw herself for a moment as she had looked then, all those years ago. Strange, she thought, that she should bear so few scars to tell the world of all she had been through. But then, she had been lucky. Others had not.

Oh Guy, Guy, why won't you leave it alone? she murmured to that other image, that other self. But the face in the mirror gave her back no answer other than the one he himself had given her.

He would do what he had to do, for himself, for his father and for the dynasty of Savigny. That he did not realise the demons he might be unleashing, the fact that he might be doing a disservice to all concerned, was neither here nor there. Apart from telling him the whole unvarnished truth there was nothing more that she could do now, and she shrank from that prospect. The man might not, after all, be von Rheinhardt. If he was not she would have broken her silence to no purpose.

Kathryn hoped fervently that the man was not von Rheinhardt.

The headlights of his car cut a swathe through the darkness as Guy navigated first the lanes and then the major roads on his way back to Bristol.

He drove more slowly than usual because his mind was busy and to drive fast, even on these quiet roads, required all his concentration.

His mother's reaction had been no more or less than he had expected – why should she change the habits of a lifetime and discuss with him now the things she had always resolutely refused to discuss? But he was disappointed all the same. Knowing her hatred of the Nazis, and this one Nazi in particular, he had hoped she might put her reticence aside when she heard there was a chance that von Rheinhardt might, at long last, be brought to face trial for his crimes. Surely, Guy had thought, she would want justice? Wouldn't that free her in some way from the ghosts of the past? But it seemed she did not want that. Not even the prospect of revenge had been able to persuade her to give up her secrets.

Well, at least he had told her what he intended to do – that he was going to take Bill's job in the Caribbean, if he could get it, and investigate the German at first hand. He wouldn't have wanted to begin something like that without telling her. Whether he had her approval or not. It was part of Guy's nature to like things straight and above board. He had hoped for her assistance, too – God knew he needed it – but that she had not been prepared to give. Well, he would have to look for the evidence he would need to establish the German's identity in another quarter. His grandfather would not be so unforthcoming, he was sure. He would go to France and talk to his French family. He had intended to do that anyway; Kathryn's refusal to help made it that little bit more necessary, that was all.

But why was she so anxious to block out the past? He couldn't understand it, never had been able to. In most matters she was as open and honest as he was, she didn't shy away from the unpleasant or try to avoid harsh reality. Just this one area was a closed book with her and nothing, it seemed, would make her turn the pages.

Guy's breath came out on a long sigh. He hated upsetting her, but his mind was made up. He would not be able to rest until he discovered for himself if the German Bill had told him about was, in reality, Otto von Rheinhardt. Any other consideration must, in this instance, be relegated to the sidelines.

3

PALE WINTER SUN filtered through the bare branches of the poplar trees surrounding the château. It lent a semblance of warmth to the pale stone walls and the dull red of the roof, it glinted on three storeys of unshuttered windows and threw poorly defined shadows in the shape of the twin towers which stood guard over the ancient building which was the ancestral home of the de Savignys and the centre of life for the village which bore their name.

In his study on the first floor Baron Guillaume de Savigny, sitting at his heavy old desk, looked up from the ledgers spread out before him and felt the pleasant diffusion of the sun warm his parchment-like skin through the glass of the window. A slight smile curved his once well-shaped but now thin lips and he turned his face towards the warmth. It was good to feel the sun; he hated being cold and in winter it seemed he was cold too often nowadays. For all the fires that were kept blazing in the grates and the central heating which he had had installed, at enormous cost, in his private apartments a few years previously, the château could still be a draughty place. He had not used to notice it, of course; as a younger man he had poured scorn on those who complained when the warm summers of Charente gave way to the chill winds and sudden harsh frosts of winter. Now, in his eighty-fifth year, he viewed things differently. The cold which he had once shrugged off crept into his bones now and worsened the ache in his arthritic hip, legacy of a fall from a horse when he had been a young man. He dreaded to see the leaves begin to change colour on the poplars which half hid the château and on the walnut trees in the valley beyond, and in spite of the fact that he was in remarkably good health for his age he always found himself wondering, a little sadly, whether he would be there in the spring to see them grow fresh green again.

The thought was seldom more than a fleeting one; Guillaume de Savigny was not a morbid man. He enjoyed comfort too much, not just the physical comforts of warmth and feather beds, good food and a glass of his own cognac, but emotional comfort too. In his opinion time spent on worrying or being miserable was time wasted and he had a facility for ignoring circumstances or events likely to upset his contented equilibrium. When things went wrong he was always initially upset, offended almost, to think that fate could be so unsporting as to play such a backhanded trick on him, but before long he would adjust his thinking to accommodate the misfortune, whatever it might be, and life would continue much as before. This facility was, in Guillaume's opinion, his greatest strength, though there were others who regarded it as a weakness. Whichever, there was no doubt it had helped him personally come to terms with what might have been crushing blows to a lesser man and probably contributed to the remarkable state of his health, both mental and physical.

He eased the rosewood chair, upholstered with ivy-green leather, away from the desk and rose slowly, crossing to the window, a spare man of medium height in a tweed suit which had seen better days. It wasn't that Guillaume could not afford to spend money on his wardrobe — money was not, and never had been, a problem for the de Savignys. Rather he liked the comfort of the old and familiar and, like so many wealthy people, could see little point in unnecessary outlay. The suit was still good; Louise, his wife, who still retained the chic that epitomised the Parisienne, could badger him all she liked to exchange it for a new one, but Guillaume could be as stubborn as he was placid. He liked the suit, there was nothing wrong with it, he would wear it with whatever shirt he chose, the warmer and the more frayed the better, and if Louise didn't like it, then — too bad.

The study was at the front of the château, overlooking the broad paved forecourt where in summer a fountain played. Now, in winter, it was still, the carved stone nymph that topped it gazing impassively down into the lichened bowl beneath. Beyond the forecourt stretched the lawns, an expanse of neatly trimmed green, and the drive, lined with tall graceful cypress, cut a grey swathe through them and the half-mile of parkland which separated the château from the main road into the village. It presented a scene of which Guillaume never tired, epitomising for him the timelessness of Savigny. For more than five centuries the château's walls had provided a refuge for his family and a linchpin for the community which depended upon them; it had survived the Revolution and two world wars, and he hoped and believed it would survive another five centuries – and that there would still be de Savignys living there to watch over it and continue the production of the cognac, made only from the vines on their own estates and sold to a discerning market under the name 'Château de Savigny'.

As usual, the very relishing of the name filled him with pride and warmed his tired body with much the same glow as did the liquor itself, and he turned back to his desk without the slightest tinge of regret. He was less involved now than he had once been with the day-to-day running of the vineyard and the processes that produced the light elegant cognac for which the château was renowned; much of that responsibility had passed now to Henri Bernard, his son-in-law. But he still liked to keep his finger on the pulse. Henri was a good businessman, shrewd and dependable, but Guillaume had never quite been able to reconcile himself to relinquishing the helm to a man who was not, by birth, a member of the de Savigny dynasty.

If his own sons had survived the war perhaps he would have stepped down and handed over to them with more grace, perhaps not – he had had little time for either of them. Charles he had considered weak and Christian feckless, and Guillaume himself was a proud and stubborn man. But neither of his sons had survived. He had seen them both taken, and the fact that in their lifetimes they had both irritated him had become an irrelevance. Both had been posthumously awarded the Croix de Guerre, but the honour had done little to compensate for their loss. His greatest hope now was that Guy, his grandson, might step into the breach when he became Baron. At present he had a restless streak, for which Guillaume blamed his English mother, Kathryn – among other things, not least of which was Charles' death. But Guy also had a strong sense of history and family loyalty and Guillaume believed that when the time came the inheritance would be safe in his hands. He had to believe it. Anything else would be a betrayal of family tradition.

It was more than a hundred years now since Guillaume's grandfather, the then Baron, had begun producing his own cognac and selling it to the most exclusive retailers in England and on the continent. It was he who had designed the distinctive engraved bottles with the heavily embossed labels, he who had laid down the ground rules which had, from the very outset, determined the quality – only grapes from their own fifty-hectare estate were to be used, no 'buying in' even in lean years, the wine to be distilled on its lees and matured for twenty years in the dank cellars that lay beneath the château. Now the estate boasted seven stills and although their output was tiny compared with many of the big-name producers in the region, the quality was such that its reputation was assured.

Because of its excellence and because it was backed by de Savigny money the cognac production had survived every crisis turbulent history had thrown at it.

Just ten years after his grandfather's first bold venture, a plague carried by a louse, Phylloxera Vastatrix, had begun to devastate the vineyards of Charente and soon the vines were withering and dying where they stood. The setback had literally broken his grandfather's heart. He had gone out one day to inspect the damage and never returned – the estate workers had found him that night lying dead of a stroke in his beloved vineyard, and the talk in the village was that Château de Savigny cognac would now be sold out to one of the wealthy merchants who were moving in to take the devasted vineyards off the hands of those growers who could no longer make a living from their ailing vines. Not that the de Savignys needed the money, of course, they had sufficient reserves to ride out the storm, but young Louis was a banker, wasn't he, who had never shown the slightest interest in his father's pet project except to drink it!

'Young Louis', however, had other ideas. He knew how much the production of his own cognac had meant to his father and he had no intention of letting it die with him. He arranged his business and banking duties to allow him more time at the château and picked up the mantle of responsibility for the vineyard which his father had let fall. For a while, like everyone else, he had searched for the right chemical to treat the precious French vines, but when this proved unsuccessful he joined an expedition to the New World to look for suitable plants to replace his own disease-ridden ones. A short time later he was back, triumphantly bearing rootstock which was to prove ideally suited to the chalky soil of Charente, then personally leading the replanting of the previously higgledy-piddledy vineyards in neat rows on the softly undulating hillsides.

Guillaume had been little more than a baby then, but he fancied he could remember the excitement as the new vines began to flourish and bear fruit.

The cognac distilled from that first pressing was still maturing in the damp cellars when the Great War ravaged France, but it scarcely touched Savigny. And later, when the depression took its toll and prohibition drove a hole through the American market, Château de Savigny once again survived, for it was sold mainly to only the most exclusive outlets in England and on the continent, to the kind of people wealthy enough to be almost unaffected by slump or boom.

Louis had followed his father to an early grave and Guillaume was the Baron de Savigny by the time war once again threatened the peaceful way of life in Charente. This time there was no escaping it; when France surrendered to the Nazi invaders the demarcation line which was drawn between occupied and Vichy territory bisected Savigny land. But once again the production of the cognac was barely disrupted. The German conquerors were too partial to the smooth golden-brown liquor to allow its demise; as long as the bottles were earmarked for their own consumption they were happy enough to allow the process to continue uninterrupted, though there were, of course, fewer young men available to do the work and the older ones and the women had to toil long and hard to ensure the vines were stripped before the frosts came to spoil the flavour of the grapes.

During those turbulent years many cognac producers had taken a great delight in cheating the Germans – inferior blends had been bottled and falsely labelled so as to be passed off as the genuine thing – but Guillaume had never been able to bring himself to indulge in such sharp practice. He was too proud of the superior quality of Château de Savigny. He couldn't bear to think of anyone, even a German, tasting it and finding it wanting.

There was no danger of that now. In the boom of prosperity that had followed the defeat of Nazi Germany and the liberation of France, Château de Savigny cognac had gained in reputation and gone from strength to strength, and Guillaume, for all the limitations advanced age had brought, still liked to retain his grip on the reins. All he hoped was that when he was gone there would still be a de Savigny to carry on his work. Henri did his best, but it wasn't the same; without the continuity of family heritage passed from father to son down the line how could it ever be?

His own sons were gone — no amount of wishful thinking could bring them back — and his daughter had only managed to produce daughters herself, and rather avant-garde ones at that. He shook his head slightly as he thought of Lise, twenty-five years old and still unmarried, seemingly more interested in left-wing writers and politicians than the family heritage, and Françoise, still studying at the Sorbonne, and looking increasingly likely to turn out the same way.

No, Guy was the one on whom his hopes were pinned — and Guy was coming to see him. With his thin, bloodless fingers Guillaume lifted the corner of his ledger and retrieved the letter which he had left on his desk top so as to be able to read and reread it at his pleasure.

It was unusual for Guy to visit at this time of the year and Guillaume allowed himself to wonder just what was behind it. That he had made up his mind at last to give up junketing about in these little twin-engined planes of his, perhaps, and move to Savigny permanently? That would be the perfect solution, the smoothest possible handover of Savigny power. It would be so good to know Guy was here, heir-in-waiting, when something happened to Guillaume, as it was bound to one day in the not-too-distant future.

I've already done a lot better than my father or my grandfather, Guillaume thought with a touch of self-congratulatory humour.

And supposed that it was Guy's impending visit that allowed him to regard his own mortality with such unaccustomed levity.

'I need to talk to you, Grandpapa. Alone,' Guy said.

Dinner was over, the formal meal so beloved of the Baron Guillaume de Savigny, reminiscent of all the formal meals he had enjoyed throughout the years. Even when he and Louise were alone they still ate in the dining room at the long refectory table which could quite comfortably seat twelve, with the solid silver candelabra placed at either end throwing a soft dancing light on their lined faces and the portraits of his ancestors looking down at them from the walls. It was the way Guillaume liked it, yet another comforting familiarity to provide evidence of continuity.

Tonight however there were six; himself and Louise, elegant as always, if a little frail, in a Paris gown of the softest black wool, Henri and Celestine, his daughter and son-in-law, who had their own suite of rooms on the second storey of the château, Lise, home from Paris for the weekend, and of course Guy. Guillaume looked at his grandson and felt himself warmed by a glow of approval. At first glance he might have been looking at his own son, Charles, at the same age, but Guy had more about him than Charles had ever had – a strength of character his father had lacked and which Guillaume found gratifying for it eased, in part at least, the disappointment and frustration which had always marred his paternal pride in Charles. Perhaps he was wrong to harbour such resentment as he did against Kathryn, he thought, for he was fairly certain that Guy's strength had been inherited from her and nurtured by the way she had brought him up. But for all that he could not forgive her for taking Guy away from Charente, and the old enmities between them went too deep for forgiveness or any hope of reconciliation now.

'You want to talk to me,' he said, swirling the last of the cognac in his glass. 'Well, I suppose I should have known you had a reason, coming here so unexpectedly. We'll go to my study.'

'Oh Guy, don't be such a bore!' Lise said. She spoke fiercely, everything about Lise was fierce these days, from her small set face to her defiantly masculine clothes. What had happened, Guillaume sometimes wondered, to the little girl who had set the château ringing with her laughter, the little girl in petticoats and flounces with ribbons in her hair? That hair was long and straight now, a sleek but, in his opinion, unbecoming curtain with a deep fringe which almost hid her eyes, and she never seemed to laugh. Her tone was always pitched somewhere between aggression and earnestness, totally lacking, he thought, in feminine charm, but he was also wise enough to know that the extra note of sharpness in it now was because Lise was disappointed that she was to be denied Guy's company, for a while at least. She hero-worshipped her cousin to the point of obsession – it had always been the same. As a small girl she had followed him everywhere like a pet puppy dog and little had changed in the intervening years. Guillaume was fairly certain she had come home this weekend especially because she had known Guy would be here; more often these days she remained in Paris with her intellectual and – in his opinion – extremely tiresome friends.

'Sorry, Lise, but it's quite important.' Guy stood up and moved toward the door, tweaking a strand of that straight dark hair as he passed her chair. 'I'll see you later and you can tell me all your news.'

'What makes you think I want to tell you anything?' she retorted, but a little colour came into her sallow cheeks all the same.

Guy allowed his grandfather to precede him along the corridor and up the curving stone staircase, matching his pace to Guillaume's.

The study was in darkness, the heavy curtains drawn against the night, and Guy went around the room turning on the lamps whilst Guillaume settled himself in his favourite chair. Then he perched on the corner of his grandfather's desk and turned to face him.

'You remember telling me, when I was a little boy, about the Nazi who was here during the war – the one who was responsible for my father's death?'

'And your Uncle Christian's, and a great many others besides.' Guillaume's voice was bitter. 'How could I ever forget?'

'Well, I can't be sure, of course, but I think I might have found him.'

For a moment Guillaume was utterly still, the unexpectedness of Guy's statement robbing him of the ability to respond in any way. Then he shook his head.

'After all this time? Impossible!'

'Why impossible? So far, I know, he has managed to hide himself away to escape having to answer for what he did, but that doesn't mean he can stay hidden for ever. The world is a smaller place these days than it was thirty years ago. Besides, they become careless, these war criminals. They get overconfident, thinking, just like you, that after so long they are safe. Hasn't Klaus Barbie been found living under an assumed name in Peru? And there are plenty of others like him. So why shouldn't von Rheinhardt float to the top of whatever cesspit he buried himself in?'

37

'That's true enough, I suppose. Somehow I imagined him to be dead, though I suppose there's no reason why he should be. He's a young man compared to me, and I'm still alive and kicking.' Guillaume's lips twisted into the ghost of a smile but the veins stood out taut and blue through the parchment skin as his hands gripped the arms of his chair. 'What made you look for him? All the stories I've told you, I suppose.'

'I didn't look for him,' Guy said. 'I have always thought I'd like to find him and make him answer for what he did but I've never actually done anything about it, apart from putting out a few feelers. I heard about this German who I think could be von Rheinhardt by sheer chance – one of those flukes that beggars belief. In a funny sort of way that, more than anything, is what makes me inclined to believe it really is him.'

'I see.' Guillaume's slightly rheumy eyes had gone very far away; what in fact he was seeing was the past. 'And what do you intend to do about it?'

'I'm going to the Caribbean myself. That's where this German is living. I want to meet him and try to establish if he is in fact von Rheinhardt.'

'And how will you go about that?'

'I shall check all available records, of course. Files, photographs, any information I can lay hands on. But I dare say he's made a pretty good job of establishing a new identity for himself, and there is another test – a simpler one. Inconclusive, of course, but it should be enough to tell me whether I'm on the right track or barking up a gum tree.'

'Which is?'

'According to what I've been told this German's house is full of treasures – artefacts which give every appearance of being French in origin. Von Rheinhardt stole things from us, didn't he?'

'He certainly did. Things which had been in our family for generations. He took over the château for his HQ, you see, and managed to spirit away anything small enough to transport which took his fancy.'

'Do you have descriptions of the missing items? Enough detail to identify them?'

'Certainly. I made an inventory when the château was returned to us after the war.'

'And photographs? Weren't there photographs?'

'Yes, there were. Photographs always seemed a sensible precaution in case the treasures were stolen. Not that I ever expected them to be looted by an occupying power, of course – more by common thieves.'

'Would you let me have them? If I could be sure the stuff in this man's house is ours then I think I could be fairly confident he is von Rheinhardt. And I think it is, Grandpapa. There's silver, there's porcelain, there's a bronze statuette. And there is a triptych.'

'A triptych!' The old man stiffened so that his spine was ramrod straight against the back of the chair.

'Yes. From my friend's description I think it might depict scenes from the life of the Maid of Orleans.'

'*Mon dieu!*' It was little more than a whisper.

'Wasn't that what our triptych represented?' Guy persisted.

'Yes. Yes. There may be others, of course, but . . .'

'But they must be few and far between. You see now why I think I may have found von Rheinhardt.'

'Yes.' The old man was silent. Guy sat watching him, sipping his brandy and waiting for what he had said to sink in. After a long while Guillaume nodded. 'Yes. If he has a triptych like that then you could be right. It could indeed be von Rheinhardt – the bastard. After all these years. I can't believe it.'

'Then you'll help me?' Guy asked.

'Oh Guy, Guy, I don't know . . .'

'But surely you'd like to see him brought to justice? You always said he deserved to pay for what he did. And you'd like to see our family heirlooms back here in the château where they belong?'

'I'd like them back, of course I would. Nothing would give me more pleasure. To see them again, to hold them in my hands. But as for the rest of it . . . I don't know. The price might be too great.'

'I don't understand. What price?'

Guillaume shook his head slowly.

'If you bring von Rheinhardt back now there would be a trial. A very public trial. It would be world news. You know how the media seize on these things nowadays. It would be most unpleasant.'

'For von Rheinhardt, certainly. Isn't that what he deserves?'

'It wouldn't only be von Rheinhardt who would suffer. We would all be forced to face things we would rather forget.'

Guy felt the beginnings of impatience. First his mother, now his grandfather, willing to let the monstrous Nazi who had marred all their lives go free rather than be made to confront the past themselves. He couldn't understand it. His mother, of course, had always refused to discuss it, but his grandfather had seemed fired up with hatred and a desire for vengeance. Now he, too, was counselling caution.

'I realise it is not nice,' Guy said slowly, 'having to remember the sort of atrocities that were committed. I realise that like my mother you have probably spent a lifetime trying to put what happened behind you. But surely it would be worth it, to know that von Rheinhardt was being punished at last?'

'I don't know. If he came to trial it wouldn't be just a case of facing him with what he did. He wouldn't be likely to just hold up his hands and admit it – he knows if he did that he would be certain to go to prison for the rest of his life. No, he'd mount a defence with the best lawyers money can buy – from what you say he's not short of a penny and there are plenty of up-and-coming young advocates who would give their eyeteeth for a chance to make their names, one way or another, in a trial that would have all the notoriety this one would have. God alone knows what they would say in his defence.'

'There's a risk of that, I realise. But you'd have nothing to fear – you did nothing wrong. My father and uncles died heroes, remember – because of von Rheinhardt. He would be the one on trial.'

The old man sighed.

'Don't be so naive, Guy. With something like this we would all be on trial. All kinds of unpleasant things would be dragged up and paraded for the world to see.'

Guy's eyes narrowed.

'What are you saying?'

'I am saying it could be very messy, that's all. I don't want the family name dragged through the mud.'

Guy levered himself further on to the corner of the desk. A finger of disturbing doubt had begun prodding at him.

'Why should it be, Grandpapa? Is there something I don't know? Something detrimental to the family that you don't want to come out?'

'No, no, of course not. We have nothing to be ashamed of. We did nothing wrong. Your father, as you know, was honoured by the Croix de Guerre. And your mother . . . well, your mother was a remarkable woman, I have to admit, though we were not the best of friends, as you must realise.' His eyes grew sharp suddenly. 'What has she told you about me?'

'Nothing,' Guy replied truthfully. 'She has never explained why the two of you didn't get on, though obviously I would be a fool if I didn't realise there was something.'

'Does there have to be a reason? Some people don't see eye to eye, that's all. That's how it was for your mother and me. We respect one another, I think.'

Guy did not reply. He was not at all sure of his mother's feelings in the matter.

'Does your mother know what you have in mind to do?' Guillaume asked.

'Yes, and she doesn't approve. But then she never wants to discuss the war. She seems to find it very painful.'

'I dare say.' Guillaume was silent for a moment, staring into space. 'What you have to remember, Guy, is that we are all human. We all have our weaknesses.'

'So you, like my mother, would rather I ignored this information I have? And let von Rheinhardt, if indeed it is him, live out his life on his Caribbean island?'

'No.' There was a quietly decisive note in Guillaume's voice now. 'You gave me a shock, Guy, coming here, telling me you think you have found that *cochon* after all this time. And I do think you should consider carefully what you are doing – it is all too easy to pursue a path so vigorously that you lose sight of the pitfalls along the way. But I would like to have our treasures back where they belong, and I would like to see von Rheinhardt pay for the lives of my sons – and all the others, too.'

He rose from his chair, crossed to a tall rosewood bureau, gleaming dully in the light thrown by the table lamp which stood on it, and extracted a large box file.

'I think you will find everything you need here – an inventory of the missing items, photographs, detailed descriptions, even the bills for the restoration work, back in the twenties, of some of the pictures that were stolen from their frames. You will also find my journals for the war years. They are not in any great detail – I've never been one for keeping detailed diaries – but at least you will be able to verify dates, should you need to. Have a look through ^nd take anything you think may be useful. In fact, perhaps you could take them to Henri's office and make copies. I think I would prefer the originals to remain here at the château. You know how to use the photocopier, do you?'

'I expect I can work it out. Thank you, Grandpapa.'

'Well, as I say, it's going to be an unpleasant business, and you know, Guy, I don't like unpleasantness. I dare say I am something of a coward in that respect. But I would like to see the family treasures back where they belong before I depart this world. Yes, it would be worth it to know they can be passed on to your children and your children's children.'

Guy smiled briefly.

'I should think that gives me ample time, then, Grandpapa. You are not going to depart this world for a very long time yet.'

'I hope not. But one never knows. Sometimes I feel very old, Guy. A man shouldn't outlive his sons.'

Certainly in that moment he did look old, Guy thought, as if the weight of the years was suddenly pressing heavily upon his shoulders.

Should I be doing this? he wondered. Should Grandpapa be worried about it at this time of life? But his desire for revenge on von Rheinhardt, nurtured throughout his childhood by his grandfather himself, was too strong. He had hated the bastard then and he hated him now. It was only the frailty of age that was making Guillaume shrink from facing again the terrible times he had lived through. And if Guy could once more return the family treasures to him it would be worth it. When he held them in his hands once more he could die happy.

'Will you do it now, Guy, or in the morning?' Guillaume asked.

'I don't have much time, Grandpapa. I'll make a start now.'

'Very well.' The old man rose and moved to the door. 'Then I think I will rejoin the others, if you don't mind. I'm very tired.'

'Do you want me to come back down with you?'

'No, no, I'm capable of managing the stairs on my own. You stay here and do what you have to.'

'All right. Say good night to the others for me if they want to go to bed before I'm finished.'

'I will.'

He left the room and Guy looked around, experiencing momentarily an eerie presentiment of the future. One day this study would be his. From here he would manage the affairs of the Château de Savigny just as his grandfather had done and his father before him. The sense of continuity was both awesome and satisfying. For a moment longer Guy allowed himself to consider it, then with a determined shrug of his shoulders he put it away and returned his attention to the task in hand.

'What on earth is going on, Guy?'

The hour was late; Guy, immersed in the papers his grandfather had given him, had not heard the door open. He looked up now, startled, to see Lise standing in the doorway.

He sat back in the chair, rubbing his eyes with his fingers.

'What are you doing here, Lise? I thought everyone would have gone to bed by now.'

'I'm a night owl, didn't you know? Anyway, you haven't answered my question yet – and I asked first!'

She came into the study and shut the door behind her, a girl of medium height, almost painfully thin, and without a trace of make-up to lend colour to her rather sallow complexion. Tonight, in deference to the occasion, she was wearing a dress, a simple shift of cream wool, and, much to her discomfort, stockings and shoes with heels. Lise did not like dressing up; she was far more at ease in the jeans and oversized sweaters and cowboy boots she usually wore in winter.

Come on, Guy, you owe me an explanation,' she persisted. 'I came down from Paris especially to see you and all you do is lock yourself away up here!'

'I had something rather important to do. The whole purpose of my visit, actually.'

'Something which has upset Grandpapa. He looked quite pale when he came down after talking to you. You shouldn't worry him, Guy. He's an old man.' She drew a packet of cigarettes out of the pocket of her dress and lit one. The pungent smell of Gaulois filled the study. 'Now, are you going to tell me about it or not?'

Guy swung himself back in the chair.

'Yes, I'll tell you. I was going to anyway. If I'm right you'll have

43

to know sometime and it might as well be now. Then you'll be prepared.'

'For what? You make this sound very mysterious.'

'It's not mysterious. Just a bit sensitive. I don't want you blabbing it to all your left-wing friends.'

'Don't be horrible, Guy!' Her mouth set in a thin line; she pulled on her cigarette. 'I'm entitled to my friends just as you are to yours. How is Wendy, by the way?'

'Wendy's OK.' He knew better than to elaborate; Lise was jealous of any relationship he had with women.

'You haven't married her yet.'

'No.'

'Why not? Is it because you don't love her?'

'None of your business.'

'I am your cousin.'

'But not my keeper. And I thought you wanted to talk about my reason for being here, not my intentions regarding Wendy.'

She smiled briedly. '*Touché*. Go on then, tell me.' She leaned over the desk to look at the papers spread out there and he caught a whiff of perfume – her mother's guest soap, he guessed, certainly not scent. Lise never used it. 'What is this?' she asked.

'Lists of the things that were looted from the château during the war. I'm sure Grandpapa has told you about them just as he told me.'

'Of course. But why are they suddenly so important?'

'Because I might be on the point of getting them back.'

She whistled softly.

'How? I thought they'd gone forever.'

'So did we all.' He went on to tell her about the information he had received and she listened intently, finishing her Gaulois and lighting another from her stub.

'So – you're going to the Caribbean,' she said when he had finished.

'I hope so, yes. The trouble is neither Grandpapa nor my mother are very keen on the idea. Mum is downright hostile – I expected that – but Grandpapa has reservations too, I think.'

'Why?' Her dark eyes were puzzled in her narrow face.

'I don't know. He seems to think it will stir up all kinds of unpleasantness. Frankly I'm a bit surprised by his attitude. He was

44

always so full of hatred for von Rheinhardt. I'd have thought he'd have jumped at the chance for revenge.'

'Oh, you know Grandpapa – what he's like. He's always hated anything to disturb the calm waters of his world and I think he's got worse as he's got older. People do that, don't they? Age only makes them more extreme, more set in whatever ways they have.'

'That's true, I suppose. But as you say, he's an old man. I don't want to upset him.'

'He didn't ask you not to go on with this?'

'No. He gave me access to this file.'

'There you are then. He's probably glad really for you to do what he can't do himself. You must try to find out if it really is von Rheinhardt, Guy. The bastard deserves everything that's coming to him.' Her voice was fierce again, that same tone that debated politics far into the night with her left-wing friends and verbally tore the old order to shreds. Guy found himself smiling now at her fervour.

'You think I'm doing the right thing, then?'

'Absolutely. I only wish I could come with you. I couldn't, I suppose . . . ?'

'No, Lise, I'm afraid you couldn't.'

'Well, keep me informed anyway. Jesus Christ, I'd like to get my hands on that German pig!'

'I'm sure you would, but if it is him I shall turn him over to the proper authorities. We live in a civilised world now, thank goodness – and thanks to the Allies.'

'And our own brave countrymen and women. Don't forget what they did. Your father, your uncle . . .'

'I know,' he said. But he felt a prickle of discomfort all the same, remembering Guillaume's warning. 'Well, I'm going to bed now. I don't think I can do any more tonight. My concentration has gone.'

'My fault, I supose,' she said ruefully.

'Not really. I was getting muzzy anyway. There's a limit to what I can absorb at one sitting.'

'What are these photographs?' She leaned over the desk again, pulling the box file towards her, partly from genuine interest and partly in an effort to prolong the late-night encounter. She wasn't ready to go to bed yet and she didn't want to miss the chance to be

45

with Guy either. Tomorrow she had to go back to Paris and he would leave for England and then, it seemed, for the other side of the world, and she didn't know how long it would be before she saw him again. His visits were too few and far between for her liking.

'Just pictures of the treasures. Haven't you seen them before?'

'No, I don't think so.' She began leafing through them, leaning so close that the curtain of her hair brushed his face. Realising what she was doing he moved away slightly.

'So this is the famous triptych,' she said, pretending not to have noticed his withdrawal.

'Yes. Scenes from the life of the Maid of Orleans. Pretty impressive, isn't it?'

'I suppose so – if you like that kind of thing.' She went on poring over the photographs, examining one after the other. 'Silver candlesticks – they must be worth a pretty penny . . .'

'It's not the monetary value that counts, though, is it? It's their sentimental and historical value.'

'. . . a little clock – Louise XIV, isn't it? – bronze statuette of Ceres . . . good grief, the place must have been quite bare when he'd finished taking what he wanted!'

'Yes, I think Grandpapa bought a good deal to take the place of what was looted. Except for the triptych, of course. He's never replaced that.'

'Wait a minute, these aren't all of artefacts,' Lise said, a note of unaccustomed excitement creeping into her voice. 'Who are these people?'

'What people?'

'Here – look. *These* people.'

She pushed a photograph towards him. A small group, standing on the forecourt of the château beside the fountain. Guy inspected it.

'Well, that's Grandpapa obviously, and that looks like my father and your mother. But I don't know who the other man is . . .' He looked more closely at the stranger, trying to identify him. It certainly wasn't his Uncle Christian, he was too tall and too fair to be a de Savigny.

'Perhaps it was one of my mother's boyfriends,' Lise suggested. 'He's very good-looking.'

'Perhaps.' But Guy was doubtful. The tiny hairs on the back of his neck had begun to tingle. 'I'm wondering if it might be him . . . von Rheinhardt.'

'Oh surely not! They wouldn't have had their photograph taken with him, would they? And he's not in uniform.'

'No, but he lived at the château, remember, and he was a frequent visitor in the days before he turned the family out and took it over for his HQ. He might not always have worn his uniform then – when he had a day off duty, for instance.'

'I still can't believe it.' Lise went on turning over photographs. 'Look, here's one of you, Guy. Oh, weren't you sweet? You must be only about a year old. Get those chubby knees!'

'Cheeky!' but he didn't feel like laughing, and a moment later he heard her draw her breath in sharply.

'You were right, Guy. Isn't that the same man? Only this time he is in uniform!'

She pushed the photograph towards him. Guy picked it up and for the first time looked at the image of the man who was his quarry, knowing with almost complete certainty that it must be him.

The photograph had been taken more in close-up than the first, every detail of the face was clear, though the original black and white had faded to give a brownish tint. Guy looked at it and felt something closing up inside him as though a giant hand had taken hold of his heart and was squeezing it tight.

Von Rheinhardt, if indeed it was he, had certainly been a handsome man. The features beneath the close-cropped fair hair were classic Aryan and the cut of the uniform accentuated broad shoulders and a powerful frame. But the beauty was marred slightly by a scar running down his left cheek and finishing at the corner of his well-shaped mouth, and Guy thought he had never seen eyes colder than these. They stared arrogantly into the camera and, it seemed, beyond it, mocking whoever it was who had clicked the shutter and now, by a process of transference, reaching out across the years to mock Guy.

'So that's the bastard I want,' he said slowly. 'I'll check tomorrow with Grandpapa, of course, but I shouldn't think there's much doubt about it.'

'If it is him it will be a great help to you, won't it?' Lise said.

'He'll be nearly thirty years older, of course, but some things don't change. He's bound to still have that scar, for a start.'

'I'd imagine so.' Guy took the photograph and slipped it into the breast pocket of his jacket, then gathered the other papers and photographs together and replaced them in the box file. 'That's it, then. I'm going to bed now. Are you coming, or are you staying here?'

'If you're going I may as well do the same,' she said reluctantly.

'I must, Lise. I'm absolutely bushed. If I don't go to bed I'll fall asleep where I am.'

They turned off all the lights, closed the study door behind them and parted in the passageway, Lise climbing the stone staircase to her parents' apartment on the upper story, Guy letting himself into the room which had once, long ago, been his father's.

But in spite of what he had said it was a long time before he fell asleep. He lay staring into the soft dark, thinking about von Rheinhardt and what he planned to do when he found him. And when at last sleep did come, it was to dream of a handsome Nazi with a scar running down one cheek and a triptych depicting scenes from the life of the Maid of Orleans.

4

WHEN HE RETURNED home from France Guy telephoned Kathryn at her shop.

'Just to tell you Grandpapa let me have details of all the missing items. I know you don't approve but I wanted to keep you in the picture. And I got something else, too – a photograph of von Rheinhardt.'

Kathryn felt her stomach fall away.

'Really? You surprise me.'

'I must say it surprised me, too. I wouldn't have expected Grandpapa to take snapshots of a Nazi, even if he was living in the château. But it's made me more convinced than ever that the man Bill met in the Caribbean is von Rheinhardt.'

Kathryn carried the telephone round her small cluttered desk and sat down in the chair behind it. Her throat felt tight.

'What makes you say that?'

'The man in the photograph has a long scar on his left cheek. That's exactly how Bill described the German he knew as Otto Brandt.'

'I see.' She swallowed hard. 'Do you know yet if you've got the job out there?'

'It's not confirmed, but it's looking good. In this business nothing is certain until it's signed and sealed, of course, but I think it's very likely. The fact that Bill has put in a word for me should go in my favour – unless he blotted his copybook while he was there, of course.'

'When will you know?'

'I'm expecting a call at any time.'

'But you won't be going before Christmas?'

'Oh no, I shouldn't think so. I wouldn't want to miss your roast turkey, anyway.'

49

He said it lightly in an effort to be conciliatory – he always tried to spend Christmas with his mother and she always spoiled him disgracefully, producing a meal that made his mouth water just thinking about it. 'Actually I could stay for a couple of days since I won't be seeing you for some time if I get the job,' he added.

'What about Wendy? Won't she want to spend some time with you if you are going away?'

'She's going to her parents in Yorkshire. You don't have other plans, do you?'

'No – I'll look forward to having you.'

'I'll see you on Christmas Eve, then. Early evening.'

'Yes. Take care, Guy.'

'And you.'

She replaced the receiver and sat for a moment with her hand still resting on it.

So – it was still going on, this relentless journey into the past. She had prayed it would stop but it had not stopped. There was still the chance that Guy might not get the job in the Caribbean, of course, and always the chance the man might not be von Rheinhardt. But in her heart she was already quite certain that he would get the job and very afraid the man was von Rheinhardt. If that was the case then she had no choice. She would have to tell him at least something of what had happened in France. She couldn't let him go blundering blindly on, oblivious of what he was about to uncover. But she didn't relish the prospect. In fact, it horrified her and she knew that it would horrify him. Perhaps, she thought, she could still stop him from going on with this. With all her heart she hoped so. But she couldn't help feeling that only the full facts would achieve that objective, and giving him the full facts was not something she was prepared to do.

Kathryn ran a hand distractedly through her hair. The ghosts of the past were very close now, filling the small room she used as an office, leering at her from the filing cabinet and the pile of catalogues, winking in the flame of the paraffin heater that was the only source of heat.

She had not wanted to face them. They reminded her too sharply of things she would rather forget – of a time when she had lived with terror and frustration, disgust and dread. France under the jackboot had not been a pleasant place to be, but that had not been the worst of it, for her at any rate. The worst had been the disillusion that had come from seeing the people she had loved and respected stripped of the niceties of their normal façade. When fear and desperation reigned the veneer of civilisation was thin indeed. She had seen those around her naked, defensive and afraid and she had not liked what she had seen. She had experienced extremes of emotion, learned both the treachery of betrayal and the extraordinary depth and meaning of true and selfless love. When it was all over there had been no going back for her. She had been affected too deeply for anything to be the same ever again. The ingenuous girl who had married Charles de Savigny and come to Charente as his bride had gone for ever, just as those who had died were gone.

Yet now, once again, they were with her in the small office behind her shop just as they had been through all the years. Charles and Christian, Otto von Rheinhardt and the man she had known as Paul Curtis. Most of all, Paul Curtis . . .

For a long while Kathryn sat quietly, lost in her memories.

'I think perhaps we should have a talk, Guy,' Kathryn said.

It was Christmas Eve; Guy had arrived, his car stacked with presents, and they had eaten a delicious meal of cold ham and jacket potatoes.

But along with the presents, he had given her the unwelcome news that his job with Air Perpetua in the Caribbean had been confirmed, and Kathryn had realised that she could no longer put off telling him at least part of the true story.

'About von Rheinhardt?' Guy stretched comfortably in the fireside chair. 'Can't we forget him for tonight at least? It's obvious it upsets you, and it is Christmas!'

'No, Guy, we can't forget it, I'm afraid. This will be the last chance we'll have to talk before you go and I think we should take it.'

Guy glanced at her, saw her serious expression, and felt a dart of apprehension.

'I take it there's something I don't know about this business,' he said.

'Let's say you're unaware of the whole truth.' She drew her russet suede waistcoat around her as if it could afford her some sort of protection and again he felt the disquiet gnaw at him.

'Perhaps you'd better tell me then.'

'That's what I am trying to do – in my own way,' she said quietly. 'So far you have heard only the best side of what happened. But there was another aspect of it – not everything was quite as you imagined. I want to tell you how things were for all of us so that you will understand and hopefully not be too shocked at the things you might learn. I ask you to be generous in your judgement and not too ready to condemn. It was a harsh world then, harsher than you will ever know. People under stress behave in strange ways, Guy, and not all of them commendable.'

Her words sounded to him like an echo of what his grandfather had said. His unease grew.

'I don't understand.'

'I am trying to tell you the way it was – to explain the position we were all in. The Nazis were in control, remember – complete control – and they were utterly ruthless. Even though the château was just the Vichy side of the demarcation line it made no difference really. Oh, compared to the occupied zone it was paradise, I suppose – in the beginning at any rate. The Germans behaved very correctly, trying to impress us with the virtues of the society they wanted to propagate, no doubt. But that didn't last very long. Whenever they came up against opposition they showed their true colours. Although the Gestapo wore civilian clothes they were there, nonetheless, doing their evil work, and because Pétain was hand in glove with the Nazis the Vichy police were working for them too in practice.'

'Mum, I already know all this,' Guy interjected. 'There's no need for you to go over it again.'

'I think there is, Guy. Because I am trying to explain to you why your grandfather took the view he did – that it was better to appease the Germans than to antagonise them.'

She saw the shocked look come into Guy's eyes and hated herself for what she was having to do.

'What are you saying?' he demanded. 'You can't be trying to tell me, surely, that my family were collaborators?'

Kathryn sighed. She would have given anything to have spared him this.

'Yes, darling, I'm afraid that's exactly what I am saying. In the beginning that is what they were.'

'I don't believe it! My father was decorated for his work with the Resistance, so was my Uncle Christian. As for Grandpapa . . .'

'Your grandpapa did what he thought best. And besides, he was a great admirer of Pétain, who had been a hero of the Great War, remember. Pétain collaborated and he made it clear that it was the duty of every right-thinking Frenchman to do the same.'

'But that is deplorable! Pétain was a traitor. And you are telling me that my own father and grandfather were as bad? I don't want to hear this!'

Kathryn sighed. She had known it would be bad, but this was worse even than she had imagined. How could she hope to explain to Guy what she had found so difficult to understand? How could she expect him to forgive what she had found unforgivable – at the time, at any rate. And how strange that she should be defending them now. At the time she had been as shocked and angry as he was now.

She looked at Guy, and his tight, shocked face reminded her forcefully of Charles. How like his father he was – physically at any rate.

'Guy – listen to me,' she tried to say. 'Please, darling, really listen!'

But for a moment no words would come. It was as if it was Charles sitting opposite her in the flickering firelight, not Guy at all, and it seemed to Kathryn that instead of being at home in the New Forest with the lights of the Christmas tree winking cheerfully across the cosy room and the greeting cards strung on a scarlet ribbon across the fire breast, she was back in the Château de Savigny in the long hard winter of 1941.

5

'**N**O, CHARLES,' SHE said. 'I won't do it. I absolutely refuse. It's bad enough having to live with the Germans everywhere, strutting about and letting us know in no uncertain terms that we have to do as they say or pay the price. But I don't have to sit down to dinner with one, and I tell you I won't do it.'

They were in the drawing room of their private apartments in the Château de Savigny on a grey afternoon in early November. Winter had come early to Charente. Those workers who had not either been whisked away to do duty for the Germans in the arms factories or gone into hiding to escape that fate had toiled long and hard to harvest the grapes before the first frosts came; now the vines, like the trees that surrounded the château, were bare beneath a heavy grey sky and an icy wind blew up the valley and rattled the doors and window frames of the château.

It was cold in the drawing room in spite of a log fire burning in the grate, but Kathryn knew that the chill making her shiver now had more to do with the cold places inside her than with the temperature of the room. She was young, she was healthy, she was lucky enough to have plenty of warm clothes in her wardrobe, acquired before they, like everything else, became unavailable, but none of these things could prevent the aura of cold that crept over her skin and ran in her veins. It had been there even in the heat of summer so that she had felt as though she were walking in a shadowed lane which the sun never reached, and as the weeks and months passed it had grown steadily worse, isolating her in an alien world.

And none of it seemed to her in that moment more alien than her husband, Charles. He faced her across the drawing room, the same slim olive-skinned man she had married, dressed, she fancied, in the exact same Breton jersey he had been wearing when she had first met him in Geneva six years earlier, or certainly one very like it. Yet the face above it was subtly different, older. His hair had receded and thinned, his forehead was perpetually creased into a perflexed frown and there was a look in the deep blue eyes that was sometimes anxious, sometimes resentful, bordering almost on the surly. There was little now of the sophisticated debonair man she had fallen in love with; occasionally, despairingly, she wondered if he had ever existed at all or if it had all been an illusion conjured up by an ingenuous teenager hungry for romance.

The ingredients for romance had been there, certainly — a handsome Frenchman, heir to a title and estates, ten years her senior — and Charles had stirred those ingredients skilfully into an irresistible recipe. He had wooed her in the French way, with flowers and presents and extravagant compliments, making her feel the most desirable woman in the world, and she had been flattered and charmed, awed by both the power she appeared to have over him and by the man himself.

But the gilt was off the gingerbread now. Six years of marriage had removed the blinkers from her eyes and revealed weaknesses in his character she had never dreamed of. She looked at him now and saw not so much a man who was his own master as the slave of tradition, weighted down by what he saw as the responsibilities of his heritage, driven more by the need to preserve the status quo than to explore uncharted territory, and anxious above all to win favour in the eyes of his father. She had felt first disappointment and impatience, then frustration. And that frustration was now, slowly but surely, giving way to disgust — and open rebellion. Kathryn was no longer the child who had come to Savigny as a dewy-eyed bride — the claustrophobic atmosphere at the château, where Guillaume's word was law, and law was the preservation of the dynasty, had begun the change in her, the birth of her son and the onset of the war had accelerated it. The arrival of the German occupying forces and the attitude of the de Savignys to them had completed the process.

'I don't understand how you can bear to be civil to them,' she said now.

Charles sighed, passing a hand through his thinning hair.

'We've been through all this before, Katrine.' He pronounced her name in the French manner. 'We have no choice but to get along with them.'

'We have every choice!' Her eyes were beginning to flash, dark brown mutating to tawny gold around the irises. 'Oh, I realise we have to have a certain amount of dealings with von Rheinhardt. He's in charge of the region now that he has replaced Buhler and as such it's necessary for your father to negotiate with him on behalf of all the people who live on the estate and in Savigny village. But he doesn't have to be so friendly with him. And he certainly does not have to invite him to dinner! It's mostrous!'

'It is also expedient. Surely you realise how awkward he could make things for us if he chose? It's important to keep him sweet, for everyone's sake.'

'That might be your way of looking at it – it's not mine.'

'Be sensible, Kathryn, I beg you,' Charles pleaded. 'Don't you see it's asking for trouble to take this attitude?'

'I don't care. I won't have dinner with that bastard. I couldn't. If I tried it would choke me. You can say I've got a headache, if you like. Say whatever you choose – I can't stop you.'

'He'll see through that. You're never ill. He will be very offended, Katrine.'

'Not nearly as offended as if I said something dreadful about Hitler, and I can't guarantee I wouldn't.' Her eyes were flashing in earnest now and Charles shook his head helplessly.

'Oh Katrine, Katrine, what am I to do with you?'

'You don't have to do anything. Just allow me my principles.'

'That's all very well. But can we afford them?'

'What has that to do with anything? The Germans are our enemies! I won't socialise with them just to please your father.'

'Not to please my father. To please me.'

'Isn't that the same thing?' she flashed.

She saw him whiten and felt a *frisson* of fear, knowing she had gone too far.

'What do you mean by that?'

'Nothing,' she said defensively. This was not the time to tell him she believed he would do anything – anything – to gain favour in his father's eyes, that he would sacrifice anything – his principles, his marriage, her respect – to be the son his father wanted. If she started down that road she would say a great deal more than she should – that it was his weakness his father deplored, his inability to stand up to him on any single issue, and that the more he strove to please, the more his father despised him. She might even tell him how pathetic she thought him, how his endless belly-crawling disgusted her — and she knew instinctively that such things, once said, could never be retracted. One day she would tell him. But not now.

'Katrine.' He was changing tack. 'You must understand why my father behaves as he does. All he is trying to do is make life bearable, not only for us, for our family, but for everyone who depends on us — estate workers, village folk, everyone. The Germans are in control, whether we like it or not, and whatever garbage Pétain spouts about "the renaissance of France being the fruit of our suffering". Don't you know what happens to those who resist? They are taken away, tortured and shot. At least this way we are allowed to get on with our lives virtually unhindered. There's a lot to be said for that.'

'Is there indeed? And when the war is over and the Germans sent packing, what will your life be like then? How will you live with yourselves, knowing you appeased the enemy — collaborated with them?'

'At least we will *be* alive!' Charles said harshly. 'Have you thought what could happen if we antagonise them, Katrine? It wouldn't be just you that would suffer, either. It would be Guy too. If you won't consider the rest of us, at least consider him. If you can't do that, what sort of a mother are you?'

The mention of her son brought a quick flush to Kathryn's cheeks.

'Don't bring Guy into this!'

'But he's in it, can't you see? The Nazis are no respecters of little children or anyone else.'

'How, then, can you possibly bear to entertain one at your dinner table?'

'General von Rheinhardt is a soldier who happens to be in control of this district. He's not Gestapo or SS. They are the real devils. And some of our own Vichy police are almost as bad, I'm ashamed to say.'

'Typical French,' she muttered under her breath.

'What did you say?' he demanded, his patience finally snapping.

She did not answer, feeling again the sharp thrill of fear, of knowing she was saying things she should not say, thinking things she should not even think, but the depth of her disillusion was too great to be stifled. She had loved France just as she had loved Charles and both had let her down. She couldn't bear to see people she had cared for and respected ingratiating themselves with the enemy.

They were everywhere, the collaborators, village girls walking out with soldiers, business people making a fast buck from their custom, and the de Savignys treating them as socially acceptable. Charles could excuse it as the manifestation of the instinct for survival, she thought it degrading and repulsive. She would rather die, she thought, than lie back and pretend to accept their dominance. At least that way she would retain her self-respect.

Charles stared at her coldly for a long moment; she stared back and saw only a stranger.

'I'm ashamed, Charles,' she said quietly at last. 'And so should you be.'

For a moment anger flashed in his dark-blue eyes and she wondered if he might strike her. He had never done so, though sometimes during their more violent arguments she had seen his hands clench into fists, but there was always a first time. He had shocked her in so many ways, why not this? In fact she thought she would prefer it if he struck her. At least hitting out was a typically masculine reaction whereas spineless appeasement put her more in mind of a frightened old woman begging not to be hurt.

But Charles did not strike her. After a moment he turned away wearily.

'I won't say any more, Katrine. I can see I am getting nowhere. But think about what you are doing, I beg you. If you are willing to jeopardise your safety, and mine, at least don't jeopardise Guy's. Now – I am going to dress for dinner. If you have any consideration for your son, you will do the same.'

He turned abruptly and left the drawing room. Kathryn stood for a moment, conquering the urge to pick up one of the priceless antiques which adorned it and hurl it after him. Then, as her anger began to ebb away, the desolation crept in, yellow and scummy like the foam on the tide, and helpless tears filled her eyes.

There was nothing she could do. Nothing. She was trapped here with her little son and it was not only the Nazis who were the jailors but also her husband and his family. How could she hope to fight all of them?

'Katrine is refusing to dine with us, Papa,' Charles said.

Guillaume looked up from his desk to see his son standing in the doorway of his study and experienced a flash of familiar impatience with him.

'What do you mean – she's refusing to dine with us?'

'Exactly that. She says she won't sit down at the same table as von Rheinhardt and I think she means it.'

'Didn't you tell her he is my guest – that if we want to keep our home we'd do well to cultivate his goodwill?'

'I've tried to talk some sense into her, yes, but she won't listen. I thought perhaps you would have a word with her.'

Guillaume's impatience grew.

'What's the matter with you, Charles? Can't you control your own wife?'

Charles said nothing. His brows had contracted, giving his face a sullen look, and Guillaume thought he looked more like a small boy afraid of being sent to his room in disgrace than a grown man, heir to the ancient Baronage de Savigny.

It had always been the same, of course. He was probably reminded of a small boy now when he looked at Charles because that was the very same expression he had worn when chastised as a child. It had infuriated Guillaume then and it infuriated him now. Did the boy have no backbone at all? Why wouldn't he let fly in return instead of standing there, taking it, and looking utterly wretched? At a very early stage Guillaume had discovered he had little time for his son – even now, across the years, he could remember with perfect clarity the first time he had acknowledged it.

Charles had been about three years old and Guillaume had acquired a pony for him. An enthusiastic horseman himself, he was keen that his son and heir should learn to ride as soon as possible. He had taken Charles to the stable block at the rear of the château, expecting him to be pleased and excited at having his very own pony. But Charles' response was quite the opposite. When Guillaume tried to lift him into the small saddle he clung to his father, white and shaking, and nothing would induce him to relinquish his grasp on Guillaume's neck.

'Don't be so stupid, boy! I won't let you fall!' Guillaume had said, less gently than he might have done because it was beyond his comprehension why Charles should behave in such a fashion. He had taken him riding plenty of times before, sitting the child in front of him on Beau, his chestnut hunter, and telling him to hold tight to Beau's mane. But of course he had never seen the terror on Charles' face as he cantered across the hillside with him and he had imagined that the tears on his cheeks when he lifted him down were the result of the wind.

'Non!' Charles had yelled, kicking so hard with his heels that he raised bruises on Guillaume's side that had lasted for days. 'Non – non! Papa – non!'

It had been the same when Guillaume tried to teach him to swim. He had hung back at the edge of the pool, screaming in terror. Eventually Guillaume had climbed out and thrown him in bodily, diving in after him and rescuing the spluttering child whose open mouth had filled with water, then wading away from him and forcing him to doggy-paddle frantically to reach the safety of his arms.

Charles had learned to both ride and swim eventually, of course, mastering his terror by the sheer force of his desire to please his father, but Guillaume's impatience with him had scarcely diminished. Rather it intensified. If the boy really did not want to do these things why didn't he at least have the guts to stand up and say so? The lack of spirit seemed to Guillaume to be almost worse than the physical fear.

As Charles grew older the relationship between them failed to improve. The boy was afraid of him, he knew, and knowing it made Guillaume despise him the more. A vicious circle was set up, Charles continually striving for his father's affection and respect, Guillaume growing colder and harder and more impatient. He could not understand why a son of his should be so spineless. His mother, making excuses for him, said he was gentle, with a kind heart and a sweet nature. Guillaume merely thought him a milksop.

Matters were not improved either by the fact that Christian, Charles' younger brother, was everything Charles was not. Christian was a tearaway, fearless to the point of recklessness, with an athleticism to match. Though two years younger than

Charles, he could soon beat him across a swimming pool, and in their rough-and-tumble games it was always Christian who came out on top. If anything he was too uninhibited, too forceful, too dismissive of authority. If he could have taken the two boys and jumbled them up a little, Guillaume thought, he might have been able to produce the perfect son. That, of course, was not possible. Unfortunately the required balance had materialised in only one of his children – his daughter Celestine, who was everything he could have wished for.

But Celestine was not only the third child and still at college in Paris, she was also a girl. The Baronage would never pass to her. He was left with doing the best he could with Charles. And an unrewarding struggle it seemed to be. Couldn't the boy get anything right? If he couldn't control his own wife what hope was there of him making a good job of running the de Savigny estates when the time came?

If the de Savigny estates were still there to be run. Guillaume gave his head a tired shake. It was more than a year now since the French army had laid down its weapons, more than a year since the lines had been drawn and the country divided up – occupied territory in the north and east, heavily policed by Hitler's forces, the rest still governed nominally, at any rate, by Pétain from his base in Vichy, the demarcation line slicing through the heart of Savigny land.

It made life difficult, that line. A pass was necessary in order to cross it for even the most mundane, everyday reason, and the border patrols were surly and suspicious. But Guillaume tried to view it as an inconvenience and no more, part of the price that had to be paid for the moment at least for having resisted the German invasion. It would not last for ever. When the conflict was finally decided things would settle into some sort of pattern closer to normality. In the meantime it was in everyone's best interests to keep on the right side of the invaders. Anything else was asking for trouble. Keep them sweet and the heritage of Savigny and all those who depended on it would be safe. Antagonise them and property would be destroyed and lives lost needlessly.

He had explained the position he intended to take to his family when France had fallen and they had gone along with it. Louise, his wife, hated violence in any form and in any case always abided by his decisions. It was a pattern that had been established early in their married life; she accepted his authority without question, content that by reason of his gender and position he must know best. Charles, typically, had agreed with him that though it was far from an ideal situation there was no point in having blood spilled on Savigny land to no useful purpose. Christian and Celestine he was less sure of – Christian was a hothead who hated living under the Nazi regime and where Christian led Celestine was likely to follow. But Christian had been wounded during his brief period of service in the French army – a serious leg wound which was taking a long while to heal – and for the present, at least, was incapable of doing anything stupid, and Guillaume was reasonably confident that the family tradition of putting duty and heritage above all else would persuade them to follow his lead.

No, Kathryn, Charles' English wife, was the greatest threat to the fragile peace at Savigny, Kathryn, whose countrymen were still at war with Hitler and who showed, by her every word and gesture, her contempt for his minions.

Guillaume experienced a stab of anger for the young woman who could so easily, he felt, do something to endanger the rapport he had established with the occupying power. Yet in spite of himself it was qualified by a grudging respect. Kathryn had spirit –that was more than could be said for Charles. He had recognised it in her the very first time Charles had brought her to Savigny and introduced her as his bride-to-be, and he had been glad. They might not always see eye to eye but if some of that spirit could be handed down to the children of the union then there might be hope yet for the Savigny line. And his hopes appeared to be justified. Already in Guy, their little son, Guillaume could see a great deal of his mother's character, though physically he was very like his father. Now just short of his fourth birthday, Guy was already bolder than Charles had ever been and showing clear signs of the self-confidence that was lacking in Charles. Guillaume knew he had Kathryn to thank for that.

But it did not mean that he intended to pander to her. She had to understand the danger she could place them all in if she continued her stand against von Rheinhardt. Already Guillaume had noticed how she had gone out of her way to avoid him and how ungracious she was about the presents of food, cigarettes and precious petrol coupons he had made to them. At the moment von Rheinhardt was well disposed towards them, appreciating the advantages of being in charge of a relatively trouble-free district, but he could turn against them just as easily if he was upset in any way and his revenge would be terrible. Kathryn must be made to realise that.

Of course, he thought, Kathryn was an optimist. If she had not been she would not have been taken in so readily by Charles' surface charms. Now her optimism refused to allow her to countenance defeat in the long term.

Guillaume was not so optimistic. He was very afraid that the old order had gone for ever and the German regime was here to stay. If so it was his duty to try to establish a place in the new order for his family and all those who depended on them. The de Savignys had discharged their responsibilities to their estates and those who lived and worked on them for more than five hundred years, providing for them in almost feudal fashion. They had survived the Revolution, they would survive the German occupation. They *must* survive and Guillaume would do whatever was necessary to make certain they did. Kathryn and her pride and obstinacy could not be allowed to jeopardise that.

Guillaume looked at his son with a mixture of scorn and pity. If Charles could not convince his wife of her duty to conform then Guillaume would have to do it for him.

'All right, Charles,' he said wearily. 'I will speak to Kathryn.'

A strange expression, half relief, half resentment, flickered across Charles' sallow features.

'It won't do any good. She won't listen to you.'

Guillaume's mouth tightened.

'Oh yes, Charles, I think she will,' he said.

The long refectory table had been set for six but as yet the dining room was empty. The de Savigny family were gathering in the salon as they always did for pre-dinner drinks. The food, when it was served, might be meagre compared with what they had been used to in the days before shortages and rationing; the old traditions were maintained nevertheless.

Guillaume and Louise had been first down, as they always were, followed by Christian, and a rather sombre Charles. All were formally dressed, as was their custom. They had been joined by

63

General von Rheinhardt, resplendent in the uniform of an officer of the Third Reich. The only member of the party who had failed to put in an appearance was Kathryn and as Guillaume poured wine, made from his own grapes, and passed it around, Charles found himself watching the door and hoping without much optimism that she might yet walk through.

His father had been up to speak to her, he knew, but he couldn't imagine that anything Guillaume could have said would make much difference. Kathryn was impossible – a law unto herself. He didn't know what had happened to the charming girl he had met and married, a girl so acquiescent and naive he had had no doubt he could mould her into the wife he both wanted and needed, a girl whose admiration of him had amounted almost to hero-worship so that she made him feel powerful, amusing and mature – all the things he had striven all his life to feel and yet which, under his father's critical eye, had eluded him.

She did not make him feel those things now. Somewhere along the line, in the six years of their marriage, they had slipped away from him. The adoration had paled in her eyes, sometimes he felt she almost disliked him, and she questioned his authority and even openly defied him at every turn. Nowadays she made him feel as inadequate as did his father, perhaps more so, because he had always been in awe of his father whilst once, not so long ago, Kathryn had been a child he wanted to pet and protect. The hurt and bewilderment burned sourly in his stomach, spoiling the taste of his father's good wine, and he found himself thinking, with longing, of Regine, his mistress and the woman he would have liked to marry if she hadn't been six years his senior and married already. Regine wouldn't have behaved in this infuriating manner; Regine would not have made him look a complete fool. She would have been there at his side, bolstering his confidence, reassuring him that he was doing the right thing, that there was nothing else he *could* do, and that anyway, in the end nothing mattered except that she loved him and they were together. He saw her now in his mind's eye, the thick blonde hair that came tumbling around her shoulders when he pulled out the pins that secured it, the generous breasts that he could bury his face in and suck on as if he were a baby again, and ached with need of her. It had always been the same – from the first moment he had met her he had wanted to drown in her pale yielding flesh and allow her to banish all the demons that haunted him. Regine had been more than just a lover to him, she had been father, mother and offspring all rolled into one, and he had worshipped her. She had taught him to make love as opposed to simply copulating, she had praised his endeavours as well as his successes, she had comforted him and cheered him when things went badly for him, she had even, sometimes, made him laugh. The one thing she had refused to do was leave her husband for him.

'I can't do that, *chéri*, you mustn't ask me to,' she had said, tenderly stroking his hand.

'Why not? Why not, Regine? It's me you love!' He had said it defiantly, but in reality he was seeking her affirmation.

'Of course I love you, but that has nothing to do with it. I am Claude's wife. I couldn't leave him and the children. It wouldn't be right. They would be hurt.'

'And what about me? Don't you think you are hurting me?'

'A little, perhaps, but that's the way it is, I'm afraid. And it's not so bad, is it? We can be together as often as you like.'

'No, we can't. I want to be with you all the time.'

She laughed; he saw the rise and fall of her magnificent breasts and wanted her so desperately he thought he would die of it.

'No, Charles, you don't,' she said. 'You'd soon be tired of me.'

'I wouldn't! I'd never tire of you, darling Regine. I wish I could be a part of you, so I could go with you wherever you go, every minute of the day. And we could make love all the time – in the bathtub, at the breakfast table, when you are working at your needlepoint, everywhere . . . anywhere!'

'Be sensible, Charles, I beg you,' she had chided him, but he knew she was pleased. 'I can't do it. You mustn't ask me. And besides, I wouldn't do for your wife. It's one thing to have a mistress who happens to be married, quite another to try to make her legitimate. Think of the scandal it would bring to the de Savigny name. Your father would be most displeased.'

'I don't care.' Needing her made him bold. 'If I had you I wouldn't care what he thought.'

'Yes, you would. And you also care about providing an heir for the de Savigny line. I can't have any more children. When I had little Gilbert the doctor was quite definite about it. I was very ill;

they told me categorically I can never have another. No, you must find a girl who will make you a suitable wife, Charles, and give you sons to carry on the name. But I will still be here for you, I promise. I will always be here for you.'

He had begged, cried even, but she had remained adamant and in the end he had seen the sense of what she said. Perhaps, he had thought, he could have the best of both worlds. The line *was* important to him, it was his duty to ensure its survival – just as long as he could still have Regine too. It was simply a matter of finding the right girl.

When he had met Kathryn he had thought she was the right girl. Strong enough to give him the sons he needed, young enough to adapt to his ways and not cause trouble, sufficiently in love with him to make him feel masterful, beautiful enough to make him proud of her.

Regine had thought so too. She had actively encouraged the match. Perhaps, he thought now with hindsight, she had considered Kathryn too naive and inexperienced to be any serious threat to her; perhaps she had thought he would lie beside Kathryn after making love to her and compare her unfavourably with Regine. Certainly in the early days she had asked him how things were in that direction, given advice and encouraged confidences that would have shocked Kathryn had she known about them.

But she had not known – at least, he didn't think so – and the arrangement had proved, in the beginning, to be very successful. Until everything had begun to go wrong.

Regine's husband, who was a wealthy wine merchant, had decided to move the centre of his operations to Paris and Regine and the children had gone with him. He still had a place in Charente, of course, and they came to stay for weekends and holidays, but somehow nothing could be quite the same. And then the war had come. Regine had been in Paris when France fell and she was there now. Regulations made it too difficult to travel, even their correspondence was curtailed. It was more than a year since he had last seen her and he ached for her with a hollow despair that grew worse rather than lessening as the weeks became months.

If only she were here now! he thought wretchedly. If only he could go to her, lay his head against her plump shoulder and tell her all his troubles. But she wasn't here. Somehow he had to bear them alone.

'More wine, Charles?'

He became aware, with a slight sense of shock, that Guillaume was addressing him. He glanced down at his glass, scarcely touched.

'No, I don't think so, thank you, Papa.'

'It's very good wine. There's no doubt about it, you French know how to do things properly.'

It was von Rheinhardt speaking. Charles looked at him, mentally appraising the new Commandant of the district.

Physically he was a fine specimen of Aryan manhood and a far more impressive ambassador of the Third Reich than Buhler, his predecessor. Where Buhler had been a very ordinary-looking man of medium height, von Rheinhardt was tall and powerfully built; where Buhler's hair had been thinning and mouse-coloured, von Rheinhardt's was thick and fair. He was better-looking than Buhler, too, with features that bordered on the handsome. But there was something about him that Charles did not care for, and the mistrust went further than simple dislike for a man whose countrymen had humbled his own. There had been something almost ingratiating about Buhler's manner – which had also irritated in its own way, he had to admit – a strange fawning respect for the aristocracy of the country over which he had power, a desire for acceptance. Von Rheinhardt was quite different. There was an arrogance about him that was apparent in every deceptively lazy moment and Charles recognised it as not only the arrogance of the conqueror. It went deeper than that. Von Rheinhardt, he suspected, came from a priviledged family himself and was in no way awed by the de Savignys. And there was something else that Charles could not quite put his finger on. He thought it might be ruthlessness. The scar did not help, of course, running from the corner of his eye to his mouth and giving him a dangerous look. But it was more than that. There was cruelty in those very blue eyes, a hard line to the set of the mouth.

Charles noted it all and tried to quell his misgivings. This man wasn't another Buhler. They were going to have to be very careful not to antagonise him. He could, Charles thought, be dangerous.

At the moment, however, he was choosing to play the part of the appreciative guest, praising the Baron for his excellent wine.

'I'm glad you like it,' Guillaume replied. 'I think you will like our cognac even more. And I hope you will allow us to go on producing it as we have done now since my grandfather's day.'

'Certainly. As long as you are prepared to share it with us, there will be no problem.' He said it pleasantly enough, but the threat was there all the same, implicit in his words, and Charles knew he did not mean only a bottle or two for him and his fellow officers at the Château François where he had his headquarters, but wholesale consignments for the hierarchy back home in Germany.

'We don't want the way of life here to suffer more than is unavoidable,' von Rheinhardt continued smoothly. 'Hopefully we can all live side by side without acrimony. I don't want trouble and I am sure you don't either.'

'No one wants trouble,' Guillaume replied. 'The people around here simply want to be allowed to get on with their lives. General Buhler found that to be the case and I am sure you will too.'

The very blue eyes narrowed a shade.

'I certainly hope so. The area is not without its problems, though, I am afraid. There will always be those who behave stupidly, those who are too pig-headed to accept things as they are – and will continue to be. General Buhler was a good man but he could be a little blind on occasions. If there are troublemakers here, be sure I shall find them, and they will be dealt with most severely.'

Charles experienced a chill of disquiet. He knew very well what von Rheinhardt meant by severe dealings. When the Nazis had first come two youths in a nearby village had tried to sabotage their operations by cutting the telephone wires. They had been caught and shot. And stories were rife of the way that any who resisted or tried to oppose the invaders in more insidious ways were treated – they were tortured before they, too, were shot, or taken away, God alone knew where.

As his father had pointed out, as yet there had been no such incident in Savigny, thanks mainly to the fact that the villagers were following the example of the de Savigny family and appeasing the enemy, but it was almost inevitable that eventually some hothead would step out of line. When one did Charles was sure von Rheinhardt would show no mercy. Unlike Buhler this was a man with a burning zeal for the Fatherland and the coldly clinical will to do whatever he had to in order to ensure everyone who came under his jurisdiction toed the line. What was more, Charles thought, he would enjoy enforcing it.

'It is good, however, to know I have your support,' von Rheinhardt continued. 'I am sure your influence will be most helpful to me in maintaining calm. It is also very kind of you to invite me to dinner and afford me the opportunity to visit your charming château and meet the members of your family socially.' He looked from one to the other of them with an almost regal smile, then his eyes narrowed a shade. 'I look forward also to meeting your daughter-in-law at last. She is English, is she not?'

'Kathryn is English-born but naturalised French,' Guillaume said swiftly. 'I am sure she will be joining us soon, won't she, Charles?'

Charles experienced another moment of something close to panic.

'She wasn't feeling too well earlier, Papa. She was suffering from a headache. I'm not sure if she will feel up to joining us.'

'Really?' Von Rheinhardt's tone was silky smooth but the undertones were unmistakable. 'That is a great pity. I do hope that I am not the cause of her indisposition.'

There was an awkward silence. Even the centuries-old walls of the château seemed to be holding their breath.

Then, as if she were an actress making a perfectly timed entrance, Kathryn opened the door and came into the salon.

'Thank God you changed your mind and came down,' Charles said. 'He had noticed, you know, and he didn't like it.'

'Really,' Kathryn said coldly.

They were in the bedroom of their apartment. The evening had passed off without incident. Von Rheinhardt had been almost genial, the de Savignys courteous good hosts; though Christian had been quieter than usual and Kathryn had hardly spoken at all, Guillaume had played the diplomat and Louise had been her charming, if rather vacuous self. The dinner, though not up to the standard of excellence offered by the superb cuisine of happier times, had still been imaginative and well presented;

Angeline, the cook, had worked miracles with vegetables from the château gardens and some of her wonderful sauces, though they were no longer rich with cream as they had been in the old days, and von Rheinhardt had appreciated the Château de Savigny cognac as Guillaume had predicted he would. There had been a few awkward moments, small silences following unfortunate nuances of speech which might have been misinterpreted, but they had been glossed over and only von Rheinhardt's thinly veiled warnings had caused any lasting discomfort.

'I understand an enemy aircraft came down about thirty miles north of here a few nights ago,' he had said, almost conversationally. 'If the pilot should come this way I sincerely hope no one in the community would be foolish enough to try to assist him.'

'Wouldn't he have been killed?' Guillaume enquired blandly.

'We don't think so. At least, no body was found in the wreckage.'

'Well, he wouldn't survive long in the open country. It's been wet and bitterly cold.'

'Exactly. Still, if someone is hiding him we shall soon find out, never fear. Then those responsible will be dealt with. We cannot, we will not, allow that sort of behaviour to go unpunished.'

'The poor man!' Louise had murmured. 'It must be dreadful to be wounded, hungry and cold in an alien country.'

Von Rheinhardt had looked at her almost benignly – Louise was quite capable of saying such things and getting away with them – but his reply was unequivocal, just the same.

'You must not think of him as a man like your own sons, Madame – he is not. He is the enemy. I hope you would not be tempted to help him.'

'Oh no, indeed not,' Louise replied, smiling at him charmingly, and Charles glanced anxiously at Kathryn, afraid of what her reaction might be.

But Kathryn had said nothing. He knew from the tightening of the muscles in her cheeks and the way she folded her hands together in her lap so that her nails bit into the backs of her hands that she was struggling to keep silent, and for that he was grateful. But he had continued to worry, all the same, that she might still say something unpardonably rash, and the evening had been a tense one for him.

Now, wearing silk pyjamas, he leaned back against the pillows and watched Kathryn getting ready for bed.

She sat at the dressing table, a rich peacock-blue kimono that he had bought for her in the East before the war covering her slender figure, but he could see that beneath it her shoulders were rigid and she was brushing her hair with unnecessary vigour.

'You did the right thing, Katrine,' he said. 'We all did. There is nothing else we can do.'

She did not answer; he tried again.

'We have to be sensible, *ma chérie*. You don't like it, I know, but what good would it do to have more French blood spilled? Life has to go on.'

Still she did not answer and he felt the familiar frustration begin to build inside him. How dare she sit there ignoring him? She was his wife, for God's sake! Surely he was entitled to a little respect? He tried to think of something grand to say, and instead only heard himself ask peevishly: 'How did Papa persuade you to come down? You wouldn't listen to me.'

Kathryn slammed the ivory-backed brush down on the dressing table and swung round. The lines of her throat above the silky kimono were taut.

'He didn't persuade me. I came because I decided to.'

'Oh really? Then what was it that affected your decision?'

'I suppose I realised I didn't have any choice – that yes, I could place Guy's life in danger if I refuse to go along with these disgusting games your family is playing. He's my son, he's half English – and the English, at least, haven't given up the fight. We're still at war with *cochons* like von Rheinhardt and that makes us vulnerable. I don't care for myself – I really don't, Charles. Personally I would rather die than kowtow to the Nazis the way you seem to be prepared to. But Guy is just a little boy. I can't take chances with his safety.'

'Good. I'm glad you've seen sense.'

'Are you? I'm not sure I am. I'm afraid for him, yes, and that is why I went along with your repulsive charade. But I can't pretend I'm proud of myself for doing it. Are you proud, Charles? Are you proud of the French capitulation?'

'I'm doing what I have to do,' he retorted, stung. 'I'm trying to save lives; to protect my heritage.'

'Oh yes, your precious heritage! What's left of it? Tell me that! You've chosen to lie down and let those bastards walk all over you and you've forced me into a position of having to do the same. And let me tell you, Charles, I find that unforgivable.'

He looked at her and felt his body begin to stir. She infuriated him, yes, especially when she talked this way, and he longed for Regine's flattery and soothing touch. But there was also something devastatingly attractive about Kathryn when she was angry, those brown eyes flashing liquid gold fire, muscles taut, breasts heaving. What was it about a woman's breasts that he found so irresistible? It couldn't be an Oedipus complex, his own mother was small, flat as a boy in the fashion of the twenties when she had been in the prime of her beauty. No, it was some other half-forgotten memory that pre-dated Regine, pre-dated even his first experiences in the high-class brothels of Paris where he had first been initiated into the pleasures of sex and learned the taste of passion.

'You knew when you married me that you were marrying into a family with traditions to uphold,' he said testily, annoyed with himself for allowing her to stir him in this way. 'You seemed happy enough with the situation then.'

'Did I? Perhaps that was because in those days I was naive enough to have romantic notions. I was stupid enough to think that your traditions, as you call them, included pride and honour. I didn't realise they meant doing anything, however demeaning, in order to save your own skins.'

'That's unfair, Katrine. It's not our skins we are trying to save – it's a whole way of life.'

'Which is obviously so rotten at the core it's scarcely worth saving.'

He sighed.

'There's no point in going over all this again, is there? You simply refuse to see that what we are doing is trying to safeguard the local community who depend on us. You were willing this evening to sacrifice your principles in order to look after Guy's best interests because he is your son. Can't you see we feel the same way about the people who work for us and live on our estates? They are a sacred trust to the de Savigny family just as Guy is to you.'

'No,' she said. 'I can't see it. I only know I feel grubby and ashamed of myself.'

She stood up, slipping off the kimono and draping it over the stool. Beneath it she was wearing a simple opera-topped nightgown; the chill in the unheated bedroom shivered over her bare arms and she moved quickly to the bed, sliding between the sheets and pulling the voluminous eiderdown a fraction higher.

'Katrine . . . you're cold.' Charles reached for her, his hand brushing her breast. 'Come here, let me warm you.'

The touch of his hand made her flinch. In the old days when they were first married she had loved cuddling up to him in their big bed, loved the warmth that was generated by two bodies pressed close together, loved the feeling of being one with the man who had seemed to her to be everything she could wish for in a romantic hero made flesh. Believing he loved her in return and wanted her physically had been a source of wonder that made her turn weak with desire and strong with a feeling of invincibility. There were differences between them, she had known that, but she had been supremely confident that their love was deep enough to overcome any obstacle and bridge the divide formed by nationality and culture and breeding.

Now she knew differently and the disappointment ached in her alongside all the other emotions.

With an impatient movement she pulled away from his questing hand.

'Don't, Charles, please.'

'Katrine . . .'

'We can't solve our problems like that. At least, I can't.'

'Very well. If that's the way you want it.' He turned away from her, hurt more by her rejection than he would ever admit.

'It's not the way I want it. It just happens to be the way it is,' she said bitterly.

Charles chose not to reply. He humped the eiderdown over him and infuriatingly soon began to snore gently. But sleep eluded Kathryn. She lay, cold still, the expanse of icy sheet which surrounded her making her unwilling to move into a more comfortable position, wondering if she and Charles would ever understand one another again. Somehow she doubted it. The chasm that had opened up between them was too great, the disillusion too damaging. Yet she had bound her life to his, he was her husband and the father of her son. Guy was a de Savigny whether she liked it or not.

73

What am I going to do? Kathryn asked herself despairingly.

In that moment the dilemma eclipsed even the day-to-day privations and fears of living in a country no longer at war, but under enemy occupation.

London, 1941

NIGHT HAD FALLEN early on London. All day a thick blanket of cloud had hung over the city, threatening snow and throwing a sombre yellowish-grey haze over the bomb craters and the shells of devastated buildings; now, though it was not yet five-thirty, the darkness was complete. Not a single chink of light showed at the windows of the hotels and houses, mostly converted into flats, which flanked Portman Square – the enforcement of the blackout made certain of that – and the sidelights of what vehicles there were had been half covered so that there was only the dimmest of glimmers to show they were there at all.

As Paul Sullivan walked briskly up the street the cold seemed to seep out of the pavements and clam in around him. He turned up the collar of his greatcoat, bending his head so that his chin was buried inside it, and thrust his gloved hands deep into his pockets.

It was, he thought, going to be a long, hard winter – and it had set in early in France, where he had spent the last months, just as in England. Though it was still only mid-November he had been out on nights much colder and darker than this one and the *frisson* of fear that always accompanied him on his missions had meant that the cold chilling his fingers and toes had been less noticeable than the aching awareness of danger that ran in his blood.

The weather assumed enormous importance in that dangerous shadowland that spanned both sides of the demarcation line between occupied territory and Vichy France, where the uniform of a Vichy policeman could be as much of a threat as that of a German soldier and danger wore a thousand different faces. A clear sky with a bright moon meant that planes could fly – friendly English planes, bearing arms and supplies and sometimes men to help him in his work. A dark night meant extra cover for operations which needed to be cloaked in secrecy. Rain misted windscreens, soggy fields muffled footsteps, frosty ground and snow meant tracks that were all too easy to follow. Paul Sullivan had seen them all and quickly learned to assess their importance – assess it so automatically that now, without even so much as glancing at the sky, his fine-tuned mind was telling him there would be no aircraft crossing the Channel tonight.

Paul thought briefly of the friends who had watched the sky with him, friends who were now dead, and felt a sickness start in his stomach. The circuit he had formed and run in north-east France was shattered, its members taken or shot as they ran on a night when no cloud had obscured the moon. He had not been with them that night. If he had been, could he have saved them, or would he too have ended up in a shallow grave? The question tormented him as it had tormented him ever since that night, and he thrust it away. To believe he could have prevented their deaths was a form of arrogance, and arrogance, in Paul Sullivan's war, was a dangerous thing.

At the corner of the square a group of Home Guard were standing outside their pillbox smoking and stamping their feet against the cold; the sight of them and the 'Mobile Mollies' – the small anti-aircraft guns – reminded Paul that the thickness of the night had a different meaning for war-torn England – tonight there would be no bombers dropping their loads of death and destruction on London. It shocked him almost that he could have forgotten so easily that here the struggle had a different face, that England was still engaged in open warfare with the Third Reich whilst France had, on the surface at any rate, capitulated. For Paul, France, where nothing was quite what it seemed, had become a way of life these last months.

As he approached the doorway that was his destination Paul glanced quickly over his shoulder, instinctively checking that he was not being followed. An unnecessary precaution here in London, he hoped, but one that had become second nature to him during his time in France. But for the Home Guard the street was deserted; satisfied, he went inside and gave his name to the doorman.

In peacetime the building had been nothing more intriguing than an elegant old house converted into flats; now several of them had been hired by the newly formed French section of the SOE.

Here agents could be seen by the home staff – much safer, for reasons of security, than allowing them to visit the SOE headquarters in Baker Street, the exact location of which was a carefully guarded secret. As a very early recruit Paul had been interviewed in a basement in Whitehall where the labyrinthine corridors were policed by uniformed soldiers, but that hidey-hole had been returned to the military now, abandoned in favour of the anonymous rented apartments, and Paul was glad. Though he would never admit it he had hated descending in the ancient creaking lift to the bowels of the earth. From childhood he had suffered from – and largely conquered – the creeping menace of claustrophobia, and the basement had reawakened his feelings of dark panic and the fear of being buried alive. He had understood, of course, that the theory was that the basement afforded protection against air raids, but he had thought he would prefer to take his chances with a bomb above ground level where at least the air was pure and escape no more than the thickness of the Ministry walls away.

He went up the staircase now to the designated apartment and knocked on the door. It was opened by a young woman.

'Captain Sullivan.' A flush of pleasure, that not even the professionalism for which she had been chosen for her special duties could suppress, coloured her cheeks and replaced some of the warmth that her khaki uniform had taken away. Paul Sullivan had this effect on most of the women he met – they warmed to his narrow face with its slightly irregular features, admired the lean frame which suggested not weakness but power, melted at the wry twist of his mouth and the way his hazel eyes crinkled when he smiled. The fact that he seldom smiled nowadays coupled with his lack of awareness of his attractiveness only made it the more potent; they longed, almost without exception, to be the one to break through that barrier of reserve. But there was a strange, still vibrance about him too and an edge of something that might almost be danger, whilst on the surface he presented an impression of total immovable calm. He might, thought the young woman, have just returned from a relaxing leave instead of a perilous mission.

'Hello, Rita.' His voice was deep, deceptively lazy. 'You're still with the department then?'

'Just let them try to get rid of me! Actually I'd say I was quite enjoying the war if it wasn't for the damage those bastards are doing! Do you know last night a bomb destroyed the church where my mother and father were married? If we don't soon put a stop to their tricks there won't be anything left worth fighting for.'

Paul's lips twisted grimly. Principles are worth fighting for, he felt like saying. The right of every human being to live their lives in freedom is worth fighting for. And people, most of all, are worth fighting for. But he did not voice the thought. He was too well aware of the desire for revenge burning inside of him to feel that such noble sentiments would be anything but hypocritical. Fine motives were all very well, but Paul knew he was driven most of all by the need to avenge his own personal loss.

Two years ago, when this bloody war had erupted, volcano-like, from the molten lava base of Nazi Germany, he'd had a wife and child who had meant the whole world to him. Now they were dead. They had been visiting Gerie's parents in Rotterdam when the Germans had attacked and they had been caught in the aerial bombardment that was known as the blitzkrieg. Desperate to discover their fate Paul had battered on every door available to him only to learn the horrifying truth – the street where Gerie's parents had lived had been reduced to a mass of smoking rubble, Gerie and his little daughter Beatrice were numbered amongst the eight hundred people who had died when Rotterdam had fallen.

'Major Fawcett is expecting me, I believe,' he said, businesslike suddenly.

The girl's eyes shadowed at the sudden end to the easy rapport of a moment ago, but young as she was she was too good at her job to allow it to show for more than a moment. Rita Barlow had been hand-picked for her qualities of efficiency and courage to do a difficult and demanding job; she would never allow what she thought of as a 'soft spot' for one of the department's agents to get in the way of duty.

'He is expecting you, yes. I'll tell him you've arrived.' She went through into what had once been a bedroom but was now coverted into an office. 'Captain Sullivan is here to see you, sir.'

'Sullivan. Come in, old chap.' The Major rose to his feet behind a desk strewn with papers he had been perusing whilst he waited for Paul; he was not a man who believed in wasting a single moment of his precious time. In an ashtray an abandoned cigar lay in a heap of pungent ash. 'Have a seat, won't you? And Rita, rustle us up some coffee. It's a cold night out there, isn't it?'

'It certainly is.' Paul unbuttoned his greatcoat and sat down in the chair opposite the Major's.

'Perhaps we'll have a tipple of something else to warm us up, too.' The Major reached into his briefcase and extracted a half-bottle of brandy. 'You wouldn't say no, I imagine?'

Paul smiled wryly.

'You're right – I wouldn't.'

The Major found two glasses in an official-looking cabinet, poured a generous measure of brandy into each of them and handed one to Paul.

'Your health. Seems as appropriate a toast as any in the circumstances.'

Paul said nothing and the Major's eyes narrowed thoughtfully. Then he put down his glass, took a fresh file from his briefcase and opened it.

'Right. Let's get down to it then, shall we? I've talked to Major Allen who debriefed you when you first got back to London and I've been through his reports and your own. You've done well, Captain Sullivan.'

Paul took a long swig of brandy.

'I'd hardly call losing an entire circuit doing well.'

'Hmm. Yes. Bad business that. It happened through loose talk, you think?'

'I've no proof, but I believe it was that, yes. For the Germans to turn up in such force at the very place and the very time we were moving the arms cache seems too convenient to be just coincidence. An odd patrol, yes. There are plenty of those. But a whole fleet of armoured vehicles . . . no, somebody talked, I'm sure of it.'

'Any idea who?'

'Try whichever of my trusted band is still walking the streets,' Paul said drily. 'No, I don't actually mean that. I don't think we were betrayed, as such. I knew my men – at least, I like to think I did. No, I think it was a careless word in the wrong ear. A wife, a girlfriend who knew too much, someone trying to be clever or impress . . . I warned them, God knows, but it doesn't come easy to simple, good country folk to mistrust people they've known all their lives. The divisions over there are so blurred. Those who want to resist, those who prefer to keep their heads down, and those who simply don't understand what all the fuss is about. There are Communists, Pétainists, those who look to de Gaulle for salvation, even Facists. There are plenty of good men, I'm sure, who only want to do what they can to overthrow the Nazis, but recruiting them is a bloody nightmare and getting them to toe the line even worse. They're still learning what it's like to live in an occupied country.'

'We are all feeling our way in a situation that is new to us.' The Major drained his glass and replenished it. 'Inevitably that will mean some blunders. And we in the SOE are fighting our own battles here at home too. The old guard believe active resistance will only stir up more trouble than it's worth. They want to restrict us to an information-gathering role. But we'll get there, never fear.'

A tap at the door interrupted his flow and Rita came in with mugs of coffee. The aroma of it filled the small room and Paul thought wryly that shortages or no shortages the hierarchy of the SOE were making sure of the supplies they needed to keep them going – and awake – through the long nights.

'You were lucky not to be taken with the rest of them,' the Major said when the door had closed after Rita once more.

'I have a punctured bicycle tyre to thank for that. It made me late getting to the meeting place. I arrived just in time to hear the shots and see the Germans arresting my men.'

'A very fortuitous puncture.'

'I suppose so.' Paul grimaced. 'It seems to me that I have a knack of being absent when disaster strikes.'

Without him having to mention them by name Major Fawcett knew that Paul was referring to what had happened to his wife and daughter.

'I can't send you back there, Sullivan,' he said abruptly. 'But of course, you must already realise that. Chances are your cover is totally blown.'

'Chances are. If they didn't already know who I was when they swooped that night they know now. At least two of my men were taken alive, and though I think they would do their best to keep what they knew secret, the Gestapo can be very persuasive.'

'So. The whole of that sector is out of the question as far as you are concerned. We shall put someone else in as soon as we can to try and re-form a circuit.'

As if he had forgotten the cigar he had abandoned in the ashtray the Major drew a fresh one from a packet in the breast pocket of his battledress and searched for matches.

'I do want to go back, though,' Paul said. 'I know it looks as if I buggered it up this time but I believe I've learned useful lessons.'

'And you haven't been put off by the fact that you only just escaped with your life?'

Paul's mouth tightened.

'I always knew the risks. I was prepared to take them. Nothing has happened to change that. Besides, how many men have you got who know France as I do and who can speak French like a native?'

The Major applied a match to his cigar.

'My father worked for the Embassy in Paris, but I spent holidays with friends all over the place and when I finished school I had a year or two of a sort of hobo existence, backpacking and getting work where I could.'

'So you think you could pass for a native anywhere?'

'I've always had a good ear for dialects, certainly.'

'That's what I was hoping you would say.' His cigar going at last, the Major tossed aside the matches and reached for another file. 'I do have something in mind for you as it happens. Do you know the west at all – Charente and Charente-sur-Mer?'

'Cognac country? I've been there, yes. I was there for the grape harvest.'

'But you're not known there?'

'No. I was just one more ex-student looking for work to pay my board and lodging. And I had a beard at the time, I think.' Paul rasped his fingers thoughtfully over his now clean-shaven chin. 'Besides, it's ten years since I was there. I don't think anyone would remember me.'

'Good. I'd like to see a circuit established there.'

'Do we have any contacts?' Paul knew that pockets of resistance were beginning to spring up all over France and that the leaders were looking to London for the supplies of guns and ammunition they needed for their work, and even the assistance of specialists such as radio operators, or 'pianists' as they were known in the field. But the French were a proud people, they did not always take kindly to taking orders from a foreigner, and to run a circuit, his way, was the only way he was prepared to work. Anything less, he considered, weighed the balance of risk too heavily against him.

'There's nothing organised in that district,' the Major assured him. 'A few locals have been engaged in sabotage, I understand – railwaymen sending trainloads of supplies to the wrong destination, that kind of thing. And back at the beginning of it all two lads were shot for tearing down telephone lines. But my information is that those who are trying to do their bit lack direction and leadership. And they could certainly use someone with your expertise.'

Paul nodded, thinking it through. To set up a circuit almost from scratch was exactly what he had been hoping for, recruiting only those he could trust – though how to be absolutely certain you could trust anyone was one of the biggest problems. Word of mouth was unreliable, certainly, and Paul preferred to rely on his own instincts. He was, he reckoned, a pretty fair judge of character and he sincerely hoped his confidence was not misplaced. His life, after all, would depend on it.

'We not only want a circuit in the area,' Major Fawcett continued, 'we want to establish an escape route too. As you know, the demarcation line cuts directly down through the region. There have to be places where it is possible to cross from occupied to Vichy France by simply walking across a field or crossing a stream. The road marks the boundary in some places – at the moment, though, my information is that they change it when the mood takes them. We need the addresses of some safe houses we can add to the list our airmen memorise in case they are shot down, and a *passeur* or two willing to show them the way across the line. I want you to take all that on board when you go.'

'Understood. If there's no formal set-up there at present I take it I'll be dropped in "blind"?'

'I'm not sure. We're working on that one. I think we may be able to arrange for the members of a cell about twenty miles from your destination to look after you initially. From there you can make your way to Charente.'

'Where I shall be on my own?'

'To begin with, yes. I do however have one name of someone who may be prepared to help you. It's a suggestion, no more, but I've checked it out as far as I am able and she seems like a good bet to me.'

Paul's eyes narrowed.

'*She?*'

'Don't say it like that, Sullivan. I happen to think women can be very good at this kind of thing. Comes from their devious natures.' He chuckled at his own joke, but Paul did not even smile. His instinctive reaction was that espionage and all it entailed was men's work. Women should not be exposed to its all-too-obvious dangers. Where possible they should be safe at home . . . His heart contracted painfully.

'Who is she?' he asked abruptly.

'An English girl – French nationalised by marriage, of course, or she'd have been rounded up and sent to a prison camp by now. Her name is Kathryn de Savigny.'

'De Savigny.' It rang a distant bell in Paul's memory.

'They are a very old French family, aristocrats, you might say. They live in a château just the Vichy side of the line, they have vineyards and produce their own cognac. Not in great quantity, but the quality, I understand, more than makes up for that. It sells, as I understand it, for a goodly sum – in peacetime it did, at any rate.'

'De Savigny!' Paul was remembering now – that long-ago summer in Charente, a centuries-old château on a hillside, fifty hectares of vines bearing grapes that made the very best cognac, and a family arrogant from an excess of wealth and privilege.

'How does an English girl come to be in that set-up?' he asked, the scepticism of his memories colouring his tone.

'She is married to one of the sons of the old Baron. Has been for the last six years.'

'I see.' Paul revised his opinion again – downwards. Not only a woman but a spoiled little rich girl to boot. He couldn't see that she would be much use in a situation like this one.

Again the Major's sharp eyes noticed, and assimilated, Paul's reaction.

'Don't dismiss her out of hand, Sullivan. The report I have on her is very favourable.'

83

'Says who?'

'Her brother.'

'Her brother!'

'He's been working for me,' the Major said, pleasantly non-committal.

'So why isn't he going to Charente?'

'Because obviously the family know him and he's less sure where their loyalties lie. They would recognise him at once and . . .'

'Fine!' Paul said sarcastically. 'He thinks the family are collaborating to save their own skins and doesn't want to risk his neck by trusting them. But you are suggesting I should do just that.'

'He trusts her, it's them he's not sure of. But you would be able to contact her without them spotting you right off. There's always a risk, of course, but personally I feel it's one worth taking. She's a spirited girl, he says, makes up her own mind about things, and is obviously pro-British.'

'You think so. She may be as eager to preserve her lifestyle as they are.'

'She may be, of course. But it's unlikely she would betray you and she may well be able to be of great assistance.'

'I'll think about it,' Paul said shortly. 'You'll let me have her details, no doubt.'

'I will indeed. Kathryn de Savigny, twenty-five years old, mother of a two-year-old son, Guy.'

'Twenty-five. And she's been in France six years, you say? She must have married young.'

'She did. Straight from finishing school in Switzerland.'

'Finishing school. Christ.'

'Sullivan, your prejudices are showing.' The Major smiled wryly. 'She may have been to finishing school but Edwin, her brother, says she was always a tomboy. A tomboy with breeding can grow up into a formidable woman.'

'If you say so.' Paul was thinking that a girl with a privileged background, married into a family like the de Savignys, was more likely to be a pain in the arse, but he kept his thoughts to himself.

The Major shuffled his papers together and stood up.

'I think that's all for the moment, Sullivan. You'll be thoroughly briefed before you leave, of course. In the meantime get some rest and recuperation and have a little fun if you can. Your apartment is comfortable, I take it?'

'Extremely so.' His London apartment belonged to the department; he had returned to it to find a refrigerator stocked with smoked salmon and good wine and cupboards full of tinned fruit and meats – luxuries indeed in wartime England. 'You look after us, sir, I can't deny that.'

The Major permitted himself another smile.

'We try. In view of the danger you will be going into we like to provide you with what luxuries we can.'

'And the condemned man ate a hearty breakfast,' Paul commented drily.

'See a show – entertain a lady. Have you friends in London or . . . ?'

'I don't need your escort agency to provide me with a date,' Paul snapped. 'It's not so long since I lost my wife, remember, and I'm not looking for a replacement.'

'As you wish. Your personal life is your own. Only remember, a little relaxation never hurt anyone.'

'I'll relax in my own way, thank you.'

The Major moved to the door, opening it.

'You know your own mind, Sullivan, I'll say that for you. It's one of the reasons you were selected for SOE duties, of course. But be careful not to let that hate burn you up. A personal vendetta can be a dangerous thing.'

Paul said nothing. If it was not for a personal vendetta he might not be in this situation at all, he thought.

In the reception room Rita Barlow was on the telephone – making an appointment with another agent, perhaps? She looked up as he came through, placing her hand over the mouthpiece.

'Captain Sullivan . . . ?'

'Good night, Rita. Take care of yourself.'

'And you, Captain Sullivan.'

He went out into the thick, dark night.

Another job, another mission, something else to fill the empty places in his heart and present him, perhaps, with the chance to extract revenge for the loss of his wife and daughter.

It was, thought Paul, all he could hope for, all he wanted.

7

Charente, 1941

THE BUS, CRAMMED with grim-faced peasants, jolted haltingly along the rutted road between bare straggling hedges and fields brown for winter. It had been raining and the slightly musty smell of damp clothing mingled with all the other smells – gasoline and garlic, cheap cigarette smoke and manure-odoured mud.

On one of the hard, bench-type seats in the rear Paul Sullivan shifted his long frame in an effort to make himself more comfortable, and decided that a journey by country bus was one of his least favourite modes of travel. Beside him a thickset man with a protesting hen wedged between his knees threw him a bad-tempered glance, but to Paul's relief it contained no hint of suspicion.

And nor should it, Paul thought wryly, glancing down at the baggy twills, shapeless jumper and serge jacket, patched at the elbows, that he was wearing. Never one to be overly concerned about his mode of dress, he had taken a great deal of care today to choose clothes unbecoming enough to allow him to merge into the persona of a country peasant at whom no one, hopefully, would take a second look. You'd have been proud of me, Gerie, he thought – proud of the effort I put into this, if not the result. The thought shot familiar pain through his solar plexus and with a determined effort Paul pushed it away. This was no time for wallowing in self-pity or indulging in grief. Every bit of his energy was needed for concentrating on what he had to do – and on simply staying alive. Shortly the bus would be crossing the demarcation line – there would be border patrols and checks and it was vital he did nothing to attract attention to himself by so much as a look or a gesture. Think French, he warned himself. You are Pierre Rousseau, farm labourer, who fought briefly with the French army, a dull uneducated fellow who simply wants to be left in peace while the psychological wounds heal. The papers in his pocket were only one of several sets provided for him by SOE in London, but the others he had left carefully concealed behind a loose brick behind the fireplace in the bedroom of the farmhouse where he was holed up. Carrying more than one set at once was a stupid and dangerous thing to do and Paul knew better than to take such a risk.

The bus rattled into a village – grey-stone houses, drab and unlovely in the rain, and a scattering of small shops. It came to a stop beside a village green which would, in summer, be pleasantly shady, but which today looked only desolate and windswept, pockmarked by drifts of decaying leaves, and two Vichy policemen boarded the bus and moved bombastically down the aisle, checking papers and passes. Paul sat staring out of the window until one came level with him, then proffered his papers with a careless movement. The policeman examined them briefly, returned them to him and moved on, and in spite of his apparent lack of concern Paul experienced a swell of relief. The forgers in London had done their work well. But even so, false papers carried an element of risk. The Germans were liable to change their format at the drop of a hat and out-of-date-styled documents would attract immediate attention.

The bus pulled away, heading north-west towards Angoulême, and Paul glanced at his watch. As long as there were no further delays he should be there in good time. Kathryn de Savigny went to the market regularly once a week, if his information was correct, getting a lift with a local farmer who had a stall there, and then spent the afternoon visiting an old woman who had been in service at the château for many years before her retirement. She lived now with her son, who owned a café. It was, Paul had thought, his best chance of snatching an initial meeting with Kathryn, well away from Savigny where a stranger might attract attention and a curious observer might wonder why a peasant should be talking to the daughter-in-law of the Baron.

Besides, it was possible that Kathryn would make things difficult for him. He was still not totally convinced of her suitability. Georges Ambert, the smallholder who had received him and put a roof over his head, had checked her out through contacts in the area and learned that the family were collaborating. But the reports on Kathryn were encouraging. She was known to hate the Germans and Georges' information was that whilst she might not actively resist he couldn't see her betraying a fellow Englishman either.

Georges was a good man, Paul thought, if a little solid and unimaginative. His heart was most definitely in the right place – he hated the Boche with a fervent loathing, his farmhouse was in a suitably isolated spot, and his brother-in-law, who hated the Germans as much as he did, was a policeman, the perfect occupational cover for resistance work since it allowed a certain freedom of movement and access to information that might otherwise be difficult to come by. It had been Georges and his brother-in-law, Yves Javaux, who had arranged the reception party when the Lysander had dropped Paul into France two nights earlier, and he had thanked God for them. On his first mission he had been dropped in 'blind', and seeing the plane turn for home and knowing he was alone in an alien country with nothing but his own wits between him and disaster had provided one of the most gut-wrenching moments of his life.

This time had been different. Georges and Yves, like so many others all over France, were anxious to resist but they needed outside help – arms and supplies from London, trained radio operators to keep the lines of contact open and the leadership of men like himself to organise their resistance, and they had welcomed him with open arms. The dual tasks of setting up a circuit and an escape route for Allied airmen shot down over France were daunting ones and he needed as many cards as possible in his hand. Kathryn de Savigny was just one of them. If she could help him, then this long and uncomfortable bus ride would have been well worth the effort.

The bus chugged temperamentally up the steep hill and into the town. Paul checked his watch again – French-made, like every one of the items of clothing he wore, from his underpants to the ancient serge jacket. Yes, he was in good time. He looked out of the windows, taking his bearings from the ornately façaded cathedral that dominated the town and mentally checking off the names of the roads against the street map Georges had given him and which he had memorised by the light of the guttering oil lamp in his room the previous evening. When the bus came to a stop he disembarked along with the other passengers into the cold grey of the early afternoon and began to make his way through the network of streets in what he judged to be the direction of the Café d'Or, using shop windows as mirrors every once in a while to ensure he was not being followed.

The café was situated on the corner of a small square, just as Georges had described. Paul went inside and sat down at a table close to the window which overlooked the square and the street down which he had just come. He ordered coffee – not real coffee, but the vile-tasting mixture of acorns and chicory that had replaced it in occupied France – and drank it, keeping an eye on the street for any approaching Germans or for Kathryn de Savigny in case she should leave through a side entrance rather than through the café. The town seemed quiet for a market day, he thought, and what people there were scurried along, heads held low, with the nervous demeanour of hunted animals. Which was, Paul mused, exactly what they were – cold, hungry, deprived of liberty, stripped of pride and afraid almost all the time of putting a foot wrong and having to take the consequences. Pressure like this affected people in one of two ways – they either became cowed and beaten or they fought back, defying the dangers. Some would betray even their own relatives and friends in order to save their skins, some would dig deep into resources of courage they had not known they possessed. What would he have done had he found himself in their situation? He liked to think he would have been one of the resisters, plotting and planning and hiding British agents just as Georges was hiding him, but in all honesty he could not be sure. All very well to do what he was doing now, driven by hatred of the Nazis and an overwhelming desire for revenge. But what if he and Gerie and little Beatrice had been an ordinary French family living under the occupation – what then? Would he have placed them at risk in order to salvage his own pride? He didn't know and the uncertainty was humbling.

Paul finished his coffee. It left a bitter taste in his mouth but he had little choice but to buy another cup. He signalled to the waitress, a young girl with straggling hair tied back at the nape of her neck, wearing a slightly grubby white apron over her black uniform skirt, and at that precise moment Kathryn de Savigny appeared from the rear of the café.

He knew it was her instantly, would have known even if Major Fawcett had not shown him a photograph of her before he left London. This was not a café that would normally be frequented by a woman wearing a Paris-designed coat, undeniably pre-war but still stylish, and he knew instinctively that she was English though he could not for the life of him have explained why. She was slim, of medium height, with thick brown hair falling loose over the collar of her coat, and she was carrying an expensive-looking crocodile-skin clutch bag. Unexpectedly he felt his throat constrict. This was it then – time for action.

'It's all right. I was just leaving,' he said to the waitress, and followed Kathryn de Savigny into the street.

She turned in the direction of the market and he followed at a discreet distance. It was about a five-minute walk, he estimated – plenty of time to get well away from the café and anyone who might have noticed his hasty exit before he approached her. She walked quite fast but with his long strides he could keep up with her almost too easily; he stopped a couple of times, once to light a cigarette, once to look into the window of a bookshop, then quickened his pace to catch up with her again.

When he judged they had covered a safe distance he pulled from his pocket a handkerchief that Georges had lent him especially for the purpose; a small square of white cotton belonging to his sister, Yves' wife. He drew alongside Kathryn.

'Excuse me, Madame, I think you dropped this,' he said in French.

She turned quickly and he saw the surprise in her eyes – brown, with golden flecks around the iris.

'I don't think so.' He knew what she was going to say and interrupted her in a low voice, though he was as confident as he could be that there was no one within hearing distance.

'*Je suis anglais.* Your brother Edwin sent me. I must speak to you.'

He saw the blank look of shock on her face and was afraid that she might do or say something that would draw attention to the fact that he was not what he seemed. Then, to his relief, she took the handkerchief from him.

'Thank you – how kind. I didn't realise . . .'

'I can't talk now.' He kept his voice low. 'You often go out alone for walks, don't you? I'll see you tomorrow at the crossroads on the hill just outside Savigny. Three o'clock. And for God's sake don't tell anyone. Not your husband, not anyone. All right?'

She hesitated for just a moment. Then: 'All right,' she said. 'But what if it's pouring with rain?'

'The first fine day then.'

'All right. I'll be there.'

'Good.' He glanced around; no one was within earshot, no one was taking the slightest notice of them, but all the same he touched his forehead in a gesture of subservience. Then he quickened his pace and walked along the street.

Next morning the wind had blown the rain clouds away. When she drew the curtains and saw the sky, higher and brighter than it had been for days, Kathryn felt her heart sink and she realised that she had actually been hoping it would be raining and she would not have to make a decision about whether or not to take the walk and keep her appointment with the Englishman who had contrived to speak to her in Angoulême.

That he was English she had no doubt − in spite of all appearances to the contrary. But she couldn't understand who he was or what he wanted with her, and she couldn't think what he could have to do with Edwin. She had not seen her brother since the beginning of the war and had heard nothing either. Was it possible that he was in France and wanted to see her? But if so, why hadn't he contacted her himself? Why send a messenge by way of a British national dressed up as a French peasant? Try as she might to find another explanation Kathryn couldn't help thinking that only one fitted the bill. Edwin was mixed up with the Resistance and the man who had waylaid her was too.

When he had left her so abruptly she had been tempted to wonder if she had dreamed the whole thing, but the square of coarse white cotton, so different from her own lace-edged lawn handkerchiefs, was all the proof she needed that she had not. Riding home in Maurice Angelot's creaking van she had been grateful for once for the farmer's relentless chatter. He always regaled her with tales of his day in the market, what he had sold and to whom he had sold it, all gritted out around the home-rolled cigarette that dangled between his weather-dried lips. Luckily for her he did not expect any reply – he thought her typically standoffish English, never realising that he drove her mad with his repetitive anecdotes – and the habit, formed over weeks and months, had given her the chance to try to organise her whirling thoughts. But it had made no difference.

What did he want with her? she asked herself for the hundredth time, and again the inescapable answer which whispered inside her head sent a chill of fear through her tense body. If he was an agent – and she was certain he must be – then he was going to ask her to help him in some way. And Kathryn was not at all sure she was brave enough – or foolhardy enough – to do it.

You are wrong! she told herself. He wouldn't be foolish enough to seek assistance from the wife and daughter-in-law of known collaborators! But the assurance could not satisfy her for long.

Supposing he did ask for her help? What the hell would she do? Resisting in any way was a terribly dangerous business – assisting a British agent even more so. And she had Guy to think about. She couldn't do anything to place him in danger . . . no, be honest, it wasn't just the thought of the risk to Guy that was making her stomach churn with fear, but the terrible prospect of what would happen to her if she were found out. The Nazis were no respecters of women. They had special ways of dealing with them, she had heard . . . She trembled, stricken with dread, yet at the same time despising herself for hesitating for even for a moment at the chance of doing something to undermine the hated Boche.

You are a hypocrite, Kathryn de Savigny, she told herself, looking at the sky and willing the storm clouds to gather so that the decision as to whether or not to keep the appointment would be taken from her. All this time you have been blaming Charles and his family for collaborating, accusing them of cowardice, and in reality you are every bit as bad!

The realisation shamed her, but there was no escaping the fact that she was in no position to do anything to help. It was far too dangerous. If he asked, she would have to tell him that.

At two-thirty the sky was still ominously clear and Kathryn knew that if she was to keep the appointment she could delay no longer.

She checked that Guy was sleeping. Although he was almost four years old he still needed an afternoon nap – because of the energy he used up, she supposed. Then she changed into a tweed skirt and walking shoes and went in search of Bridget, who was, since the war had begun, one of only three servants at the château which had once employed more than twenty.

'I am going out,' she said. 'Listen for Guy when he wakes up, please.'

'Wouldn't he like to go with you?' Bridget was cheeky where the older servants never were. 'The fresh air would do him good.'

Kathryn resisted the urge to argue with her.

'Just do as I say, Bridget, please.'

She fetched her coat and hat, her stomach churning with nervousness.

Don't let him be there! she prayed as she walked down the drive, bordered on both sides by winter-brown parkland. If he's not there that will be the end of it. But at least I'll be able to live with myself, knowing I did what was asked of me.

The chill wind cut through her coat and Kathryn shivered. Telling herself she was doing what had been asked of her was cold comfort indeed.

At two-thirty Paul Sullivan was cycling up the hill towards the crossroads outside Savigny. He had intended allowing himself a full hour to hide himself and his bicycle in one of the thickets overlooking the whole valley to make as certain as he could that there were no traps waiting to be sprung on him; he didn't yet know whether Kathryn de Savigny was to be trusted and if she had told anyone of their planned meeting there might be a patrol of German or Vichy police waiting to pounce. But it had taken him longer than he had anticipated to cycle the twenty kilometres; the road was undulating, and even in his present peak fitness he had been unable to maintain the speed he needed. There was, in any case, the danger that the Germans, if they did know about him, would time their arrival for exactly three o'clock, but it was a risk he had to take and on balance he was inclined to trust Kathryn. Her swift reaction when he had approached her the previous afternoon had impressed him and his instinct was that she would not knowingly betray him. Generally speaking Paul trusted his intuition. It rarely let him down — more often it was the reasoned judgement that did that.

Paul dismounted, pushing his bicycle up the last, and steepest, part of the hill and looking for a way to get into the thicket that breasted it. He found a track and gateway but discounted them – too soft and muddy after the recent rain. His bicycle would leave telltale tyre marks and the mud would cake on his shoes, clear evidence for anyone who cared to look that he had not remained on the roads where he should have been. A little further on was a gap in the hedge and Paul settled for that, lifting his bicycle through and then manhandling it into hiding.

From this vantage point the whole of the valley with its little winding roads was spread out beneath him and he knew he had chosen well – the safest possible place for a meeting as risky as this one. To his left, along the ridge, he could see the towers of the château rising above the trees, beneath him the fields fell away to the village – the collection of grey-stone houses and the church, its spire pointing up towards the thicker grey of the sky. Everything was quiet, everything appeared as normal as it could be – no enemy patrols, as yet at any rate. He leaned against the bole of a tree, lighting a cigarette and constantly scanning the vista for any sign of danger.

Just before three o'clock he saw her approaching along the road from the direction of the château and realised that until that moment he had not been certain whether or not she would come. She was wearing a trench coat and a soft felt hat that covered her hair, her head was bent and she was walking purposefully. He remained under cover, watching her, more alert than ever. At the crossroads she stopped, looked around uncertainly. He let her wait for a full five minutes. Once he thought he heard the sound of a car and stiffened, peering down the valley. But it was only a farm truck; it chugged away and all was quiet again. He saw her look at her watch and wondered how long she would be prepared to wait. The timing of the meeting was a gamble, as was the decision whether or not to take his bicycle with him when he broke cover. On balance he decided to leave it where it was. If a patrol did come there was no way he could outrun it on a road, bicycle or no bicycle, and at least hidden in the thicket it did not attract attention.

Paul saw her glance at her watch again and then look around. He was close enough to be able to see her perplexed expression.

She was pretty, he thought, in a typically English way that bordered on the beautiful. She also looked classy. She moved from one side of the crossroads to the other, clearly uncertain what to do, then turned as if to go back the way she had come. Paul checked the valley once more, and decided it was time to take the chance and pray she had kept the meeting to herself. He left the cover of the thicket and climbed back through the gap in the hedge.

'Good afternoon, Madame de Savigny,' he said.

Kathryn swung round, taken by surprise.

'I thought you weren't coming. You said three o'clock.'

He smiled briefly, apologetically.

'Precautions. I couldn't be sure you'd be alone.'

'Oh! Surely you didn't think I'd . . .'

'I had to be certain. This is a dangerous game we're playing.'

'What is all this about?' she asked fiercely. 'You said something about Edwin.'

Paul Sullivan glanced up and down the road. It was making him nervous standing in the open. He touched her elbow.

'Let's go into the woods. We're too conspicuous here.'

She hesitated.

'It's all right, I'm not going to attack you,' he said shortly.

'I didn't think for one moment that you were. I was worried about snagging my coat.'

'Ah, your coat.' He said it sarcastically, thinking that he had been right first time – she was just a spoiled little rich girl with nothing more important than her expensive wardrobe on her mind.

She shot him a glance.

'If I go home with twigs caught up in it I shall have some questions to answer,' she said curtly, and he knew she had read his thoughts. So – she might be spoiled, she was certainly one of the privileged classes, but she was not stupid. But then, he had already known that.

'Don't worry, we'll make sure there aren't any telltale signs,' he said. 'But I really would rather be out of sight of the road.'

'All right.' She followed him through the hedge back into the thicket, her shoes squelching in the leaf mould. 'Who are you?'

He turned to face her.

'I must ask you a question first. How do you feel about the German occupation?' He saw the guarded look come into her eyes, and said in English: 'I must know which side you are on.'

Her mouth tightened a shade.

'Which side do you think I'm on? Not those Nazi butchers, for sure.'

'You'd like to see them driven out of France?'

'I'd like to see them exterminated. Does that answer your question?'

He smiled briefly.

'I think so. The next question is, would you be willing to help do it?'

Though she had been expecting something of the sort, his words still shocked her.

'What do you mean?'

'Exactly what I say. I'm here to try to organise local resistance and also an escape line for British airmen. I need to recruit people I can trust. Your name was suggested to my head of department by your brother.'

'Edwin. Is he involved in this?'

'I don't know,' Paul lied.

'I'll bet he is! Where is he? Are you sure you don't know?' Kathryn was overwhelmed by a sudden rush of longing. She and Edwin had been close once, in spite of their day-to-day squabbles, and she missed him.

'I'm sorry, I really don't know,' Paul said. The eagerness in her face had given her an air of vulnerability that was at odds with the poise and sophistication of her outward appearance and made him regret, for a moment, that he could not help her. Then he thrust his sentiment away. Emotions of that sort had no place in the job he had to do. 'Look, I haven't time to beat about the bush. Will you help me?'

She shook her head. 'I couldn't.'

'That's a very hasty refusal.'

'I've had all night to think about it. I more or less guessed what was coming after you spoke to me in Angoulême yesterday. I'm not a fool. And I'm sorry, but there's nothing I can do.'

'I see.'

'No, you don't. My husband's family are collaborators. I'm not proud of it, but it's a fact. General von Rheinhardt, who is in charge of the district, visits the château socially – my father-in-law invites him to dinner sometimes and he reciprocates by loaning us his official car if we need to make a journey – petrol is in terribly short supply, you know. I think von Rheinhardt actually likes coming to the château – he's certainly a frequent visitor, anyway, so it would be far too dangerous for me to be involved in any subversive activity.'

'I see the risks, of course. I also see that having the General at such close quarters could be a wonderful cover. He wouldn't expect anything to be going on right under his nose.'

'But I wouldn't be able to deceive my husband and the rest of the family. We live as a very close unit. They wouldn't agree to any sort of resistance, I know. They take the view that it is safest for everyone to keep their heads down and pretend friendship, at least. And they certainly wouldn't allow Allied airmen shelter under their roof. It would be far too great a risk. The penalties for such a thing are very extreme.'

'Certainly the château as a safe house was more than even I dared hoped for. Well, I'm sorry I dragged you out here for nothing, Madame.' He hesitated. 'You wouldn't know, I suppose, of anyone in the locality who might be more sympathetic to the cause?'

'I would have said the whole neighbourhood is more or less completely united in wanting to avoid trouble.'

'Following the example of your husband's family, no doubt.' He should not have said it, he knew, but he found the jibe irresistible all the same, and experienced a sense of satisfaction when he saw the quick colour flood her cheeks.

'That's unfair,' she said. 'You haven't had to live with these bastards breathing down your neck, threatening your safety and the lives of your children. If it was your son who might be torn away from you in the middle of the night, perhaps you would understand how they feel – how *I* feel.'

The blackness was there inside his head.

'Perhaps I understand more than you think,' he said harshly. 'But if you won't help, you won't. I can't force you to – I wouldn't want to. Resistance demands very special qualitites, not the least total commitment to the cause. Anything less is a recipe for disaster.' He turned, easing his bicycle out of the undergrowth where he had hidden it. 'I take it I can at least count on your discretion about this meeting?'

'Yes, of course! What do you think I am?'

'I think,' he said, 'that you are a woman who could be a great help to the Allies if you put your mind to it. I think you are clever and resourceful and possibly all kinds of other things as well. But if you have no will to resist then there really is no point pursuing it.'

He turned, looking down the valley again. All was quiet. Well, at least he had been right to trust her. She hadn't betrayed him.

'Goodbye, Madame de Savigny.'

'Wait!' He was on the point of lifting the bicycle through the hedge when that one word stopped him. He looked round. Kathryn was standing, one hand jamming her felt hat down on to her head, the other stretched out towards him in a gesture that was half imperious, half pleading. 'Don't go for a minute, please!'

He said nothing, just looked at her, and after a moment she said: 'What is it you would want me to do?'

He set the bicycle down again.

'At the moment, nothing.'

'Nothing?'

'At this stage I simply need to know who I can count on for help.'

'And later?'

'People first. As I already said I hoped you might be able to give me the names of anyone sympathetic to the cause – anyone already resisting in some way perhaps. We need men who can move about without arousing suspicion – railwaymen, for instance, with their "love bird" passes and a sound knowledge of goods movements, policemen, priests – anyone with a legitimate reason for being out and about after curfew or in out-of-the-way places. We need safe houses, for agents as well as escaping Allied airmen. We need a whole network, eventually building to an undercover army. I need a register of people brave enough to allow their premises to be used for transmitting radio messages to London. My "pianist", when he arrives, will have to keep on the move – too many transmissions from any one place can be traced by the detector vans. It may be someone with a loft, it may be a farmer prepared to turn a blind eye to what goes on in his barn after dark. I also need the advice of someone with a detailed knowledge of the locality and the terrain – I thought you might be able to help me there.'

'I know the district well, certainly . . .'

'You would also make an ideal messenger. It's unlikely that any German would question why someone in your position should be visiting, say, retired employees of the estate.'

'We do try to keep an eye on them, yes – especially if they are old or sick.'

'And last but not least I would like you to help me check the validity of any Allied airmen whom we are preparing to pass down the escape line, once it's established. The Germans have been known to use plants in order to infiltrate the system. As you are English you would be able to ask the kind of questions that would establish whether an airman was genuine or not – you'd spot a foreign imposter immediately. So would I, of course, but I may be too busy with other things to be able to conduct the necessary interview myself.'

'But if he was an impostor he'd know from the very fact that I was interviewing him that I was working for the Resistance!'

'True. But we would ensure he was dealt with before he could do any real harm. There is a risk, of course. I won't pretend there is not. But I promise I would do everything in my power to minimise it.'

'Can I think about it?'

'Of course, but don't think too long.'

'Where can I contact you?'

He smiled. 'Oh no, I'm afraid I can't tell you that yet. Maybe I never will. The smaller and tighter and more self-contained each cell, the safer it is. What people don't know they can't be persuaded to tell. Will you be going to Angoulême again next week?'

'Yes. It's a regular thing with me.'

'I'll see you then.'

'When? Where?'

'Leave that to me. Just do as you always do. Don't look for me or do anything different from usual. But don't be surprised if I'm not in my French peasant's gear. It is a little difficult for such a rough fellow to talk to a beautiful and aristocratic lady without attracting attention. Now – you'd better be getting home before they send out a search party for you.'

They scrambled back on to the road, Paul holding the branches aside for Kathryn to squeeze through.

'I'm sorry to be so indecisive,' she said. 'It's not just me I'm worried about – I have my little boy to think of too.'

'I know. Well, at least you came . . .'

He broke off as the sound of an engine cut through the stillness of the winter afternoon. A car was coming up the hill – Vichy police!

'Get down!' he hissed at Kathryn.

He saw the startled look on her face and realised she had frozen. He tossed his bicycle back over the hedge, grabbed Kathryn and threw her back into the thicket, hurling himself after her. They landed in an untidy heap and as Kathryn tried to rise he caught her shoulders, pushing her down into the soft leaf mould.

'Stay down!' he ordered.

Frightened, Kathryn did as he said. She could not in any case have moved. The weight of his body prevented it. The sound of the engine grew louder as the car came closer up the hill. She could scarcely breathe and her heart was pounding like a hammer. The car approached, passed, turned right at the crossroads. As the engine note grew fainter, dying away into the distance, Paul relaxed his hold on her and sat up, and Kathryn did the same. She realised she was shaking all over.

'I'm sorry,' Paul said roughly.

'Why did you do that?' she gasped, though of course she knew why. 'I'm filthy – look at me!'

She was brushing the leaf mould off her hands, reaching for her hat which had come off and rolled into the brambles. Her hair, released, tumbled untidily around her face. He felt a jolt of some primal, half-forgotten emotion, and then, as quickly, it was gone.

'It wouldn't do for us to be seen together. That's the price you pay, I'm afraid, for getting mixed up with someone like me.' He got up, gave her his hand and pulled her up too. 'Perhaps that will make up your mind for you.'

'Well, I'm certainly not used to being thrown through hedges!' Fright, and another emotion she did not bother to identify, made her tone sharp.

'I know. I said I'm sorry. But I had no choice.' He retrieved his bicycle. 'I'm going now, before that patrol comes back. You had better do the same. Is next week still on?'

She looked at him, at that very ordinary face grown almost dangerous suddenly, at the lithe athletic body beneath the scruffy peasant clothes which had, a few minutes ago, been pinning her to the ground, and experienced a moment's total recklessness.

'Yes. It's still on.'

'Good.'

He mounted his bicycle, lifted his hand to her in a mock salute, and was gone, speeding away down the hill.

'Mummy! You're bleeding!'

Guy caught at Kathryn's hand as she absently splashed him with bubbles in his favourite bathtime game, turning it over to expose the network of scratches on her palm.

Kathryn winced and tore her hand away.

'It's nothing,' she said, but she was uncomfortably aware of Bridget standing beside her, holding the big white bath towel ready to dry Guy. 'I slipped when I was out on my walk this afternoon and skagged myself, that's all.'

'It looks nasty,' Bridget said. 'You should put some iodine on it.'

'It's nothing,' Kathryn said again. Her hand was smarting, it was true, but she had scarcely given it a thought. She had been too preoccupied with the other implications of this afternoon's encounter to worry about such a minor discomfort.

What was she doing getting mixed up in something like this? she asked herself. She should never have kept the appointment, much less made another. The Englishman, whose name she did not even know, spelled danger – danger for her, for Guy, for the whole family. Supposing the Vichy patrol had seen them hiding in the thicket – how would they have explained themselves? And supposing the stranger had been picked up as he cycled back to wherever it was he had come from and been interrogated – would he tell them why he had been in Savigny and who it was he had come to see? A haze of perspiration broke out on Kathryn's forehead and she closed her eyes momentarily, feeling sick with dread. She shouldn't have done it, shouldn't have put Guy and the others at risk in this way. All very well to blame Charles' family for collaborating, suddenly she could see all too clearly just why they did it.

And yet . . . in spite of her fear Kathryn felt a knot of resolve hardening within her. That was precisely the reason why they should resist. It was demeaning, having to live beneath a regime that made it impossible to go where one wanted, talk to to whom one wished. Sometimes it was necessary to take risks in order to preserve one's self-respect. At least today she had shown some defiance of the state of affairs that existed, rebelled in a minor way against their German masters. The Englishman, whoever he was, was risking his life for their freedom and it could be that her own brother was doing the same. It wouldn't surprise her – it would be very like Edwin. If so, the least she could do was offer what help she could. But if she did she must be very, very careful. She must not trust anybody, not Charles, not Bridget, perhaps not even the stranger himself. She had a week in which to make up her mind. But somehow, in her heart of hearts, Kathryn knew she had already decided what she was going to do.

8

THE FOLLOWING WEEK Paul Sullivan took the train to Angoulême. Today he was using a different persona – that of a travelling salesman in pharmaceuticals – and he thought that in his suit and overcoat he might look too conspicous on the country bus. Besides, the train was quicker, provided there were no unexpected delays, and time was beginning to be precious.

He had not wasted the week since he had cycled to Savigny to see Kathryn. She had been his first choice of contact but he could not rely on her too much. He did not know yet whether or not she would help him, and in any case he could see the difficulties that living in a house of collaborators would pose if she did. How much she lived her own life would have a bearing on that, he supposed, but there was a limit to the number of walks she could take, especially at this time of year. When summer came it would be easier, but summer was a long way off.

Paul had gone back to scratch and started his recruiting drive using Georges and Yves as the centre of a web, building outwards from them step by step. They were outside the area he had been dropped in to develop but they were keen to resist and needed direction and assistance. Using the radio transmitter he had brought in with him rather than their rather amateurish radio link, Paul had been in touch with London to ask for a drop of arms for their use, and he was tuning in nightly to the BBC, waiting to hear the coded message that would tell him it was on its way. Listening to the BBC was, of course, forbidden, but it was a small risk compared with transmitting himself. Paul was not the most adept of operators, barely competent, and he looked forward to the day when London sent him in a properly trained 'pianist'.

He had also made a start towards the setting up of an escape route. He had enlisted the help of a *passeur*, a farmer whose land straddled the demarcation line, and a parish priest willing to allow the crypt of his church to be used for hiding Allied airmen until they could be passed on. There was, of course, a limit to how much of the line he could personally oversee. There was no way he could check it out all the way to Switzerland or the Spanish border; for that he had to rely on each member of the chain establishing the next link for themselves, but at least he could do his best to ensure that the escapees he pushed their way were genuine fugitives, not German plants. The sense of responsibility weighed heavily on him and he prayed he would not let them down. Try as he might to tell himself it had not been his fault, he still felt a sense of guilt about losing his last circuit. He wanted to do all he could to ensure he did not have other arrests or executions on his conscience.

But all these things were secondary almost to his main plan to form a circuit within Savigny itself. And for that he needed Kathryn's help.

As he was in good time Paul decided to try and see Kathryn before she paid her visit to the old woman who lived at the café. He had already planned to meet her in a different setting – much safer than repeating an exercise if there had been any breach of confidence. He made his way to the main street leading from the market to the café, fairly certain it was the route she would take, and mingled with the shoppers whilst he waited.

After a while he saw her coming up the street, the wind blowing her hair which had escaped from the same felt hat she had been wearing the last time he had seen her. He walked towards her, then stopped, turning as if he had only just noticed her.

'Katrine! What a surprise!'

He saw from her startled look that she had not immediately recognised him in his different persona but she quickly recovered herself.

'Oh – hello!'

'Fancy seeing you here! It's a very cold day, isn't it? How would you like a nice hot cup of coffee?'

She looked around nervously – he must warn her, he thought, not to do that. But no one appeared to be taking any notice of them.

'Yes, that would be nice,' she said.

He cupped his hand around her elbow, propelling her back up the street to a café he had noticed earlier. They went inside and he chose a corner table, almost hidden from the rest of the café by a large potted plant.

'Well?' he said when they had ordered. 'Have you thought things over?'

'Yes, I've thought.'

'And?'

'And I've decided I'll do what I can to help.'

Briefly his hand covered hers.

'Good girl.'

'I don't know how much use I can be.' Her tone was sharp. She could not understand the strange, almost electric thrill that had run through her at the touch of his hand, understood even less the regret she felt that he had removed it. As she spoke she found herself looking down at his hand, broad, flecked with tiny dark hairs, wishing he would touch her again. Mentally she gave herself a small shake. 'It will be very difficult for me to do anything at all, but if you have anything specific in mind let me know.'

'I have.' His voice was firm and low. It sent another shock wave through her. 'I need a base in Savigny. Could you get me into the château?'

Her eyes widened.

'What on earth do you mean?'

'Exactly what I say. Savigny is the exact hub of the area I want to activate. If I was staying at the château it would place me right at the nerve centre.'

'You're mad! I told you – my husband's family are collaborators and General von Rheinhardt is a frequent visitor.'

'All the better. They would think no agent in his right mind would operate in such a hive of enemy industry.'

'They'd be right – no agent in his right mind would!'

'I believe in bold moves,' Paul said. 'I'd need a good cover story, of course, but I think I have one. You were in Switzerland at finishing school, right? You met me there. I am a Swiss national, though my father was English. My name is Paul Curtis and I am a teacher by profession. You have been thinking for some time that you should arrange for a tutor for your little boy. You persuade your husband I am the right man for the job.'

She shook her head, totally bemused by this unexpected turn of events.

'But Guy is only three years old!'

'Almost four.'

'How do you know that?'

'You'd be surprised how much I know about you, Kathryn.' For a moment a humorous light flickered in his eyes. 'You think it would be an excellent idea to have Guy start lessons with a tutor who speaks not only English and French but German too.'

'And you do?'

'Yes.' He drew out a pack of cigarettes. 'Would you like one?'

She didn't often smoke but just now she thought she could do with one.

'Thank you.'

He flicked his lighter on and leaned across the table. As he lit her cigarette his hand brushed hers again but this time she was too preoccupied to feel any response.

'But what are you supposed to be doing in France?'

'I was teaching at a small private school near Bordeaux. Because of the war it has had to close down. Oh, don't worry, the story holds up. There was such a school and if asked the principal will confirm I was on the staff there. It was all checked out and carefully set up before I left London.'

'I can't believe it!' she said. 'You really had all this worked out!'

'In the hope that you would help me, yes. The SOE might be a relatively new organisation but it's learning fast. They don't leave anything to chance.'

'Well.' She drew on her cigarette and coughed slightly. 'I still think it's crazy, but if I should agree to it, how would I explain your sudden appearance?'

'You bumped into me today. Coincidences like that do happen, believe me. Do you think you could carry it off? You'd have to be very convincing.'

'I don't know . . . I'm not used to telling lies . . .'

'But you are resourceful.' He looked at her steadily. He was already convinced that if she decided to go along with the plan she certainly was capable of carrying it off. Until he had met her he had withheld judgement – something like this required very special qualities if it was not going to end in disaster. Now his early doubts had vanished. She was the right type to get away with it; all he had to do was convince her of that. The one absolutely necessary ingredient lacking was confidence. By letting her know he was willing to place his life in her hands he was doing all he could to instil it in her, but that alone was not sufficient. The rest she must do for herself.

'What did you say your name was?'

'Paul Curtis. I was working as a barman in the Hôtel Belles Fleures in Geneva for about six months while waiting to go to college. We'll go over the full story later. We need to agree on every detail.'

'Yes, of course, I'm not stupid . . . Look, I shall have to go. Anne-Marie will think I'm not coming.'

'All right. I'll contact you again.'

'I haven't made any promises, mind . . .'

They stubbed out their cigarettes and went out into the street. As the door closed behind them Kathryn stiffened suddenly.

'Oh my God!'

'What is it?'

'Over there – on the other side of the street – Charles' brother, Christian. I think he's seen us. Yes – he's coming over! What do we do?'

His hand went under her elbow. He could feel her trembling through the thick cashmere of her coat.

'Bluff it out.'

'How?'

'Just be natural. I'm an old friend, remember.'

Christian had almost reached them. Any further conversation was impossible.

'Christian! What are you doing in Angoulême?' she said, endeavouring to hide her nervousness.

'I had to see someone on business. I can give you a lift home if you like, instead of you having to travel in Maurice Angelot's old rattletrap.' But as he spoke he was looking at Paul and Kathryn could see the unspoken suspicion in his eyes.

'This is a very old friend of mine – Paul Curtis,' she said swiftly. 'We knew one another in Switzerland. Paul – my brother-in-law, Christian de Savigny.'

'Pleased to meet you.' Paul held out his hand without a flicker of hesitation. 'Katrine and I happened to run into one another in the market. It must be eight years at least since we last met – in very different circumstances. It's a small world, isn't it?'

'Yes,' Christian said with a touch of irony. 'Yes, it is.'

Kathryn could feel her heart pumping uncomfortably yet suddenly her mind was crystal clear. Without stopping to give it a moment's further thought she heard herself say: 'It really is a stroke of good fortune. Paul is a teacher and he has just lost his job when the school where he was working in Bordeaux closed. I was just saying to him it's high time Guy had a tutor. I'm going to ask Charles if we couldn't offer him a position.'

One corner of Christian's mouth lifted in a slight smile.

'Were you indeed! I wonder what he will say?'

'I very much hope he will agree,' Kathryn said with acerbity. 'I know Paul would be very good for Guy.'

'Yes.' But the small smile was still there, faintly mocking. 'What about it then, Katrine? Can I give you a lift home or not?'

'I'm not ready to go yet. I still have to see Anne-Marie and in any case Maurice would be offended if I didn't ride home with him.'

'Very well. I'm just leaving myself. I'd like to get home before it begins to get dark – my lights are not as good as they might be.' Christian held out his hand. 'Nice to have met you, Monsieur. Perhaps we shall meet again before too long.'

Then he was gone, swallowed up by the market-day crowds.

Kathryn looked at Paul, the fear naked in her face now.

'Oh my God, do you think he . . . ?'

'Not here!' Paul warned her. 'You did well, Kathryn. You see – I told you you could do it.'

'I feel like a jelly!' she confessed. 'But I suppose that's it, isn't it? Decision made. And I hardly had time to think about it.'

'You must go now. Speak to your husband – you'll have to now, or your brother-in-law will do it for you. And I'll call the château in a few days.'

'When . . . ?'

'Just leave that to me.' Then he too was gone, a tall figure in an overcoat and soft trilby hat disappearing down the street just as Christian had done.

Three days later Paul telephoned the château as he had promised.

'Well?' he said when Kathryn came on the line. 'Have you spoken to your husband about me?'

'Yes.'

'And?'

'He wants to see you. I'm to make an appointment for you.'

'Good girl.'

'I don't know about that . . .' Kathryn stopped abruptly, realising that she must not say anything out of keeping with the charade she had begun. One never knew who might be listening. 'My husband will be free all day tomorrow. Could you come then? About eleven, say?'

'Make it later. I'm not sure how I'll get there. Two would be better.'

'All right. I'll tell him. I'll see you then, Paul.'

She replaced the receiver. Her hand was trembling. She was in this now up to her neck and she was still not certain she had done the right thing. It was, she knew, very dangerous.

Talking to Charles, however, had been surprisingly easy. She had put the suggestion to him that same night after running over and over the story so often in her mind that she had felt like a gramophone record stuck in a single groove. But at least there had been no indecision, no wondering when would be the right moment. The fact that Christian had seen her with Paul had forced her hand.

'I really think it's an opportunity we can't afford to miss,' she had said and Charles, somewhat preoccupied and distant as he so often was these days, had nodded.

'Well, it would seem to be. It won't be entirely easy to get Guy a good education with things as they are these days. This Paul Curtis would be suitable, you think?'

'I do, yes. I can't actually speak for what sort of a teacher he is, of course, but it was certainly always a vocation with him.'

'He's Swiss, you say?'

'Yes. Would you like to interview him, Charles?' she rushed on, turning the conversation away from awkward details; she was not sure enough of Paul's cover story to want to answer too many questions on his background.

'Yes, I suppose I'd better if we are entrusting him with our son's education,' Charles said. 'Arrange it, would you, Katrine? You can check my diary for a suitable date.'

So – it was done, and still she did not know what had possessed her. The need to do something positive in the struggle against the Nazis after the months of frustration and shame at her husband's acceptance of them, she supposed.

And refused to admit to herself that the fact that she wanted to see Paul Curtis again, very much, had anything to do with it.

'So – this tutor you are engaging for Guy is a good man, is he?' Guillaume asked.

Dinner was over; they were in the salon enjoying a cup of coffee – real coffee, supplied by von Rheinhardt.

'I think so, yes,' Charles said. 'He is fluent in three languages and he has a degree in mathematics. He impressed me very favourably.'

Kathryn sat very still, holding her hands twisted tightly together in her lap. Paul had impressed her, too, when he had come to the château for his interview with Charles, but for quite different reasons. It was his sheer nerve that had taken her breath away, the confidence and total credibility of his performance. He would certainly have convinced her he was exactly who he said he was if she had not known differently.

'But surely Guy is a little young for that sort of thing?' Louise said. 'He's just a baby. He can't even do simple sums yet – it will be years before he's ready for higher mathematics.'

'He's a bright child,' Guillaume said. 'The sooner he begins lessons the better – it will keep him out of mischief. And Charles is quite right to ensure he has the best tuition from the very start. How he copes later on will depend very much on the early foundations.'

'I suppose so. I still think that all he really needs at the moment is a playmate.' Louise glanced meaningfully at Kathryn. It's high time Guy had a brother or sister, that look said.

Kathryn averted her eyes. There was scant chance of that, when she couldn't bear Charles even to touch her. But she did not want her mother-in-law to know that. She and Charles still retired to their rooms together each night as they had always done. It was only when the door closed behind them that she dared to let her disgust with him show.

'He's going to live in, is he, this tutor?' Christian asked.

'Yes – he can have the blue room on our floor,' Charles replied laconically – domestic arrangement bored him. 'And the little room next door can be used as a schoolroom. It should be quite convenient.'

'Very convenient, I'd say.' Christian sounded almost amused.

Kathryn looked up sharply and found his eyes on her. His glance matched his tone – the amusement was there in his eyes, but there was something else, too, a glimmer of something that might have been not so much suspicion as understanding.

Of course he had seen them together outside the café and although they had been at pains to explain that, Kathryn realised with a quicksilver dart of fear that he had known there was more to it than a chance meeting between old friends.

I shall have to be very careful of Christian, she thought, and I must warn Paul to be wary of him too. But then perhaps Paul did not need warning. Perhaps he was used to subterfuge where she was not. Certainly his performance this morning had suggested as much.

Paul moved into the château a week later, his belongings packed in a battered brown suitcase. He also brought with him a pile of books and a Gladstone bag, purporting, Kathryn supposed, to be full of teaching materials. In fact it contained his little two-way radio for contacting London, as she discovered when she showed him his room and they were alone.

'Don't worry, I won't use it here at the château,' he assured her. 'I don't want to put you at risk if there are any detector vans in the vicinity.'

'Where will you use it then?' she asked.

'I have a few spots lined up.' He didn't want to tell her about the farmer who had offered the use of his hay loft, or the station-master's office – the less she knew the better. Not that he didn't trust her, but what people didn't know they couldn't tell under pressure.

'I'm a little worried about Christian,' she said. 'I may be wrong but I think he's a bit suspicious about you. Be careful, please.'

'I will be. Don't worry about me. Worry about you. You must stop thinking of me as anything but Guy's tutor. If you're anxious it will show.'

'Has it, do you think?' she asked nervously.

'No. You're doing marvellously.' He smiled at her and something in his eyes sparked a response in her. For a moment the conspiracy was there, linking them. Her heart thudded. Then with an abrupt movement, as if he too was aware of it and had decided to put a stop to what was happening between them, he turned away. 'We'd better get the details of the story ironed out. What have you said about me?'

'Nothing, except what we agreed.'

'Not even to your husband?'

'No. Charles and I don't . . . talk much any more.'

It was there in her voice, the bleakness of their relationship laid bare momentarily.

'The man's a fool,' he said bluntly

'No . . . no, he's not . . ' To her astonishment Kathryn found herself defending him. 'He's just toeing the family line – doing what he thinks is for the best.'

'Yes. I shouldn't have said that.' He did not explain that he had not been talking about Charles' collaboration but the fact that he had somehow let a woman like Kathryn slip away from him. All the more reason why he should not have said it, should not have thought it even. One of the first rules of the SOE was not to become emotionally involved. However attracted he might be to Kathryn – and he had to admit he was attracted to her – she was off limits.

'I'll fill you in on the life and times of Paul Curtis,' he said roughly. 'Listen carefully. It's vital that our stories coincide.'

'I know. Go on – I'm listening.'

As he talked she stood by the door, one ear to the crack so as to hear any sound of movement in the passage outside that might warn of someone coming. When he had finished she nodded.

'Right, I've got all that – I think.'

'I hope so. Now you'd better go before anyone thinks you've been spending too long with me. Where is Guy?'

'Bridget has taken him for a walk. When they get back I'll bring him up and introduce you to him.'

'Good. Just one more thing. Does that wireless set work? He indicated a crystal set in the corner of the room.

'It should do. Unless the batteries need recharging. Why?'

'I'll need to listen out for messages sometimes. It's illegal to tune in to London, of course, so I'd be grateful if you'd make sure there's no one within earshot around seven each evening. Can you do that for me?'

'I'll do my best.' She half opened the door to leave, then closed it again. 'It will be all right, won't it?'

'I hope so.' His face was serious. She felt a dart of panic at what she had done.

'What do you mean — you *hope* so?'

'Kathryn, you know as well as I do that there are no guarantees with this. It's a dangerous business. I'll do everything in my power to make sure no harm comes to you, but I am here to do a job.'

'But you promised! You said . . .' She was angry suddenly.

'I said I would be careful. That's the best I can do. But think of the alternative. If we don't beat the Germans one way or another, nothing in the western world that we value will be worth a candle. Think about that.'

'I am thinking. And I'm suddenly seeing it from Charles' point of view. At least we'd be alive!'

'And what about all the innocent people who have died already?'

'I don't know anyone who has died — not really.'

'Then you're lucky.' He was thinking suddenly about Gerie and little Beatrice and the memory added bitterness to his voice.

'But what about Guillaume and Louise, Celestine — Guy? Most of all, Guy.'

He gripped her arms.

'You're doing this for Guy. Remember that.'

He had meant to calm her by his touch. He had no way of knowing the ferment of emotion it unleashed in her. He felt her tense, rigid almost.

'I'll go through with it,' she whispered through gritted teeth, 'because somehow you've backed me into a corner and I can't change my mind now without bringing everything crashing down. But all I can say is it had better be all right. It had just better!'

She pulled free of his grasp and ran from the room.

In her own suite Kathryn tried to collect herself. She was shaking from head to foot and tears were very close. How dare this man place her in this position? How dare he put them all in such terrible danger? She hated him – hated his self-assurance and that edge of arrogance that assumed that any risk was worth taking for the greater purpose. It wasn't his child who was being used as a pawn in the game. It wasn't his family who might be dragged away to face a firing squad.

She pressed her hands against her eyes, trying to dispel the nightmare vision and replace it with a positive one – a France returned to its former glory, a safe and happy home for her to raise her son, a heritage he could aspire to which meant something, not simply a place to exist as the chattel of an alien regime.

But she couldn't dispel the antagonism she was experiencing for the man in the room next door, and she realised that it was not only the position he had placed her in that was firing it, but the ferment of confused emotion that he had aroused in her too.

What the hell was the matter with her? She blamed Charles and his family for their attitude towards the Nazis, yet she was now desperately wishing she had adopted the same position – and stuck by it. She despised Charles for his inaction and at the same time she hated Paul for quite the opposite reason. What *did* she want?

Slowly Kathryn's anger ebbed away until nothing but despair remained. There was, it seemed, no way out of the terrible mess they were all embroiled in. Whatever action she took or did not take, there was no escape. She could only go on living from day to day and hope that in the end there would be some light at the end of the tunnel.

9

PAUL'S FIRST WEEKS at the château passed off peacefully enough and Kathryn found herself relaxing a little. Paul had been accepted into the household, using the room next door to Guy's which Charles had suggested would be suitable for him and taking his meals with the family, and a routine had been established – Paul took Guy for lessons twice a day, sessions short enough not to overtax his brief attention span, and the remainder of the time the child played in his room or out of doors if the weather was fine with either Kathryn or Bridget, leaving Paul free to come and go as he pleased.

With the continuing labour shortage Guillaume and Charles were kept too busy at the distillery to be much concerned with what was going on in the nursery, and in any case now that Charles had approved the employment of a tutor for Guy he was inclined to leave the practical details to Kathryn. The raising of a child as young as Guy was, he considered, her domain, and the tensions between them caused by their continuing estrangement made him uncomfortable and bad-tempered in her presence. At least whilst he was working he was able to forget for a little while that his wife apparently despised him; when they were together there was no avoiding the hostility in her eyes and in every move she made.

Kathryn, for her part, was busy avoiding Paul as much as possible. The less she knew about what he was doing the better, she thought, and he must be of the same opinion. He went out a great deal but he never told her where he was going or why, never explained himself when he returned.

There had been a few unpleasant moments – the day when von Rheinhardt had come to lunch had been one of them. She had held her breath when Paul was introduced to him, horribly certain that von Rheinhardt's sharp eyes would see through the charade, but Paul had, as usual, been utterly convincing, every inch the rather dull tutor, and she had breathed again.

It was still Christian who worried her most. Sometimes she would look up unexpectedly and find his eyes on her, and the knowingness of his gaze sent a shiver of fear through her.

At other times the whole situation seemed vaguely unreal, a bad dream from which she would surely soon awake. Then one day when she went to collect Guy from his lessons Paul drew her to one side.

'A word, Kathryn.'

'About Guy?' she asked. But she knew it was not about Guy. Paul's serious tone had already told her that.

'No. Something I want you to do for me.'

Apprehension flared in her.

'What?'

'Could you go to Périgueux – take a message for me?'

'I don't know . . .'

'Mummy! Mummy!' Guy had pushed back his little chair and was running across the room to them waving a sheet of paper on which he had been drawing with bright crayons. 'Look – see what I've done!'

She bent down, scooping him up, glad of the interruption.

'Oh Guy, it's very good. What is it?'

'It's General von Rheinhardt.' The name was too difficult for him to pronounce, it came out as 'Wine-hat'. 'And there's the sun – and that's a tree . . .'

'I need to speak to you in private. I wouldn't ask, but it's important,' Paul said.

She looked up at him over Guy's small dark head. A pulse was beating in her throat.

'All right. I'll come to your room as soon as I've taken Guy back to Bridget.'

Fifteen minutes later she tapped on the door of his room. He opened it immediately and stepped aside for her to go in.

Anxious as she was she could not help noticing how much he had made the room his own during the few short weeks he had been there. Few as his belongings were, they somehow impressed an unmistakable maleness on the previously anonymous guest room.

'I couldn't finish what I had to say in front of Guy,' he said. 'We don't want him repeating conversations.'

'I hope he doesn't mention that I was coming to your room,' she said. Nervousness and something else – the sudden overwhelming awareness of him – made her tone sharp.

'Is he likely to?'

'You're his tutor. What do you think?'

'I think you had better have an excuse ready, just in case. And I'll be as brief as I can. I need to get a message to someone in Périgueux who is working for me and it's urgent – too urgent to leave it in our usual letterbox.'

Kathryn knew he was referring to the series of hiding places in dry-stone walls and hollow tree stumps where agents of the Resistance hid messages if they needed to pass on information. She bit her lip, desperately trying to think of an excuse to make the journey to Périgueux.

'What would I tell Charles?'

'Do you have to tell him anything? You two don't talk much, do you?'

'I'd need to take the car. He'd certainly wonder why.'

'All right – Plan B. I'll provide the excuse if you can provide the car. You can say I need to pick up some more books to help me with Guy's education from a friend there. Drive me in and I'll deliver the message myself.'

'You have got this well worked out, haven't you?' she said drily.

'That's my job – the reason I'm here. Well, what about it?'

She thought for a moment.

'All right, we'll try it. Who do you have to contact?'

'I'll tell you that when we get there. But we'd better make an early start. I shall need to be in Périgueux by ten-thirty at the latest.'

'That shouldn't be a problem. Charles is working long hours.'

'I'll leave the arrangments to you then.'

'I'll do my best.'

'What the devil do you want to go to Périgueux for?' Charles exploded when she broached the subject.

'I told you – Paul has some materials at a friend's house there that he wants for Guy. Why do you have to question everything I want to do?'

'It sounds like a waste of petrol to me – joy-riding all that way.'

'Don't be so mean-minded, Charles. Surely Guy's education is important enough to justify a little drop of petrol? Anyway, you can always get more from your friend General von Rheinhardt, I expect,' she added tartly.

'Von Rheinhardt is not my friend. But I've no intention of going over all that again.'

'Well, can I have the car or can't I?'

'I suppose so.' Charles sighed wearily. He hated this constant bickering. 'Just as long as you're sure that's the reason you're going.'

Her blood ran cold. 'What do you mean by that?'

'Nothing. But you're too friendly with this Paul for my liking.'

His eyes were dark, not with suspicion so much as jealousy. Christian! Kathryn thought. What has he been saying? Aloud she said: 'Don't be ridiculous. He's Guy's tutor and an old friend, that's all.'

'I hope so,' Charles said tiredly. 'I certainly hope so.'

They started out early, Kathryn driving Charles' Hispano. Spring had begun to turn the valley green, the first faint shoots spiking the trees and hedgerows, but the previous night there had been a frost which made everything sparkle in the first rose-pink rays of the morning sun.

Kathryn, who had always enjoyed being allowed to drive the Hispano, made the most of the opportunity which was, these days, all too rare, and the miles disappeared swiftly beneath its wheels.

Like so many old French towns Périgueux was dominated by its cathedral, a huge white Byzantine building crowning the hill. In happier times Kathryn had enjoyed visiting it, parking in the tree-lined boulevard and walking through the old town where the brownish-red roofs were dwarfed by the majesty of the cathedral with its dozen elegant minarets, five shimmering domes and a four-storey bell tower topped by a conical stone spire on a lantern of slender pillars. Today however she scarcely noticed it. Her mind was elsewhere.

'Where do you want to go?' she asked Paul.

'Puy St-Front. You know it?' He was sitting, remarkably

relaxed, in the passenger seat, enjoying the comfort of the soft leather.

'Yes. But you'll have to direct me when we get there.'

'I will, don't worry.'

In spite of the war the streets were busy. Kathryn was forced to concentrate on negotiating the traffic and pedestrians.

'Turn left. Here. Stop where you like. I have to pay a visit to the doctor's.'

He opened the passenger door and got out, walking along the narrow street, his rather worn brown suit with a shirt buttoned to the neck French-style blending perfectly with the surroundings.

As she waited Kathryn found herself wondering about him again. He had come into her life and turned it upside down, made her question all her fine principles, insinuated himself under her roof – and yet she knew so little about him. Perhaps it was safest that way but she couldn't help being curious – and suspecting that under any circumstances he would still be a very private person. The air of mystery was not only attractive but also strangely disconcerting.

After a while Kathryn began to be concerned. Paul had been gone a very long time. A Vichy police car turned into the narrow street and her heart leaped into her mouth. Supposing they stopped and asked what she was doing here – what would she say? To her relief it did not stop but cruised by.

Just when she thought he never would, Paul reappeared, coming out of the peeling brown-painted door with its tarnished brass plate.

'Where have you been?' she hissed at him as he slid into the passenger seat beside her. 'I wondered what ever had happened to you!'

'I told you – I had to visit the doctor. One has to wait one's turn.' His unruffled manner, when she had been so worried, annoyed her.

'That's all very well, but I thought I was going to be questioned by Vichy police.'

'You weren't, were you?'

'No.'

'That's all right then, isn't it?'

She pursed her lips angrily. It was impossible to argue with him and not very prudent either here in the middle of a busy street. She started the engine.

'Hang on,' he said in English. 'Where are you going?'

'Home, of course.'

'Don't you think perhaps we should visit a bookshop first and buy some books? It will look a little strange if we arrive back without any, since that was our excuse for coming.'

'I imagined you had some. You seem to think of everything,' she snapped, annoyed at her own lack of thought.

He ignored the jibe and his continued determination not to be ruffled annoyed her still further. She knocked the car out of gear.

'What do you want to do about it then?'

'Drive on,' he said, 'but slowly. Stop at the first bookshop you see.'

'Which way?'

'I thought you said you knew the place. All right, turn left here, then right . . . slow down, can't you! Here . . . stop!'

She did as he said, seething inwardly and trying not to show it. His sharp eyes had noted a second-hand bookshop; he got out and disappeared inside. A few minutes later he was back with an armful of battered volumes.

'That should do the trick.' He deposited them on the rear seat. 'All right, we'll go home now.'

'I wish you'd stop treating me like a chauffeur,' she snapped.

She drove in silence until they were outside the town and heading back towards Savigny. Her knuckles gripping the steering wheel were white, her neck and shoulders a hard line of anger and tension. Out in the country, miles from anywhere, he touched her arm lightly.

'Stop a minute, Kathryn.'

'Why?'

'Just do as I say for once without asking questions.'

Still fuming she pulled into the side of the road. The sun had melted the frost from the hedgerows now and the green shoots were clearly visible.

'Well?'

'Kathryn, would you rather I left the château?'

'Sometimes I wish to God you'd never come.'

'That's neither here nor there though, is it?' He pulled out his cigarettes and lit one without offering the packet to her. 'I thought you'd be able to cope with me being there but now I'm not so sure. You seem very . . . strung up. That's a dangerous thing to be.'

Hot colour suffused her face and neck. Little as she wanted him there she wanted even less to be judged and found wanting.

'I just wish I knew a little more of what was going on,' she said.

'I've been keeping you in the dark for your own safety.'

'That's not what you said in the beginning. Then you were full of all kinds of things you wanted me to do.'

'That was before I decided to go ahead with asking you if I could use the château as a base. You've provided me with a good cover, which is probably just about the most important thing you *could* do. But for all our sakes the less you know about what I'm doing the better. It's dangerous to have too many agents under one roof. As things are, if I was captured you could plead ignorance. My cover story will hold up, I assured you of that. If you stuck to it no one would have any reason to disbelieve you.'

'Unless you were to betray me.'

'I wouldn't that.'

'Brave words. But I've heard how the Gestapo persuade people to talk, putting out their eyes with a naked flame, cutting off their genitals. How would you hold out against that sort of torture?'

'They wouldn't take me alive. I have a cyanide capsule in my cuff link.'

And still he said it with that infuriating calm, talking about killing himself with deadly poison in the same casually conversational manner he might use to discuss a trip on a cross-channel ferry. She looked at him sharply.

'Who are you?'

'You know better than to ask me that.'

'Oh, I don't mean your real name. I know you won't tell me that. No, what I actually mean is – why are you doing this? Why you putting your life on the line in this way?'

'I have my reasons.'

'Which are?'

He opened the car window and flicked out the cigarette end.

'Let's just say that I do understand your concern for your family – especially for your son. If the Nazis did something terrible to him how would *you* feel – besides being devastated, of course?

Wouldn't you want revenge? You wouldn't care about yourself then, would you? All that would matter would be doing all you could to help drive the bastards back into the sewers where they belong and screw the manhole covers down so tight they could never get out to wreak that kind of terror and destruction ever again.'

His hands were balled now in his lap, his voice, though quiet, held such undercurrents of anguish that the last remnants of her anger died, replaced by dawning horror.

'You mean . . . ?'

'I don't want to talk about it,' he said roughly. 'But I understand those feelings only too well.'

For a moment she could not speak. She only knew that suddenly she was seeing him in a totally different light.

'I'm so sorry,' she said. 'Please tell me . . . what happened.'

'I said I don't want to talk about it. Suffice it to say that when this damned war started I had a wife and daughter. Now . . . well, I haven't.'

'I'm so sorry,' she said again, knowing it was totally inadequate. She reached out and covered his hand with her own, the only way she could begin to express the emotions that were flooding through her – regret at having misjudged him, shame for her self-centred reactions and an empathy so profound it was as if she herself had already lost those dearest to her. For a few moments they sat without moving, locked together by a common bond, nothing physical now, in spite of the contact of their hands, more a meeting of two souls offering and receiving comfort.

Paul was the first to move. He turned his hand over, squeezed her fingers lightly, then placed her hand on the steering wheel.

'I think perhaps we ought to go back to Savigny now,' he said.

Two nights later Paul came to her suite as she was getting ready to go down for dinner.

'Charles isn't here, is he?' he said softly when she opened the door.

'No – he's gone on down to discuss business with his father.'

'I thought I heard him going downstairs and I wanted to speak to you. I have to go out tonight.'

'Now?'

'No – later. After dinner. If it looks like being a long session I'll excuse myself by saying I have some work to prepare. But if there should be any questions asked I'd be grateful if you'd cover for me.'

'Yes, of course.'

She knew better than to ask why he had to go out, what he planned to do. But when he had gone again she looked out of the window. It was dark already but a clear night, the stars shining in the velvet blackness and a moon making the beginnings of a frost shimmer on the bushes. A perfect night for some kind of resistance operation. A perfect night to die.

Kathryn didn't know why she should have heard those words so clearly in her mind. She only knew that a shiver ran through her and a feeling of dread began to close in. But this time, she knew, her fear was not so much for herself, for the family, or even for Guy. It was all for the man who called himself Paul Curtis.

A few minutes before half past eleven Paul quietly closed the door of his room behind him and crept along the passage and down the stairs. The château was dark and silent but for the occasional settling of a timber and he blessed the luck that had sent the family early to bed this evening. Not that it was only luck, of course – they were all tired from the long hours they were working – but he had not wanted to trust to that. He had made sure his window was unlatched – the creaking of the heavy catch would have been a dreadful giveaway on such a cold, crisp night – and tested again the heavy creeper covering the wall outside which he had checked out as a possible escape route the first night he had been in the room. He did not relish the prospect of having to descend that way unless it was absolutely imperative. It might take his weight, but then again it might not. But at least tonight he had been spared having to find out. When the house was quiet he had changed into a black roll-neck sweater and a pair of dark corduroy trousers and rubbed charcoal over his face before checking the pockets of his jacket to make sure his torch, gun, and a hip flask filled with brandy were there. Now, carrying his shoes in his hand, he made his way out of the château by the back door.

The air was still and crisp and moonlight illuminated the garden, making it easy to find his way across the central courtyard to the outbuilding where his bicycle was stored. It was, he thought, a perfect night for flying. He had been almost certain, even before he had tuned in to the BBC that evening, that the operation would be on and the coded message which he and he alone understood had confirmed it. '*Le bébé s'appelle Jacques*' might sound like incomprehensible rubbish but to Paul it made perfect sense. Tonight a Lysander would be leaving England with his fully trained radio operator and a demolition expert to join his team. He must be there to meet it.

Adrenaline surged through his veins and he pedalled faster than he needed to, watching the dark sky for any arcing headlights that might warn of a police patrol and listening for the sound of engines. All was quiet. Again he ran over the details of the operation in his mind, details he had planned and set in motion by his visit to the doctor's surgery in Périgueux two days earlier. His men were briefed and ready – Albert, a farmer who owned a pick-up truck that was to be used to ferry the two new arrivals to their safe houses, Jean Lussac, the stationmaster, who hated to be left out of anything, and two local lads whom Albert had vouched for to act as lookouts. They had only had to listen to the BBC as he had done to know that tonight was the night. Just as long as they had heard it, he thought wryly. He didn't much fancy having to meet the Lysander all by himself with no way of transporting the new agents. But at least they would be put down in comparative comfort, not dropped by parachute into a ploughed field as he had been when he had first come to France.

As he approached the field selected as a landing ground Paul saw the pick-up truck parked, as planned, in a gateway, and felt a surge of relief. Albert, at least, had heard the message and presumably would have passed it on. Paul dismounted, laying his bicycle against the hedge, and approached the van.

'You're here, then.'

'Yes, but Jean won't be able to make it. He's caught flu.'

'Never mind. We'll manage without him. It's a perfect night. The pilot shouldn't have any trouble following the landmarks if he's done his homework properly. They'll be on time. I should think.'

'As long as they can keep out of the way of the flak.'

Albert was a dour man, though a reliable one, who hated the

Boche with a fervour that had stirred him out of his mundane existence into active resistance. At the moment his mouth was full of bread and cold sausage so that his words came out thickly.

Paul flicked his lighter and checked his watch.

'Let's get the landing site marked out. You can finish your supper while we're waiting.'

Albert packed the remains of his bread and sausage into one pocket of his coat and a flask of coffee into the other. He and the two village lads, who had climbed into the truck with him whilst they waited, joined Paul and together they crossed the fields to the one they had chosen for the landing strip. Bounded on three sides by hedges, with a line of trees at its far end, it was reasonably flat but low enough for the flares to be invisible from any direction except overhead. Paul and Albert set out the lamps that Albert had brought in his truck in the shape of an 'L', whilst the two lads took up positions from which they could keep a good lookout. There was nothing to do now but wait.

They talked little, Albert stoically finishing his sausage and Paul taking a few swigs of stomach-warming brandy. Paul checked his watch again – a few minutes after midnight. The tension of waiting prickled over his skin. Somehow it was almost impossible to imagine the plane ever arriving. If it did not he would have to risk another direct contact with London, he supposed, but he did not like using his radio more than he could help. He was not fast enough at it and every minute spent transmitting was another minute when he might be detected. He didn't care much for himself but he did care about the danger to which it would expose his circuit and most especially the danger to the de Savignys – and Kathryn. With an effort he pushed the thought aside. No point worrying about it yet – worry about it tomorrow when he knew for certain something had gone wrong with the drop.

And then, just when he had almost given up hope, he heard the unmistakable sound of an aircraft engine. He thrust the hip flask back into his pocket with fingers gone stiff from the cold.

He signalled to Albert, lit the lamp closest to him and grabbed his torch, flashing the agreed letter in Morse Code, whilst Albert, moving swiftly for once in spite of his bulk, hurried to light the other two.

The Lysander came overhead, skimming the tops of the trees.

Paul signalled again, the Lysander replied, and its landing light blazed into life. Paul watched it make its circuit and come in in a descending turn towards the first of the lamps. It seemed to be going very fast. Paul found himself holding his breath and hoping fervently that the field was long enough. Then wheels touched grass, the Lysander bounced once, then steadied, braking into wind, turning around the lamp furthest from it and taxiing back across the field.

The hatch opened and the pilot's head emerged.

'Hi, fellas. Nice landing site.'

Simultaneously the first of the two passengers scrambled from the plane, revolver at the ready, and the second handed down the baggage to him. Scarcely were they clear of the aircraft than the pilot called a farewell, closed the hatch and put on full power. He took off, skimming the hedges, and Paul approached the newcomers.

'Welcome. I am Paul Curtis.'

'I'm Jacques – your radio operator. This is Maurice.'

'Good. We'd better get moving, though, in case anyone spotted the aircraft. Albert here will take you to a temporary safe house. I'll be in touch shortly.'

They made their way back across the field to where Albert's truck was parked and piled inside. The engine coughed to life and Paul watched it disappear down the lane before recovering his bicycle from the hedge. The two village lads who had acted as lookouts had already gone, sure-footed shadows swallowed up by the darkness.

So far so good. The operation had passed off more smoothly than he had dared hope. Paul mounted his bicycle and started up the lane in the direction of the château. The silence of the night was unbroken and he began to relax. He pedalled on, unaware of just how close he was to disaster.

The German patrol vehicle must have been coasting down the hill with its engine and headlamps switched off. Why it should have been doing so he never knew but afterwards he could not imagine any other reason why he should not have heard its approach. It rounded the bend without warning, a dark, squat bulk in the moonlight. Without stopping to think Paul threw both himself and his bicycle into the hedge, but he knew with a cold certainty that transcended the sharp gut-churning fear that they must have seen him. The headlamps came on full beam, shockingly bright, as he scrambled through the hedge. Twigs tore at his coat, he wrenched himself free and rolled into the long frosty grass, inching along on his stomach. Then he heard the car door open and the shouts in German: 'Here! Just here! It's a bicycle!'

His heart was pounding, sweat pouring down his face. He crawled on along the perimeter of the field. Not far ahead of him was another hedge, dividing this field from the next. If he could get through it perhaps there was a chance for him. The only alternative he could see was a small wood at the far side of the field. Beyond it, he knew, was a river and the outskirts of the de Savigny estate. But the field between was an open expanse of no man's land. He'd never get across if he simply made a run for it, and even if he did he would be leading the Nazis direct to the château. No, there was nothing for it but to attempt to stop his pursuers. He did not know how many of them there were, didn't know how many he could get before they got him, but there were six bullets in his gun.

Paul rolled closer to the hedge, adopted a crouching position, drew his gun out of his pocket and released the safety catch. The first German emerged from the shadow of the hedge and without a moment's hesitation Paul fired. Even from this position and at this distance his aim was excellent; he had been shooting since he was a boy and he had a natural eye for it. The first German fell with a startled scream, clutching his stomach. Another German blundered through the hedge and Paul fired again. The first shot missed or merely winged him, Paul was not sure which, and he spun round firing back indiscriminately. Machine-gun bullets raked the grass and Paul felt a sudden sharp pain in his arm followed by total numbness. He froze, merging into the shadows. The German approached along the line of the hedgerow, gun at the ready, but he did not fire again. He thinks he got me, Paul thought. He waited, forcing himself to keep absolutely still, until the German was so close he could make out his fleshy features in the moonlight. Then he pulled the trigger.

The German crashed to the ground with scarcely a sound, shot through the heart. Paul waited a few moments. Were there any more of them? But there were no more shouts from the direction of the lane, only the groans of the first man he had shot threshing about in the grass. Paul knew he did not dare leave him alive. He crossed to him and without giving himself time to think about what he was doing, shot him in the head. The man jerked once and was still.

Paul looked around. His heart was hammering and he was as out of breath as if he had just run a mile. Lucky for him there had been only two of them, but he had to get away before reinforcements arrived.

His first instinct was to make a run for it across the fields but he knew he must not leave his bicycle. One bicycle here in the country was very like another but there was always the risk it might be identified. Somehow he crawled back through the hedge and ran up the lane to where the scout car had come to a stop. The engine was still running and the doors swinging open. He reached inside and switched off both engine and lights. It wouldn't be long before it was found in any case but the less attention it attracted the more precious time he would gain.

He lifted the bicycle out of the ditch and mounted it with difficulty. His arm was throbbing violently now and his fingers were sticky with blood that was pouring down. Gritting his teeth he began to ride, wobbling badly, along the road back to Savigny.

Kathryn had been unable to sleep. For a long while she had lain staring into the darkness wondering what Paul was up to, and once she thought she heard the sound of a plane overhead.

Beside her Charles was snoring gently – a habit Kathryn found repulsive these days. She pushed aside the covers and got out of bed, reaching for her kimono and pulling it on. The bare boards of the bedroom floor beyond the rug struck cold; she found her slippers, pushed her feet into them and crossed to the window.

Bright moonlight illuminated the parkland and Kathryn glanced up at the sky. No sign of a plane now, just the stars shining brightly and a scattering of high cloud. For a long while she stood there, looking out and thinking about Paul. What he had told her – or rather *not* told her – about the fate of his wife and child had affected her deeply and she found herself wondering about them too. It was difficult to imagine that hard, seemingly nerveless man as a loving husband and father, yet he had cared for them very deeply, she was certain, and grieved for them with an intensity that was almost beyond her comprehension. With something of a shock Kathryn realised just how limited was her own emotional experience. She loved Guy, of course, with the deep protective and proud love of a mother, but that was perhaps the extent of it. She had thought she loved Charles, but that love had died, not in an explosion of pain but rather petered out like a damp squib, leaving only regret and resentment that he was not the man she had thought him to be and probably never had been. Otherwise her emotions were mostly negative, futile ones – loneliness, longing and, since the war had come, anger and fear. Measured against Paul's obvious depth of feeling they seemed shallow and selfish.

Kathryn shivered. The thin silk kimono was no protection against the frosty night. If she didn't go back to bed she'd catch a chill. But she did not want to go back to bed. The thought of lying there, listening for the small sounds that would tell her Paul had returned, was not an inviting one.

Suddenly a movement on the drive caught her eye. She leaned forward against the windowsill, peering out. Paul – it had to be! She experienced a rush of relief and then, as suddenly, the first creeping fingers of alarm. His progress was erratic, he was pushing the bicycle in a way that looked more as if the bicycle was supporting him than the other way around, and his other arm looked strangely awkward. Something was wrong. She knew it with instinctive certainty and knew, just as surely, that she had to find out what it was.

Charles was still sleeping soundly, his snores softened into deep, regular breathing. Kathryn padded into the dressing room and found a coat. Then she changed her slippers for a pair of flat-heeled shoes, let herself out of the bedroom and crept down the stairs.

The back door of the château was unlocked, evidence that he had intended to return that way, and she crossed the courtyard to the shed, the door of which was ajar. She pushed it open and as she did so heard the click of a gun being cocked.

'It's me!' she hissed urgently. 'Is that you, Paul?'

'For God's sake! I almost shot you!' His voice was thick.

'Are you mad?' she whispered, shocked.

The shed was very dark after the bright moonlight outside but she could just make out the figure leaning heavily against the wall, clutching his arm.

'Paul?' she said. 'Are you all right?'

'No, I'm bloody not. I nearly got caught, dammit. I killed two Germans. And one of them got me in the arm.'

'On my God!' Kathryn went hot, then cold, and for a moment she thought she was going to faint. Never in her life before had she experienced such overwhelming terror. 'You killed two Germans? Paul – you'll bring the roof in on us!'

'Never mind them for the moment. It's me I'm concerned about. I'm dripping blood everywhere and I think my arm is broken.'

'Oh my God!' she said again. Her eyes were beginning to get used to the light now. She went over to him. 'Show me.'

'This one. Christ!' He winced as she touched it.

The thick material of his jacket felt soggy and sticky to her touch; a dark pool of blood had dripped on to the floor.

'Stay here,' she said. 'You can't come back into the house while you're bleeding like that. I'll get something . . .'

She left him in the shed and flew back into the kitchen. A few minutes later she was back with a thick towel.

'Can you take your jacket off?'

He groaned as he eased it off his shoulder; she peeled the sleeve back down his arm, wrapping the towel around it as firmly and gently as she could.

'That should take care of it for a minute or two. Let's get you inside.'

She put her arm around him, supporting him, and he leaned against her gratefully. Every last reserve of his strength had gone into getting back to the château and now he felt weak and shaky.

'Can you make it up to your room?' she asked when they were back in the kitchen. 'I'd better do something about the blood in the shed.'

'I'll make it,' he said through gritted teeth.

She filled a bucket with water, found a scrubbing brush and took both out to the shed. In the half-light she was not sure how good a job she would be able to make of clearing up but at least she had to try. After a few minutes' work the floor looked reasonably clean again. She scattered some sawdust which she found in a sack by the door over the wet patch and rearranged a couple of sacks to half cover it. The bicycle she stowed away against the far wall. Then she emptied the bucket down a drain in the yard and went back into the house, bolting the door behind her and creeping up the stairs to Paul's room. He was sitting on the bed cradling his arm, which was still swathed in the kitchen towel. His face was drawn into tight lines of pain and lacked any vestige of colour.

'You look terrible,' she said.

'Thank you very much!'

'Don't be flip. What are we going to do about your arm?' She crossed to him, sitting on the bed beside him and trying to unwrap the towel. He winced.

'Leave it, can't you?'

'No, I can't. Let me look at it.'

He allowed her to unwrap the towel, wadding it underneath to prevent blood dripping on to the floor. It was an ugly wound but at least she did not think the arm was broken.

'I'll try to clean this up,' she said, 'but you are going to have to get it seen to professionally.'

'And how the hell do I do that?' The pain was making him sharp and snappy, loss of blood and exhaustion fogging his brain.

'What about your doctor friend in Périgueux? I'll take you there tomorrow. But you'll have to keep out of sight. Thank goodness they are all busy at the distillery is all I can say. And thank goodness I happened to see you coming back!'

He said nothing. It was alien to him not to be in control but for the moment he was glad to be able to leave it all to her.

Kathryn went back downstairs for a bowl of water and disinfectant – she was afraid to use the bathroom in case someone heard her. Bad enough running water at all in the middle of the night – the ancient plumbing could make ghastly noises in the pipes. When she returned she bathed the wound as best she could, steeling herself to ignore Paul's muffled groans of anguish. When she had finished she bound it up with yet another clean towel and secured it with a long silk scarf around his neck. Then she helped him to lie down on the bed, fully clothed, and covered him with the eiderdown.

'I don't suppose you'll sleep much but do at least try,' she said. 'I must go to bed myself now or Charles will miss me. I'll bring you breakfast in the morning and we'll work out a plan of some kind.'

He nodded, reaching out a hand to her.

'You know, Kathryn, you're quite a girl.'

'Yes,' she said drily. 'I surprise myself sometimes.'

But there was a glow in her, a tenderness erasing the anxiety momentarily. It went with her as she returned to her bedroom, hanging up the coat and draping her kimono over a chair. As she slipped into bed Charles stirred, reaching for her in his sleep. She eased herself out of his reach but for a moment she found herself imagining that the body beside her, emanating warmth, was not Charles but Paul. She lay, savouring the illusion, too tired to wonder at it let alone try to evaluate or understand. But still sleep would not come. Every time she closed her eyes she was reliving the events of the last hour and soon the pleasant illusion was overtaken by anxiety once more – anxiety for Paul, anxiety for herself, for what she had to do and how she was going to achieve it. And then, just at the point when sheer exhaustion was about to claim her, heart-stopping terror.

Paul had killed two Germans, he had said. Whether they knew he was responsible or not, what dire consequences would that have for them all?

Dawn was breaking, silver and pink, before finally Kathryn managed to grab a couple of hours' desperately needed sleep.

WHEN SHE WAS sure that the coast was clear Kathryn went to Paul's room.

He was lying on the bed dozing but the tumbled eiderdown and pillows told her he had, not surprisingly, spent a bad night. As soon as he realised he was no longer alone he jerked violently, groaned and tried to sit upright.

'How are you feeling?' she asked.

'Lousy.'

'I can see that. Look, I've brought you a cup of coffee. We have to talk. We must decide what to do.'

She set the cup down on a small table within reach of his good arm, glancing, as she did so, at the towel with which she had bound up the wound. Though a dark patch of blood was visible it was not as large as she had feared it might be.

'At least the bleeding seems to have stopped,' she said, 'but I still think you should get it seen to. It could turn septic. And the trouble is I can't ask a doctor to call here. We daren't draw attention to the fact that you need treatment, and in any case I'm not sure how far Dr Artigaux is to be trusted. I'll have to take you to Périgueux. I only hope there's enough petrol left in the Hispano.'

'No,' he said. 'I can't ask you to do that, Kathryn. I've had a chance to think now – I've been awake most of the night. The best thing would be for me to get of here altogether. Then if the Gestapo come asking questions about the murder of two German soldiers they won't find you sheltering an enemy agent under your roof.'

'But where would you go?' Instead of relief Kathryn was experiencing a sinking feeling in the pit of her stomach.

'I have other contacts. They'd hide me and I can change my identity. Now this has happened I can't endanger you any more than I already have done. With hindsight perhaps I shouldn't have come back here last night at all but there are things I need to remove. They are well hidden but if the Germans made a really thorough search I wouldn't like to guarantee they wouldn't find them. Besides, I was worried about the damn bicycle – I thought it might be identifiable.'

'Oh Paul, I don't know ... The very fact that you had disappeared would be suspicious. How would I explain that?'

'You wouldn't. You'd just have to plead complete ignorance, pretend you were as taken in as the rest of them. Even if your family had doubts they wouldn't betray you, would they? And to the outside world the fact that they have been such good citizens of the new France should stand you all in good stead.'

'I don't know,' she said again. 'I don't like it.'

'Neither do I, but it's the best we can do. If the Boche come here asking questions tell them about me as openly as you can without incriminating yourself. Christ, it's a mess, I know. I'm sorry, Kathryn. It was a mistake on my part to involve you.'

'It's a bit late to worry about that now,' she said. 'In any case you didn't make any promises about it being easy. You did warn me it would be dangerous.'

'I also said I'd do what I could to protect you. So far I've made a balls-up of that. I don't want to get you in deeper.'

'If you were to go like this you'd be picked up in no time.' She couldn't believe how much it suddenly mattered to her that he should not be picked up – and not because she was afraid he might talk under pressure, for she knew he would not allow that to happen. If questioning and torture became inevitable he would simply take the cyanide capsule that he carried in his cuff link –and it was that very possibility she could not bear to think about. 'Please – let me take you to Périgueux and see if the doctor can patch you up enough to bluff it out. I'd never forgive myself if I turned you out now, just when you need help and support more than ever.'

'And I'd never forgive myself if anything happened to you because of me.'

It was a truth he was no longer able to ignore, but which had shaken him nevertheless and cost him a great deal to admit, even to himself. He cared very much what happened to Kathryn. He had come here half expecting a spoiled little rich girl of the type he despised most and found instead a woman of character and spirit, scared to death yet brave enough to risk the consequences in order to help him. He had used her ruthlessly, knowing he was placing her in a position of great danger and accepting that the ultimate sacrifice might be the result. If he was to be successful he could not afford to think about that. She was just one woman; the stake he and others like him were playing for was a whole continent of men, women and children. The trouble was that he had committed the cardinal sin of espionage. He had ceased to see her as just one woman.

Tossing and turning through the long painful hours of the night he had seen her face, heard her voice, wished irrationally that she was still there with him instead of lying beside her husband, even though, like most wounded animals, his primary instinct was to want to be alone with his pain. But somehow thinking of her had eased the agony. The realisation had come as a shock to him. In the dark and lonely hours it had always been Gerie's face that had been there before his half-closed eyes, Gerie's voice speaking inside his head. Now he discovered to his dismay that he was unable to visualise her clearly. With infinite care he sketched the details in his mind like an artist working on a portrait – the flaxen hair, her china-blue eyes, her creamy skin and the flush of pink colour in her cheeks. Baby-face, he had used to call her teasingly. But try as he might the picture refused to take shape, the details refusing to blend into a whole. And with a sickening sense of betrayal creeping around his heart Paul realised it was Kathryn's face that was real to him now.

It was this realisation that had made him decide he must leave the château. On a professional front it was dangerous to feel this way about any one person – the caring made one too vulnerable. But from a personal point of view too he wanted to escape. He did not want another face replacing Gerie's in his mind's eye, did not want anyone else impingeing on the place in his heart that belonged to her alone. It was too soon, much too soon, an insult to all they had shared.

'I have to go,' he said now. 'It's the best chance for all of us.'

Kathryn raked her fingers through her hair. She felt close to tears, helpless and frightened.

'Well, I don't agree with you. But if your mind is made up I suppose I can't very well stop you. But at least have something to eat first.'

'All right,' he said. 'Then you must go out. Take Guy with you. When you get back I'll be gone. Tell someone straight away. Pretend surprise — bafflement. And then forget all about me.'

She nodded, knowing he was asking the impossible. It would be difficult to enough to carry off such a charade, but she supposed she could manage it. What she would not be able to do was forget him.

As she went down the stairs the study door opened and Christian came out. She jumped guiltily; she had not known any of the family were still in the house.

'Christian — I thought you were at the distillery!'

'I'll bet you did. You've been visiting the tutor again, have you?'

She froze, her hand gripping the banister.

'What do you mean by that?'

'Don't you know?'

'No, I don't. I've been to see Paul, yes — he's not well this morning. He won't be able to take Guy for his lessons.'

'I see. And I suppose he wasn't well last night either.'

She could not answer. Her mind was racing in wild circles.

'You might fool Charles, Katrine. You don't fool me.' Christian sounded almost amused, but she could hear the stern undertone. 'There's something odd about that man. I've always thought so. And I've seen the way he looks at you, too. Is he your lover?'

'No!' Hot colour flooded Kathryn's cheeks and ebbed away again. 'No — of course he's not!'

'Really? You find it necessary to discuss Guy's education in the middle of the night then, do you? I couldn't sleep last night. I got up to fetch a drink of water. And I saw you come out of his room. Don't deny it, Katrine. I'm not given to hallucinations.'

So I was right to be worried about Christian, Kathryn thought. I was right to think he was suspicious. The confirmation of her fears was making her feel sick and shaky, yet at the same time it was almost a relief. Kathryn hesitated, weighing up what she should say to him. Should she pretend that Paul *was* in fact her lover and then, when he disappeared, let Christian think he had gone because their alliance had been discovered? Or should she tell him the truth and ask for his help? Of all the family Kathryn felt that Christian was the most likely to be sympathetic. He did not like what his father and Charles were doing, he had showed it often enough. He hated the Boche, hated von Rheinhardt. And he was something of a rebel, she knew.

Quite suddenly Kathryn felt unable to go on with the charade alone. She needed an ally. Without further ado, she made up her mind. She would trust Christian with the truth and pray to God he would not fail her.

'Can I talk to you, Christian?' she said.

His brows came together. 'Now?'

'Yes, now.'

'It's private, I take it?'

'Very much so.'

They went into the study and closed the door behind them.

'*Mon dieu*,' Christian said when she had finished. 'Well, I knew there was something going on but I never for one moment expected this!'

'Thank goodness you didn't. It probably means no one else suspects either. But what are we going to do? Paul is insisting on leaving, but he's not fit. He'd be caught in next to no time.'

'Then he'll have to stay here. If he came to France to help us, the least we can do is help *him*.'

Relief flooded her. Christian might very well have taken the easy way out, refused to do anything to put the family in greater danger than they already were. He could have replied that Paul had known the risk he was taking and brought it all on himself. He could have – but he had not. In that moment she felt closer to Christian than at any time since she had come to Charente.

'He needs to see a doctor,' she said. 'That's the first priority, I think, and I don't know if we can trust Artigaux. I was going to take him to a contact of his in Périgueux but I'm not sure if there's enough petrol in the Hispano.'

'I have some petrol in my car,' Christian said. 'But if he intends leaving I should think the first priority is to persuade him not to. Then we'll work out some kind of plan.'

'Will you come and talk to him with me? I was going to get him something to eat – give me a few minutes and then come up.'

'Very well. But Papa is expecting me back at the distillery. I'll telephone and say I've been delayed.'

Kathryn left him and went down to the kitchen, fortunately deserted at this time of day. The breakfast dishes had been washed and put away and Bridget would now be with Guy, Kathryn knew. She made coffee and found some bread and home-made preserve, wishing she had confided in Christian earlier. She should have known that a man who had fought with the French army could be relied upon.

He was still in the study when she went back upstairs with Paul's breakfast tray – she could hear his voice on the other side of the door though not what he was saying – and as she went along the upper landing she heard the sound of Guy giggling helplessly.

'Bridget – stop it! You're tickling me!'

A brief smile touched Kathryn's lips. Bridget was very fond of Guy and played games with him all the time. Please God don't let anything happen to turn his laughter to tears! she prayed.

The door to Paul's room was closed. She turned the handle and pushed. Nothing happened. She pushed harder. Still the door would not budge. Something was jamming it.

'Paul!' she called, softly, urgently.

No reply.

Alarmed, Kathryn set the breakfast tray down on the floor and pushed at the door with both hands. It opened a crack, no more, but it was enough for her to see what was holding it jammed closed. It was Paul's body.

'Oh my God!' she whispered.

Leaving the tray where it was and praying that Guy and Bridget would not come along and find it she ran back down the stairs.

Christian had finished his phone call; she met him in the doorway of the study.

'What's wrong?' he asked, seeing her frightened face.

'Come quickly, Christian. It's Paul. I think he has collapsed.'

He preceded her up the stairs, taking them two at a time.

'You're right.' He dropped to his knees, managing to get the door open enough to force his arm inside. Useless. There was no way he could move Paul's inert body.

'Paul! Can you hear me?' Christian called in a low voice.

Miraculously he was rewarded by a low groan. Paul must be beginning to regain consciousness.

'Try to roll away from the door!' Christian hissed.

After a moment Paul managed to do as he said. The door, with Christian's weight behind it, opened all of a rush and he practically fell into the room, Kathryn close behind.

'Paul!' She dropped to the floor beside him. He was pale as death, every vestige of colour drained from his face. 'For God's sake, Paul, are you all right?'

Paul ignored her, looking up at Christian in horror.

'What are you doing here?'

'It's all right, Paul, he knows. I've told him.' Suddenly she remembered the breakfast tray, still in the corridor, and ran to fetch it.

Christian helped Paul to his feet, supporting him back to the bed. The fall had started his arm bleeding again – Kathryn could see fresh scarlet staining the towel.

'What happened, Paul?' she asked, closing the door behind her.

'I tried to get up. You were such a damned long time. I got as far as the door and then . . . I couldn't get any further.'

'You fainted,' she said. 'You're weak from loss of blood. Now do you believe me when I say you can't possibly go wandering off on your own? Christian is going to help us. I have told him everything and he is with us.' She tried to sound calm and reassuring, though in fact she only sounded panicky.

'Why the hell didn't you say something before?' Christian said. 'I've been wanting to do something for the Resistance for a long while but I didn't know who I could trust in this nest of collaborators. You can count on me.'

'Christian says he has petrol in his car. We can get you to the doctor.'

'I'll take you,' Christian offered.

Momentary relief flared in Paul's foggy eyes, then he shook his head.

'It's too dangerous. If we should be stopped . . .'

'For heaven's sake, man, what choice have you? You've got to get patched up. If we're stopped, let me do the talking. I'll say you put your arm through a window. It's all right – stop worrying. I'm well known round here.'

Paul laughed harshly.

'That won't do you much good. Two Germans were shot last night. Didn't Kathryn tell you? Patrols will be everywhere.'

'Do they know that whoever did the killing was also shot?'

'Not unless they have seen the blood on the road. But I think I managed to stem it until I got to the crossroads, then I cut across the fields. I was bleeding like a pig by then.'

'So they have no reason whatever to link the shooting of the Germans to the château?'

'No. Let's face it, if they did they'd have been here by now.'

'True,' Christian agreed ruefully. 'That's it, then. I'm getting my car out, then I'll come back for you. Give me five minutes.' Paul tried to say something but Christian cut him off. 'You're in no shape to argue. You have already discovered you can't go anywhere by yourself and it's in our interests to make sure you are all right. The last thing we want is a dead body with a gunshot wound we can't explain on our hands.'

'He's right,' Kathryn said when Christian had gone. 'Not very tactful, perhaps, but right.'

'You told him about the doctor in Périgueux,' Paul said belligerently. 'You shouldn't have done that.'

'I had no choice but to trust him. You must see that.'

'I suppose so. I'm sorry, Kathryn.'

'Is there anything else we should know about what happened last night?' she asked, thinking of the aircraft she had thought she heard.

'Not at the moment. The less you know the better. If we get away with this and I'm laid up for any length of time there may be things I shall have to ask you to do, though.'

'Anything,' she said. 'Your colour is beginning to come back now. Try to drink some coffee.'

She poured some into a cup and sat down on the bed beside him, steadying his hand while he drank it. When he had finished she set the cup down but remained sitting beside him, covering his hand with hers, and a sense of closeness enveloped them both. In spite of her anxiety, in spite of her fear, she felt a surge of fierce joy.

When Christian returned and found them sitting there his brows lifted slightly but he said nothing and they did not even realise how obvious was the bond between them. Not a word had been said but no words were needed. They were reaching out to one another on a level so basic that words would have been totally superfluous.

'I've brought the car round to the door,' Christian said. He had taken charge with a swiftness and a decisiveness that surprised Kathryn – he had always seemed such an easy-going character, interested only in enjoying himself.

'Shall I come with you?' she asked, unwilling to let Paul out of her sight.

'Better not. There's no point putting you at risk as well. You can stay here and cover for us if necessary. When we've gone, break a window just in case I have to tell someone that's why Paul's arm is bleeding. I'd do it myself but I don't want to alert anyone by the sound of breaking glass before I've got him safely downstairs and into the car.'

'But won't they think it odd they heard glass breaking *after* you'd gone?'

'True. Perhaps it would be better to leave that. After all, if the Boche are suspicious enough to check on a broken window they'll be suspicious enough to examine Paul's arm, and I don't suppose a gunshot wound could be confused with a bad cut. The bullet isn't still in it, is it?'

'I don't know. I haven't felt up to investigating.'

'All right. Check the coast is clear for us, Kathryn, then stay here to ward off Bridget should she come out of Guy's room. And don't worry!'

He helped Paul up and supported him along the passage and down the stairs. A few minutes later Kathryn heard the sound of the car starting up and watched from the window as it passed below. She could see Christian's face, tense with concentration, but not Paul's. He was hunched in the seat, leaning his head against the glass.

Don't worry! she thought in anguish. All very well to say that – she would not be able to stop worrying until they were safely back again. And even then there would be a new set of problems to confront.

But at least this way Paul stood a chance and at least she had an ally in the camp. That alone would make things easier.

When the car had disappeared down the drive Kathryn spent a few moments collecting herself and then went in search of Guy and Bridget.

The hours passed more slowly than Kathryn would have believed possible. She was nervous as a kitten, jumping at every sound and watching the drive long before she knew she could reasonably expect them back.

'What's the matter, Mummy?' Guy asked, noticing. 'You're funny!'

'No I'm not. Don't be silly, Guy.'

'Where is Paul? Aren't I having any lessons today?' He looked forward to the sessions with Paul; they stimulated him in a way Bridget's games never could.

'Paul has gone out with Uncle Christian,' she said vaguely, praying they would be back before Charles and Guillaume came home from the distillery and there were more questions to answer. 'I'll take you for some lessons,' she went on. 'Fetch your book and you can read to me, show me how you are getting on.'

It would keep him quiet and take her mind off the waiting, she had thought. But sitting beside him, watching his small plump finger trace the words, she was not sure it was such a good idea. She could not concentrate and every time he stumbled and she had to correct him she wanted to scream.

'That's enough for now,' she said when she could stand it no longer. 'Why don't you put on your coat and go out to play for a little while?'

'I don't know what to do.'

'Guy, you have a hundred and one things to do. Go and ride your tricycle in the yard. It's a lovely day – the fresh air will do you good.'

She buttoned him into his coat and got out his tricycle, relieved momentarily at the prospect of at least being able to worry uninterrupted, then thinking anxiously that perhaps she should have kept him indoors so there was no danger of him seeing Paul and Christian return . . . when they returned . . . *if* they returned . . .

She watched the window, she watched the clock, she sat down, she stood up, she paced from room to room. Something had gone wrong. It must have. They should have been back by now.

Lunchtime was approaching and there was every chance that Charles and Guillaume would come home for something to eat. Her anxiety began to turn to panic.

And then, just when she was almost beside herself, she saw Christian's car coming up the drive. All her instincts were to run and meet them but she knew that what she must do was make sure Guy and Bridget were out of the way.

She ran to the courtyard, scooped up Guy and called to Bridget.

'Could you come in here for a moment? I'm sure I saw a mouse behind the grand piano! Come and help me see if we can catch him.'

'I'll set a trap,' said Bridget, who was not keen on the idea of a mouse scuttling around her feet, but when Kathryn insisted, she came anyway and Kathryn kept her there until she heard footsteps in the passage and on the stairs. The door opened and Christian came in.

'What's going on here?' His tone was jovial, and his exhilarated expression told Kathryn that all was well.

'A mouse,' she said. 'At least, I thought so. I must have been mistaken. We'll set a trap like you said, Bridget. See to it, will you?'

She followed Christian back into the passage. Bridget, relieved but grumbling, returned to the kitchen, leaving an eager Guy still hoping he might catch the mouse.

'Well?' she questioned Christian with her eyes.

'All passed off without incident. Paul has gone up to his room to rest. Go up if you like. I have to get back to the distillery.'

Her feet flew up the stairs. Paul was sitting on the bed, his arm bound with a bulky bandage completely covered by a voluminous fisherman's sweater. He was still pale but he managed to smile at her.

She ran to him, relief of tension removing the last barriers of reticence, and put her arms around him.

'Oh Paul, I was so afraid I'd never see you again!' she said.

For the moment nothing else in the world mattered.

Kathryn was having lunch with Guy and Bridget in the kitchen when Charles came home. She looked up as the door opened and knew at once that something was wrong. His face had the sort of hang dog expression he wore when he was worried and Guillaume was not with him.

'I must talk to you,' he said with a sidelong glance at Guy, indicating that whatever it was he wanted to say, he did not want it to be in his son's presence.

Kathryn's heart came into her mouth.

'Don't you want something to eat?' she asked.

'No, I'm not hungry. I'll be in the salon.'

'I didn't do lessons today, Papa!' Guy said. 'Monsieur Curtis wasn't very well.'

'Never mind, there's another day tomorrow.' Charles ruffled Guy's hair absently as he passed his chair.

Kathryn put down her soup spoon.

'Finish your lunch, Guy. I'll be back in a minute.'

'Aren't you hungry either, Mummy?'

'No, not really. Now do as you're told, there's a good boy.'

She went through into the salon. Charles was standing by the window, hands thrust into pockets, looking out across the gardens. He turned as he heard her come in.

'What is it?' she asked. 'What's the matter?'

'There was an . . . incident . . . last night. Two German soldiers were shot in a field not very far from here. Von Rheinhardt came to the distillery. There is a big inquiry going on, naturally. Von Rheinhardt wanted to know if we knew anything about it.'

'You told him we didn't, of course.' Kathryn was very cold; she twisted her hands together to keep them from shaking.

'Of course. But he won't let matters rest there.'

'Who do you think could have done such a thing?'

'I don't know. I thought everyone round here had more sense than to get involved in something like this. That's what I told von Rheinhardt too, but of course he's not satisfied. There is going to be hell to pay if he doesn't find the person responsible.'

'What do you mean?'

'Oh Kathryn, do I have to spell it out? They'll take hostages, I shouldn't wonder. This is just the kind of trouble we have been at pains to avoid. And that's not all. A plane was seen, flying very low. They think someone or something may have been dropped in last night.'

'A plane. Yes, I heard it.' He glanced at her in surprise and she felt guilty colour rise in her cheeks. 'I couldn't sleep. It never occurred to me though . . . They think it might have been an agent?'

'An agent or ammunition and supplies for someone already operating round here somewhere, yes. It might not have been, of course. There were no reports of anyone seeing it land or parachutes or anything of that kind. It could merely have been reconnaissance. But whether it was or was not, the fact remains that someone shot two Germans. And the people round here – our people – will have to pay for it.'

'Can't you persuade von Rheinhardt that it couldn't possibly have anything to do with the villagers?' she asked.

'I did try. To be honest he was in no mood to listen.'

'Hmm. So much for your friendship,' Kathryn said bitterly.

Charles' eyes narrowed. He looked, momentarily, as he might have done if she had struck him, and in spite of herself Kathryn felt a little ashamed of twisting the knife when he was so clearly worried.

'He is not my friend,' Charles said, his voice low and angry. 'I hate the Germans being here as much as you do. It's my homeland that's being raped, remember.'

'Not so much raped as lying down and begging for it!' She knew she shouldn't say it but she could not help herself. 'Oh, I know we shall pay for it, but at least whoever shot those Germans was putting up some kind of a fight.'

Charles sighed.

'You won't see, Katrine, will you, the futility of that sort of gesture? Killing two men out of thousands won't do anything to change the situation and it may result in the deaths of innocent people. I wonder if you will still feel as bullish if you have to watch them tie up two poor villagers in front of a firing squad? Now, I am going back to the distillery, but I thought I should let you know what had happened in case von Rheinhardt comes here. I wanted you to be prepared.'

'Very well, I'm prepared.' But he had shocked her with his talk of villagers being shot in retaliation. The very thought made her stomach turn over.

'Was Christian at the distillery when von Rheinhardt came?' she asked suddenly as he crossed to the door.

'Yes. Why do you ask?' He fixed her with one of his penetrating looks.

'I thought I heard him at home during the morning, that's all.'

She knew she should not have drawn attention to Christian but she needed to know if he too had been warned.

'I'll see you this evening. We may have von Rheinhardt as a dinner guest. We invited him in the hope we can talk him out of reprisals. He wouldn't commit himself, of course – with all this going on he may be too busy. But perhaps you could warn Bridget we may be one extra.'

'I'll tell her.' She was shaking again at the prospect of Paul, with his injured arm, and von Rheinhardt under the same roof.

She went back to the kitchen. Guy had finished his soup and was helping Bridget with the dishes, wiping up plates and cutlery with exaggerated care. Kathryn's heart lurched. He was such an adorable little boy, sometimes so serious, sometimes brimming over with high spirits, and in his jersey and shorts he looked wholesome and innocent. Her every instinct was to scoop him up in her arms, protecting him as best she could from all the dangers that threatened him and taking comfort herself from the feel of his firm little body close to hers. But she did not want to frighten him.

'If you like we could have a game of ludo,' she offered.

'Oh yes! Yes please!'

'Go and get it then.'

His interest in the drying-up forgotten, Guy dropped the cloth and ran off. Left alone with Bridget, Kathryn told her as briefly as possible what had happened and also informed her that von Rheinhardt might make an extra one at dinner.

'That man – I don't like him!' Bridget said, then clapped a hand over her mouth. 'I'm sorry, I shouldn't have said that. It's not my place.'

'It's all right, Bridget, I don't like him either. But the Baron and Monsieur Charles think it's best we don't show it.'

'He frightens me,' Bridget went on. 'Oh, I know he is very generous but he has the coldest eyes I've ever seen. When I see him playing with Guy I want to snatch the child and run away with him.'

'I know. I feel just the same. But we must be strong.' Kathryn could hear Guy coming back. 'Will you entertain Guy for just a few minutes? I want to take some of this soup up to Monsieur Curtis. He hasn't been well this morning.'

Bridget's eyes sharpened.

'I'll take it if you like.'

'No, it's all right. You go on with what you are doing,' Kathryn said quickly. Guy came running in, clutching the board and a bag containing dice and counters. 'Get it all ready, Guy. I'll be back in a minute,' she told him.

There was no reply at first when she tapped on Paul's door. Anxiously she turned the handle, half expecting a recurrence of this morning's drama, but the door opened without hindrance. Paul was lying on the bed, dozing.

'Ah – lunch!' he said with an attempt at a smile.

'Yes. It's only parsnip soup, I'm afraid.'

'It smells very good. And I must say I'm hungry.'

She set down the tray on his knees.

'They have found the Germans.'

'Well, yes, they were bound to, weren't they? I'm only surprised we didn't meet road blocks and God knows what this morning.'

'Charles thinks there might be reprisals. He's invited von Rheinhardt to dinner tonight to try and appease him. You'd better stay here out of the way.'

Paul thought for a moment, then shook his head.

'No. No, I can't do that. He'd think it very odd if I didn't show up.'

'But your arm . . .'

'We'll put it in a sling and say I've sprained my wrist. From what you say they are looking for someone who was dropped in last night. I've been here long enough now to be part of the scenery – as long as we're careful.'

'It's terribly risky . . .'

'Yes, I'm afraid it is. But there really is no alternative. We just have to be bold, bluff it out. Charles doesn't suspect anything, does he?'

'I don't think so . . .' She broke off, her hand flying to her mouth. 'But why did he come home especially to warn me? Oh my God, do you think he might . . . ?'

'You're the best judge of that. What would he do if he did suspect?'

'I honestly don't know. But I think he might turn you over to the Germans to try to avoid them taking hostages.'

'I suppose,' he said slowly, 'you think I should turn myself in for the same reason.'

'No!' she said sharply.

'Yes you do. I can see it in your eyes. If I thought it would do any good I'd do just that. But I'm not sure it would and it would be bound to bring suspicion on you. If Charles betrayed me that would be different. You could pretend you had been taken in by me just like the others.'

'I couldn't!' Tears were pricking her eyes, lack of sleep and the stress of all that had happened weighing heavily on her. 'I honestly don't think I could do that!'

'Yes you could. You'd have to. Oh sweetheart, don't cry . . .'

The endearment slipped out quite unintentionally and he reached for her hand, pulling her towards him. He had intended only to comfort her but as his fingers closed over hers he experienced a powerful wave of emotion. Christ, but he wanted her! He shouldn't, but he did. And the wanting was not only physical, either, but a potent mix of the desire to protect her and make her happy coupled with his own need of her. He held her, feeling the softness of her hair against his chin, smelling the faint sweet perfume which clung to it, knowing he was overstepping all the boundaries he had set himself and wondering if she knew it too.

Perhaps she did, for with abrupt suddenness she pulled away.

'I'm sorry . . . I'm being stupid. The tray . . . you'll spill your soup . . .'

'Never mind the soup, it's you I'm concerned about.' The desire of a moment ago gave a hard edge to his voice. 'It's not easy, I know, and I can't in all honesty promise you it's going to get any better. I'm afraid you'll just have to be brave.'

'I'm trying. I really am. But I'm so bloody scared! Oh hell, I don't seem to have a handkerchief . . .'

'Here, have mine.' He pulled one from the voluminous sleeve covering his injured arm and gently wiped her eyes with it. 'Better now?'

'Yes. I must look a fright . . .'

Impossible, he thought. Aloud he said: 'No you don't. You look fine. You'd better go now or someone will wonder where you are.'

'Yes, I'd better. Will you be all right?'

'I'll be OK. But could you come back late afternoon and help me fix the sling when I'm getting ready for dinner?'

'Of course. Though I'm still not sure it's a good idea . . .'

'Bluff, remember? Off you go now.'

The door closed after her and he laid his head back against the pillow, closing his eyes and wondering what was the best way to deal with this turn of events. He should have got out, of course, as soon as he had realised he was beginning to have feelings for Kathryn, but he hadn't got out. Circumstances had conspired against him and now it was too late. He cared for her more deeply than he had imagined he would ever care for anyone again. It was a reality he could not avoid; he would simply have to deal with it the best way he could.

11

'MUMMY – MUMMY – GIVE me your counter. Look – I won again!'

Guy tapped out the spaces to the centre of the board, laughing in delight. Three games in a row and he had won every one of them!

'All right, Guy, I give in. You're the champ,' Kathryn said, laughing a little at his obvious pleasure and knowing that his triumph could be accounted for not only by luck but also by her own total inability to concentrate. 'I think that's enough for one afternoon, don't you? Off you go and find something else to do.'

'I'll give you a game if you like, Guy,' said Bridget, who had just finished preparing the vegetables for dinner. 'See if you can beat me too.'

Kathryn smiled at her and escaped gratefully. She did not think she could have played another game if her life had depended on it –and, she thought grimly, perhaps it did, since the ability to behave normally was an absolute necessity. It was also a charade that was difficult beyond belief – and not merely for the obvious reasons. Yes, she was still desperately worried about what was likely to happen, not only this evening but in the future too. Yes, she was terrified that Charles might be beginning to be suspicious of Guy's tutor. And yes, she was sick with dread as to what von Rheinhardt might do in retaliation for the killing of two of his men. But in spite of all that, in spite of the nightmare that had closed in around her, she was also irrationally, singingly happy. It bubbled in a deep well somewhere inside her, that crazy feeling of anticipation, inexplicable even if everything had been normal, and given the present circumstances, quite ridiculous. But there was no denying it, and she knew that the reason for it was what was happening between her and Paul.

Crazy as it might seem, dangerous as it certainly was, she was falling in love. She had not experienced anything like it since she had first met Charles, and she had forgotten how potent an emotion it could be, like drinking a glass of her father-in-law's fine brandy too quickly. Her head was spinning, she felt like a young girl again, and all the privations of the past year, all the resentment and helplessness, all the fears for the future, paled into insignificance beside it. She was falling in love. That was the reality. Upstairs was a man who had touched her heart in a way she had forgotten it could be touched. The wonder of it transcended everything else.

At five she went to his room. It was too early by far to be getting ready for dinner but she wanted to fix the sling before Charles returned from the distillery. She did not want to have to worry that he might wonder why she should be visiting Paul's room, and in any case she could not wait another minute to see him again.

The château was quiet. Guy was in the kitchen, having his tea under the supervision of Bridget, who was preparing dinner. Kathryn knocked on Paul's door, feeling shy suddenly.

'Come in.'

The sound of his voice made a pulse beat deep within her. She opened the door.

He was standing by the bed and had obviously begun the process of getting himself ready for dinner. He had changed from the sweater and cords into a pair of dark trousers and a white shirt, the sleeve of which strained over his bandaged arm, and which was still open at the neck. His efforts – and the resultant pain – had made him pale again, but he smiled at her and she found herself marvelling at his resilience.

'Hello.'

'Hello. How are you feeling?'

'Don't ask! I'm sure you wouldn't want to know.'

Oh, I do! she thought. I want to know everything about you. Aloud, she said: 'I've brought this scarf. I can make a sling with it – if you're sure you can go through with tonight.'

'I have to. You haven't heard yet whether we are to have the pleasure of von Rheinhardt's company?'

'I haven't heard, but I should think it's likely. He doesn't usually pass up an opportunity to dine with us. He's a cultured man, which is more than can be said for some of his friends. I think he enjoys our company.'

'He certainly enjoys yours,' Paul said drily. 'I've seen the way he looks at you.'

'Don't be ridiculous! I hate the man and he knows it.'

'Perhaps knowing you hate him adds a certain spice. And besides, you are a very attractive woman.'

She felt the colour burning in her cheeks and changed the subject abruptly.

'What are we going to do about your arm, then?'

'First see if I can get a jacket on over the bandage. I couldn't manage it myself. If it's too tight a fit we'll have to think again.'

The jacket was hanging over the rail at the foot of the bed. She picked it up, resisting a crazy urge to bury her face in it.

'Let me help you then. Left arm first.'

She eased his hand through the armhole, trying to wriggle the sleeve on without hurting him too much, but the wad of the bandage prevented it. He swore, a mixture of frustration and pain.

'We'll have to take off some of the bandage.'

'But supposing it starts bleeding again?'

'It won't if it's up in a sling. Anyway, I can hardly go down to dinner wearing a sweater.'

'All right. I'll get some scissors. But don't try to do it yourself. Leave it to me.'

A few minutes later she was back with her dressmaking shears. She rolled up his shirtsleeve, took out the safety pins securing the bandage and began to unwind it. The doctor had done a thorough job; soon the wad was considerably thinner and the dressing still not exposed.

'Let's try the sleeve again.'

She was bending over, concentrating on fixing the safety pins neatly, when she felt his good arm go round her waist. For just a second she froze, her heart pounding, then she pushed the pin into place and fastened it.

'Try that.'

She looked up, straight into his eyes. He was gazing down at her, not moving, not speaking, but his look said it all.

'Paul . . .' she said, a catch in her voice.

His arm tightened round her waist; he leaned towards her very slowly. Her throat felt constricted; she could scarcely breathe. His face was close now, going out of focus, yet somehow she could see him more clearly than ever before, every line, every shadow. She knew she should pull away, end this now, but she could not. She stood, mesmerised, still holding his bandaged arm carefully, and felt the first gentle touch of his lips on hers. Just a brush, the smallest, lightest caress, yet it started a fire within her. She stood unmoving, savouring the tenderness of the moment within the maelstrom of seething emotions, feeling as if she were suspended somewhere in space with only the stars for company and the terrors of the past twenty-four hours nothing but a dark shadow on the earth far beneath. He lifted his mouth momentarily and she wanted to cry out at the loss, then he was kissing her again, harder, deeper, and she moved her own mouth in response, returning the pressure, parting her lips beneath his.

When he released her she was breathless, dizzy, achingly aware yet somehow unreal.

'I've been wanting to do that for days. Longer. I've been wanting to do it ever since I first met you.'

'Have you?'

'Yes. I want you, Kathryn.'

'And I want you.' It was little more than a whisper.

'But this is not the right time. I have a job to do and so do you.'

'Yes.' He was right, of course, but she still felt bereft. Her whole body was alive with the urgent need of him, every nerve ending tingling with sharp awareness, every tiny muscle straining towards him as if drawn by a powerful magnet, and aching with desire. She longed for him to kiss her again, longed for the feel of that hard seeking mouth on hers, and more, much more than that – his hands on her breasts and between her thighs, his body against hers, in her. Without a single coherent thought she knew she wanted all these things more than she had ever wanted anything in her life. Yet at the same time she knew he was right – this was not the time or the place.

As if understanding and responding to her longings he tilted her chin up with his hand, looking deep into her eyes.

'When this is all over, Kathryn. If we get out of it alive.'

He kissed her again, lightly this time, subjugating his own desire with the iron will that was so much a part of his make-up. For a few moments he had allowed his personal need to rule his professional judgement. It must not happen again.

With a movement almost brutal in its decisiveness he pulled the jacket round his shoulders, forcing his injured arm into the sleeve. She fixed the scarf around his neck to form a sling but like a sleeper awakening from a dream she did not feel in full control of herself. Her hands were clumsy, not deft, and with the new awareness each touch revived the desire, sparking it to new life so that normality was merely a pretence, a thin veneer covering the seething cauldron of her emotions.

'That's fine,' he said briskly when it was done. 'I'll see you at dinner.'

He touched his finger to his lips then pressed it briefly against hers.

'Be brave, Kathryn,' he said.

By dinner Kathryn's nerves were taut as a well-strung violin and she did not know how she was going to get through the evening. Charles had come home and told her von Rheinhardt had still not confirmed acceptance of his invitation.

'Does that mean he won't come, do you think?' she asked hopefully.

'It means I don't know,' Charles snapped. He was a worried man and anxiety made him ill-tempered. 'He's still busy with the investigation into the deaths of his men, I suppose, which is hardly surprising. If I were in his position I would feel exactly the same—that everything else had to take second place to finding the murderer.'

'It's quite different!' Kathryn flared back. 'If it was your men who had been shot you'd be concerned because you cared for them and their families. Von Rheinhardt isn't. He simply sees it as an insult to him, to Nazi Germany and the efficiency of his forces. That most of all. Inefficiency is the most heinous of crimes to the Boche, isn't it?'

'For God's sake, Katrine,' Charles said wearily. 'You never give up, do you? Not even when the lives of your own family might be at stake.'

A cold shiver ran over her skin.

'What do you mean? He isn't holding any of us responsible for what happened, is he?'

'I don't know. But he is a powerful man and you would do well to remember it.'

How could I forget? she thought bitterly. But at least perhaps all the activity meant von Rheinhardt would not come. She prayed he would not.

They had still not received word one way or the other by the time they assembled for dinner. Christian was first down; he was already in the salon with a drink in his hand when Kathryn and Charles went in, and she was glad to know that at least she had an ally in the camp.

'How is Monsieur Curtis' arm?' Christian asked with perfect naturalness and a tiny conspiratorial glance at her that was quite unnoticeable to the others.

'Painful, I think,' she replied carefully.

'What is wrong with Monsieur Curtis' arm?' Guillaume enquired, coming in with Louse in time to catch the end of the conversation.

'He fell off his bicycle and sprained his wrist.' Her voice was tight but fortunately Guillaume was scarcely listening.

'This is a bad business,' he said, pouring a sherry and handing it to Louise. 'I dread to think what the outcome of it will be.'

'How could anyone be so foolish as to shoot German soldiers?' Louise wondered aloud, sipping her sherry. 'Such a very dangerous thing to do.'

But as always she looked remarkably unworried. Louise hasn't a brain in her head, Kathryn thought irritably. To her the most trying aspect of the war is the fact that she can't go to Paris and order a new wardrobe of fashionable clothes each season as she used to.

'I'd put my money on it being someone from outside the district,' Guillaume said testily. 'I'm sure everyone around here has too much sense.'

'Especially considering the example you set them,' Louise murmured.

'I just hope to God von Rheinhardt gets whoever was responsible. Coming here and making trouble! If he doesn't, we may well see the innocent pay the price for the guilty.'

As he said it the door opened and Paul came in. Kathryn's heart seemed to stand still, partly from nervousness, partly because the sight of him was making her stomach turn somersaults.

'Good evening,' he said pleasantly. 'I hope I'm not late. It took me a little longer than usual to get ready tonight.'

'You fell off your bicycle, I hear,' Guillaume said. 'How did you manage to do that?'

Paul was saved from replying by the sound of a car coming up the drive. They all looked towards the window. Bright lights were cutting a swathe through the darkness, a large black staff car drawing up outside.

'Von Rheinhardt. He's here then.' Christian spoke for all of them.

Otto von Rheinhardt swung his tall frame out of the staff car and straightened, looking for a moment at the château and absorbing, as he always did when he came here, the sense of history that emanated from every stone of the centuries-old building.

What was it about great institutions, he sometimes wondered, which could inspire him with such passion? Where his fellow human beings were concerned he had no feelings at all. His men he treated like robotic machines, nameless ranks who were there to do a job and who he would see were severely disciplined if they failed in their duty in even the smallest degree. The French natives were the enemy, but for the most part, in his opinion, were stupid and weak, unworthy of anything more than his scorn – unless, of course, they stepped out of line, in which case he would exert his authority with cold fury. Even his family, at home in Germany, meant little to him. His mother had died some years ago and he and his father had little in common. Otto senior was a coffee importer – the coffee he selected and distributed was drunk in the finest establishments across Germany and Austria – and he had always been too concerned with the business to have much time for building a close relationship with the son he found hard-hearted and aloof.

Not even the women in von Rheinhardt's life had the power to stir anything more than superficial emotions – occasional lust and the sense of satisfaction and pride that came from having a beauty on his arm – as Ingrid, the fiancée who adored him, would testify. She had his ring on her finger and waited for him in war-torn Germany, but she could never be sure of him, for even loving him as she did she was aware of his total detachment, though she would never have admitted to it or to the basic truth of the matter – where people were concerned von Rheinhardt was totally without care or compassion.

All his energy was reserved for the furtherance of his career and in this he had been outstandingly successful, gaining his promotions in the army of the Third Reich by his single-mindedness and a determination which even his superiors had found daunting. He was hard, he was cold, he was ruthless. He dealt with those who opposed him as he would have dealt with a fly that annoyed him, swatting it to the ground and crushing it underfoot with never a thought for human misery, and not caring, or so it seemed, for the fact that he was almost universally disliked. No, people did not matter to Otto von Rheinhardt. Only Aryan supremacy and his place in the order it created were important to him.

Yet for all his apparent heartlessness, beauty and culture and a sense of history touched him in a way nothing else could. His home he loved, not for its memories of the happy childhood he had spent there, but for its aesthetic value, and the Château de Savigny stirred him in much the same way. Its faded grandeur pleased him – the square-turreted building, the courtyard and well, the fountain, the moat which had repelled other invaders, but not him. And within its walls he was continually finding new things to pleasure his senses. Whenever he visited he hungrily devoured the treasures it housed with his eyes, feeling his spirits raised by the beauty of the glowing paintings and works of art, the silverware, gleaming dully in the soft lamplight, the delicately fashioned porcelains, the chunky wholesome bronzes. He looked at them and coveted them, promising himself that one day, when he was finished with soldiering and had a home of his own, he would fill it with just such treasures.

He seldom refused an invitation to the château and in fact actively sought excuses to visit this oasis of culture in an alien land. He had thought that tonight he might he unable to take up the Baron's offer of dinner – two of his men had been shot last night and as a result he had spent a trying day in an effort to discover who had perpetrated this outrage, which he looked upon more as a threat to his control of the area than a tragedy for the men concerned. But thanks to his efforts that matter now appeared to be well on the way to being satisfactorily resolved and he had felt able, after all, to keep the engagement.

A small cruel smile played around von Rheinhardt's mouth. He straightened his uniform jacket and walked towards the château.

As Guillaume ushered von Rheinhardt into the salon Kathryn found herself moving to Paul's side. Imperceptibly he squeezed her arm. Courage, that squeeze said. Stay calm and everything will be all right. She wished she could be so sure.

'Can I get you a drink?' Guillaume was asking.

'Yes. Thank you.' His tall courtly figure dominated the room. Each of them, for their own reasons, was looking at him, each asking their own silent question.

'We weren't sure if you would be able to be here,' Guillaume said. 'You have been very busy, I am sure.'

'Busy, yes.' Von Rheinhardt took a deep sip of his drink. 'But also, I am glad to say, successful. Thanks to some good work on the part of my officers we have apprehended an enemy agent who was, I believe, dropped into the area last night. He has been found at the house of a farmer, about twenty kilometres from here.'

Kathryn glanced at Paul. His face was expressionless and she could only guess at what he was thinking.

'How do you know he is an enemy agent?' Guillaume asked.

Von Rheinhardt laughed. It was not a pleasant laugh, something between a derisive snort and a chuckle.

'He was in possession of not one but two sets of papers – false, obviously. And hidden in his belongings was a radio transmitter. Fairly conclusive proof, wouldn't you say?'

'What has happened to him?' Christian asked.

'He has been arrested, naturally. And the farmer stupid enough to harbour him has been arrested too. They will pay the price for their folly – in full. But before we execute them we shall endeavour to find out if anyone else is involved in this criminal resistance. We need to know – I need to know – if they were working alone or whether there are others.'

'Surely not,' Guillaume said. 'I can't believe there can be many people who would act so irresponsibly.'

Von Rheinhardt drained his glass.

'I hope not. So far I have been treating the people well. But if they are going to behave like rebellious children then I am afraid the kid gloves will have to come off.' He said it casually, but there was no mistaking the ruthless cruelty beneath the smooth exterior and Kathryn shivered violently.

'At least this means though that you are satisfied you have found your murderer,' Guillaume said. 'At least – I presume so? There will be no reprisals on innocent villagers?'

'For the moment, no. If anything of the kind happens again, then I shall have to consider teaching them a lesson they won't forget. But we don't want to talk about this now, do we? Let us hope last night's incident was an isolated one. I don't want trouble. You know that.'

'Of course,' Guillaume said with an ingratiating smile. 'Let's have dinner – such as it is.'

He steered von Rheinhardt towards the table and the others followed, Kathryn and Paul bringing up the rear.

'Better start praying,' Paul said softly in her ear.

She looked up at him questioningly.

'That they are able to kill themselves before they can be persuaded to talk,' he whispered.

For Kathryn the evening passed in a haze of unreality. Uppermost in her mind was the terror inspired by Paul's whispered words. Supposing the farmer who had been captured did talk? What would happen to them all? What would happen to Guy? It was all she could do to stop herself from jumping up from the table and running upstairs to take him in her arms, holding him close and assuring herself of his safety. But she knew she must not. For his sake – for all their sakes – she must hide her dread and continue to act normally.

Later, however, lying in bed beside Charles, she found certain vignettes returning to her, illuminated in her mind's eye as clear and frozen as lantern slides. Von Rheinhardt was there, handsome, distinguished even, the candlelight making his close-cropped fair hair appear almost white, a gleam of self-satisfied triumph in his very blue eyes; Guillaume, the perfect host, almost jocular in his relief that disaster had been, as he thought, averted; Louise, flirting in a genteel but thoroughly sickening way with von Rheinhardt; Christian, putting on the act of his life as he strove to be his usual debonair self. And Paul – most of all Paul – ice-cool, parrying questions about his arm, hiding all his emotions beneath that inscrutable exterior. She could only guess at what he must be feeling – dismay that he had lost his new radio operator before so much as a single transmission had been sent, anxiety not only for the unknown agent's fate but also for his own, worries as to how he should proceed next. All these things must, she knew, have supplanted any thoughts he might otherwise have had about her and what had happened between them. Unlikely now that he would look at her and remember a kiss when he had so many other things of paramount importance on his mind. And crazy that, in spite of everything, it should matter so much to her that he should.

She had looked at him across the table and felt her heart melting. She had passed him the bread, felt her hand brush his, and thought it was like the touch of bare electric wires. He did not love her yet, of course, it was too soon by far for that. What they felt for one another was most likely an attraction born of shared danger. Yet her heart was telling her otherwise – that it was far, far more than that.

'When this is all over, Kathryn,' he had said, and though he had left it unfinished she felt she knew what he had been saying and hugged the words to her. 'When this is all over . . .'

The unexplained promise was to her like a lantern shining brightly in a dark world. And though it could not eclipse her fear of what might have to be lived through before that time came, what might happen to prevent the promise ever being kept, as well as lighting her world it warmed her and made her brave.

It was several days before they heard of the fate of the two men who had been captured, several days of waiting in a state of unimaginable dread, wondering if they had talked. If they had, the cell, if not the entire circuit, would collapse, going down one by one like a set of ninepins, and at the end of the line Paul for certain and possibly Kathryn too. She was under no illusion now; all very well for Paul to say she could pretend to have been taken in by him but she did not think it would cut any ice with von Rheinhardt. He knew she was violently anti-Nazi – she had never troubled to conceal her hatred of him – and worse, she was English-born. Kathryn knew that the only reason she had escaped trouble before now was because she was Charles' wife and Guillaume's daughter-in-law. But if Paul was unmasked that would not save her. Nothing would.

And so she waited, the tension mounting with every passing day. That first night the intoxication of what had passed between her and Paul had blinded her to it; now, as the first exhilaration faded no matter how she tried to cling to it, the fear began to creep in, cold and debilitating.

Yet if they had talked, reason told her, Paul would have been picked up by now, or at least some of the members of the cell would have been.

Three days later Christian risked taking Paul to Périgueux again for a check-up on his wounded arm, and the doctor was able to provide them with some details. Someone in the village, when questioned, had reported seeing the farmer's truck pass by his cottage soon after the aircraft had been heard overhead; a search of the farm had uncovered the presence of the agent with his incriminating papers, and the discovery of the radio set had turned suspicion into cast-iron certainty. The agent and the farmer had been taken away; nothing had been heard of them since.

'Can't we do something for them?' Kathryn had asked when Paul told her, anguished at the thought of the torture the two men were, in all probability, enduring.

'There is nothing we can do,' Paul replied. 'They are beyond our help. Von Rheinhardt's HQ is as secure as Fort Knox. All we can hope for is that they have an opportunity to take their own lives before they suffer too much. Anything else would put the rest of the circuit at risk.'

'Surely it is at risk if we don't help them?'

'There's nothing we can do,' Paul repeated, his voice hard. 'As for ourselves – we can only sweat it out.'

And so the waiting went on, debilitating and seemingly endless. The news, when it came, was from von Rheinhardt himself.

He visited the château on the Sunday morning, driving up in his big black staff car. The family had been to church as was their custom and Kathryn, never the most religious of women, though she had converted to Catholicism when she married Charles, had prayed as she had never prayed before.

Von Rheinhardt came into the salon where they were gathered, picking up Guy and swinging him round while he screamed with laughter, and Kathryn longed only to snatch him from the arms of the man she thought of as a monster.

'Oh, by the way,' he said casually, putting Guy down at last, 'I think we can say the episode of the enemy agent is over.'

'Why? What has happened?' Guillaume asked.

'He killed himself the same night we took him. He must have had a death pill concealed on his person.'

'And the farmer?' Christian asked.

'Unfortunately the guards treated him too roughly. He died before they could persuade him to talk.'

'So you couldn't discover if anyone else was involved?'

'No. Sadly. But if there *was* anyone else involved I think they will have learned their lesson,' von Rheinhardt said smoothly. 'I don't think we will have any recurrence of trouble, do you?'

Kathryn's rush of relief was tempered by a chill of fear. It seemed to her that as he spoke von Rheinhardt was looking directly at her.

12

SPRING CAME SUDDENLY to Charente. Almost overnight it seemed the small green shoots burgeoned into full growth, the fields were lush and the trees a mass of blossom beneath a sky that was clear and blue. The rivers ran full and deep from the winter rains between banks heavy with bulrushes, and the air began to feel softer and warmer, even after the sun had gone down.

With the passage of the weeks some sort of normality had returned to the château. There had been no more alerts and no more incidents in the village, except for the sudden appearance of anti-Nazi slogans painted overnight on the walls of the bakery. Guillaume had called the youth of the village together and pointed out, with some severity, the error of their ways, the slogans had been painted over and there was only a block of fresh whitewash to show they had ever been there at all.

Unobtrusively Paul had continued to build up his circuit. Known to him and to London by the code name 'Mariner' it consisted of five quite separate cells, the leaders of which reported directly to him through Christian, who acted as courier, and who was able to move about the district freely without arousing suspicion.

London had sent a new agent to replace the one captured so disastrously soon after his arrival, and though Paul still blamed himself for the débâcle he tried to put it behind him. In time of war, working in a country occupied by the enemy, these things happened. It was futile to waste time and energy worrying about it. The best one could do was learn from one's mistakes and move on, and the new agent was a good man, quick, intelligent and slippery as an eel. In peacetime he had been a musician and the fingers that had once deftly plucked guitar strings now transmitted messages to London with the same effortless grace. His code name was Alain; Paul did not actually like him very much but that was neither here nor there. He was good at his job – that was all that mattered.

As for Paul's arm, that was healing nicely now, thanks to the doctor at Périgueux and also to Kathryn, who had changed the dressings frequently enough to ensure that infection did not set in.

Paul knew he had been lucky. At best the wound could have meant he would have had to ask to be lifted out, at worst any part of the disastrous incident could have cost him his life. But luck, he knew, played a vital part in the success or otherwise of any agent. So far it had been on his side. He only hoped he had not used up whatever portion fate had allocated him, for he was going to need it in abundance soon. He was setting up an operation which would, if it worked, cause the Boche a considerable amount of trouble, but which was going to be difficult and dangerous.

One afternoon in May while Guy was out for a walk with Bridget, Kathryn came to his room as he had asked her to in order to talk about it.

'I have a job planned and I think it would be best if I went away for a while,' he told her.

Kathryn did not ask the reason. She knew that as usual Paul was trying to distance the activities of Mariner from the château; should anything go wrong he did not want her involved. His concern warmed her heart but did nothing to make the prospect any easier. Already she knew how it would be when he was gone – the same worrying, the same waiting that she had to live through every time he went out 'on business', wondering what he was doing, watching for his return tense with fear that he might, this time, be caught. And if he intended going away for a while it would be a hundred times worse, for the waiting would go on much longer and she would have no way of knowing if the operation had been a success or even if he had fallen into the hands of the Boche. But she knew better than to argue. Kathryn, who disputed every single decision Charles made, had learned that she must accept Paul's judgement as final.

'Where would I say you'd gone?' she asked.

'To Bordeaux to visit a colleague I used to teach with. I have everything planned. I'll take the train out in case anyone is watching, then, when I'm sure I'm not being followed, I'll make my way back. Don't worry. I'll be out of sight – or unrecognisable, anyway. All you have to do is cover for me.'

'When do you leave?'

'On Monday, so we should tell the others tonight that I am going. I don't want it to appear too sudden a decision.'

She nodded. Monday was four days away.

'You will be careful, won't you?'

'Of course.' He was standing by the window. The sun, slanting in between the slats of the blind, was throwing stripes of shadow across his face and white shirt, open at the neck, and accentuating the thin covering of dark hairs on his forearms. Her heart lurched as it so often did when she looked at him, and now, more sharply then ever, her longing was tinged with fear for him.

'I don't know what I'd do if anything happened to you,' she said huskily, and it was no more than the truth.

She saw his face soften, saw the mask of total implacable control slip a little, revealing the man behind the automaton he sometimes appeared to be. There had been other moments such as this in the weeks that had passed, moments of tenderness and mutual understanding, moments when the closeness between them was so real as to be tangible, moments when their very souls seemed to meet, sparking the depth of feeling that they shared more violently even than the light accidental touches or the quick squeeze of a hand. But there had been no more passionate kisses – by mutual agreement they had been postponed for a future they both knew might never come.

'I mean it,' she said. 'I really couldn't bear it, Paul.'

'You would.' His voice was low, detached. Only his eyes were betraying him. 'If anything happened to me you would have to be doubly strong, to avoid suspicion falling on the rest of the family.'

She wrapped her arms around herself. Through the thin cotton of her dress her fingers encountered her ribs, prominent as a fisherman's creel. She had lost a lot of weight recently and knew it was not only due to the fact that good nourishing food was beginning to be in really short supply. Mostly it was because she was living on the edge of her nerves.

'I don't know that I could, I really don't. Sometimes, even now, I don't know how to go on. The strain seems to get worse all the time. Instead of getting used to it it's as if each time I'm worried or frightened it goes into a reservoir inside me that's just getting deeper and deeper.'

His brows furrowed slightly.

'Kathryn — you're not going to crack, are you? Because if it is that bad perhaps I should move out permanently.'

'No!' she said quickly. 'You mustn't do that.'

'But if it's getting to be too much for you it's the only thing I can do. Everything depends on your keeping up the charade. You know that as well as I do. If your nerves start to show it could be the end — for all of us.'

She breathed deeply, steadying herself. He was right, of course — he always was. But the thought of him going — the certainty of not seeing him any more — was worse even than the constant anxiety.

'I'll be all right,' she said. 'I guess I'm tougher than I think I am. I'm just so terribly afraid of what might happen to you.'

'Come here,' he said.

She looked at him, startled almost — in spite of the strength of feeling between them, the habit of restraint was so strong it was almost impossible to break.

'Come here,' he said again.

The longing to feel his arms around her overcame the self-imposed reserve. She went to him.

He held her gently at first, massaging her shoulders until he felt the tension begin to ease, then, as the awareness began to awaken both their bodies, he pulled her closer. Her hair smelled sweet — he buried his face in it and felt its softness against his cheek; the yielding pressure of her breasts against his chest started a fire within him. He moved his hands over her back, tracing the line of shoulder blades and spine, moving down to her waist, so small he felt that to snap her in two would be easy. Yet there was still a softness to her, a supple curve to her hips that was totally feminine, a warmth and a promise of passion that was making him forget all his good resolutions.

She moved a little in his arms, arching her neck and pressing her body close to his. He kissed her forehead beneath the soft fringe of hair, then her nose and lastly her lips. They were moist, trembling slightly with all the pent-up longing of the past weeks and months.

'Kathryn,' he whispered against them, then parted them with his tongue, thrusting into her mouth.

She pressed herself more closely against him, moulding her body and legs to his. His hand moved to her breast, squeezing, caressing, locating the buttons at the neck of her dress and unfastening them to slip his hand inside. Her flesh was slightly moist from the heat of the afternoon, her nipples firm and erect beneath his touch.

He wanted her now with a ferocity that banished all caution; the fire within him making him forget everything but her nearness and his need of her. Gerie, the wife he had adored, his little daughter Beatrice, his hatred of the Nazis, the work he had come to France to do, the mission, dangerous but worthwhile, which faced him, all were relegated to the periphery of his consciousness. Kathryn was the only reality, his fierce longing for her the only thing of importance.

Her tea dress was not belted; he ran his hand on down over her stomach, softly rounded between the jut of her hip bones. In spite of the warmth of the day she was wearing stockings — not to do so at the château would be unthinkable for a lady — and the wisp of suspender belt cut a slight dent into her stomach. He touched her thighs, brushed the soft tuft of hair between them, and began to ease her gently towards the bed.

And then, with a suddenness that shocked, he felt her tense.

'No!'

He moved his head slightly, looking at her. Her face had gone shut-in and she appeared to be on the verge of tears.

'We want one another, Kathryn,' he said in a low voice.

'I know, but we mustn't. We agreed. You know we did.' She pulled away from him. 'We agreed!' she said again, stubbornly repeating herself.

'OK, so we agreed,' he said harshly. Frustrated desire was making him angry; he simply could not understand how one moment she could be so eager, so yielding, and the next so cold and unassailable, as if someone had simply tripped a switch and a light had gone off. 'It didn't seem like that a minute ago.'

'Paul, don't be like this, please . . .'

'I'm not being like anything.'

'You are. You're angry. I'm sorry. I'm really sorry . . .'

He sighed, running a hand through his hair, turning away from her.

'For God's sake — *you* don't have to be sorry. It was all my doing. I was the one who broke the rules.'

She buttoned her dress, took a step or two towards him. He could feel her there, feel her outstretched hand with every tiny nerve ending, but he continued to stare out of the window, not because he did not want to look at her or touch her, but because he wanted to – too much.

'I'll go,' she said in a small voice after a moment.

'Yes – sure. I'll see you at dinner.'

He heard the door close after her and swore. What the hell had got into him? She was right, of course. They had agreed. But he had wanted her so much that agreement – and any other consideration – had ceased to matter. He had thought she felt the same way. Obviously she did not. Well, the heck with it. He would do well to put the episode behind him and get back to concentrating on the job in hand.

But he knew it would not be that easy. For the moment the fire might have been doused but beneath the surface it would continue to smoulder.

He wanted Kathryn, wanted her with a ferocity that denied all reason. Nothng could change that.

Kathryn closed the door and stood for a moment leaning against it. She was trembling violently and close to tears. Dear God, how she loved him! It would have been easy, so easy, to let him make love to her. She had wanted it with every fibre of her being, just as she had wanted it every time she had looked at him these past weeks. Caring so much for him and yet unable to express her feelings by anything more than a look, being so close yet not daring to touch him in anything but the most platonic way, had driven her crazy, so that the love and the longing had intensified way beyond the bearable. And for a few wonderful, exhilarating minutes there in his room everything – anything – had seemed possible.

But of course it was not. Thinking that it could be, even for a moment, was madness, and not only because it would interfere with the job he had to do. That was only a part of it – a small part. Kathryn, with her innate loyalty and well-developed sense of right and wrong, took her marriage vows very seriously. Whatever she might feel for Paul, however desperately she might want him – love him, even – she was Charles' wife. Perhaps their marriage had become a sham, perhaps Charles was not, and never had been, the man she thought him, but she owed him a duty nonetheless. She had promised faithfulness and it seemed to her that that promise encompassed not only Charles but Guy also. He was her son, Charles was his father. His heritage was here at Savigny; her duty to him by proxy, as it were, of her vows to Charles meant the sanctity of the family unit.

She had, Kathryn thought, already betrayed both of them in her heart over these last weeks and months. She must not do so with her body.

She straightened, tidying her hair with her hands and checking again that her dress was buttoned properly. Then she went along the passage to her own room and opened the door.

'Well,' said a voice from within. 'You have decided to come back then.'

She jumped as if she had been shot. Charles was standing in the doorway to his dressing room. He was wearing the lightweight tweed suit he used for work but had removed the jacket. His hair was untidy as if he had been running his fingers through it and an expression of barely controlled fury contorted his features.

'What do you mean?' she demanded. She had begun to tremble again.

'Don't play the innocent with me, Katrine. You've been with him, haven't you – Paul Curtis – in his room. Has he been making love to you?'

The proximity of the truth made her cheeks flame.

'No!' she cried. 'No – he hasn't!'

'Liar!' His voice was like a whiplash. 'It's written all over you. How long have you been cuckolding me with him, Katrine? How long, eh?'

'I haven't, I tell you!'

'And I don't believe you. Perhaps he was your lover in Switzerland, before we met. That's it, isn't it? That's why he's here. You couldn't stay away from one another.'

'No!' But in the midst of her dismay and fear of this new, violent Charles, was a nugget of relief. Better that he should think that of her than suspect the truth.

'No wonder you won't let me touch you!' he said bitterly. 'As far as I'm concerned you act like a bloody vestal virgin and all the time your lover is just along the passage. What a fool I've been! Going off to the distillery, leaving you alone with him . . . that was just what you wanted, wasn't it?'

'For the last time, Charles, he is not my lover!'

'Huh!' he snorted furiously.

'Well if you won't believe me, you won't,' she said, trying to gain some control over the situation. 'I suppose you'll throw him out now.'

'And have the rest of the family know what a fool he has made of me? Not likely! No, he can stay. But a few things are going to be different round here.'

'Oh really?' She felt a flash of scorn. How like Charles to be more concerned about his father's opinion than about making sure she never had another opportunity to – as he thought – make love with Paul. Any other man, thinking his wife was conducting an affair, would give her lover a bloody nose and the hell with who knew about it. Not Charles. Appearances were all-important to him, saving face was his prime consideration. Any other man would have kicked Paul out of the house and thrown his belongings after him. But Charles was not any other man. In fact, Kathryn was beginning to wonder if he was a real man at all.

'So – what is going to change?' she asked. 'Do tell me.'

He heard the derision in her voice and understood – stupidity was not one of his failings. His brows lowered, his mouth set in a hard line.

'All right, Katrine, I will tell you. Firstly, *ma chérie*, you are going to begin being a wife to me again – a proper wife, if you understand my meaning.'

Her palms were damp; she made fists of her hands so that the nails pressed into them.

'And if I refuse?'

'You won't refuse, Katrine. I shall not allow you to.'

'You'll look a pretty fool if I start screaming.'

'On the contrary, you are the one who will look a fool. Whoever heard of a wife refusing to allow her husband his marital rights? And besides, you would only frighten Guy. You wouldn't want to do that, I'm sure.'

'You wouldn't dare force me!' she said with more bravado than she was feeling; she did not care for the look on Charles' face.

'Why not, Katrine?' He smiled, but it was not a nice smile, simply a humourless movement of his mouth which did not reach his cheeks, let alone his eyes. 'I have been very patient for a long time – too long. I don't feel like being patient any longer. In fact I think it is time we had a little practice.'

'Now! Surely you can't mean now?' Involuntarily she took a step away from him.

He ripped off his shirt. She saw that his chest was heaving.

'Why not? There's no time like the present. Oh, I don't suppose you feel like it, having so recently been with your lover, but I do feel like it. Knowing you were with him woke me up, if you like. Yes, it woke me up.'

He advanced towards her, grabbing her by the shoulders and tearing open the buttons of her dress.

'Don't!' She tried to pull it together, sickened by the thought of Charles' hands touching her where such a short time ago Paul had caressed her with such tenderness, and at the same time afraid that the evidence would somehow be there for him to see.

'Take it off!'

'No!'

'If you won't then I shall do it for you.' He caught at her dress, ripping it as he yanked it down over her shoulders, then threw her bodily on to the bed.

'Charles, please . . . !' She was struggling to sit but he held her down with a strength she had not known he possessed, one hand on her throat whilst with the other he tore at her clothes and his own.

'You're my wife, Katrine!' he rasped. 'Just remember that!'

She was sobbing now but no sound came, and though she wanted to scream she dared not. She was remembering what he had said about frightening Guy and afraid too that if she cried out Paul might hear and come to investigate. If he found Charles forcing himself on her it could mean disaster for all of them. But she fought him all the way all the same, clawing at his back, kicking out and twisting her head violently from side to side on the pillow.

Useless. He was too strong for her. He caught her flailing arms, twisting them above her head and parting her legs with his knee. Anger had given him a more satisfactory erection than tenderness had ever done and he drove into her protesting body with a savagery that made her cry out in spite of her determination to keep silent. But his mouth stifled the cry; he bit at her lips, pumping for what seemed to Kathryn to be hours but was in reality only a few brief minutes.

When it was over he rolled off her, panting.

She lay too shocked even to weep, scarcely able to believe that he could have done this to her. But the evidence was unmistakable enough – the burning in her throat where he had restrained her, the throbbing pain in the deepest part of her where his violence had bruised her, and the sticky wetness on her thighs.

He sat up now, this Charles she did not know any more, glancing at her with an expression midway between triumph and hatred.

'Not bad for a practice run,' he said unpleasantly, fastening his trousers.

Kathryn sat up too, trying to cover herself with the tattered remnants of her clothes.

'I hope you're satisfied.' Her voice was bitter.

'For the time being. But you may as well realise that that is the way it's going to be from now on if you continue to refuse me my rights.'

'Oh no,' she said determinedly. 'That is the first and last time you will ever use me like that. You just killed any love I had left for you, Charles. I have been faithful to you, whether you choose to believe it or not. The fact that I am your wife still meant something to me. Not any more.'

He stared at her, shocked by her tone and the depth of feeling it conveyed, experiencing for the first time a shard of something close to fear.

'What are you talking about?'

'If ever . . . ever . . . you lay a finger on me again I'll leave you and take Guy with me. And I won't go quietly, either. I'll tell your father exactly what sort of a man you are and why I can no longer live with you. I mean it, Charles – one finger! Believe me, I mean it!'

And quite suddenly he was in no doubt. She did indeed mean it. The balance of power had shifted. Charles felt the shard of fear pierce him again, so sharp he could scarcely breathe, and a wash of scalding shame bathed his whole body.

In that moment he became a small boy again, hauled up before his father for some misdemeanour, seeing the accusation in the wise old eyes, and worse, the disappointment. He had always disappointed his father, he knew, and the knowledge caused him deep-rooted insecurity. But if Guillaume should find out about this it would be more than disappointment he felt, it would be disgust. Charles' failings as a man and a husband would be exposed totally to anyone to whom Kathryn cared to tell her story. They would all despise him. But it was the fact that Guillaume would despise him that mattered most of all.

'For God's sake get dressed, woman,' he said angrily.

But as he turned on his heel and left her there it felt to him that he was the one who was naked.

'What's wrong, Kathryn?' Paul asked softly.

It was the next evening and she had taken her coffee outside, feeling that she could not bear the claustrophobic conversation of the family a moment longer. She was sitting on the wrought-iron bench at the edge of the lawn, looking out over the moonlit parkland, and she had not heard him come up behind her until he spoke.

She looked up. In the moonlight his face was very strong, all planes and angles. Her heart reached out to him.

'Nothing's wrong.'

'You're very quiet. In fact you've hardly said a word all day and it was the same last evening. It's not because of what happened between us, is it?'

'No, of course not.'

'I didn't mean to upset you. It was just that I wanted you so much.'

'I know. And I wanted you too. I *do* want you, more than anything . . .'

And that was the essence of it. Soaking herself in her bath, trying to wash the last traces of Charles from her body after his brutal attack on her, she had found herself questioning the loyalty that had made her refuse to consummate her love for Paul. Perhaps she had been something less than a good wife to Charles, but she had tried, God alone knew, and at least she had been faithful to him. But for what? So that he could use and abuse her like a common whore, demanding his rights and forcing himself on her in a way that made a total mockery of loving and caring?

The resentment had grown, eating like corrosive acid into her intention not to betray him. In her own way she had fought to cling to what she had believed to be right, even when love and respect had gone. Now she wondered bitterly what that sacrifice had been worth.

She had told him he had destroyed the last of her feelings for him but it was more than that. He had also destroyed her loyalty. She owed him nothing now, for he had demanded and taken what she had been unable to give.

He thinks Paul is my lover – then why shouldn't he be? Kathryn had thought angrily, and the very passage of the words through her mind had both excited and comforted her.

Why shouldn't she make love with Paul? It would be the one sure way to erase the humiliation of Charles' attack from her mind and her body, superimposing passion on degradation. She loved Paul and wanted him. In three days he would be leaving, going into God alone knew what danger, from which he might never return. And the thought of never having known him physically was more than she could bear.

But in spite of her change of heart the self-imposed constraints were still strong. How could she simply go to him and say: 'Paul, I've changed my mind'? It wasn't so easy. Kathryn stood on the edge of a precipice and knew it. One step over the edge and there could be no going back – ever.

On one point only had she totally made up her mind. Paul must not know what Charles had done to her. There were some things which must be between a husband and wife and no one else, not even a man for whom she felt as deeply as she felt for Paul, and this, too, made her hesitate. Wouldn't Charles' assault be there, written all over her body? When she lay in Paul's arms, how could she hide it from him?

Now, however, sitting beside him in the moonlight, every such consideration seemed suddenly quite unimportant. She wanted him. He wanted her. And in two days' time he would be leaving, perhaps forever. She laid her fingers on his thigh, feeling the hard muscle beneath the rough cotton.

'I'm very afraid for you, Paul,' she said.

'Don't be. I'm only doing what I came here to do.'

'I know. They should be thanking you for it. One day perhaps they will. In fact I'm sure they will. But I was thinking, Paul, if you don't come back . . .'

'Don't say that. I will.'

'But if you didn't . . . you and I . . . we'd never . . .'

'That's true enough,' he said with grim humour. 'You're a deep thinker, I see, Kathryn.'

'Don't joke!' she said sharply. 'What I'm trying to say is . . .'

Footsteps on the gravel; Christian coming towards them.

'Wait for me tonight,' she whispered. 'I'll come to your room.'

She saw his look of surprise. But there was no time to say anything else before Christian joined them.

As on the previous night Kathryn was half afraid that there might be an argument with Charles trying to insist on his conjugal rights, but once again it had not happened. Charles was being almost conciliatory, a little like a child who has misbehaved and wishes to curry favour, but she had continued to treat him with all the coldness she felt for him and very soon he had been snoring with the intensity of a man who has consumed too much wine and brandy. He was, she thought, unlikely to stir for hours.

She opened the door softly and looked back. He had not moved. She slipped out into the passage. The night was soft and warm, the scents of evening carrying in through the open windows and mingling with the faint garlicky smell left over from dinner. She went along the passage, her bare feet making no sound, and tried the door of Paul's room. It was unlocked. She pushed it open and went outside.

'So – you came.'

He was standing by the window, still fully dressed though he had removed his jacket.

'Yes,' she said in a whisper.

He crossed the room, taking her in his arms, kissing her hair, her face, her lips. She buried her face in his chest, feeling the hair at the open neck of his shirt tickle her face, and smelling the maleness of him mingled with the clean scent of soap.

'What made you change your mind?' he asked softly.

She suppressed the urge to tell him.

'Does it matter? I'm here.'

'And this time you won't tell me no?'

'No.'

'No, you won't tell me no?'

'Yes — no — I want you to make love to me, Paul.'

'Come to bed then.'

He unfastened the tie of her kimono and slid it from her shoulders. In the moonlight her body gleamed white and smooth. He held her away, looking at her, drinking her in.

'You are beautiful, Kathryn.'

He ran his hands slowly over her breasts, her hips, the curve of her thighs. She stood quivering slightly, her hands on his shoulders, loving the taut feel of his muscles beneath the smooth cotton. She did not speak. She did not want to break the spell of the moment. After a while she slipped her hands down to the buttons of his shirt, unfastening them and running her fingers over his bare chest, then pressed herself lightly to him, glorying in the touch of flesh on flesh, warm and slightly sticky. Unhurriedly, she found the fastening of his trousers and undid that too. As they pressed together, completely nude, and she felt the hardness of his body against her, the quiver deep within her began to become urgent desire, but still they held back. So long had they waited for this that to rush it now would be to spoil the perfection. There could only be one first time for them, perhaps only one time ever. Let it last until forever, it would still be over too soon.

Only when the anticipation became too much to bear did they move. He lifted her gently with one arm behind her knees and carried her to the bed, laying her down and covering her with kisses. She arched her neck luxuriously against the pillow, feeling every bit of her body come alive beneath his lips, as if silken cords joined each secret place he touched to the very core of her. Her breasts tingled now with sensitised awareness, her thighs were peppered with a million nerve endings, all fine-tuned to a pitch of sensual delight. Only when his mouth moved to the soft tuft between her legs did she moan softly, moving with the rhythm of his lips.

She wanted him now so desperately that the wanting was a fever. She reached out for him, pulling him down on top of her, winding her arms around his neck, loving the feel of this body, hot and hard, where his lips had been. He thrust his tongue into her mouth as he thrust his body into hers and the delight was so complete that for a moment it seemed to her as though the world stood still. Then they were moving in unison, slowly at first like the waves lapping the beach, then more urgently. Those waves took her over now; she rode them, floating, swirling, higher and higher until she thought she would drown in the glory of it. No more, no more! she wanted to cry. It is too beautiful to bear; I'll die with the beauty of it! But at the same time she wanted it to go on forever, bearing her up, sweeping her away, making her forget everything but two bodies, close as human bodies can ever be, two hearts beating as one, two souls reaching out to touch one another and cling because they knew, without question, that they were meant for one another.

At the last she cried out, a sob deep in her throat, a sob for the unbearable bittersweet ecstasy of it, and also a sob because it was slipping away from her, going, perhaps, for ever.

They lay then in one another's arms, their moist bodies clinging, their heads side by side on the pillow. For a long while they did not speak. Then at last he said: 'Are you glad you came to see me, then?'

She laughed softly.

'What do you think?'

'I think you're glad. I certainly am.'

'Mm.' She was beginning to be drowsy now. She wanted to throw caution to the winds and fall asleep here beside him but she knew she must not. 'I want to stay with you,' she whispered, 'but I can't. I have to go.'

'Yes,' he said. 'Yes, you do. But I will tell you something, Kathryn de Savigny. When this is all over I shall come back for you. I shall come back for you and nothing and nobody will make me leave you ever again.'

'I love you,' she whispered.

'And I love you. But now you have to get back before your husband wakes up and finds you missing.'

'I know.'

He helped her up, watched as she slipped on her kimono and fastened the tie around her waist. Then he kissed her once more, gently loosening her arms from about his neck when she seemed reluctant to release him.

'Good night, my darling. Sleep well, and remember – you may be with him but you and I both know – you're mine.'

She nodded, her face rosy and rounded with satisfied love.

In the doorway she looked back once more; he was standing there, still naked, in the moonlight. He looked young and strong and invincible, like a statue of a Greek god. She blew a kiss and left the room.

Charles was still sleeping. He stirred slightly as she slipped into bed beside him. She turned her back on him, folding her arms around the body Paul had so lately loved and hid herself away in a world that held nothing but her dreams.

13

TWO DAYS, TWO wonderful stolen days, snatching what time they could to be together. It was all they might ever have and they both knew it.

The knowledge gave an edge of bittersweet poignancy to their lovemaking, the danger of discovery added a spice. In the afternoons whilst Guy played in the garden, watched over by Bridget, Kathryn went to Paul's room and they made love with the curtains pulled against the bright sun, locked in a world of their own; at night when Charles was sleeping she crept away to where Paul lay waiting for her. On the second morning they took Guy for a walk in the burgeoning countryside, sharing his delight in the butterflies that flittered in the sunshine and the discovery of poppies, blazing scarlet in the fields of sprouting crops. They walked, not touching, yet the bond between them was so real it was as if they were joined by invisible strings, and when their eyes met Kathryn felt as if her body was melting, leaving her spirit free to reach out to his. Once when Guy ran on ahead Paul caught her in his arms, kissing her quickly, furtively, one eye on the small figure lost in the waist-high grass, and she laughed, revelling in the thrill that came from daring to risk the forbidden as well as the joy that came from loving and being loved in return.

I feel young again, Kathryn thought. After the years of disillusion and dissatisfaction and the recent long, stressful months of the occupation it was an exhilarating feeling.

But the brighter the sun the longer the shadows. At first, determined not to allow anything to spoil these precious days, Kathryn tried to ignore them as she might walk down a tunnel of sunlight never looking to left or right into the forest that bordered it. Yet it was there, all the same, on the periphery of her consciousness, and when the lovemaking was over, she found the courage to explore it willingly, for it was not only his body she wanted to know well but everything about him, everything that made him the person he was.

In some ways those conversations brought them closer than any more physical union could. He told her about Gerie and his daughter, and his pain became her pain.

'You must have loved them very much,' she said softly, stroking the back of his hand with her fingers, wanting him to know she was there for him and would be as long as there was breath in her body.

'I do love them still,' he said. 'Just because they are dead I haven't stopped loving them.'

'Of course you haven't.'

'Everything we had, all the things we did together, nothing can take them away.'

She felt a moment's jealousy for a part of his life she could never share, a brief treacherous ache that this unknown woman, Gerie, had once been with Paul as she was now, only more so, because she had been his wife, and was instantly deeply ashamed. Just because she had never known love like this before did not mean he had to be an emotional virgin too. Loving Gerie had been one of the things that made him the man he was, losing her had brought him to France – and to Kathryn.

'It must have been dreadful for you,' she said.

'It's a pain that never goes away. But life goes on. What we can't change we must accept and put to good use. I am determined to do what I can to make the Nazis pay for what happened to Gerie and Beatrice. That way, at least, I can make sure they did not die in vain.'

'I think you are very brave.' She twined her fingers in his.

'No, I'm not. Bravery is doing something when you are afraid of the consequences but doing it all the same. I came to France not really caring what happened to me because I had nothing left to lose.'

And now? she wanted to say. Don't you have something now you would care about losing? But she did not. In spite of the closeness between them she did not feel she had the right. This thought cast yet another small shadow on her fragile happiness and she tried to thrust it to the back of her mind. These days, these moments, were too precious to spoil with negative emotions, with regrets about the past and fears for the future. Take them, enjoy them for what they are, and be grateful.

But they slipped by, all the same, those precious days, with terrifying speed, the days became hours – hours she could count on the fingers of her hand.

The night before he was due to leave she stayed as long as possible in his room, knowing that this was their last chance to be together – at least until his next mission had been completed.

She still did not know what it was or precisely where he was going. She knew it would be pointless to ask – he would not tell her, for her own good as much as the good of the operation. But the not knowing made her feel trapped and helpless and there was one question she could ask.

'How long will you be away?'

'Two weeks – maybe three. If I was to turn up back here immediately after the job is done it would look too suspicious – someone might put two and two together and make four. Besides I need to do some co-ordinating in . . . one of my more far-flung kingdoms. I can't get there very often, this gives me the opportunity. I can't tell you more than that, Kathryn. Don't ask me, please.'

'I won't. I'd make a good gangster's moll, don't you think? Very discreet, very loyal and . . . very willing.' She said it lightly but there was a sickness inside her, a weight growing heavier by the second.

He trailed a hand across her stomach.

'You know very well what I think.'

'No I don't. Tell me.'

'Kathryn – you are insatiable. Very well. I think you are beautiful and brave and loving. You also have a streak of deceitfulness.'

'That's not very nice!' she said, peeved.

'Perhaps not. It may, however, save your life.'

'Oh Paul, I'm so frightened! For you, for me, for all of us . . .'

He pulled her close, not offering any words of comfort but running his hands over her body in the way that could usually make her forget everything else. Now, however, it merely deepened her sense of foreboding. It was, she thought, as if he was committing every line, every curve, to memory, something to take with him in case they should never again be together in this very special way.

'You'd better go now,' he said suddenly. 'We don't want Charles waking up and finding you missing. At this stage that could be disastrous.'

'For us, you mean?'

'For what I have to do. Go now, there's a good girl.'

He had, she realised, ceased to be her lover and became once again the SOE agent, thinking only of his mission. It was, of course, the reason he was here, his whole reason, perhaps, for being. But it hurt her nonetheless and she felt that although he would not actually be leaving the château until the following morning he had left her already.

It was, she thought, the loneliest moment of her life.

'The Resistance is becoming very troublesome,' von Rheinhardt said. 'There was a huge explosion last night in an arms dump not far from here – in the next district, as a matter of fact. We are quite certain it was the work of saboteurs. They do not seem to realise how futile such action is.'

Kathryn glanced quickly at Christian, who was sitting across the table from her, but he was looking not at her but at von Rheinhardt, his good-looking features quite impassive, and she was grateful for it. A look between them might have been noticed, such indiscretions were unforgivably foolish, but she had simply been unable to control that quick instinctive reaction. The past week had been a nightmare of worrying and wondering without so much as the slightest indication of where Paul was or what he was doing, whether he was alive or dead even. She knew, of course, that it was no more than she could expect – Paul would never risk either them or this operation by trying to make contact – but that did not make it any easier. Now at least she knew – or thought she knew – what it was he had set out to do, and that it had been successful.

'You didn't catch whoever was responsible?' she asked, trying to keep her voice level.

Von Rheinhardt glanced at her sharply and for a terrifying moment as his ice-cold blue eyes bored into hers she was quite certain he was seeing right through her.

'No,' he said after a moment. 'No, we didn't. Our men gave chase, of course, and there was some shooting, but they got clean away. Heads will roll for such abominable security arrangements – the officer in charge of the arms dump is already under arrest. But the real fault, I think, lies in the fact that we have been treating you people too well. We have tried to be reasonable and this is all the thanks we get. It is time, I think, to show those who wish to resist the error of their ways.'

'And how will you do that if you don't know who is responsible?' Christian asked. His tone was a little belligerent and von Rheinhardt's mouth hardened.

'What Christian means is – you have a problem punishing someone if they have escaped your net,' Guillaume said quickly. 'I am sure Christian accepts that the culprits deserve to be punished, don't you, Christian?'

'Of course,' Christian agreed, but Kathryn knew what the attitude of subservience was costing him.

'There is only one way to persuade renegades like that into line,' von Rheinhardt said, cutting vigorously into a piece of pork. 'That is to show them we will not stand for this kind of thing. It is certainly what I would do if anyone in my district were foolish enough to try anything of this sort.'

'You mean . . . ?'

'Reprisals. Every time something of this kind occurred I would take a dozen hostages from the village closest to the outrage and have them shot. I think that would soon put a stop to such nonsense.'

He said it almost totally without emotion, calmly eating his pork. Kathryn's blood ran cold and she felt the shock run around the table, touching each and every one of them.

'But those people might be totally innocent!' Guillaume protested mildly. 'The chances are they would be villagers who had done nothing wrong at all.'

'Perhaps. It would be unfortunate for them, I agree. But I'll guarantee that with such a threat hanging over them people would soon miraculously remember suspicious incidents they had chosen to forget and tongues would be loosened. I would get my saboteurs, I think – and if I didn't, then the people of the village would know what to expect if such a thing happened again. It would, I think, make a very effective form of control.'

Control by fear, Kathryn thought. That's what this Nazi regime is all about.

'Perhaps, my dear Baron, you will explain this once again to your own people when next you speak to them. It would give me no pleasure to have to arrange the deportation or execution of men, women and children from Savigny.'

But you'd do it anyway, Kathryn thought. And I don't believe you when you say you wouldn't enjoy it – you most certainly would! Already, simply stating his intentions, von Rheinhardt had a salacious look about him.

How could Guillaume continue to fraternise with such a man? All very well to pretend it was expedient – from what he had just said it was obvious that von Rheinhardt would not be swayed in the slightest from his purpose by any supposed friendship. He would go right on with running the district in whatever way he considered most appropriate, and if that meant taking lives or property then he would do it just the same, pretending regret but secretly enjoying every sadistic moment.

Suddenly she could not bear to sit at the same table as him a moment longer. She felt nauseous and dizzy and her stomach was revolting against the food she had already eaten.

'Please excuse me for a moment,' she said, pushing back her chair and rising unsteadily to her feet.

She fled to the bathroom and was violently sick.

As she made her hasty exit Louise turned to Charles, a sharp, almost knowing look replacing her usual vacuous expression.

'Is Kathryn all right, do you think? She looked very pale and she has hardly eaten a thing.'

'I don't know, Maman. She's not herself these days.'

'A very highly strung girl,' Guillaume remarked, helping himself to more potatoes. 'Spends too much time alone or with the child, if you ask me.'

'And what else is she supposed to do?' Christian demanded.

'She could keep me company,' Louise grumbled. 'She has never been the wife I would have wished for you, if I am honest, Charles. I had always hoped that when you married I would gain another daughter. But Kathryn . . .' she hesitated, her face becoming even more vixenish, 'why, she seems to spend more time with Guy's tutor than she does with any of us. I'm surprised you allow it, Charles.'

The familiar shut-in look darkened Charles' features.

'For heaven's sake, Maman, what are you suggesting?' he demanded.

'Nothing, nothing at all . . .'

'Guy's tutor. We do not have the pleasure of his company tonight,' von Rheinhardt remarked casually, but his eyes were sharp.

'He went to visit friends in Bordeaux,' Christian said quickly.

'And probably won't be coming back,' Charles said.

They all turned to look at him.

'What do you mean?' Guillaume asked.

'I'm not very happy with his work. I don't think he's the right tutor for Guy. I've been meaning to talk to you about it, Papa.'

'Really?' Guillaume remarked mildly. 'I thought he was very good with Guy.'

'He's well qualified I know, but his speciality is dealing with much older children. I am seriously considering dispensing with his services when he returns . . . if he returns, which I somehow doubt. I imagine he is as bored with Guy as Guy is with him.'

'You surprise me,' Christian said sharply, alarmed at the prospect of Paul losing his base here at the château. 'Like Papa, I thought he was just the man to give Guy a good start. What does Kathryn think? Have you discussed it with her?'

'No, I haven't.' Charles' tone was bombastic. 'Kathryn is unreasonably biased, since he's an old friend of hers. I think I am the one to judge what is best for my son's education.'

'We don't have to discuss it now, though, surely?' Louise put in with an anxious look at von Rheinhardt. 'We shouldn't be boring the General with our domestic trivia. And Charles, I really think you should go and see if Kathryn is all right. She didn't look at all well to me.'

'Stop fussing, Maman,' Charles began irritably, then broke off at the unexpected sound of voices raised in greeting in the passageway outside the door and the clatter of high heels on the flagstoned floor. 'What is going on out there?'

The door opened; a slender girl with long straight hair stood there. Her eyes were red-rimmed with dark shadows beneath, her cotton blouse and skirt crumpled, and she clutched a canvas holdall to her chest.

'Celestine!' Louise gasped. 'I don't believe it! You are supposed to be in Paris!'

She spoke for all of them.

'I've come home,' Celestine said. 'I couldn't bear it any longer. It's terrible there. I got a train but it was delayed and . . .' She broke off, suddenly becoming aware of von Rheinhardt. His back was towards the door but like the others he had turned his head. Celestine's already pale face turned even whiter.

'Who is he? What is a German officer doing here?'

'Celestine!' Louise spoke sharply, warningly, and Guillaume tried to intervene.

'My daughter is obviously tired. She doesn't know what she's saying.'

But nothing and no one could stop Celestine.

'I don't believe it!' she cried. Tears had begun to run down her face. 'You get everywhere, don't you? Even here in my own home! Oh, I can't bear it! The Boche – even in my own home!'

It was the first time that anyone at the château had actually voiced aloud a condemnation of the Germans. It hung in the air like a portent of what was to come.

'Celestine – darling – come and sit down.' Louise, surprisingly, was the first to recover, perhaps because, naive as she was, she simply did not fully realise the possible ramifications of Celestine's outburst. She rose from her chair, a slight figure in an extravagant pre-war Paris creation, putting her arms around Celestine's thin shoulders and leading her to the chair Kathryn had recently vacated. 'Bridget will set a place for you. You're hungry, I'm sure, if you have travelled all the way from Paris.'

'No – I'm not hungry.' Celestine tried to shrug her off. 'I just want to go to my room, Maman. I just want a bath and a sleep.'

'Celestine, do as your mother says and sit down!' Guillaume ordered. It was seldom he played the authoritarian and when he did the effect was startlingly positive. Celestine looked at him from beneath her slightly hooded eyelids and subsided into a chair, still clutching her holdall. Christian, sitting next to her, relieved her of it, placing it on the floor. It was, he thought, surprisingly light if

Celestine had come home for any length of time, but then that was typical of her. She had never been one to bother her head much about possessions.

As she sat von Rheinhardt made to rise.

'I think perhaps I should thank you for an excellent dinner and leave,' he said. 'This is obviously a family occasion.'

'Otto – no!' Guillaume protested, rising also. 'Please do stay until we have finished the meal, at least. It does seem to be turning into something of a farce, I agree, but . . .'

'Not at all,' von Rheinhardt said, correct almost to the point of overpoliteness, though his eyes were very cold, very hard. 'I do not wish to intrude or to cause distress to a young lady. And besides, I have a great deal of work to do. As I told you, saboteurs are beginning to cause us trouble. I want to ensure that nothing of this sort occurs in my district. I will bid you all good night.' His eyes narrowed a fraction. 'I do hope Madame Kathryn will be feeling better soon.'

Guillaume accompanied him to the door.

'I am so sorry – I hope you will come again to visit us soon . . .'

'I hope so too.'

As the big black staff car pulled away down the drive Guillaume returned to the dining room. His eyes were blazing with rare fury.

'What on earth were you thinking of, Celestine? Surely you should know better than to speak to a German officer like that? How did you get here anyway? It's after curfew.'

'The stationmaster brought me. He was very kind,' Celestine said, huddling into her chair. 'As for speaking as I did, yes, I shouldn't have done it, I know, but I'm fed up with having to kowtow to the Boche. Paris is full of them – it's dreadful. And it was such a shock, finding one here, in my own home. What was he doing sitting at our table?'

'We have to keep on his right side,' Charles told her. 'He's in charge of the district. God knows what damage you have done, Celestine, speaking to him like that.'

'I know . . . I'm sorry . . .' She was close to tears now. 'I just don't know how you can bear it, any of you.' She looked around. 'Where is Kathryn?'

'Kathryn was unwell,' Louise said gently. 'Please tell us why you've come home, Celestine. It's lovely to see you but it's such a surprise when we thought you were in Paris. What about your studies?'

'What do my studies matter now, Maman?' Celestine asked bitterly. 'What is the point of anything any more?'

'Don't talk like that, darling,' Louise chided her. 'I know how it seems to you at the moment but you have all your life in front of you. You can't give up just because things are not as they used to be.'

'Really?' Celestine laughed harshly. 'Forgive me, Maman, but you don't know what you are talking about. Tucked away down here in comfort you don't know anything about it.'

Louise bristled.

'Really, Celestine, we have our privations too.'

'No, she is right, Maman,' Christian said. He squeezed Celestine's thin arm. 'We are sheltered here. The Boche don't bother us much. They've been anxious to be good gaolers. I expect it's a different story in the cities.'

'It certainly is. If you saw Paris now you'd hardly recognise it – swastikas everywhere, troops parading, French people not allowed to go into some of the streets, nasty little men in Homburg hats and raincoats watching your every movement.'

'Homburg hats and raincoats?' Louise repeated blankly. 'What do you mean?'

'She means secret police,' Christian said. 'You see, Maman, she's right, isn't she? We *are* sheltered here.'

'Then there is the Gestapo HQ in the Avenue Foch,' Celestine continued. 'Those who are taken there don't come out. Oh, I hate them! I hate every one of them! If you knew what they were really like you'd never have one under your roof!'

'Otto von Rheinhardt is a soldier, not Gestapo,' Guillaume pointed out.

'He's still a German,' Celestine said passionately. 'That's enough for me.'

'I can see you are upset, Celestine, but I must ask you to try and contain yourself.' Guillaume spoke gently, for he loved his daughter, but there was no mistaking the firmness in his tone. 'You may not like it, none of us do, but there are some things we have to do to ensure our survival and the survival of our heritage. I am sure if you think about it you will realise the sense in it.'

'You mean I should want the Château de Savigny to be here for my children?' Celestine flared back. 'Well, I don't, Papa – not if it means fraternising with those pigs and having them as house guests.'

Guillaume shook his head wearily.

'You are young and full of fire, *ma petite*. When you have a child of your own you will feel differently, you'll see.'

'You think so, huh?' Celestine drew herself upright in her chair, holding on to the arms so tightly that her knuckles showed white.

'I know so. When the time comes . . .'

'Let me tell you, Papa, the time is a great deal nearer than you think. And I still feel the same. I don't want the Boche around my child – I'd rather die! That's the reason I've come home from Paris, don't you see?' She broke off. They were all gazing at her in disbelief. She gave a little laugh. 'I'm sorry. I didn't mean to tell you like this. I didn't mean to tell you at all just yet. But there – it's done now. I'm pregnant. I am going to have a baby.'

The silence seemed to go on forever, broken only by Louise's small strangled cry. She pressed a napkin to her mouth, her cheeks as white as the square of starched damask. Then Guillaume spoke.

'Is this some kind of joke, Celestine? Your way of getting back at us for having von Rheinhardt here to dinner? If so, let me tell you . . .'

'It's no joke, Papa, I assure you. I'm sorry but there it is.'

'I can't believe this! The shame!' Louise whispered. She looked on the point of fainting. 'Who is the man? Where is he?'

'Maman – for God's sake!' Christian rose, standing behind Celestine and placing his hands protectively on her shoulders. 'Celestine, little one, you don't have to say anything now if you don't want to.'

'It's all right.' Celestine smiled up at him weakly. 'I'll tell you. His name was Julien Didier. He was a student too. We loved one another. But he's dead now – at least, I am almost certain he is. You see – he was a Jew. The Boche took him. They came to our apartment and took him. They beat him up in front of my eyes . . .' Her voice began to falter; Christian held her more tightly. 'They beat him with the butts of their guns,' she went on reciting it like a litany. 'His face was just a pulp. They kicked him until he couldn't stand up and then they threw him down the stairs. I saw it all. The apartment was spattered with his blood. Then they bundled him into one of their vehicles and drove him away. I couldn't find out where they had taken him but I can guess. I haven't seen him since. I won't, I know. What they started in the apartment they will have finished now. He's dead, I know it. And you wonder why I hate the Boche!'

Suddenly, explosively, her unnatural calm shattered and she began to cry, huge gasping sobs that racked her body.

'The bastards!' Christian grated. He crossed to the chiffonier, poured some cognac into a glass and pressed it into Celestine's trembling hands. 'Drink this, little one. It will do you good.'

'Oh my baby!' Louise, her outrage at Celestine's indiscretion temporarily forgotten, found her own maternal instincts aroused in the face of her daughter's distress. 'This is terrible . . . terrible!'

'Maman, why don't you take Celestine to her room?' Christian was taking charge of the situation. 'We'll talk about this in the morning when we are all calmer.'

'Yes. Oh my darling, you need to rest . . .'

When Celestine and Louise had left the dining room Guillaume covered his face with his hands. He looked old suddenly, a broken old man, his authority washed away like a sandcastle by an incoming tide.

'Whatever next?' he asked, more of himself than the others. 'What else are we expected to bear?'

'Perhaps,' Christian said, 'you will begin to see the Boche as they really are – an army of butchers.'

'But Paris is Paris . . . it's different here in Savigny . . .'

'Is it? Is it really? And how long will it be before they exert their savagery here too? They are drunk with power but they want more, still more. Surely you must see, Papa, they will never be satisfied, until they grind us into the dirt.'

'I don't know, Christian, I don't know anything any more,' Guillaume muttered.

Charles said nothing at all.

'Charles, what did you mean by telling Papa that you are not satisfied with Paul as a tutor?' Kathryn demanded angrily.

It was the following evening and Charles was dressing for dinner when Kathryn burst into the room. He looked up, startled, still holding one gold cuff link half slotted into the cuff of his white evening shirt.

'Christian has just told me about it,' Kathryn rushed on. 'How dare you do something like that behind my back?'

For a moment Charles looked almost shamefaced, then he recovered himself.

'It wouldn't have been behind your back if you hadn't absented yourself from the table so rudely.'

'I was sick!' Kathryn flared. 'Not that I'd expect any sympathy from you. But that's beside the point. If you're not happy with Paul as Guy's tutor I'm the one you should be discussing it with, not your father and the rest of the family, not to mention von Rheinhardt!'

'I have not discussed it with you since I wouldn't expect you to be objective about the matter.'

His voice was very cold and Kathryn felt a chill of alarm.

'What do you mean by that?'

Charles laughed shortly.

'You really think I don't know what was going on between the two of you? You swore to me, Kathryn, that he was not your lover, but you were lying. I'm not the complete fool you seem to take me for. I know you were visiting him in the middle of the night before he left, and I'm not prepared to put up with it any more.'

Kathryn was so taken aback she was unable for the moment to find words to reply, and Charles continued: 'I should have thrown him out there and then but I didn't want to cause a scene and have my father know the sort of woman I am married to, so I thought it better to do it in a roundabout way.'

'You bloody hypocrite!' Kathryn grated. 'You don't give a damn what they think of me. It's *you* you're concerned about. You don't want to look a fool in front of your father, that's all. Paul is good for Guy and you know it. You've no business lying about his abilities as a tutor.'

Charles' lip curled.

'From the reception my suggestion received it seems the others agree with you. I've not pressed the point at the moment, but at least I have laid the foundations. If your Monsieur Paul returns –

which he won't if he has any sense — and if you resume your nocturnal visits to his room, I assure you I shall have no hesitation whatever in making sure my wishes are observed. I'll have him thrown out, make no mistake of it. Do I make myself clear?'

Kathryn returned his glare defiantly but inwardly the fight had gone out of her and she felt trapped and helpless. This was the moment to have it out with Charles once and for all, tell him that she and Paul were in love and that when all this was over she was going to leave Charles to be with him. But she dared not. Too much depended on Paul's remaining at the château, and not only her own peace of mind and the comfort of seeing him, however fleetingly. It had become Paul's base, a secure place from which he could conduct his operations, as well as a permanent cover for his resistance work. She must not do anything to threaten that.

She looked at Charles, seeing a man she had once loved but now despised, and knew that for the moment at least he had won.

'You make yourself perfectly clear, Charles,' she replied quietly.

In the long days and weeks that followed it was Celestine who provided the diversion which made life bearable for Kathryn. The two girls had always been good friends, now Kathryn discovered that talking with Celestine and trying to help her come to terms with what had happened enabled her to forget, for a little while, the constant nagging fear for Paul's safety and anxiety for the future.

Celestine's moods swung between fiery defiance and black despair. She was suffering from shock and grief as well as the more normal roller-coaster emotional swings that pregnancy inevitably brings, and she was by turns insecure and bullish.

'I don't understand how they can accept the Boche,' she said over and over again. 'They are monsters! Maman and Papa, well yes, I suppose Maman sees only what she wants to see, and nothing but the survival of Savigny matters to Papa. But Charles and Christian . . . I'd never have expected them to take it lying down. They have gone right down in my estimation, I can tell you. How can they call themselves men?'

Kathryn hesitated, tempted to tell her that Christian was working for the Resistance, but deciding against it. Though she knew she could count on Celestine's support, for her own safety it was better she did not know.

'Don't judge them too harshly,' was all she said.

'You wouldn't say that if you saw what the Boche did to Julien!' Celestine's eyes filled with tears and she turned away, lost in her own private hell, and Kathryn put her arms around the thin shoulders, knowing there were no words which could ease her suffering and comforting her in the only way she knew how.

'I loved him so much,' Celestine said through her tears. 'You can't imagine what it was like, seeing them treat him like that and not being able to do anything to help. I just had to watch them beat him up and drag him away . . . I wasn't even there when he died. Oh, I can't bear it! He was so beautiful, so clever . . . I was so proud of him. I don't know what he saw in someone like me.'

'You are beautiful and clever too, Celestine.'

'No I'm not. I'm plain and I'm certainly not clever. He used to help me with my studies so that the tutors wouldn't know how stupid I was. And he was brave, too. He knew the dangers of being a Jew. He should have run away, tried to get out of the country, but he just wouldn't believe they would take him like that. "Those stupid strutting little men don't frighten me," he used to say. He was proud too, you see, proud of being Jewish. I was afraid for him but he wouldn't listen to me.'

'At least you have his baby,' Kathryn said. 'They can't take that away from you.'

'That's true.' Celestine lifted her chin, pursing her lips so that her small face was a mask of defiance. 'Maman and Papa are ashamed of me just now. They think I have let them down. But one day they will be proud. And so will I. I know my son will be the very image of his father.'

'I'm sure he will be,' Kathryn said, but suddenly she was very cold inside. The baby Celestine was carrying was half Jewish. It had not occurred to her before and she did not suppose it had occurred to any of the rest of the family either. It hadn't seemed important – only comforting Celestine had mattered. Now she realised with growing disquiet just how very important it might be.

'Does anyone in Paris know you are pregnant?' she asked, trying not to let her anxiety show.

'My friends know – Agnes and Françoise. And of course the doctor. It wasn't common knowledge and I'm not showing yet, but word gets around. Why do you ask? You're not afraid of the scandal too, are you, Katrine? I wouldn't expect that of you.'

'No, of course not. It's just that . . . I don't think you should tell anyone outside of the family that Julien was Jewish.'

'Oh my God, I never thought!' Celestine's hand flew to her mouth, her eyes wide with dawning horror. 'You mean . . . if they knew, my baby might be in danger too! Of course – of course! People in Paris with Jewish blood generations back have been trying to hide their ancestry. Suppose those bastards who took Julien find out I'm pregnant! They might track me down here! They might . . . God knows what they might do!'

'I'm sure that is not going to happen,' Kathryn said, with more confidence than she was feeling. 'I do think you must be very careful from now on, though. At least you can talk about Julien without giving the game away. His name doesn't sound Jewish.'

'No, but . . . everyone knew. He had to wear a Star of David. Oh Katrine, if the Boche find out he is the father of my baby . . . what will I do?'

'Don't upset yourself,' Kathryn said. 'That won't help anyone – least of all your baby. Just carry on as normally as possible and try not to worry. I'll think of something.'

But even as she tried to sound consoling she knew with terrifying certainty that if the Nazis did indeed discover that Celestine's baby was half Jewish there would be nothing she could do to save her, and the realisation added a new dimension of horror to the nightmare that was slowly but relentlessly engulfing them all.

14

IN THE SMALL anteroom of the doctor's surgery at Périgueux Paul sat waiting his turn. In the rough trousers and collarless shirt which he wore in his persona as country peasant he blended perfectly with the other patients – a middle-aged man with a heavily bandaged hand, a little old lady dressed all in black who huddled, shivering in spite of the heat of the day, a heavily pregnant girl, shifting her bulk uncomfortly and trying, without much success, to control the two small children who ran riot and clung to her skirts by turns. As he waited Paul coughed occasionally, and the feigned spasms sounded sufficiently sepulchral to make the other patients keep their distance. No one wanted a serious chest infection to add to all their other problems.

At last it was Paul's turn. Dr Ventura was writing, bending closely over his desk to enable him to see what he was doing. He needed to get his glasses replaced by stronger ones, he knew, but at present he had too many things on his mind to bother about what was no more than an inconvenience, and he wasn't at all sure that new spectacles would be available anyway. Precious little was, these days. As Paul entered the surgery he looked up, a big bluff man well past his first youth, dressed in a worn tweed suit.

'Paul – you're back then.'

'I'm back. How have things been in my absence?'

'Ticking over. We got three parcels away down the line.'

Paul nodded. He knew that the doctor was referring to Allied airmen being passed along the escape route.

'Any problems there?'

'I don't think so. No thanks to them, though. We put them up at Madame Poire's guesthouse and they got hold of a bottle of pinot and got very drunk. One of them was singing in English, if you please. Then one of the others decided to take a walk around town and got himself lost. God, it's frightening when you think that idiots like that are flying about the skies in great lumps of metal!'

'They got away though?'

'From here they did – with a good ticking-off about their behaviour. I've never been so glad to see the back of anyone in my life. I only hope I made them see the error of their ways or they'll put someone else in danger further down the line. Stupid fools.'

'They are very young, most of them, and probably very frightened,' Paul said, feeling ashamed of his countrymen.

'That's no excuse. They should realise they are endangering the lives of those helping them by their irresponsibility.'

'I know. Anything else?'

'I've recruited a couple more local lads. We'll have to watch them, they're a bit hot-headed, but they are keen and strong – they have youth on their side. And the parish priest at Bouley. He's a good sound man, should be useful. But there's something else I think you should know. It seems that an SS major by the name of Heydrich, who is based in Paris, has taken over a house at St Vincent as a sort of weekend retreat. He's a great friend of von Rheinhardt, he came down to visit him, saw the place and fell in love with it. It had been empty and boarded up for some time but it's been opened up again and all kinds of supplies have been going in through the front door – the sort of luxuries the rest of us haven't been able to get our hands on for years. From what I hear he intends installing his floozy there and coming down to stay whenever he can – which, knowing the way the SS are a law unto themselves, will probably be pretty often.'

Paul swore. An SS major on the doorstep was something they could all well do without and he said as much.

'There's more,' the doctor said, stretching back in his swivel chair. 'And it's serious. The Communists have got wind of what's going on and word is they intend to dispose of him.'

'You've got to be joking!'

'I wish I was.'

'How do you know this?'

'I had it from Madame Yvette. One of her girls heard about it from a client. And those girls are pretty reliable, as you know.'

Paul nodded. Madame Yvette's was a brothel, but the girls who worked for her were among the bravest and most patriotic he had met. As a result of the intimacy they shared with men from all walks of life and every political persuasion they made wonderful informants, and their pillow talk came from not only Frenchmen but Germans too. More than once he had had reason to be grateful to Madame Yvette's girls and he knew that he would sooner trust his life to one of them than to many so-called 'respectable folk'.

By the same token he had a healthy mistrust of the Communists. They were a motley crew, a law unto themselves. In the beginning they had even sided with the Nazis, seeing their rule as a way of destroying the old order, but now that they had defeated Russia the Communists had turned against them. But they still refused to work alongside the Resistance, preferring to run their own show, though they expected to be helped out with supplies of arms and ammunition to carry out their campaigns. They were, Paul considered, at best a nuisance and at worst a danger, for they tended to allow themselves to be carried away by the grand cause to the point of recklessness.

This plan was nothing if not reckless.

'They must be stopped,' he said now. 'Don't they realise the kind of trouble they'll unleash if they assassinate an SS major? The reprisals will be terrible. Von Rheinhardt would make sure of that, especially if it's a friend of his who's killed. And it wouldn't stop there. They'd have the Gestapo here in force faster than you could say the word. They'd line up local people in their hundreds and shoot them down in cold blood.'

'I know all about that,' the doctor said. 'But how the hell can we stop them? I've already talked to Gaultier the local leader, but he wouldn't listen. He as good as told me to mind my own business. You can try if you like. He might take notice of you, though I somehow doubt it. They have the bit between their teeth and all they can see is the satisfaction they'd get from watching a prominent SS major crawling for his life.'

'I know how they feel,' Paul admitted. 'But he is only one man. Get rid of him and someone else just as bad would soon take his place. It's crazy. They might just as well turn their own guns on the local people. They would be sentencing them to death just as surely.'

'Well I hope you can stop them. I couldn't. Now you'd better go. I have other patients waiting to see me. They'll begin to wonder what's taking you so long.'

'All right, *mon ami*. I'll be in touch.'

Paul rose and laid a hand briefly on the older man's shoulder. He was very aware that if the Communists went ahead with this act of folly he might never see him again. The mayor, the doctor and the priest were always amongst the first to be taken when the Nazis required a blood sacrifice. And if the slightest suspicion fell on him, he too might be among those to pay the price.

In the doorway he paused.

'By the way, should anything happen to me I've primed Christian de Savigny to take over the circuit. He's a good man, quick and resourceful, and he has the lovebirds on his papers.'

The loverbirds was a stamp of authorisation which enabled the holders of a pass bearing it to move about freely, even in the forbidden coastal zones.

The doctor nodded. 'Let's hope it won't come to that.'

'You and me both, but you never know.' Paul opened the door, touched his forehead and said loudly and hoarsely: 'Thank you, Doctor. If it's no better I'll come back in a few days. *Bonjour*.'

Then, with a loud simulated cough, he left the surgery.

Pedalling back to the outlying farm cottage where he had been lying low Paul felt his shirt, wet with perspiration, clinging to his back and knew it was not just the hard cycle ride in the heat of the midday sun that was causing him to sweat.

He would go and see the Communist leader right away, he decided, but he did not hold out much hope of persuading him to abandon his plan. Gaultier would not take kindly to what he would see as interference from a rival organisation – and one headed by a foreigner at that. If he wanted this SS major badly enough nothing on earth would stop him. But as Paul had said to Dr Ventura, the repercussions would be terrible. A hundred French lives for the life of one German officer was the going rate, he had heard, and who knew where the axe would fall? Supposing Kathryn was amongst those taken? She was, of course, a de Savigny, the daughter-in-law and wife of known collaborators, but if something like this happened, would that save her? She was English, and a prominent citizen. It was always possible that von Rheinhardt might choose to make an example of her, and if he did not, then the death squads, who he knew would inevitably be brought in, might. And she was doubly at risk because of her connection with him.

As he thought of her and the fate which might be lying in store for her, Paul's fingers tightened around the handlegrips of his bicycle so that the old rubber, already disintegrating from age and from the heat of the sun, attached itself to his sweating palms.

He was in love with her. He shouldn't have allowed it to get this far but it had happened all the same and the weeks he had been away from her had done nothing to alter that. Even whilst he had been fully occupied with the things he had to do she had been there, a sweet shadow at the edges of his consciousness, an aching longing in the dark reaches of the night. He loved her, there was no denying it, and the thought that some harm might befall her was more than he could bear, especially when he knew that if it did he, more than anyone, would be to blame.

Now he thought again of the terrible retribution that would follow if the Communists could not be dissuaded from their maniacal plans and feared for her with a fear that was sharp and all-consuming. The sweat stood out in beads on his forehead as he pressed down hard on the pedals, and by the time he had reached the cottage he knew what he had to do.

Kathryn was in the garden watching Guy chase butterflies with the net on a stick that Bridget had rigged up for him. The sun was bright and hot, drawing perfume from all the plants that had once been nurtured and cared for but which now ran riot, and Kathryn thought she preferred it that way. Too much order was against nature; she liked the wild feel the garden had nowadays.

'I've caught one, Mummy!' Guy called to her. 'Look, isn't he beautiful?'

Kathryn smiled at his excitement.

'Yes, darling, he is. Much too beautiful to put in a jar. He needs his freedom. Now that you've looked at him, I think you should let him go.'

Guy's small face clouded.

'But I don't want to!'

'You mustn't only think of what you want, Guy,' she told him. 'How would you like to be shut up in a jam jar?'

'Not much,' he admitted.

'Let him go, then, there's a good boy.'

After a moment's thought Guy released the butterfly. It fluttered up into the clear air, a tiny speck of brilliant blue, and Kathryn wished that she, too, could escape as easily from all the things that troubled her. Yet watching the butterfly enjoy the return of its freedom her spirits lifted and for a moment it seemed to her as if she was flying with him, one of those brief experiences of pure joy which owed nothing whatever to circumstances. She settled herself more comfortably on the old wooden seat, kicking off her shoes and wriggling her bare toes in the scratchy dry grass, happier than she had been for days for no reason that she could think of.

Could it be, she wondered, that Paul was coming back? It seemed a fanciful thought, that she could somehow know without the smallest scrap of evidence, just by this sudden inexplicable feeling of joyous anticipation, yet she had experienced similar moments, of utter wretchedness as well as exhilaration, as if her very soul touched infinity and was granted a glimpse of the future.

Perhaps . . . perhaps . . . she thought, and smiled at herself for even thinking such a thing. But even when she and Guy went back indoors the warmth of the sun seemed to go with them and when night fell it was still there, somewhere within her, a tiny candle flame in the darkness all around.

'I don't understand you, Christian,' Celestine said. 'I honestly, truly can't understand how you can be nice to the Boche.'

They had gone for a walk after dinner in the cool of the evening and from the top of the hill overlooking Savigny the scene below them was one of perfect peace. The valley, stretching away into the distance, was dappled with soft shade, the uninterrupted green of the fields, the unchanging beauty of the château nestling behind the trees, the animals gathering beneath the trees, all so reminiscent of happier times that it seemed impossible to believe that life was not going on as it always had. This was the Savigny of her childhood and for a little while her troubles seemed no more than a terrible nightmare fading with the rosy light of dawn. And then a German patrol rumbled into view, squat grey vehicles despoiling the peaceful scene like pustules on a beautiful woman's skin, and the horror returned, rushing in all the more disturbingly because of the recent respite, brutally reminding her that it was no nightmare but reality, harsh and inescapable.

'Papa has explained to you,' Christian said, pulling a grass from the hedge and shredding the seed heads between his fingers. 'It's for the best.'

'No!' she said, her voice sharp with tears. 'It's not for the best. It's degrading – horrible. And I'm the one who knows what I'm talking about, remember. I'm the one who saw Julien dragged away. But at least he died with his pride intact. At least he won't have to live knowing he kowtowed to these monsters.'

'You mustn't talk like that, Celestine,' Christian warned her. 'It's very dangerous. You must try to control yourself.'

'Must I? Why? Because Papa says so, is that it? Oh, I know what he is like. I know where his priorities lie. And he's getting older. Any fire he ever had in him has long since gone. But you and Charles . . . I don't know how you can lie down under it, I don't really. I never expected you to be so subservient – my own brothers! You make me ashamed. Ashamed to be a de Savigny.'

Christian looked at her small set face and the spark of hatred in her haunted eyes and understood how she was feeling. Hadn't he felt exactly the same before Paul came and gave him the chance to do something about it? He knew, too, why she was especially angry with him. He had always been her hero, the big brother she had attached herself to so that sometimes he had felt like screaming at her to go away and leave him alone. But he never had. He loved Celestine fiercely and had grown in stature in her unquestioning worship. The years had done nothing to change those feelings – he still valued her unstinting regard and it hurt him to know that she was looking at him and finding him wanting.

'I never thought I'd feel ashamed of you, Christian,' she said again and suddenly his pride could take no more. He could trust her, couldn't he? She was his sister, after all . . .

'Celestine, not everything is quite as it seems,' he said slowly. 'We are not all the collaborators you take us for.'

She stopped dead in her tracks, staring at him.

'What do you mean?'

'There are more ways than one to kill a pig,' he said. 'Sometimes secrecy and stealth work better than outright aggression. You have heard, I expect, that there are Resistance cells all over France.

Well, let me just say that one of them is not a million miles from here.'

He was rewarded by the light beginning to come into her pinched face.

'You mean . . . you . . . ?'

'There's a man living at the château who is not what he seems. He is away at the moment, but . . .'

'You mean Guy's tutor?' Suddenly there was animation in her tone. 'Guy's tutor is. . . ?'

'You mustn't ask me,' Christian said. 'It's better you don't know anything. But I am working with him against the Boche. Let's just leave it at that.'

'Oh Christian!' Her voice was full of the old admiration again; it warmed him. 'Christian, I *knew* you couldn't just let this happen! I knew it!'

'You must keep this to yourself, Celestine. Not a word to anyone, remember. Papa knows nothing of this. If you let one mention of it slip we could all be dead. Promise me, now, you'll put it out of your mind and never speak of it again.'

'Of course, Christian! Of course I promise!'

'Just as long as you remember that,' he said. 'Now, perhaps, it is time we went home.'

'Mummy! Mummy!' Guy came running up the stairs to the bedroom where Kathryn was sorting clean clothes into piles ready to put away. 'Mummy – it's Monsieur Paul! He's back!'

Kathryn's heart gave a great leap of joy.

'Monsieur Paul?' she repeated breathlessly.

'He's in the kitchen with Bridget. I'm going back to talk to him!' He clattered back down the stairs, almost falling over himself in his haste.

Kathryn set the pile of underwear in the drawer with exaggerated care and closed it. Her hands were trembling slightly, her pulse racing. It hadn't misled her then, that moment of intuition the previous afternoon. He was back, and somehow, inexplicably, she had known it.

She glanced in the mirror, tidying her hair swiftly with her fingers, noticing the flush of pleasure colouring her cheeks and the sparkle in her eyes. Dear God, she must be careful or someone else would notice too! She took a few deep breaths, attempting to compose herself, and went downstairs holding tightly to the banister because her legs felt unsteady.

He was in the kitchen, leaning casually against the table and talking to Bridget whilst Guy interjected his own bits of news wherever possible. At the sight of him her heart turned over again and she longed to run to him, throw her arms around him, bury her face in his shoulder, feel the strong lines of his body against hers and his mouth in her hair. But she knew she could not do that. She smiled at him and as their eyes met the electricity arced between them, invisible bridges of sparking current.

'So – you're back,' she said. 'How was Bordeaux?'

'Much like everywhere else – riddled with Germans.'

The conspiracy was an extra bridge between them.

'We've missed you,' she said.

'Good. It's nice to be missed.'

'Bridget made me a butterfly net!' Guy was jumping up and down. 'It works, too.'

'Why don't we go and catch some butterflies then?' Over Guy's head his eyes met Kathryn's – I want to be alone with you, they said. As much alone as we can be at the moment . . .

'Mummy won't let me.'

'I didn't say you couldn't catch them, Guy, just that when you have you must let them go,' Kathryn said, laughing a little, because laughter seemed the only way to let out some of the fierce joy that was bubbling inside her like vintage champagne.

'But keep them long enough to show me,' Paul said. 'I'll just take my valise up to my room and I'll join you in the garden.'

Again his eyes met Kathryn's, again longing sparked within her. I'll come with you! she wanted to say, but she knew she must not.

'Come on, Guy,' she said. 'Let's see what we can find for Monsieur Paul.'

Already the sun was hot. She found a seat in the shade, pretending to watch Guy's wild lunges at the butterflies that flittered from blossom to blossom but actually watching the path, waiting for Paul. When he emerged from the house he had changed into a short-sleeved shirt. He came and sat down beside her and though they did not touch she felt the closeness of his bare arm to hers with every nerve, every pore.

'I was afraid you might not come back,' she said when Guy was safely out of earshot.

'I nearly didn't.' His voice was very low, very serious. 'I have to talk to you, Kathryn.'

'Talk away then,' she said gaily. She was too happy to see him to allow his sombre tone to affect her. 'Where have you really been? Did you have anything to do with blowing up the arms dump?'

'You know better than to ask me that.' He gave her a sideways look. 'And what I want to talk about is the future, not what's over and done with.'

The first bolt of alarm darted within her.

'Look, I'll be as brief as I can in case Guy comes back,' he went on. 'I'm worried about your safety, Kathryn.'

She raised a hand to brush her hair away from her face; the sun caught the tiny golden hairs on her arm, making them shimmer.

'I don't understand.'

'I'll try to explain.' He repeated what Dr Ventura had told him and saw the slow-dawning horror come into her eyes.

'But that would be crazy! Heaven knows what the Nazis would do if one of their high-ranking officers was murdered here, in Savigny!'

'Exactly. But try telling the Communists that. And of course, what makes it even worse is that this Heydrich is a personal friend of von Rheinhardt. He'd stop at nothing to find out who was responsible and if he couldn't do that he wouldn't care who was taken by way of revenge.'

'My God!' She was very pale, remembering the promises of reprisals she had heard from von Rheinhardt's own lips. 'They've got to be stopped!'

'I don't think they can be.'

'Supposing Charles talked to them – or Guillaume. They might listen to them.'

'I doubt it. They'd look on it as interference by known collaborators. They are fanatics and the danger with fanatics is their absolute conviction that they are right and everyone else is wrong.'

Guy came running towards them, clasping his butterfly net.

'Look – look – I got one, Monsieur Paul! Isn't he a beauty?'

For seemingly endless minutes they examined Guy's prize, Kathryn marvelling at Paul's ability to appear totally normal. Her own brain was spinning and she was trembling inwardly. When at last Guy ran off again Paul turned to her.

'Look, Kathryn, I want to get you out of this. I want to pass you and Guy down the escape line to Spain. From there you could get back to England – and safety.'

Her hands flew to her mouth, pressing her nails into her lips. Then she shook her head.

'I couldn't do that. I couldn't just walk out on all of them. I'd feel like a traitor.'

'That's all very well, but they are adults and citizens of France. Don't you think your first consideration should be for your son?'

'They wouldn't hurt Guy . . . would they?'

'I wouldn't like to guarantee it. They can be total unconscionable bastards. If they want to teach someone a lesson they won't have a single scruple about how they do it. And even if they didn't touch Guy, what would happen to him if you were taken?'

Her nails picked nervously at her lips, her eyes flew to Guy, happily chasing yet another butterfly. If anything should happen to him . . . But she couldn't believe it. She couldn't envisage the German officer who played games with Guy doing anything to harm him.

'I'm sure he'll be all right,' she said stubbornly. 'And whatever you might think, I do owe a debt of loyalty to my husband's family. Things are bad enough here as it is without me making them worse.'

'What do you mean?'

She told him about Celestine.

'She needs me here,' she finished. 'She is in a terrible state about what happened in Paris and frightened out of her wits in case the Germans discover that her baby is half Jewish. Now there's someone who should be passed down the escape line if it could be managed! But to be honest I don't think her state of health would allow it. She's not fit to hide in barns and woods or walk for days on end. She'd never make it. When you meet her you'll understand what I mean. Oh – here she is now!'

Celestine had emerged from the house and was coming towards them. In her blue cotton frock she looked thin and frail but the bulge of her stomach where her baby was growing was beginning to protrude.

Paul touched Kathryn's arm urgently.

'Promise me you'll at least think about what I have said.'

'I'll think about it.'

'Well, don't think for too long. I don't know how much time we have before the balloon goes up. When it does, it will be too late to do anything about it.'

She nodded and raised a hand to her sister-in-law.

'Celestine – over here!' she called. 'Come and meet Guy's tutor!'

For the moment the time for confidences was over.

'So – he's back,' Charles said. His face wore its now customary shut-in look. 'I hope you haven't forgotten our conversation about his future, Katrine.'

Her lips fastened in a tight line.

'How could I possibly forget?'

'Good. Remember, if you give me the slightest cause to think you have resumed your liaison I'll have him out of here so fast his feet won't touch the ground.'

'Don't worry, Charles, I won't give you cause. I, at least, have my son's welfare at heart.'

'I hope you stand by that.' He turned away and Kathryn felt the jaws of the trap closing in around her once more. Would this nightmare never end? She thought again of the conversation she had had with Paul, his fears for Guy's safety and his suggestion to get them away. His talk of the Communists' crazy plans and the reprisals which would follow had frightened her badly but she had also found herself wondering, unreasonably she knew, how he could want to send her away if he wanted to be with her as much as she wanted to be with him.

Now, on top of everything else, here was Charles reminding her how impossible even the smallest contact would be if she was not to endanger Paul's position at the château.

Kathryn covered her face with her hands and wondered, not for the first time, just how much more she could take without breaking, and where it would all end.

15

IT WAS A beautiful Sunday morning and the family were returning from church when von Rheinhardt's big black staff car overtook them on the drive.

'What's he doing here?' Celestine demanded, her thin frame stiffening.

'Celestine, please!' Guillaume cautioned her. 'Don't make more trouble, there's a good girl. Heaven knows what damage you have done already.'

Celestine's mouth tightened rebelliously but there was a frightened look in her eyes. Since her outburst it had been noticeable that von Rheinhardt had visited the château less often, and when he did, some of the cordiality had gone from his manner. She had offended him deeply, Guillaume was sure, and although he had tried to explain that his daughter had been tired and unwell, besides being in a delicate condition, he was not at all sure that von Rheinhardt accepted the explanation. The result was an awkwardness which Guillaume found surprising; he had thought von Rheinhardt's skin was thicker than that, but he could not help wondering if the Nazi had in fact realised that Celestine had merely voiced what they were all thinking beneath the pretence of friendship, and he was very afraid that she had undone much of the hard work he had put in to establish a good relationship.

'It's all right, Celestine.' Kathryn linked her arm through her sister-in-law's, but inwardly she too was quaking. Two weeks had passed since Paul had warned her of the Communists' plans to murder Heydrich and so far there had been no developments, though whether that was because they had been persuaded to change their minds or whether it was simply that the opportunity had not yet presented itself she had no way of knowing. Now, with a cold wash of fear, she found herself wondering if something had happened in that direction. It was, after all, a weekend, just the time when Heydrich was likely to be staying at the cottage he had commandeered. Was it possible that the hotheads had struck and von Rheinhardt's unexpected visit was the result of it?

The Nazi emerged from his car and stood waiting for them, an impressive figure resplendent in his uniform, stern and unsmiling.

'Otto! What brings you here?' Guillaume greeted him. 'It's a beautiful morning, isn't it? I would have thought you would be taking advantage of the weekend to relax a little.'

'I am afraid the commandant in charge of a district has very little time for relaxation,' von Rheinhardt returned stiffly. 'This isn't a social visit, either. I want to talk to you about certain things that are disturbing me.'

'Oh dear, that sounds very serious,' Guillaume said casually, but Kathryn was not deceived by the lightness of his tone.

'It's serious,' von Rheinhardt agreed. 'I would like to talk to you and Charles in private.'

The lump of nervousness tightened in Kathryn's throat. She steered Guy past the car, which always made him goggle-eyed with admiration, and up the steps to the front door of the château.

'Come on, darling, I think you should get out of your best clothes before you start playing in the garden.'

She took him upstairs and her hands were unsteady as she unfastened the buttons of his shirt and helped him into clean shorts and a casual top.

'I want to play with my toy farm,' Guy announced.

She got it out for him, then, leaving him to arrange the little tin animals, she went along the passage to Paul's room. There was no reply when she knocked at the door and after a moment she opened it and looked in. The room was empty. He must have gone out. Where? she wondered, her anxiety growing.

On the stairs she met Christian.

'Father has taken von Rheinhardt into his study,' he said.

She nodded, pale and tense. She and Christian stood for a moment outside the door, trying to listen. But the murmur of voices from the other side was unintelligible.

'There is an agent working in this vicinity,' von Rheinhardt said.

Guillaume and Charles exchanged glances.

'Surely not,' Guillaume said at last. 'I can't believe it.'

'There's no doubt, I'm afraid.' Von Rheinhardt was standing in front of the window, and the sun, slanting in, caught the buttons on his uniform and refracted the light. 'We have picked up radio transmissions which are being made to London on a regular basis.'

'From here? But where?'

'That we do not yet know. Obviously the transmitter is being moved about. Several times our detection vans have been on the point of finding it but always the transmission ends before they can close in. It is just a matter of time, though. We will find it, and when we do the illegal operator will be dealt with with the utmost severity.'

'As he deserves!' Charles said harshly. They both looked at him and he cleared his throat. 'This kind of behaviour undermines everything we are working to achieve. What can they hope to gain?'

'A little victory of some kind, I imagine.' Von Rheinhardt's tone was grim. 'It is of course futile. The Third Reich will never be threatened by anything so puny. But they must be taught that we will not tolerate this kind of insubordination.'

Guillaume spread his hands.

'I'm sorry I can't help you. I have no idea who could be doing such a thing.'

'As I say, our detector vans will find them before long. But I thought a warning to you would not come amiss.' As he spoke von Rheinhardt reached out and picked up a porcelain figurine which stood on the mantel shelf, his thick fingers stroking the delicate china with something close to tenderness. Then he replaced it, his eyes growing hard once more.

'If there is a Resistance cell working in this district the chances are that the radio transmissions are only a small part of their activities,' he went on. 'As I have said before, these resisters are becoming very troublesome and I will not stand for that. You had better warn your people and tell them to spread the word. If anything untoward happens here I shall see that the perpetrators pay the price – in full.'

'And if you cannot find the perpetrators?'

'Then I shall make an example of whoever I think fit. The axe will fall where I consider it will have most impact.'

He was looking directly at Guillaume and there was a barely veiled threat in his cold blue eyes.

From the window of her bedroom Celestine saw von Rheinhardt leave. She stood, rigid with fear and hatred, her arms wrapped protectively around the growing bulge of her stomach, watching the big black car disappear down the drive between the tall cypress trees, and as the tension slowly ebbed from her body she began to cry, softly at first, then harder as she relived once more the horror of what had happened in Paris. Her thin shoulders shook and her body seemed almost to fold in on itself, racked by grief that was a physical pain.

Oh God, would this nightmare never end? She had thought that if she came home she would find escape from it, as if somehow Savigny, peaceful haven of her childhood years, would have survived exactly as she had remembered it, an oasis in a war-torn world. She had fled here blindly, desperate for the balm she had believed she would find to soothe her jangling nerves and help mend her breaking heart, and she had been devastated to find that here too the domination of the Nazis was complete.

Walking through the door and seeing von Rheinhardt sitting at her father's table had been a shock on every possible level and she had thought that night that she now knew what it felt like to be raped. Her refuge had been violated. Added to that was the desperate fear for her unborn child. Lying sleepless night after night Celestine had wondered if she might be losing her mind. One thing was certain – the laughing, carefree girl she had once been had gone for ever.

As her sobs began to ease Celestine heard footsteps on the stairs; she went to the door and opened it to see Charles coming up. He looked weary, she thought, old beyond his years, his hair receding prematurely from a face that had forgotten how to smile and a stoop to his shoulders as if he was bearing an unseen burden. The Nazis had done this too, she thought, wrought their evil on all her family so that they were subtly changed from the people she knew and loved.

'He's gone then, the pig. I saw the car drive away,' she said, but she was peering past him down the staircase as if she still expected von Rheinhardt to materialise there.

'Yes, he's gone. Celestine, *chérie*, don't be afraid. He won't hurt you.'

'How do you know that? You can't be sure . . .' She was crying again. He put his arms around her, trying to comfort her.

'He's all right. He trusts us, I think – as far as the Nazis trust anyone.'

'But you can't trust them,' she sobbed. 'You can't, Charles – you must not! And if he was to find out what you're doing . . .'

Charles stiffened slightly.

'What do you mean – what I'm doing?'

'Oh . . .' Celestine raised her head. Her eyes, swollen from crying, looked into his pleadingly. 'I'm sorry, Charles, I know I'm not supposed to know, but Christian told me.'

His fingers tightened on her arms.

'Christian told you what?'

'About how Guy's tutor is really a British agent and you are hiding him here and working with him. I'm glad, of course – I hated to think that you were all just lying down and taking it, even entertaining Nazis under our roof. You don't know what a relief it was to find out that that is just a cover. But I'm frightened all the same. If von Rheinhardt should discover what you are really doing, right under his nose . . .'

'I see,' Charles said. His eyes had grown very hard.

'Don't tell Christian I told you, will you?' Celestine begged. 'He made me promise not to tell anyone. He'd be angry if he thought I'd spoken of it, even to you. I expect he thinks you want to keep me in ignorance to protect me in case anything . . . should happen.'

'I expect so,' Charles said.

Celestine was too upset to notice the odd tone of his voice. She found a handkerchief in her pocket and blew her nose.

'I want you to know though that I'm proud of you, Charles,' she said, the defiance beginning to return. 'We have to drive those bastards out of our country somehow. I just hope we don't all die doing it.'

'You can be sure, *chérie*, we all hope that.' He touched her hair tenderly. 'Are you all right now?'

She nodded.

'I suppose so. As right as I'll ever be until this is all over.'

'In that case I am going to change my clothes. I'll see you at lunch.'

He left her on the stairs and went on up to his apartment.

As he passed the door of his son's room Charles heard the voices coming from inside – Kathryn playing with Guy. He hesitated, his hand hovering over the handle, then he changed his mind and went on to his own room.

Sunlight was slanting in, bathing the old brocade of the drapes in a golden glow and making the dark wood gleam richly. He took off his jacket, hanging it up with exaggerated care, and unbuttoning his shirt. He felt weighed down suddenly by the knowledge that Celestine had unwittingly revealed to him.

So – Paul Curtis was an agent. Deep down he had suspected it for a long while but he had been so obsessed with Kathryn's infidelity that he had allowed himself to be blinded to the possibility. Even now the thought of them together was so upsetting to him that it threatened to obliterate all other considerations, and Charles bent his head, massaging the nape of his neck, swamped by pain and self-recrimination.

For too long, he thought, he had refused to acknowledge that he had played his part in the failure of their marriage. He had been all too ready to lay the blame at Kathryn's door, telling himself she should be grateful for the things he had given her – a more than comfortable lifestyle, a secure future with the promise of a title, and a son she adored. He had been impatient with her expectations of him, considering her yearning for physical affection to be a sign of her immaturity, responding to her pleas for him to give more of himself to her with an almost calculated indifference. Later, when she had begun to turn against him, he had grown even more annoyed, putting her reaction down to a mixture of a total lack of understanding and a fit of childish pique and comparing her unfavourably with Regine. Only when he had seen the way she glowed when she was with Paul and noticed the looks that passed between them had he begun to see her in a different light and discovered, to his chagrin, that he was jealous. She was his wife, for God's sake! She shouldn't be playing up to another man! Yet still he had refused to accept any responsibility for what was happening.

Now, for the first time, Charles found himself wondering if he had been quite fair to her. It wasn't her fault she was not Regine. Perhaps when he had married her he should have made some effort to put his mistress out of his mind instead of continually hankering after her and drawing comparisons. But he hadn't. He had been so sure that Kathryn would still be there at his feet grovelling for his affection, grateful for the crumbs he might throw to her, he simply had not envisaged a time when the tables might be turned.

Well, they were turned now, all right – and Charles had discovered he did not like it one bit. Bad enough that the wife he had looked upon as his personal property should have sought solace with another man. But what he had just learned inadvertently from Celestine made it a thousand times worse. The man was not only a threat to his marriage but also a British agent who could bring disaster to them all. He had made a fool of Charles twice over. How dare he! How bloody dare he!

Charles straightened, his blood boiling with fury, wondering what to do. He could, he supposed, pursue his previous plan to have him thrown out of the château on the grounds of his incompetence. He could go to his father and denounce him as an agent. But it was always possible that Guillaume would take Paul's part – his fondness for collaboration seemed to have waned since Celestine had returned and told her story – and if there was a showdown there was always the chance that the truth about Paul's relationship with Kathryn might come out. And besides, simply getting rid of Paul Curtis was no longer enough for him. His desire for revenge was too strong.

No, there would be a better way if only he gave himself the time and space to plan for it.

Charles rose, his face a mask of hatred. His time would come and he would make Paul Curtis wish he had never set eyes on any of the de Savignys. All he had to do was to be patient for a little while and continue to play the part he had been playing now for so long that it had become second nature.

It was mid-afternoon when Paul returned. Christian saw him coming up the drive and managed to be outside by the time he reached the château.

'I must talk to you. Go round to the stable block – there won't be anyone there at this time of day. I'll join you in a minute.'

Paul's eyes narrowed but he knew better than to pursue the conversation here in full view of the house. He did as Christian suggested, putting his bicycle away and waiting in the cool interior of the stables. Outside the paved yard glared white, reflecting the hot sunshine, and he mopped his face and neck with his handkerchief as he waited. He wished he had not had to go out today – he hoped no one had wondered about his absence – but there had been urgent arrangements he had to put in hand. The message had come through that London were going to send in a consignment of arms and ammunition that he had asked for, and looking at the clear sky Paul had known it could be very soon. It had been imperative he prepare the reception party and Pierre, the boy Paul had been using as a messenger, had needed to be alerted. But Pierre had been in the next village, visiting his girlfriend, and his parents had insisted Paul share their midday meal of bread and cheese whilst he waited, so that the whole exercise had taken a great deal longer than he had intended.

At last Christian rounded the corner of the château. His serious expression alarmed Paul further.

'Has something happened?' he asked.

'Von Rheinhardt has been here,' Christian said bluntly. 'He spoke to Papa and Charles. It seems they have picked up radio transmissions and they are going all out to trace them.'

Paul swore.

'It was bound to happen sooner or later, I suppose. They're getting very sharp about that kind of thing. But I could have done without it just now, when we are expecting an arms drop. I must get a message to my pianist and warn him to be extra careful and keep on the move. Is there any chance you could do that for me, Christian? I've already been out and about today more than seems feasible.'

Christian nodded. 'What do I do – just leave a message in the letterbox?'

Paul thought for a moment. He had told Pierre to check the letterboxes twice daily now that the arms drop was imminent – a message placed there now should be picked up this evening and was probably safer than Christian having to seek out a member of the cell on a Sunday afternoon when the de Savignys enjoyed a day of relaxation and would not normally be expected to be out visiting villagers.

'Yes,' he said. 'Use the one closest to the château.'

'Leave it to me.' Christian rubbed his jaw with his fingers. 'I have a horrible feeling, Paul, that things are going to get pretty hot round here.'

'I agree. I'm especially concerned about Kathryn and Celestine if the dung hits the fan, Kathryn being English and Celestine carrying a Jewish baby. I'd like to get them away, but obviously Celestine isn't strong enough to make it down the line and Kathryn won't leave without her.' He paused, a sudden thought striking him. 'Perhaps I could get them out by Lysander. The plane bringing the arms and ammunition will be landing in the field just up the valley. He could take them back with him – if they'd go.'

'I think Celestine would,' Christian said eagerly. 'She's terrified for her baby. I'm not so sure about Kathryn.'

'She should think of Guy,' Paul said harshly. 'If the Communists do as they are threatening and murder Heydrich I wouldn't like to answer for what might happen.'

'Is there any news on that front?'

'Heydrich hasn't put in an appearance yet. He's been busy in Paris, from what I can make out. But when he does come I'm very afraid they are going to do what they are threatening. They're a lot of madmen.'

'Damn Communists!' Christian took out a packet of Gauloises, offered one to Paul, and lit them both. 'I wonder if it would help if I talked to Kathryn?'

'It's worth a try.' Paul's face set. He had had so little time alone with Kathryn since his return. She seemed to be àvoiding him. 'Persuade her that Guy could be in very real danger – and also tell her that Celestine would need someone to look after her. It might just work.'

'I'll do that. I'd better go now. We don't want to be seen together.'

Paul nodded.

'You're right. But you'll leave the message in the letterbox?'

'Yes. And I'll talk to Kathryn and Celestine.'

Paul laid a hand on Christian's arm.

'You're a good man.'

'I have to do something to make up for the rest of my family,' Christian said wryly.

Christian was not the only person from the château to take a walk that afternoon.

Charles was still seething with anger over the morning's revelations, and leaving the château slumbering in the heat of the early summer afternoon he walked across the fields and up the rise to a spot that had been a haunt of his since childhood days. There, in the shade of a clump of trees, he had taken his schoolbooks to study in perfect undisturbed peace. Later he had gone there with his first girlfriend, a second cousin named Isabelle who had come to stay in the summer when he was sixteen. He had snatched his first kiss there, explored for the first time the soft exciting curves of a female body, lain in the sun with his shirt open to the waist, glorying in the warmth on his skin and drunk on the fresh sweet smell of the grass and the nearness of Isabelle. From this vantage point the château and its grounds were spread out in a panorama beneath him, de Savigny land as far as the eye could see, and he had thought: One day this will be mine. The knowledge had touched a nerve of anticipation within him, filling him with pride and a sense of awe. The past and the future had seemed very close, as if he could reach out and encompass both, the unchanging heritage of generations. Savigny, beautiful Savigny, home of his forefathers, which would one day be the home of his children and their children; Savigny, an obligation, his birthright, a sacred trust.

This afternoon, however, as he climbed the ridge, his anger began to turn in on itself, filling him with despair and self-loathing. He was a failure, an utter failure. His father was right to despise him. And not only his father. They all despised him – Kathryn, Christian, perhaps even Celestine. They had all known what he had not – the truth about Paul Curtis. Perhaps they also knew about Kathryn's affair with the damned man and were laughing at him behind his back. The thought made the sweat break out on his forehead and sent a rush of hot shame through him.

Long before he reached his favourite spot his legs were aching but he drove himself on, refusing to slow his pace, until he reached the clump of trees. Then he stopped, breath coming hard, stretching his neck back to relieve the ache of tension in his shoulders. The trunk of one of the trees lay where it had fallen many years earlier; Charles perched himself on a flat ledge of it, resting his back against the gnarled old wood.

In the quietude he could hear the sounds of nature, the crickets, the bees, the flies swarming beneath the overhanging branches. It took more than a German invasion to stop them going about their business, he thought, a tired smile playing about his mouth. No matter what happened the world of nature went on renewing itself. But would his children be there to see it? Supposing when all this was over Kathryn should leave him for Paul Curtis and take Guy with her?

He would fight her, of course, with all the resources available to him. Guy was a de Savigny, nothing could change that. But in this uncertain world, who knew what the outcome would be? Nothing was as it should be any more; Charles felt as if he had somehow stumbled into a mire of quicksand and he did not know which way to turn to stop himself from sinking.

For a long while he sat staring down into the valley. Then a movement on the drive to the château caught his eye. A figure on a bicycle – Paul Curtis returning from wherever he had been. A rush of anger made the brightness of the afternoon turn black before his eyes. The bastard! He'd like to throttle him with his bare hands. Curtis disappeared and still Charles sat, unwilling to go back, wanting to be alone a little longer before he had to resume the façade that was his armour.

He was still there when he saw a figure he recognised as Christian emerge, walking down the drive. Another wave of resentment overcame him. Christian too was deceiving him and their father. Everywhere he looked, it seemed, those familiar to him were displaying a secret side to their natures.

Christian was walking purposefully – nothing so strange in that, Christian never ambled when he took a walk, always striding out energetically. But with his heightened sense of persecution Charles found himself watching his brother's progress with suspicion. Where was he going? Charles shaded his eyes against the sun, watching. For a few minutes Christian disappeared out of sight beneath a knoll in the rising ground and when he reappeared he was almost at the lane that bounded the edge of the parkland.

There he stopped, crouching down beside the low stone wall. Charles strained his eyes. What the hell was he doing? Tying a shoelace, perhaps? But no, he appeared to be doing something to the wall itself.

After a moment he straightened up and continued down the lane, and though he still walked fast it seemed to Charles that there was a subtle difference in his demeanour. He puzzled over it and when his brother was out of sight, walking in the direction of the village, he got up from his seat on the fallen tree and made his way diagonally down the grassy slope towards the spot where he had seen Christian fiddling with the wall.

A slight sheen of perspiration had begun to bead Charles' forehead. He took out a handkerchief to mop his face and found his hand was trembling slightly, though for the life of him he could not understand the reason. Some sixth sense was stirring like a jagged nerve deep within him.

At first sight there was nothing remarkable about the wall, no obvious reason for Christian's interest in it. Looking around to make certain there was no one about, Charles crouched down to examine it. The stones were old, creeper and tiny weeds grew between them. But one, Charles noticed, looked slightly different. The plants had been disturbed, dry crumbling plaster was exposed. He ran his fingers around it and with a jolt of excitement found that it was loose.

Crouching lower he eased it out. There in the hollow was a small packet. A postbox! Charles thought. The fools were using this place, right on the edge of the grounds, to pass messages! He unwrapped the package, his fingers clumsy with eagerness.

The note was not even coded. Perhaps whoever it was meant for was not clever enough to decipher codes.

'Warn the pianist only transmit in emergency. Detector vans active.'

Well, at least they had the wit to be cautious. Perhaps it would curtail their activities if they knew that the Germans were on to them. Carefully he replaced the note and pushed the stone back into place. This time he'd leave it so that it would be found by whoever it was intended for. He did not want Christian to know he had discovered his secret. But Charles' mind was made up. He would keep an eye on the letterbox. That way he would stay ahead in the game.

Kathryn heard Paul come upstairs and hurried along the corridor to his room.

'Paul – thank goodness you're back! I was so worried about you! Von Rheinhardt has been here and . . .'

'I know,' he said. 'Christian told me. Everything is under control, don't worry.'

'Don't worry! It's easy to say that! I was frantic!'

He held out his hand to her.

'Come here.'

She hung back, looking over her shoulder nervously though she knew Charles had gone out.

'What's the matter?' he asked. 'You've been avoiding me.'

'Charles knows,' she said softly, urgently. 'He couldn't have been as fast asleep as I thought he was when I came to your room. He has already tried to get you thrown out of the château. I was afraid if I did anything else to upset him he would try again and succeed.'

Paul snorted; his opinion of Charles was very low.

'Don't worry about that. To be honest I think I should leave anyway. There are far too many of us under one roof here.'

'Oh Paul, no! Please don't go . . .'

'I want to talk to you, Kathryn. But first do as I say and come here. It's been far too long since I kissed you.'

She glanced over her shoulder again, then her longing for him overcame her fear. She pushed the door closed behind her and went to him. He held her, pressing her to him, running his hands lightly over her back and legs as if rediscovering every line. She buried her face in his shoulder, then turned her head so that her lips tasted his throat. They kissed, deeply, urgently, but the tension was still tingling in her, marring the sweetness of the moment.

'Kathryn, listen.' He held her away slightly so that he could look at her. 'I'm expecting a Lysander very soon with an arms drop. I could arrange for it to take you, Guy and Celestine out. Don't answer too quickly. I know you said before you wouldn't go, but I really think you should consider it, for Guy's sake, if nothing else. And it would ensure Celestine's safety too – no struggling down a difficult escape route. But she'd need you, Kathryn, pregnant in a strange country.'

She hesitated.

'You don't think the Boche would turn on the rest of the family if we suddenly disappeared?'

'I don't know. They'd have to pretend you'd gone to stay with relatives or something. I've already discussed it with Christian and he agrees with me. Guy must be your first priority now – and Celestine's baby. If the others care anything for either of you they'll understand that.'

'Yes, I think Guillaume and Louise would. I'm not so sure about Charles, but . . .' She broke off, unable to bring herself to say what was in her heart – that she no longer cared what Charles thought, though she did still care what happened to him. For a few moments she was silent, deep in thought, then she nodded. 'All right.'

He looked at her, startled. He had expected her to argue again. She laughed shortly.

'Don't look like that. I thought you wanted me to go back to England.'

'And I thought you would almost certainly refuse to go. What brought about this change of heart?'

She shrugged. 'Oh, I don't know – I've had time to think about it, I suppose.' It was not the whole truth but there were some things she was not yet ready to share with anyone – even Paul. 'Suppose someone should hear the plane?' she went on swiftly. 'Mightn't they be suspicious?'

'That's a chance we have to take.'

'Supposing they connect it with you?'

'As I've already said, I think it's time for Paul Curtis to make his exit. You taking Guy away will give me the perfect excuse. I'll hardly be needed any longer as his tutor if he's not here, and I'm sure Guillaume can convince the authorities, if needs be, that he thought I was genuine.'

'Do you know yet when it will be?'

'Not precisely, but it will be soon. Warn Celestine and have a bag packed and ready. I'll give you as much notice as I can but it may be only a few hours.'

'I understand.'

'I love you,' he said. 'When this is all over we'll be together, I promise.'

'Oh I do hope so!' she whispered. 'I love you too, Paul.'

She was beginning to ache now with need of him but she knew that for the moment it could not be. Their time would come, if the gods were on their side. He held her for a few moments longer, gently massaging the knots of tension in the slope of her shoulders, kissed her again, and put her away gently but firmly.

'Be brave.'

Tears ached in her throat.

'I'll try. But I don't feel very brave.'

'You will be,' he said, 'I know it. You are a very special woman, Kathryn. I never expected to feel this way about anyone, ever again. But there it is – I do.'

'And I never knew it was possible to feel this way at all.'

'There you are then. Anything else is a bonus.'

'I suppose so. What a time to find out though!'

'That is often when it happens – when we are afraid there might be no second chances.'

'Oh Paul . . .'

'Go on now,' he said gently. 'Go and talk to Celestine.'

She went. Alone, he thought: Thank God for that! At least when I know she is safe I'll be able to get on with the job in hand.

But the relief did nothing to ease the ache in his heart that came from knowing that within a few days she would be gone.

Kathryn found Celestine in the walled garden, sitting on the old stone seat and staring into space. Kathryn sat down beside her.

'I think I've found a way to get you and your baby out of reach of the Nazis. I'm going to take you to England.'

Celestine's eyes widened, huge dark-blue orbs in her sallow face.

'England? But how? They'd never let us go.'

'Look, you have to keep this completely to yourself, not mention it to Maman or Papa or anyone. There's an English plane coming to drop supplies for the Resistance. We are going to take Guy and fly out on it.'

'Oh!' Celestine was silent for a moment, digesting the information, but instead of bombarding Kathryn with the questions she had expected, she only smiled slyly. 'It's Paul's doing, I suppose.'

It was Kathryn's turn to be surprised.

'How do you know about Paul?' she asked sharply.

'Christian told me. He's an agent, isn't he?'

'Yes, he is. But Christian shouldn't have said anything.'

'It's all right.' Celestine laughed a little nervously. 'You can trust me. I hate the Boche too, remember.'

'I know you do, but all the same . . .' Kathryn checked herself. No point agonising over it now; there were too many important plans to be made. 'You do want to go?'

'Of course I do! Oh Kathryn, you've no idea what a relief it would be to know I didn't have to worry any more about them finding out my baby is half Jewish! Just to think he can be born in a free country . . . you can't imagine what that will mean to me.'

Kathryn hesitated. It was on the tip of her tongue to say that she knew exactly what Celestine meant; that she felt exactly the same way. For Kathryn was beginning to be fairly certain that she, too, was pregnant.

It had been a long while before she had recognised the signs. At first she had put the constant nausea that was troubling her down to the fact that she was so worried, though she now wondered how she could have beem so naive, considering she had felt exactly the same when she had been pregnant with Guy. Never one to be bothered with counting days she had not noticed either that her period had not come, until one day she woke up and thought in a rather puzzled way: When did I last have the curse? She began calculating, trying to tie it in with some event or other, only to realise that it must be almost two months ago. She had panicked then, examining her body for telltale signs, and when she found that her breasts had begun to change, the nipples harder and darker, the breasts themselves fuller and more tender, she knew in a minute without any doubt what she had failed to suspect for so long.

She had stood staring at herself in the mirror, too stunned for the moment to think straight. When she had been pregnant with Guy it had been the fulfilment of a dream and she had been filled with joy. Now she felt only apprehension. This was no world into which to bring a new baby, this cauldron of suspicion and fear.

And worse, she was not even sure who had fathered the tiny new life beginning within her. She would like to think, of course, that it was Paul. If it was, she would have something of his to carry into the years ahead, whatever might happen. But she could not be certain that the baby was Paul's. Too vividly she remembered the occasion when Charles had forced himself on her. Charles had given her Guy within the first year of their marriage. Was it not quite likely that he might also be the father of the baby she was now carrying?

Uncertainty and doubts plagued her and she had kept her own counsel about her condition. Would she have told anyone had she been sure who was the father? she wondered. Certainly she would have longed to share the news with Paul if she could have been certain the baby was his, but didn't he have enough to worry about without that added complication? And to tell him now, with her hovering doubts, would mean admitting that single disgusting episode with Charles. As for telling Charles himself, she shrank from it. She felt too angry with him, too full of cold dislike, to want to share anything with him, much less this.

She wouldn't be able to keep it to herself much longer, of course. Soon it would be obvious for all to see. She wallowed in indecision, wondering how to deal with the situation.

And then like the answer to a prayer Paul had offered her the flight out of France and Kathryn had known what she must do. Being away from Savigny would give her a breathing space. In addition, her baby, whoever had fathered him, would be born in freedom. England might still be at war, but the dangers were clean-cut ones, not an ideal world but far preferable to the privations and insidious perils of occupied France. Besides, Kathryn thought with wry realism, if she remained here she might not even live to give birth to her child. She was, after all, involved with the Resistance. If that fact was discovered her chances would be slim indeed.

She said none of this, however, to Celestine.

'Get a few things together,' she told the girl. 'Not too much, we'll have to travel light.'

'I left most of my things in Paris anyway.' Celestine sounded almost light-hearted. 'The only thing that is important to me is what I'm carrying right here.' She patted her stomach with fondness and pride and Kathryn felt a moment's envy for the simplicity of her priorities.

'It might be dangerous, of course,' she warned. 'The plane will have to fly through flak. There's always the risk of being shot down.'

'We'll get through,' Celestine said. 'I know it. Oh, Kathryn, this is the best news I've had since this nightmare began.' Her face clouded slightly and she ran a hand through her straight dark hair. 'What will Maman and Papa do, though? I won't even be able to say goodbye to them!'

'They'll know it's for the best. With any luck the war will soon be over and we'll all be able to be together again.'

Celestine nodded.

'What will we do when we get to England?'

'We'll go to my parents. They'll let us stay with them for the time being. They live in the country, well away from the bombing – or at least, I hope it is!' She hugged Celestine briefly. 'Be ready the minute I say the word. And remember, it would be safest not to mention this to anyone, even Christian.'

Celestine hugged her back.

'I understand. I won't let you down, Kathryn. And you know something? I don't think Charles realises for one moment how lucky he is to have you as a wife.'

Kathryn smiled wryly.

'I'm not sure he would agree with you about that,' she said.

The remark was totally ambiguous.

Every day on his way to the distillery Charles checked the letterbox in the wall; every night on his way home he checked it again. He made excuses to Christian and his father for walking alone – easy as far as Christian was concerned, for he seemed to want to go off on his own far too often for Charles' liking, much more difficult to get away from Guillaume. But somehow he managed it. Checking the box had become an obsession with him.

For the first few days the tiny cave behind the stone was empty and Charles began to wonder if they had stopped using this particular hiding place. It would make sense, he knew, to keep changing the letterboxes, and the valley between the château and the village was full of possibilities.

Then one evening his seeking fingers encountered something that felt like folded paper. He pulled it out and unfolded it, trembling with excitement at his find.

Once again the message was simple and uncoded.

'Listen for message, *Le bébé s'appelle Beau*. Act after dark same night.'

Charles' eyes narrowed. So, in spite of all his warnings, some kind of operation was being planned and, if the message was to be believed, imminent. If it went ahead von Rheinhardt would be furious; Charles had no doubt he would make reprisals as he had threatened. Unless the perpetrators were caught. Charles replaced the message and the loose stone and walked on, deep in thought. He had already decided he would have no compunction about betraying Paul. Not only would it save the innocent, it would also give him deep personal satisfaction. The bastard had played him for a fool in more ways than one and Charles was consumed with the desire for revenge. If he could be caught in the act of whatever foolishness he was planning, so much the better. All he, Charles, had to do was to listen for the message – *Le bébé s'appelle Beau* – and he could warn von Rheinhardt that something was in the offing.

That night at seven o'clock he went to the small room he used as a study and tuned the wireless there to the BBC. He knew that was the time messages were transmitted – he had listened to them before, fuming at the multitude of coded gibberish which had increased dramatically over the past months. Half France must be resisting, judging by this evidence – including his own brother, which, of course, presented a problem. Charles had no wish to see Christian taken. He must, he thought, ensure that Christian played no part in whatever operation was planned. As for the others – well, they would get what they were asking for.

Without the slightest compunction, Charles began to lay his plans.

Guy was running around the garden pretending to be an aeroplane, arms stretched wide, humming loudly in an effort to imitate the sound of an aero-engine.

Watching him, Kathryn had to bite her tongue to prevent herself from shouting at him to stop. With nerves stretched to breaking point by the days of waiting, it seemed to her that he was announcing to all the world that very soon an aeroplane would play a very important part in his life.

That was nonsense, of course. He knew nothing of what was planned. It was simply a game played by a small boy for whom a fascination with flying was fast replacing his interest in his toy farm. But it jarred on her all the same.

'Kathryn.'

She looked up, startled, to see Paul at her side. He must have followed the path from the house that was obscured by the thick hedges and his shoes had made no sound on the grass.

'You made me jump.'

'Sorry. Listen – I just heard the message on the wireless. If it is repeated tonight that means the drop is on.'

'For tonight.'

'Yes. I've arranged for Albert to be at the gates with his truck at twenty-three-thirty hours. I didn't think it was a very good idea for you to have to trek across the fields with Guy. Will you tell Celestine?'

'Twenty-three-thirty hours – you mean half past eleven?'

'Yes. You must be on time – he won't be able to hang about.'

'We will be.' But her heart was hammering uncomfortably. After all the waiting she could hardly believe the time had arrived; now that it had, she did not know how she could bear to leave him. She looked at him, at every line of the face she loved with a depth she had never believed possible, and felt her heart would burst within her. If only she could tell him about the baby! If only she could be sure it was a part of him she was taking with her! But she could not be sure and she knew she must keep her secret.

Until this moment he had been brisk, efficient, thinking only of the arrangements he had to make. Now, seeing her look, his own heart twisted.

'Kathryn, don't,' he said. 'We will be together again one day, I promise you.'

He gently brushed her hair away from her face, letting his fingers linger on the base of her neck. She raised her hand to place it on top of his and after a moment he turned it over, curling his fingers around hers. Such a little touch, yet it epitomised all the depth of the feeling they shared, as if the whole of their beings was there concentrated in the small area where their fingers brushed, generating warmth and electricity and mutual understanding. She learned towards him, oblivious to everything else, lost in a world where there were only their two selves. His lips found hers and they kissed with all the desperation of two people who knew that their time together was short and that soon they would be denied even the shared secret glance, the clandestine touch.

'I love you,' she whispered, and her breath on his cheek was like a sigh. 'You will take care, won't you? Promise me?'

'I'll be all right.' But they both knew it was a promise he might be unable to keep.

'Mummy?' Guy's voice, questioning, broke the spell. She turned quickly to see him standing there, arms still outstretched like wings, small face perplexed. She felt a rush of guilt. How much had he seen?

'Guy – you startled me!'

For a moment Guy regarded them solemnly, looking from one to the other. He could not understand why they were sitting there like that, so close together. He'd never seen his mother so close to anyone – he was the only one she cuddled. He experienced a flash of something close to jealousy, then, as quickly as it had come, it was gone again, along with his interest in an unfamiliar scenario.

'Look at me, Monsieur Paul!' he shouted. 'I'm an aeroplane!'

'Oh, are you?' Paul's voice sounded level as it always did. Only Kathryn was aware of the slightly rough edge betraying his inner feelings.

'Yes – watch me! Watch me!'

And he was off again, wheeling around the garden in a huge circle.

'He saw us,' Kathryn said.

'It doesn't matter. One day soon he'll have to get used to it, won't he?'

She laughed nervously.

'I suppose so.'

The thought lifted her spirits. For a moment it put her in touch with a future where there would be no more fear, no more pretence – and no more partings. She held on tightly to the illusion, knowing she needed it to give her courage for what lay ahead.

16

WHEN HE JOINED them for dinner that evening Paul's eyes sought Kathryn's and he gave her a tiny, almost imperceptible nod. Nerves fluttered in her stomach as she realised what it meant; the drop was on for tonight.

As they sat down to eat her thoughts were racing, checking over the preparations she had made – a bag packed with the few things she was able to take, Guy's clean shorts and a warm jumper laid out ready to dress him in when the time came to wake him and lead him quietly out of the house. But at least Charles had taken to sleeping in his dressing room – if they still shared a bed the whole plan would have been much more difficult to execute.

She had primed Celestine too, and now, glancing at her sister-in-law, she saw her own nervous tension reflected in Celestine's pale face and edge of palpable excitement.

'Yes – tonight,' she whispered to Celestine as she leaned towards her to reach for the salt, and heard the quick intake of breath.

Was Celestine, too, thinking that this would be the last time they would all sit around this table together for dinner? Kathryn wondered. She doubted it. To Celestine this was merely a temporary escape. One day soon when the Allies had driven the Nazis out of her beloved France she would come home again and everything would be as before. But Kathryn knew that whatever the outcome she would never again return to Savigny as the daughter of the house. That part of her life was over forever and she could not regret it. She had never felt truly at home here even in the days when she had been in love with Charles. Now, despising him, she could feel only immense relief that the charade was almost over. But it was a strange feeling, nevertheless, knowing that a ritual which was now so totally familiar would soon be consigned to the past.

Occasionally as they ate she glanced at Paul, but he was avoiding looking at her. It was Charles whose eyes seemed to be on her whenever she looked in his direction, and the expression on his face frightened her a little. It was almost as if he was gloating, she thought – that hooded glance, that twist to his lips that might have been mistaken for a smile if one failed to notice that it did not reach his eyes. Had Guy said something to him about finding her practically in Paul's arms? Surely he was too young to understand the significance of what he had seen. 'I saw Mummy kissing Monsieur Paul.' It could have been that. But in that case surely Charles would have looked angry, not so . . . triumphant.

She gave herself a small mental shake. No point worrying about it now. If all went well in a few hours' time she would be leaving Savigny – and Charles – forever.

The meal proceeded at its usual leisurely pace. For generations the de Savignys had been taking their time over enjoying the fine food and wines that graced their table and although the fare was now frugal by comparison the habit of lingering over dinner was too much a part of their routine to be altered. Kathryn kept an eye on the elegant cased clock which stood on the mantel shelf as one course followed another, and thought it must be playing tricks on her. Sometimes the hands seemed to have moved scarcely at all, sometimes they had raced with frightening speed through another half-hour. Her throat felt tight with nerves, her mouth so dry it was difficult to swallow. She sipped at her wine, wishing she could drink more and knowing she dared not. She needed to be sharp for what lay ahead, not fuddled from the effects of alcohol however calming it might be to her tight-drawn nerves. Instead she filled her glass from the pitcher of water, fresh from the well in the central courtyard and icy cold in spite of the searing temperature of the day, and saw Charles watching her again.

'Water, Katrine?' he drawled in an amused tone. 'That's not like you.'

Colour flooded her cheeks.

'Why shouldn't I drink water?'

'No reason at all, except that you usually prefer wine.'

'Well tonight I feel like water. Anyone would think I was an alcoholic to hear you talk.'

'Not at all, my dear. But you must admit you took to the French customs very readily.'

The edge was there between them, obvious to everyone around the table. There was a moment's awkward silence, then Charles turned to his brother.

'I feel like a game of chess, Christian. It's been a long while since we played. What do you say we get the board out after dinner?'

Kathryn felt her throat constrict again. Since Paul had told her the drop was on she had not had a chance to talk to Christian and she did not know if he had a part to play in the night's operation. If he did, starting a game of chess with Charles could make things difficult. It was true they did not play often nowadays, but when they did the games were long-drawn-out affairs lasting into the small hours. But Christian nodded, picking up a crumb from the table beside his plate and rolling it between his fingers.

'All right, you're on. Last time we played you beat me, I seem to remember. Tonight it's my turn to trounce you.'

His readiness to accept the challenge reassured her a little and when a moment or two later their eyes met and he gave her an almost imperceptible wink she understood. Christian was not a necessary part of the operation and he was making the most of the opportunity to ensure that Charles was occupied at the relevant time. It would, they both knew, make it much easier for her to slip out unnoticed.

When at last the meal was over and the coffee pot empty, Kathryn rose.

'If you'll excuse me I think I'll have an early night.'

Celestine, too, pushed back her chair.

'Me too. I'm very tired.' Her voice was a trifle unsteady and Kathryn saw the way her hand shook as her fingers pressed on to the polished surface of the table. She hoped no one else had noticed but if they had perhaps they would attribute it to Celestine's condition. Since returning to the château she had been so unlike her former self it was hard to believe that this was the same girl who had left two years earlier for Paris, full of the joy of life and hopes for the future.

Kathryn went to Charles, kissing him lightly on the cheek as she had done every night since their estrangement, a charade of dutiful uxoriousness which fooled no one, with the possible exception of Louise.

'Good night. I'll be asleep by the time you finish your game with Christian, I expect.'

'I'm sure you will,' he said drily. 'I'll sleep in the dressing room so as not to disturb you.'

Another piece of luck! Silently Kathryn thanked the providence that had made him choose this very night to challenge Christian to a game of chess.

As the door closed after them Celestine grabbed her arm in a vice-like grip.

'It's on then?'

'Yes. Be outside the gates at half past eleven and for God's sake don't be late. Albert won't be able to wait. He's taking a risk coming here for us at all.'

'I know. And it's for my benefit, isn't it?'

'Yours – and Guy's too.'

'Don't worry, I'll be there. I feel like going out now, just to be sure.'

'You mustn't do that. Don't do anything to attract attention to yourself. If a patrol was to pass and see you out after curfew . . .' She shuddered at the thought of the consequences.

'I know,' Celestine said again. 'I'm not stupid.'

Her voice was sharp but Kathryn did not take offence at it. The strain they were all under was enough to make anyone snappy.

She left Celestine at her door and followed the passage around to their own wing, looking into Guy's room as she passed. He was sleeping soundly, one arm lying over the covers, the other bunched up to allow his thumb into his mouth. Guy always sucked his thumb when he was tired or sleeping and though Kathryn had tried everything from bitter aloes to a thumbstall tied to his wrist in an effort to break the habit she had been unsuccessful.

'I *like* sucking my thumb,' he would say with perfect reasonableness.

Now, looking at him, her heart filled with love. Please God, let everything go well tonight, for his sake if nothing else, she prayed, and knew that as far as Guy was concerned she certainly was doing the right thing. France under the jackboot was no place for a small child – especially one who was half English. If the situation took a turn for the worse Guy could find himself in as much danger as

Celestine's unborn baby; Kathryn had simply not wanted to acknowledge that fact.

In her own room she checked again that the bag she had prepared contained all the bare essentials they would need, together with the few personal effects she wanted to take with her – a drawing of Guy's, her birth certificate and papers, the earrings her mother had given her for her twenty-first birthday. Her engagement ring and the pieces of jewellery Charles had given her she placed in her jewellery case and left in a prominent position on her dressing table. She did not want them any more and she wanted Charles to know she had left them behind. Then she laid out a dark silk sweater, trousers and jacket, undressed to her underwear and lay down on the bed, pulling a single coverlet over herself. There was nothing left to do now but wait.

At eleven-fifteen Kathryn got up, dressed and crept out of her room, peeping into Charles' dressing room as she passed. Yes, his bed was still empty as she had thought it would be. She had heard Paul come upstairs half an hour earlier, the old floorboards protesting a little beneath his tread, but there had been no telltale sounds of Charles coming to bed. He and Christian must be still engrossed in their game.

The house was dark and quiet with only the occasional creak of a settling timber to disturb the silence. Outside Paul's door she hesitated, longing to go in on the pretext of asking whether everything was going according to plan, knowing that in reality what she wanted was to be in his arms one last time. But she knew she must not. To deviate now from the arrangements was to court trouble.

Guy was sleeping soundly. She knelt down by his bed, shaking him gently.

'Guy – darling, wake up.'

He stirred. She pulled back the covers, easing him into a sitting position in her arms, talking to him softly all the while, soothing him.

'We're going to have an adventure, darling. I want you to be very quiet – not make a sound. I'm going to get you dressed and then we are going to see an aeroplane. You'd like that, wouldn't you?'

'Mummy . . . I'm tired!' His voice was thick with sleep.

'Shh! Not a sound, remember! Hold up your arms now – off with your pyjamas – come on, there's a good boy.'

She pulled the sweater over his head, buttoned his shorts and eased his feet into his sandals. He stood like a stuffed toy, letting her do it, his small hands, balled to fists, pressing against his sleepy eyes.

She glanced at her watch. It had taken much longer than she had expected to rouse him and get him dressed. The hands of her watch which earlier had seemed to be motionless had taken wings.

'Darling, come on, please . . .'

She opened the door cautiously and looked out. The house was still silent. She picked up the bag and taking Guy by the hand led him out of the bedroom and along the passage. He stumbled beside her, still half-asleep, and she wished she could pick him up and carry him, but she did not think she could manage both him and the bag down the back stairs. He was a big boy for his age and the stairs, uneven in places, would be treacherous. Kathryn was taut with nerves. Supposing Charles should finish his game with Christian and come to bed in the next few minutes? She wouldn't run into him this way – he would use the main staircase – but there was always the chance he might look into her room or Guy's and find them gone.

The bolts on the kitchen door had been pulled back; either Paul or Celestine must have already left this way, she guessed. She opened it as quietly as she could and led Guy out into the narrow passageway. The moon was shining brightly but here the walls of the château cast huge sharp shadows and the air was heavy with the scent of honeysuckle. She pulled the door to behind her and took Guy's hand again.

'Come on, darling. Isn't this exciting?' she cajoled him.

A figure emerged from the deep shadow ahead and her heart leaped into her mouth. Then with a rush of relief she recognised Paul. He must have been waiting for her in one of the archways, she realised.

'Paul! You gave me a fright!'

'Sorry. I thought you might need some help with Guy.'

'Monsieur Paul?' Guy said wonderingly.

'Shh! You must be quiet, Guy!'

'We'll cut across the parkland,' Paul said softly. 'With the moon this bright the drive is all too visible from the house. Come on, Guy, you want a piggyback?'

He swung the sleepy child easily on to his shoulders and they set off across the rough grass, talking little, concentrating on keeping in shadow as far as possible until the trees blocked out the windows of the château.

Paul walked fast; by the time they reached the lane Kathryn was breathing heavily.

'I hope Celestine isn't late,' she panted.

'If she is we'll just have to go without her.' Paul's voice had the hard edge to it that she had come to know; Paul the man and Paul the agent were two quite different people, and she loved both of them. But she hoped fervently that Celestine would be on time, for she had no doubt that if she was not Paul would carry out his threat and go without her.

When they turned into the lane, however, Celestine was already there, standing in the shadows.

'Thank God! I thought you would never get here!' she greeted them, her voice shaking with nervous tension. 'I've been here ages!'

'You haven't seen anyone?' Paul asked sharply.

'No, it's all as quiet as the grave . . .' She broke off, biting her lip at the awkward analogy.

Paul set Guy down, sitting him on Kathryn's bag underneath the low wall. He curled into it, holding on to Kathryn's leg for comfort.

'Now, you both know what you have to do, don't you? When the Lysander arrives keep well clear whilst we unload the supplies, but be ready. The minute that's done they'll drop a ladder and you get in as quickly as you can. The pilot won't want to wait a minute longer than absolutely necessary.' He checked his watch. 'Albert should be here at any moment.'

Hardly had he spoken than they heard the roar of an engine, loud in the silence of the night.

'This could be him now. But keep out of sight just in case it's not.'

They drew back into the shadows, Kathryn holding Guy very close. At the gates the van juddered to a stop. It was Albert. Paul leaped forward and opened the rear doors.

'Come on, quick as you can. Lie on the floor in case there's a patrol about.'

They did as he said, tumbling inside and huddling in the dark interior which smelled of cheap fuel and rotting vegetables. Paul climbed into the front beside Albert and they were off, jolting away along the rutted lane.

'This is it, then,' Kathryn said unsteadily.

Neither Celestine nor Guy, wide awake now, but round-eyed with puzzlement and frightened by the tension he sensed in the adults, made any reply.

From the top of the ridge the German patrol, parked with its lights off, had followed the erratic progress of the truck in the valley beneath. Now they watched it turn east, heading deep into the country on the unoccupied side of the line.

'Do we go in now?' one asked.

'No. Our orders are to follow it and liaise with the others. One sprat may lead us to a lot of mackerel.'

The men laughed and the observer reached for his radio telephone. This was going to be good sport – a much more interesting way to spend a night than the usually excruciatingly boring hours between dusk and dawn, the hours of curfew when everything should be quiet – and usually was.

'They are heading your way,' he said into the telephone. 'You should see them any minute now. But don't do anything – just follow at a discreet distance. We want to know where they are going.'

'*Ja*, I know,' came the reply. '*Ja* – I have them now.'

Unaware of being watched and followed, Albert continued to drive towards the field where the Lysander was to land.

The landing site was the same one Paul had used on the night he had been shot, and as Albert pulled into the gateway and cut his engine and lights Paul experienced a moment's *déjà vu* as he saw the other members of the reception party, huddled together smoking and eating their supper of bread and cold sausage just as they had that night. Paul picked up Guy, carrying him across the rough ground towards the field. The men's faces expressed surprise as they recognised Celestine, but they knew better than to make any comment.

'We're all right now you're here then, my friend,' one of them said to Paul, referring to the fact that following a few unfortunate experiences the Lysander and Hudson squadrons had stipulated that they would only fly in when the operation was under the direction of a properly trained agent.

In spite of her nervousness Kathryn felt a glow of pride as she watched Paul take control, checking wind direction and working out the positions of the lights that would be used to make the touchdown and turning points for the aircraft. Then, once again, there was nothing to do but wait.

'They will come, won't they?' she whispered to Paul.

'I certainly hope so!'

But they both knew it was possible they might not; a wrong heading, a change in wind direction which would throw the Lysander off course, the flak fields over the French coast – there were any number of hazards which might jeopardise the success of the operation. And if that happened – what then? There would be nothing for it but to go back to the château, back to Charles – who might, even now, have realised they were missing – and try to make certain Guy said nothing about his midnight adventure, make fresh plans, go through all this again . . . She didn't think she could stand it.

The hum of an aero-engine suddenly impinged on the silence. Kathryn turned, straining her eyes in the direction of the sound, and saw it come into view like a great bird swooping in above the tops of the trees.

She turned to Paul, torn between relief that the aeroplane was here and the sudden bleak realisation that the moment of parting was very close. She longed to touch him and feel the reassurance of his arms around her one last time but Paul had moved away, resuming the professional role that made him a stranger to her.

With his pocket torch he signalled in Morse to the pilot, and the moment the pilot returned the signal the three landing lights flared into life. The pilot overflew the field, checking it out, and turned downwind. To Kathryn it seemed he was already very low and she held tight to Guy, who was now practically jumping up and down with excitement.

'You see – I told you we were going to see an aeroplane,' she said to him, but her voice was all but drowned out by the noise of the engine as the Lysander turned and came in, dropping fast now that its flaps were fully extended. It touched down, bumping a little on the rough ground and braking gently at first, then harder as the second lamp passed beneath its port wing and the border of trees came rushing up to meet it. It turned and taxied slowly back to the point of touchdown.

The field was a hive of activity now, the reception committee running to unload the plane. Kathryn saw Paul climb on to the undercarriage housing to speak to the pilot and when several cartons had been passed down to the ground he waved to her.

'Time to go.'

They ran across the field, Kathryn holding tight to Guy's hand. Paul jumped down and she ran to him, not caring any more who saw, throwing herself into his arms.

He held her for a moment, kissing her, and in that brief embrace it seemed to her that time stood still.

'Take care, my darling.'

'And you. I love you, Kathryn.'

'And I love you . . .'

Momentarily engrossed in their snatched goodbyes, neither saw the lights approaching down the lane and the sound of the vehicles was drowned out by the racing aircraft engines.

It was Albert's shout which alerted them. They jerked apart. And in that same moment, it seemed to Kathryn, all hell broke loose.

Afterwards she remembered only a scene of total chaos, a nightmare come to life which she would relive over and over again, fragmented pictures of vehicles roaring into the field and men running, of shouts and screams and gunfire. Some of the reception committee dashed for the shelter of the trees – they knew they stood no chance of making a fight of it with the Boche arriving in such strength. But Paul did not run. He was there beside her, throwing Guy into the Lysander to Celestine's waiting arms.

'Get in!' he shouted to her, pushing her bodily up the little ladder.

'You come too . . .'

'Don't be stupid . . . get in! Close the hatch!'

'Paul!' She was almost hysterical. 'For God's sake, Paul!'

It was Celestine who restrained her, Celestine who dragged her into the Lysander and pulled up the ladder. Then the hatch was closed, the engines roaring as the pilot applied full power and the plane began to move forward over the rough ground.

'Paul! My God – Paul!'

She could hear shot peppering the fuselage of the aircraft but she no longer cared about her own situation. All she could think of was that Paul was still out there in the moonlit field and the Germans had come. He couldn't escape. There was no way . . .

Guy was crying. Somewhere on the periphery of her mind she could hear him and she reached out for him blindly, holding him tight to her while she shook and sobbed. The wheels left the ground, somehow, miraculously, they were airborne, climbing away, and she knew with sick certainty that when the plane was out of range the Boche would turn their guns on Paul. If they had not already done so. And if they didn't . . .

From a cold place somewhere deep inside her she seemed to hear his voice speaking to her in what seemed now to have been another lifetime.

'They'll never take me alive.'

The memory cut through her hysteria and froze her sobs, turning the whole of her body into a solid block of ice through which breath had to be forced and blood could scarcely flow. She could not move, could not think, but thought was unnecessary. Knowing was enough – knowing indisputably, with every fibre of her being, that this could end in one way only.

Maybe at this very moment Paul was dying or already dead. She would never see him again, this man whom she now knew she loved more than life. It was over.

With an instinctive movement she pulled Guy close so that her face was buried in the soft soap-scented cap of his hair. Her little boy – her son – somehow she had to be strong for him and for the unborn child she was carrying within her.

They were all that was left to her now.

17

Bristol, 1971

'SO,' KATHRYN SAID, looking steadily at Guy, 'now you know. In the early part of the war, at least, your father and grandfather were collaborators. They positively encouraged von Rheinhardt and called him their friend. That much, at least, is bound to come out if the man you have found living in the Caribbean is von Rheinhardt and if you bring him to justice.'

She was standing now beside the fireplace, leaning back against the stone ledge that ran from the overmantel to the wall. Whilst she had talked she had prowled around the small comfortably furnished living room as if she could not bear to be still; now only the fact that she fiddled incessantly with the bracelets that hung around her wrist beneath the sleeve of her cream sweater gave any indication of the agitation she had experienced reliving the events that had turned her world upside down more than a quarter of a century ago.

For long minutes Guy was silent, sitting in the fireside chair, one leg crossed over the other, nursing his chin in his hand whilst his elbow rested on his knee. Because his head was bent forward his face was in shadow and Kathryn could not read his expression. But she knew her revelations had been a shock to him – how could they possibly have been anything else, raised, as he had been, on stories of his family's heroism? And she still had not told him all of it. The part about his father's treachery she had kept back. She herself had learned of it only after the war was over from a broken Guillaume, who could no longer bear alone the guilty knowledge of what his son had confessed to him. 'It was my doing, Papa,' Charles had told Guillaume. 'I didn't know Kathryn and Guy would be there, of course, but that's no excuse. I was mad with jealousy and I was responsible for the deaths and torture of men who had only the good of France in mind.' He had done his best to make up for it, of course. When the Communists had carried out their unsuccessful attempt on the life of Heydrich, the SS officer, and hostages had been taken, Charles had offered himself in place of one of them. It had been a brave gesture but she did not want Guy to know the truth of it – that it had been Charles' way of ending his life because he could no longer live with the terrible guilt of what he had done. She hoped with all her heart that what she had told Guy would be enough to make him forget his plans to rake up the past. Then there would never be any need for him to find out the truth about his father.

She looked at him, sitting there assimilating all she had said, and felt her heart swell with love for him just as it had swelled that long-ago night when she had looked into the bedroom at the small sleeping figure with a thumb pressed into his mouth. Guy was a grown man now but that did not mean the maternal instinct was any the less strong. She could still sense the vulnerability beneath the hard masculine exterior, all the more poignant because of it, and she still wanted to protect him. It was different now, of course, and in a strange way she felt even more helpless than she had done all those years ago when all she had wanted was to keep him safe from harm. She had been afraid then of circumstances beyond her control, but one could at least manipulate a child into the position which afforded the best protection. It wasn't possible to do that when the child was grown. They went their own way – that was as it should be and she had learned to accept it. Throughout his first forays into the adult world, his first motorcycle, the first times away from home, the first broken heart, she had trained herself to stand back on the sidelines. She had offered advice but never tried to enforce her will, for she felt her role now was reduced to a loving, supportive one, counselling, standing back, and if necessary comforting and being there to pick up the pieces. But it didn't make it any the easier, didn't mean that her heart did not bleed for him or that she felt for him any the less acutely. One still wanted everything to be right for one's children, no matter how old they might be. It would be the same, she suspected, if she lived to be a hundred.

Eventually Guy looked up at her, still massaging his jaw with long fingers the exact same shape Charles' had been.

'So – early in the war they collaborated,' he said. 'It's nothing to be proud of, I agree, but I don't see it's such a big problem as you are making it out to be. They thought it was for the best. They were mistaken, of course, but knowing what Savigny means to them I can almost understand it. And it wasn't so long after that that my father died a hero's death. When the chips were down, when the hostages were taken and shot as a reprisal for the attempt on Heydrich's life, my father offered himself in place of one of them. You can't get braver than that.'

'No,' she agreed. 'You can't.'

'So why should I or anyone else be ashamed of what went before? It's not very nice, I admit, to think of them entertaining Nazis in the family home but I'd already guessed that much from the photographs I found in Grandpapa's box, and quite honestly I think my father more than made up for that by giving his life in exchange for the life of one of the hostages.'

Kathryn ran a hand through her hair, the bangles jangling cold against her hot face. It was as she had feared, Guy wasn't convinced by half a story. Unless she told him the rest he would refuse to see it any differently. And telling him the rest was not something she could bring herself to do, though she was very much afraid that it would all come out if von Rheinhardt was brought to trial.

'Uncle Christian was a hero, too,' Guy went on. 'He went on working for the Resistance until he was captured and executed. No, what has really shocked me is that you betrayed my father with the British agent – Paul Curtis, or whatever his real name was. How could you do it, Mum? I'd never have believed it of you.'

His eyes met Kathryn's in a cold blue stare and she experienced a wash of horror. He wasn't seeing things from her point of view at all but from his father's. She should have known, of course, that he would. His father had been a hero-figure to him for too long, canonised almost by his heroic death, and she had encouraged that, feeling that Guy needed it and driven also, perhaps, by a guilt she had been unwilling to acknowledge. She had loved Paul so much that it had never seemed sordid or wrong to her – on the surface anyway. But that wasn't the way it looked to Guy. To him it was simply a betrayal of the father he idolised. And perhaps, deep down, she felt it too – that she had been guilty of a disloyalty too deep to contemplate and had, in her own way, been as responsible for what had happened as Charles had been.

'You never saw him again, I take it?' he said. His voice was cold; she did not think she could ever recollect having heard him use this tone with her before.

'I never saw him again,' she agreed. 'He died the night we escaped to England.' She hesitated. 'You should thank him for that, at least, Guy. If he had run with the others he would have stood a chance. As it was he stayed by the plane, shooting at the Germans to keep them back until we were able to take off.'

'We shouldn't have been there at all,' Guy said harshly. 'We shouldn't have deserted Papa. Our place was with him, at the château.'

'You were a little boy, Guy. I was afraid for your safety. And Celestine was desperate. The Nazis might have taken her if she had stayed. They would certainly have taken her baby. Your cousin Lise is half Jewish – the Nazis would have taken them away to the death camps when they realised it.'

'And your baby?' Guy asked in the same cold, hard voice. 'What happened to that? Do I have another brother or sister somewhere I know nothing about?'

'Of course not!' Kathryn flared. 'I lost my baby that night.'

She closed her eyes momentarily, reliving it. She had been so dazed with shock she had not even really been aware of the flak as they passed over the French coast or the desperate ducking and weaving and low flying the pilot had engaged in to avoid it, much less the first warm trickle of blood that had heralded a miscarriage. Celestine had told her afterwards of the hazards of that flight; she had crouched in the Lysander holding Guy tightly in her arms, thinking that the dull ache in the pit of her stomach was the beginnings of grief and not noticing the hot wetness between her legs until she was soaked with it. They had taken her to hospital in Tangmere when the Lysander landed and they found the floor awash with blood, but it was too late. She had lost the baby and scarcely even cried for it. All her tears were for Paul and for a future in which she would never see him again. It was only much later that she started to grieve for the little life snuffed out before it had begun, but even then she had not really known what to think about it. If she could have been sure it was Paul's child she would have welcomed it, cherished it as a part of him left to her. But she was not sure and she did not think she could have borne to live with a constant reminder of the night Charles had raped her.

'Well that's something, I suppose.' Guy stood up. 'I think I need a drink. Can I help myself?'

'Of course you can. This is your home!' she said defensively.

He glanced at her. Is it? that look seemed to say. I'm not sure of anything any more. But he said nothing, simply crossed to the sideboard and took out the bottle, pouring himself a generous measure and tossing it back.

'You can get me one too,' she said.

He poured some whisky into a glass and passed it to her. She sipped it, neat, feeling the liquor burn her throat and stomach and spread a little warmth through her veins.

He was refilling his own glass.

'Don't have too much, Guy. Remember you have to drive.'

He did not answer, carrying the glass over to the window and looking out at the winter-bare garden.

'What are you going to do?' she asked after a moment.

'What am I going to do?' He repeated it almost reflectively. 'I'm still going to the Caribbean, of course. I still want the man who murdered my father and I still want the family heirlooms he stole back where they belong. He took over the château for his headquarters soon after all this happened, I suppose.'

'Yes. But you already knew that. He ordered the family to move into the *gîte* where the attempt was made on Heydrich's life and moved his own staff into the château. He'd always coveted it – you could see it in his eyes – and I think it was a double pleasure for him, knowing the de Savignys were having to live in the house that had seen the attack that cost your father his life. Heydrich, understandably, didn't want to use it any more and it satisfied von Rheinhardt to know that every time they looked at the bullet holes in the walls they would be reminded of the folly of trying to kill a Nazi general.'

'The cruel bastard.' Guy set his glass down on the table with a thud. 'If anything, I want him more than ever.'

'What he did was unforgivable,' Kathryn said. 'But I still wish you'd let the past lie.'

'I'm sure you do.' Guy's voice was hard, full of hidden meaning. She looked at him questioningly and he went on: 'Are you sure you've been honest with me, Mum? Are you sure the reason you don't want any of this to come out isn't because you don't want anyone to know about your indiscretion?'

'Guy!' She was shocked now. 'How could you think such a thing?'

'I'm sorry, but that's the way it looks to me. In any case, nothing you've told me changes the way I feel. I hate the Nazis and I hate von Rheinhardt in particular. I'd bring every last one of them to justice if I could. I can't do that but I can go after this one.'

'I hate them too, Guy,' she said. 'I have more reason for hating them than you know.'

His eyes narrowed.

'What do you mean?'

She shook her head. It was something else she had decided a long while ago never to tell him – or anyone. Like so much else it was her closely guarded secret. She had her reasons and though those reasons had rebounded on her now it made no difference.

'I just think that sometimes it is best to leave the past where it belongs,' she said lamely.

'That is where we shall have to agree to differ,' Guy said. 'Look, Mum, I suggest we forget all about this now and try to enjoy the rest of the holiday. It's Christmas Day, for goodness' sake.'

'Is it?' Kathryn glanced at the clock, the hands of which now showed ten past midnight. Christmas Day had arrived whilst they were talking and she had not even noticed it!

She opened her arms to him pleadingly.

'Happy Christmas, darling.'

'Happy Christmas.'

But there was something less than his usual warmth in his embrace and Kathryn's heart sank. She had tried her best and failed. Now there was a barrier between them which might never be broken down.

I have lost him, Kathryn thought wretchedly. I have lost him as surely as I lost Paul, and to no avail.

Suddenly she wanted to weep.

Guy left on Boxing Day afternoon. The holiday had been a less than comfortable one and now his thoughts raced as he drove home towards Bristol.

He had known, of course, that things were not right between his mother and his French family but, fool that he was, he had never guessed the real reason. No wonder she didn't ever want to talk about the war, no wonder she had tried to stop him exhuming the past.

He should have guessed, of course. The small clues had been there, half buried in his childhood memories, impressions, perhaps, more than clear pictures, but none the less telling now that he came to think about them.

Was she being entirely truthful, he wondered, when she said she had never seen the man he had known as Monsieur Paul after the night they had flown out of France? It seemed reasonable to suppose that he had indeed been killed if things had happened the way she had told it. And yet . . .

She had been absent for a long time during his early childhood, he remembered. For several years he had lived with his English grandparents whilst she was, supposedly, working for the Ministry of Defence in the wilds of Scotland. Now he found himself doubting even that. If she could have concealed her affair from him all these years could she also have concealed something else? He had the unmistakable feeling that there was something she was not telling him. Could it be that Paul had actually escaped too and she had . . . gone off with him? As recently as two days ago he would never have believed such a thing of his mother, now he was no longer sure of anything. She had become an enigma to him and he realised that in spite of having lived with her for so many years he really did not know her at all.

And there was something else, too, tugging at the edges of his memory – something that was, for the moment, eluding him.

Still, he wasn't going to worry about that now. Better to give his full attention to trying to find out once and for all if the German on the Caribbean island was, in fact, von Rheinhardt, and if it was, to bring him to justice and recover his family's stolen treasures.

He owed it to his father's memory. Kathryn might have been unfaithful to Charles; Guy at least was going to ensure that he did not let him down.

He pressed his foot down hard on the accelerator again and headed for Bristol.

PART TWO
Retribution

18

New York, 1971

THE LETTER BEARING the exotic Caribbean island stamp was the first one Lilli Brandt noticed when she picked up her mail, and immediately she experienced a pang of homesickness.

She had been in New York for almost four years now, but her longing for the island paradise where she had been born and raised was as sharp as ever, particularly on days like this one when the streets of Manhattan were cold and windswept and the thick blanket of grey cloud that hid the tops of the skyscrapers threatened snow. Simply holding the envelope in her hands conjured up a vision of palm-fringed beaches and sea as blue as sapphires, the balmy warmth of the sun on bare skin and the scent of nutmeg and frangipani, and made her ache with longing. That her departure for New York had been in a haze of emotional pain made no difference, nor the fact that as she had looked down through the window of the little twin-engined plane at the speck of land in that sapphire-blue sea growing smaller and smaller she had promised herself that she would never go back. If anything it made it worse, for the pain was superimposed on memories of a childhood idyll and beneath it the nostaligia for those lost years of innocence ached and throbbed all the more poignantly.

Madrepora, my island paradise, thought Lilli, shivering in the biting cold of a New York winter. Madrepora, where the shutters at the window are to keep out the blazing sun, not the icy wind. Madrepora, where I lay on the beach with the gentle surf breaking over my sun-warmed limbs, where I snorkeled in water so clear I could see right down to the stony coral that gave the island its name. Madrepora in the days when my father was my hero, indestructible, and master of all he surveyed, and my mother was a beautiful memory, a hybrid of saint and movie star, a beautiful dark-skinned princess with scarlet lips and nails, enveloped in a haunting perfume as exotic as the islands, who had died, as all the best heroines should, before the years could fade her beauty and humble her with the ordinariness of old age. Madrepora in those blissful days before my father married Ingrid, the days when it seemed childhood would never end. Before I was forced, so brutally fast, to grow up. Before Jorge. Yes, most of all, before Jorge.

The memory of him hurt her even more than the wave of homesickness for the island had done and impatiently Lilli pushed it away. She wouldn't think of him. She dared not. He had lied to her, deceived her, broken her heart. Worse, he had sullied every aspect of everything she had loved. No – that was not quite true. The imperfections had been there all the time – Jorge had merely opened her eyes to them. He had been the catalyst. She couldn't forgive him – she couldn't forgive any of them – and yet she loved them still. That was her cross, weighing heavily upon her slim shoulders. That was what made it so hard to bear.

Lilli took off her coat, a thick warm duffel in ochre wool, and hung it carefully in the closet. Her reflection in the mirrored door met her head-on, throwing back the image of a tall slender girl with thick dark hair tumbling over the polo-neck of a black cashmere sweater and eyes of so dark a brown they were almost black. Lilli had inherited her looks from her Venezuelan mother; there was about her nothing of the fairness of her Aryan father. She had long legs and a slim, almost boyish figure that would have looked totally at home on the thoroughbred horses her mother's family had bred on their sweeping estate in the Andes. She had all their grace coupled with their toughness and their air of compelling mystique. Even in cosmopolitan New York her exotic beauty was remarkable and she was shrewd enough to realise that it was an asset in her job as a PR girl for a small publishing house. Those who met her did not forget her easily and her charm and good looks opened doors which might otherwise have remained closed.

In the tiny kitchen of her apartment Lilli turned up the central heating and poured herself a glass of wine. It would have been sensible, perhaps, to make a pot of scalding coffee, but Lilli enjoyed the ritual of a glass of Chablis at the end of a working day.

She sipped it appreciatively, topped up the glass and carried it over to the peninsula counter, sliding herself up easily into a tall high-backed stool.

The letter with the Caribbean postage stamp lay on the counter where she had put it down. The writing on the envelope, round and childish, was instantly recognisable.

Josie, her lifelong – if, in her father's eyes at least, totally unsuitable – friend. Josie, whose mother had been one of the maids at her father's villa, had become to Lilli the sister she never had. No matter that at times her father had put his foot down and forbidden them to play together, they had found ways. No matter that Lilli was spoiled and petted and wanted for nothing whilst Josie's family was unashamedly poor. The bond had been forged between them and had never been broken. Lilli had been sent away to be educated in Venezuela whilst Josie had attended the little island school which was run for the benefit of the local children, but whenever Lilli returned home they had picked up their friendship exactly where it had been left off.

Josie was married now, to one of the gardeners on Lilli's father's estate, and she had a baby son – born not on Madrepora but on St Vincent, since Josie, like all the locals, had been sent away from the island for her confinement. Lilli's father did not want the complication of native-born Madreporans staking claims of birthright to his island if such a thing could be avoided. But though Lilli was no longer living on Madrepora Josie had written to ask her to be godmother, and though she knew her father would be furious Lilli had been delighted to agree, making her vows by proxy.

The two girls corresponded regularly if a little infrequently and Josie's letters were always full of news of her family, of little Winston's progress, and, in her last letter a few months ago, the announcement that she was pregnant again. But she rarely mentioned Lilli's father or Ingrid, whom she knew Lilli disliked, and she never mentioned Jorge.

Lilli tore open the envelope and extracted the two sheets of paper covered in Josie's meticulous childlike hand. She sipped her wine as she perused details of Winston's latest mischief, Josie's advancing pregnancy and the fact that Abel, her husband, had been promoted to chief groundsman in charge of the island's one and only hotel as well as general estate duties. As she read, Lilli's feeling of homesickness deepened and she saw again in her mind's eye the manicured lawns, the flowering shrubs, neatly pruned yet riotous with colour, and the tennis courts rolled to the smooth emerald velvet of a bowling green.

A small wistful smile lifted the corners of her mouth as she remembered the afternoons when she and Josie had gone to the hotel and hidden in the shrubs which surrounded the large open-air swimming pool, spying on the guests as they exposed their pale flabby bodies to the sun on the loungers beside the pool or executed flat belly-flop dives into the azure water, and giggling together at the men's ineptitude. The guests had always been a source of amusement to the girls. They were the very epitome of middle-aged sobriety, talking to one another in German, a language Lilli did not understand although it was her father's native tongue, and almost paranoid about their privacy. Lilli had known that her father would be furious if he knew she and Josie were spying on them, though the hotel itself was not forbidden to her as certain parts of the island were. It was simply that he would have disapproved of her having fun at their expense and encouraging Josie to do the same – Josie, the local, who should have known her place.

Now Abel, Josie's husband, was tending those very shrubs, supervising the cleaning of that very pool, while the same guests, or some very like them, allowed their fair-skinned bodies to turn salmon pink under the hot Madrepora sun like pigs roasting on a spit. The irony of it made Lilli smile again and she read on, hungry for the words that evoked so vividly her memories of the island.

A few paragraphs on, however, and the tone of the letter changed. Even before she read what Josie had to say Lilli sensed it, as if her friend had become awkward suddenly, wondering how to proceed, and her anxiety had transferred itself to the page in a way that was more mystic, more nebulous, than mere stilted words.

'There is something, Lilli, which I think you ought to know. Your father has not been at all well. He has become very thin, very drawn, most unlike himself, and the maids at the villa say he needs to rest a lot. I did not mention it before because I did not want to worry you, but a week or so ago he flew to the mainland and Abel heard he was going to a hospital for tests. When he returned he looked worse than ever. I tried to find out what is wrong – not easy, your father is a very private man. But Abel's brother, Noah, who has been working at the villa, thinks the doctor your father went to see is a cancer specialist. He may have been in touch with you himself, of course, but knowing the situation I somehow doubt it. Besides, your father hates to be ill, doesn't he? Anyway, I thought you should know.'

Her serious news imparted, Josie returned with obvious relief to other lighter topics, but Lilli scarcely bothered to read them.

The cold of the early evening seemed to have got right inside her suddenly, chill fingers touching her spine and sending shivers of dread through her veins to dispel the initial reaction of utter disbelief.

Her father ill – perhaps very ill – he couldn't be! It was unimaginable. In all her life Lilli did not think she could ever remember him having so much as a headache. He had, to her, epitomised power and strength. As a child she had been a little afraid of him, respectful of his sudden changes of mood and the flashes of temper that erupted if she misbehaved or displeased him, always in awe of his indisputable air of authority. Even later, when she had discovered that he had not been as much in control of everything in his life as she had believed, he had still remained a towering personality, flawed a little, perhaps, but still a force to be reckoned with. She had seen him grow older, watched his fair hair turn white, seen the lines etch themselves more deeply on his face and the veins become more prominent in his hands, but it simply never occurred to her that the years would take their toll on his body as on everyone else's. Time, it had seemed to her, had passed her father by. He was still tall and straight, his voice still firm and unwavering, his will as indomitable as ever. Sickness and death were misfortunes that befell other mere mortals, weaknesses with which he would have no dealing. He defied them, and it had seemed to her that he would go on defying them to time immemorial.

Now, with a sense of utter shock, it came home to her that he was not, after all, immune.

She reread Josie's letter, her sense of foreboding growing. However close their friendship, Josie knew better than to interfere in family matters. She would never have taken the step of breaking news such as this unless she thought it absolutely necessary, especially when what she actually knew was little more than supposition and hearsay, and the very unsensational matter-of-factness of her words made them all the more chillingly convincing.

He should have let me know! Lilli thought, a terrible sense of isolation overwhelming her. And if he wouldn't do it, for all the reasons Josie mentioned, then Ingrid should have. They should have told me! I am his daughter, for God's sake! I have a right to know!

She sat for a few moments longer, turning the glass between her hands, steeling herself to do what she knew she had to do – speak to them herself and find out the truth. Then she got up, crossed to the telephone and called the operator.

'I want an international call, please, to Madrepora in the Windward Islands.' Her throat felt tight as she gave the number, once so familiar, but now rusty on her tongue, lost beneath the layers of other, more recently used numbers – her New York friends, her business acquaintances.

'All lines are busy at the moment. I'll call you back.'

The unconcerned implacability of the operator increased her feeling of helplessness. How long would it be before she was able to get through? But there was nothing she could do about it. She replaced the receiver, went to get herself another glass of wine, then changed her mind. She could do with something stronger. It was much too early, of course, but still – tough! She unstoppered the gin bottle, poured a good measure into a fresh glass and topped it up with tonic water. Then she gulped at it like a lost traveller at a St Bernard's life-saving brandy flask.

The telephone, when it began to ring, made her start. Perhaps it wasn't the call to Madrepora, she told herself. Perhaps it was one of her friends suggesting a movie or a drink.

But it was the call to Madrepora.

'Connecting you now,' the operator told her, and she heard the whistles and the hollow echoings, which reminded her oddly of the surf on the beach, and then, as if from a long way off, the ringing of the bell.

After a few moments it was answered by one of the maids – Lilli knew it must be one of the maids because she recognised the slightly singsong patois.

254

'I'd like to speak to Herr Brandt,' she said.

'Who is calling, please?'

'It's his daughter.'

'Lilli! Miss Lilli – is that really you?'

'Patsy?'

'Yes, Miss Lilli, it's me. Oh, it's good to hear your voice!'

'And yours, Patsy.'

Memories, rushing in; a smiling black face, a broad bosom in which Lilli used to bury her face – Patsy, her nurse, closer to her in many ways than her own mother had ever been. When Magdalene had died it had been Patsy who had picked Lilli up and cleaned her grazed knees when she fell down, Patsy who had braided her hair, Patsy who had tucked her up in bed at night, crooning to her in a low tuneless voice. Even before Magdalene had died Patsy had been the one Lilli could run to, dishevelled and crying, knowing that unlike her mother there would be no protests about her crumpling her dress or planting sticky kisses on her cheek. Dear, dear Patsy. But Lilli knew she could not spend time in idle chatter however much she wanted to. The lines to Madrepora were not very reliable. This one could break up at any minute and it was important she speak to her father.

'Is Daddy there?'

'He's here, Miss Lilli, but I'm not sure . . . He's been ill, you know. I think he may be resting.'

'Frau Brandt then?' Lilli suggested.

'Oh yes, speak to Frau Brandt, Miss Lilli.' The relief in Patsy's voice was obvious. 'I'll fetch her. Oh, I'm so glad . . .'

Lilli took another gulp of gin as she waited. She felt a little calmer now – hearing Patsy's voice had done that.

She heard voices, too indistinct to be able to make out what they were saying, then what sounded like footsteps on the tiled floor of the villa. And then, unusually clearly, as if she were in the next room instead of half the length of a continent away, Ingrid's voice.

'Lilli.'

Just the sound of it conjured up a picture of her. In imagination Lilli saw her standing there, holding the receiver in her smooth beringed hand, stroking it lightly with nails varnished to a pale pearly pink. Ingrid was fifty-six years old but she looked ten years younger, her pampered plumpness denying the wrinkles the chance to deepen and giving her a statuesque poise. Ingrid never allowed her fair skin to be exposed to the hot Caribbean sun but she glowed with an aura of health and sophistication, dressing with a flamboyance that was striking but never tarty. She was charming and well bred and Lilli did not think she could ever remember having heard her voice raised in anger. But she had long believed that Ingrid was a schemer and that the surface charm, projected with such apparent sincerity, hid a single-minded and selfish nature. Lilli had endured Ingrid because she believed Ingrid was good for Otto – he had had too many lonely years since Magdalene's death and too much pain – but she did not like her.

'Ingrid,' she said. 'I had a letter from Josie.'

There was a small pause – a lag on the line, or Ingrid gathering herself together? Then Ingrid said: 'I see.'

She wasn't going to make this easy, Lilli realised.

'She tells me Daddy is ill. Is it true?'

Another pause. Then: 'Yes, it's true,' Ingrid said.

'How ill?'

'Very. He may have only months to live.'

Lilli's blood turned to ice. From the moment she had read Josie's letter she had feared the worst, but having it confirmed so baldly was still a shock.

'Why didn't you let me know?' she demanded. 'If he's so ill . . . if he's going to die . . . You should have told me!'

'He didn't want you to know,' Ingrid said. 'You know your father – he despises weakness in himself as in others. He prefers to believe he is going to get well.'

'But he's not?'

'Miracles can happen, I suppose. But to be honest, I don't think so.'

'So what is it?' Lilli asked, willing herself not to break down in tears. 'What's wrong with him? Josie mentioned a cancer specialist.'

'You can't keep anything private here, can you?' Ingrid said with a touch of bitterness. 'Yes, it is cancer, I'm afraid.'

'But isn't there something that can be done? Drugs . . . an operation?'

'The specialist was willing to attempt it, yes. But he thought things had gone too far. And in any case your father won't contemplate an operation.'

'But surely – if there's a chance . . .'

'You know how he is about hospitals. He hates them. He insists on fighting this his own way.'

'What good will that do?' Lilli burst out. 'Oh, I know Daddy thinks he can do anything, but still . . .'

'I've tried to talk to him, Lilli, but he won't listen, any more than he would listen when I told him I thought we should get in touch with you. No, I am afraid we must resign ourselves to the fact that your father may have no more than six months at the outside to live.'

'Dear God,' Lilli said. She could hear the line beginning to break up and made up her mind. Jorge, infidelity, betrayal, the secrets of the past and the awkwardnesses of the present all paled into insignificance in the face of this one devastating fact. Her father was dying. Nothing else mattered.

'Ingrid,' she said, her voice steady now with resolve. 'Ingrid . . . I'm coming home.'

Ingrid Brandt replaced the receiver and stood for a moment with her hand still resting on it. Her clear blue eyes had narrowed slightly – the closest she ever came to frowning – and a pulse fluttered faintly at the base of her throat, the physical reflex of the tightness in her stomach that had gripped her the moment Patsy had come to tell her that Lilli was on the telephone.

Lilli always affected her this way. Useless to tell herself that Lilli was just a young girl – or had been when she left Madrepora – and that she was Otto's daughter and had every right to be at the centre of his life. Lilli was not only Otto's daughter, she was also Magdalene's. She was the living image of her mother and she reminded Ingrid too sharply of all the things she preferred to forget. In Lilli's presence all the old hurts resurfaced, robbing Ingrid of her carefully nurtured self-possession and making her as vulnerable as the heartsick young woman she had once been. Seven years of marriage to Otto, seven years of living a life of luxury with him when he had given her everything she could wish for, had done nothing to change that, and now that she was on the point of losing him again she knew nothing ever would.

Ingrid released her grip on the telephone and raised a hand to smooth her thick fair hair back into the sleek chignon at the nape of her neck. Not a strand had escaped, except the tendrils she intended to be there, softening the outline of her face, but it was an instinctive gesture of self-protection to reassure herself that on the surface, at least, she was as poised and perfectly turned-out as ever. Then she walked through the villa, through the soft patches of light and shade thrown by the half-drawn shutters, and into the salon.

Otto was on the veranda, sitting propped up in a recliner with a long cool drink and the day's newspapers on a rattan table within easy reach beside him. Ill as he was he had refused to take to his bed. Each day Basil, the local who had served him faithfully for twenty years, bathed and dressed him and settled him here where he could look out over the gardens, shaded from the heat of the sun by the hibiscus-entwined trellis; each night he put his master to bed and wondered sadly, but with the implacable resignation that is part of the Caribbean islanders' character, whether he would ever leave it again.

As Ingrid approached Otto turned his head towards her, but she could see that even such a small movement required a good deal of effort on his part and her heart twisted with pain for him – and for herself, because it brought into sharper focus the sickening knowledge that she was soon going to lose him.

'Who was on the telephone?' he asked. His voice was still surprisingly vibrant, as if he concentrated all his scant reserves of energy into it, determined that even if his body was betraying him, at least he should not sound like a sick old man.

She came around and sat in the rattan chair beside him, pouring herself a glass of the iced lemon drink spiced with cognac which stood on the table.

'It was Lilli.'

'Lilli!' A spark of light came into the blue eyes, dulled now from too many hours of coping with too much pain. 'You should have called me!'

'The line was breaking up. You'd never have got to the telephone in time.'

'God in heaven – I'm not dead yet! I could have tried!'

'It's all right, Otto.' She leaned forward, placing a hand on his arm, telling herself she did it to calm him but knowing deep down it was also a proprietorial gesture to reassure herself that he belonged to her now. 'You'll be able to talk to her soon, face to face. She's coming home.'

Beneath her fingers the sinews of his arm tensed and he shifted himself fractionally in the lounger as if to rise and physically intervene.

'She can't do that! Why didn't you stop her?'

'How could I? She's hundreds of miles away. She said she was coming home and then the line went dead. She's heard you are ill, Otto. She wants to see you. It's only natural.'

'How did she find out? You didn't let her know, did you? I told you not to!'

'She'd had a letter from that friend of hers, that local girl — what's her name?'

'Josie. Dammit — are they still in touch?'

'Obviously. Don't upset yourself, my darling. It will be all right, I'm sure. Lilli has a whole new life now. That business with Jorge was over a long time ago.'

Otto's hands, lying in his lap, balled into fists.

'It's never over with Jorge. Never! He's not the sort to let anything go when he thinks of it as his, whether he wants it or not.'

The pain and anger was there in his face, superimposed upon the lines of that other, physical, pain. It tore at Ingrid, resurrecting her own insecurity.

'Well, there's nothing you or I can do to stop her now,' she said, resorting to the brisk yet placid approach that was her stock-in-trade. 'She's coming home and that's all there is to it.'

He was silent for a moment while the conflicting emotions fought within his disease-racked body. In spite of everything he did very much want to see Lilli again. She was his daughter, his little girl, and she came to him sometimes when he lay sleepless in the long reaches of the night because he refused, whenever possible, to take the drugs that had been prescribed for him. He saw her then as the child she had once been, daughter of his beloved Magdalene. She had been born when he had reached an age when he had never expected to have a child, and he loved her with the fiercely protective love that made him vulnerable. Lilli, so like her mother that she could have been Magdalene reincarnated,

Lilli, totally unaware of the implications of that legacy, Lilli, whom he had missed more than he would have believed possible. Otto was a hard man, ruthless and without conscience or scruple, but two women had found a chink in the armour. One had been Magdalene, the other Lilli. But much as he longed to see her smile, hear her low infectious laugh, hold her slim brown hand in his, he would have died rather than expose her again to the dangers that had claimed her mother's life. He should have died! he thought fiercely. If the disease had tightened its hold more quickly or if he had put his gun to his head when he had first found out about it Lilli would not be coming home now. Or would she? Madrepora was her home. For all that had happened there – was still happening – she might still have come. And he would not have been here to warn her and try to protect her.

'When is she coming?' he asked. His voice was tired now, resigned, his energy ebbing with the anger.

'She didn't say. There wasn't time.'

His hands unclenched, stroking light little patterns on his linen-covered knees.

'Call her back, Ingrid. Find out what her plans are and then arrange for the air taxi to meet her.'

'I'll call her tomorrow. She won't have had time to book a flight yet.'

'But do it!' His voice rose again with an echo of the old iron will. 'Make sure she is met by our pilot. I don't want . . .' He broke off as a wave of pain caught him, pressing his forearm hard against his stomach.

Ingrid pretended not to notice. That was the way Otto wanted it. He hated sympathy. But mentally she completed the sentence he had left unfinished. She knew without being told the reason he was so anxious an air taxi should meet Lilli at Barbados International Airport. He did not want it to be Jorge waiting there for her. He did not want her seeing him a moment sooner than she had to – and certainly not before he had had a chance to talk to her first. For now that he was dying there were things Lilli had to know, for her own safety and for all their sakes.

'Don't worry, Otto, I'll do it,' she promised him.

Little as she wanted Lilli here, it was the least she could do.

*

Guy de Savigny completed the entry in his log book – Madrepora to Caracas, Caracas to Madrepora – waited for the ink to dry, then closed the log book with a snap and stowed it in his leather flight bag alongside his map and headset. He tidied the papers on his desk, securing them with a bulldog clip and hanging it on the appropriate hook below the notice board. Then, with relief, he headed for the door.

In the heat of the Caribbean afternoon the little hut on the perimeter of the landing strip which served as an office for Air Perpetua resembled an oven – even with the windows and doors fully open and the ceiling fan twirling, the temperature inside must, he reckoned, be in the hundreds. His short-sleeved pilot shirt was sticking to his back and he wanted nothing so much as a cold beer and the chance of a swim in the pool at the little house that had been put at his disposal. But it would be an hour or so yet before he was free to go – he had reported a magneto drop on his aircraft when he had landed after the trip to Caracas and he wanted to check with the engineer that it had been sorted out before he left the airstrip and headed home.

Outside the hut Manuel Santander, his fellow pilot, was stretched out in a white plastic chair, legs propped up on the low picket fence, swarthy face upturned to the sun. Guy dropped down into the chair beside him, pulling it back a little to get the best of the shade.

'Y-up.' It was Manuel's customary greeting and pretty much the extent of his vocabulary. Though Guy had been working along-side him now for almost three weeks there was precious little communication between them and it added to Guy's mounting sense of frustration. For in spite of living and working here, flying in and out of the tiny airstrip which lay at the very edge of the ocean, the island was as much a closed book to Guy as it had ever been. He had met Fabio Sanchez, whose family, it seemed, owned Air Perpetua along with various other business interests in South America and the Caribbean, but his conversation with him had been limited to what was expected of him in return for his short-term contract as a pilot. He had drunk at a bar on the other side of the island run by a local known as Johnny Shovelnose because, it was said, he had once had a close call with a shovelnose shark and was missing half of one foot to prove it, but the patrons there were, for the most part, too drunk or too high on drugs to be able to sustain a sensible conversation. And he had not been able to get any closer to the villa than flying over it at eight hundred feet when he approached the airstrip from the northern side of the island. He had looked down on the fine two-storey building with its hibiscus-covered veranda and spacious well-tended grounds and itched for an opportunity to get inside to see for himself the treasures Bill had described and meet the German who lived there. But he had had no opportunity to do so and any questions he had asked of Manuel had met with the blank wall of the other pilot's surly refusal to communicate.

In all his years as a pilot Guy had never met as unfriendly a fellow pilot as Manuel and he cursed his luck in having run into one here just when he wanted to learn as much as possible about the island and its inhabitants. Pilots were, on the whole, a gregarious lot, given to talking too loudly and too much, but Manuel was the exception to the rule, and try as he might Guy could not like him. Manuel had a thin weasely face, a thin drooping black moustache and thin lips. His long fingernails were as carefully manicured as a woman's but his personal hygiene did not extend to deodorant – expensive and difficult to come by in the islands – and on the occasions when he had flown with Guy the cockpit had been filled with the sickly-sweet smell of sweat, both fresh and not-so-fresh, and Guy had had to turn his head away, opening the side vent to take a few breaths of untainted air.

Although Manuel sometimes flew with Guy as a safety pilot when he was ferrying passengers, Guy had never flown with Manuel, and this he found surprising. As the senior pilot of Madrepora, Guy would have expected Manuel to take the passenger trips whilst he was left to fly the freight, but this was not the case. Though Guy had done one or two trips to the mainland for supplies it was Manuel who came in and out in an Islander loaded with cartons and cases, whilst Guy's aircraft, a Twin Otter, was mainly used as a taxi service.

'What the hell do they do with all that stuff?' Guy had asked Manuel one day, watching the local workers unload Manuel's aircraft into a truck. 'I brought in a load of food for the hotel only yesterday and I would have thought the natives lived mostly off local produce.'

Manuel had shrugged.

'It's business.'

'What business, for Christ's sake?'

'Oh, this and that.'

His face wore its usual closed-in look and Guy knew he would get no more from him.

Packages left, too, in Manuel's aircraft.

'Batique cloth wear,' Manuel had said when Guy questioned him. 'It's manufactured here. The old man deals in it – that and his rare stamps.'

'You'd need a hell of a lot of rare stamps to fill your aeroplane.'

Manuel shot him a strange look, his small black eyes all but disappearing in the swarthy skin that surrounded them.

'So who is the old man?' Guy enquired, glad of the opportunity to ask some questions about the man who was his quarry.

'Herr Brandt? He's a German. In partnership with the Sanchez brothers, Jorge and Fabio, and their father, Fernando.'

'Do we ever get to fly him?'

'Not much. When he leaves the island, which isn't often, Jorge Sanchez takes him. That's Jorge's plane – the white Beechcraft Baron.'

It was probably the longest speech Manuel had ever favoured him with.

'So we see the old man down here at the airstrip sometimes then?' Guy persisted, encouraged.

'We have done. He's ill now though. Won't be going anywhere for a bit.'

'Ill?' Guy repeated sharply. 'What's wrong with him?'

'I couldn't say. I mind my own business.'

The implication was clear. I mind my business and you should mind yours. Guy's dislike for Manuel grew, fuelled by the feeling of frustration. He was within spitting distance of the man who might very well have been responsible for looting his family's heirlooms and taking the lives of his countrymen – his own father and uncle included – but he might as well still be in England flying the mail for all the good it had done him.

He held on to his patience with difficulty.

'Well all I can say is there must be a pretty good living in batique cloth and rare stamps,' he said laconically. 'They're hardly short of a penny or two, are they, any of them?'

Manuel refused to answer, simply burying his head in one of the paperback Westerns he read when he had nothing better to do.

There was a paperback book lying on the ground beside his chair now, propped open at the page he had reached, and as Guy sat down he picked it up, pointedly discouraging conversation.

Guy shrugged mentally. He had given up trying to get anything out of Manuel. But where, he asked himself, did he go from here?

Inside the hut the telephone began to ring, a shrill tinkling sound. Manuel continued to read his book. Guy glared at him, annoyed by his attitude, then got up himself and slammed into the office, reaching across the desk for the telephone.

'Air Perpetua.' The black bakelite was so hot it was almost burning his hand.

'Who is that?' It was a woman's voice, low and educated, with the faintly guttural sound of a German accent. Guy felt the tiny hairs at the back of his neck rise.

'This is Captain de Savigny.' Guy winced at the sound of his own name. He wished he could have changed it so as not to alert von Rheinhardt to his presence, but having to produce his pilot's licence when applying for the job made such a thing impossible.

'Ah — good. Frau Brandt here. I would like you to meet a passenger who will be arriving in Barbados from New York tomorrow. The flight is due in at two-forty in the afternoon and the passenger is to be brought directly here. We will have our car waiting for her at the airstrip when you land. Is that all right? You are not already busy tomorrow?'

'No, I'm not busy tomorrow.' Guy didn't mention the fact that he had been due to take a day off the following day. 'Who is the passenger?'

'Her name is Fraulein Lilli Brandt. She is my stepdaughter. Please take good care of her.'

'I never do anything else,' Guy said, but it was all he could do to keep the jubilation out of his voice. He'd just been wondering how the hell he could make some contact with the Brandt family and now, totally unexpectedly, fate was handing him the opportunity on a plate.

'Fraulein Lilli Brandt . . . my stepdaughter,' the woman had said. That could mean only one thing. Fraulein Lilli Brandt must be the old man's daughter.

Thank God the call had come in this afternoon! If it had come tomorrow when he was taking a day off – *wasting* a day, swimming and lying in the sun – he would have missed out. Thank God, too, for the faulty magneto which had delayed him at the airstrip, and for Manuel's bolshy attitude. For once the man's surly behaviour had worked in Guy's favour.

At last he was going to meet one of the Brandts, as they called themselves. Tomorrow he was going to fly the old man's daughter.

'I've booked the air taxi to meet Lilli,' Ingrid said.

Otto nodded without raising his head from the back rest of the lounger supporting it. Today he had had Basil settle him in the salon rather than out on the veranda; even given the shade of the hibiscus he hadn't felt able to endure the brightness of the sun outside. He had slept badly – thinking about Lilli coming home had kept his mind active and wide awake even between the bouts of pain that came more and more frequently, and he felt weak and exhausted by it, a pale shadow of his old vigorous self. It was, he thought, as if his illness had drained him not only of his strength but also his personality, turning him into a figure of pathos to be pitied and humoured instead of respected and feared. That, most of all, he found insupportable.

'Who did you speak to?' he asked, gathering himself together with an effort. 'Not Manuel, I hope?'

'No. But it wouldn't be him doing the trip anyway, would it? He works mostly for Jorge, doesn't he? This was the new pilot, I think. Do you know anything about him?'

'No. Fabio engaged him since I was . . . ill. Why do you ask?'

'I just wondered. He sounded English – very English – but he had a French-sounding name. I didn't quite catch it.'

Otto's eyes narrowed in his wasted face, his mind, a little fuddled because of the drugs he had been forced to take this morning, wandering to the past. France during the war, a château in Charente, vineyards and cognac, an aristocratic family. Memories from another lifetime, before his Führer had been humiliated, before the Fatherland had fallen, before he had fled to South America with the help of his old friend Vicente Cordoba, and long before Cordoba acquired Madrepora on his behalf. Before Magdalene, before Lilli . . .

His eyes strayed to the treasures filling the salon – the silver candlesticks, the bronze statuette of Ceres, the little Louis XIV clock and the beautiful glowing triptych he always referred to as 'Lilli's triptych'. They had surrounded him now for so long that he had forgotten they had once belonged elsewhere, in a château in Charente. Strange he should find himself thinking of it now.

With an effort Otto dragged his hazy thoughts back to the present and savoured the relief that came from knowing that Lilli would be flown in, not by Jorge or one of his cronies, but by the new pilot, whatever his name might be. He hadn't been in Madrepora long enough yet to be involved with Jorge and his dangerous games – at least Otto assumed he hadn't. That meant that for the moment, Lilli was safe. To Otto, nothing else mattered.

19

AS THE AIRLINER took off from Kennedy, gaining its cruise
level and heading south for the Caribbean islands, Lilli sipped
a glass of champagne and made a conscious effort to relax.

Not easy. Since talking to Ingrid she had scarcely slept. Now,
though she felt spaced and exhausted, the adrenaline was still
flowing in unsteadying bursts, making her flesh tingle and creep
every time she thought of what she was doing, and she knew that
in spite of the comfort of her seat in First Class she would not be
able to sleep during the flight.

That, of course, was what she had had in mind when she booked
it – the prospect of arriving fresh and rested in Barbados had
overcome her natural reluctance for what she thought of as
needless extravagance. Lilli had been brought up on nothing but
the best – and the best meant first-class travel amongst other
things. But the easy living had not spoiled her. If anything it had
given her a fierce determination to stand on her own two feet and
do without those luxuries she was unable to afford on her own
salary, rather than supplementing it with hand-outs from her
father.

On this occasion, however, she had weighed up all the factors
and decided that the extravagance was justified. She simply could
not face the journey any other way.

The in-flight meal was served – *haute cuisine* on bone-china
plates – but Lilli ate only a few mouthfuls before pushing it aside.
She had hardly eaten, either, in the last two days and now the
smoked salmon and chicken à la King tasted like cardboard and
stuck in her throat. She leaned back in the comfortable seat,
closing her eyes and giving way to the mêlée of thoughts that
chased one another around her sleep-starved brain.

Overlying them all, of course, was concern for her father. The devastating news that he was desperately ill had dominated her thoughts and emotions waking and sleeping ever since she had spoken to Ingrid. As she had made her arrangements the only thing that had seemed of any importance at all was that she should get home to be with him as soon as possible. Perhaps, she had thought, she might be able to persuade him to undergo surgery where Ingrid and the doctors had failed. If so, time was of the essence. And in any case, she simply wanted to see him, to be near him. The distance between them had suddenly been unbearable and she wavered between the totally irrational hope that simply by being there she could avert disaster and the sickening fear that if she did not get home quickly she might be too late. If Josie had not written to her he could have died without her even knowing he was ill and the realisation of how long it had been since they had been close had awakened urgent longings which had negated all her reasons for leaving the island.

Now that she was actually on her way, however, all the other implications of returning to Madrepora were there too, silent ghosts creeping up on her almost unawares and jangling her already taut nerves. Would Jorge be on the island? He wasn't always. He divided his time between Madrepora, Venezuela and Florida. But if her father was ill the likelihood was that he would be there, overseeing his business interests, and Lilli felt a shiver of apprehension at the thought of seeing him again.

Dear God, I still love him! she thought. In spite of what he is, in spite of what I now know about him, he still has the power to make me want him so much it hurts. I can despise him, fear him even, and it makes no difference. I still turn into a jelly of desire, as if my bones were melting, just thinking about him.

It had always been that way and Lilli was beginning to be afraid it always would. She had thought that leaving Madrepora would cleanse her, exorcise him from her heart, but it hadn't. True, she had been able to put him out of her mind as she had put him out of her life, but the memory of him was still there, not dead but only lying dormant, and she knew in her heart that when she saw him again the attraction he held for her would be as potent as ever.

How will I cope? Lilli wondered in panic. What will I do if he still wants me? And how will I be able to bear it if he does not?

She had been just five years old when she had first decided she wanted to marry Jorge, and the memory would have amused her now if it had not been such a presentiment of what was to follow.

In her mind's eye she saw him now as she had first seen him, in the company of her mother on the veranda of the villa in Madrepora. The sun had fragmented through the hibiscus-covered trellis to dapple him with light and shade, a tall, strongly built man in a white shirt and bleached cotton jodphurs. It seemed to her now that he had not changed one iota in all the years, but she knew that was simply because she was superimposing the face of the forty-four-year-old man he now was on to the image. Or perhaps he really hadn't changed. Perhaps he was one of those people for whom time stands still between maturity and old age. Certainly she was sure he had always had those hard lines between nose and mouth, etched deeply into his darkly tanned skin, the colour of mahogany, the texture of leather, and the pouches beneath his eyes which suggested too much hard living, but which seemed oddly to enhance his amazing good looks rather than detracting from them.

She had looked at him that day and felt a strange excitement building inside her. She had been far too young to identify it of course, she had only known she wanted to go to him, to join him and her mother on the veranda, more than she had ever wanted anything in her life. She had skipped out through the archway, her sandalled feet slapping on the tiled floor, then stopped, shy suddenly.

'Lilli!' her mother had said. 'I thought you were down at the beach with Patsy.'

Her voice, low and musical, was tinged with surprise. She was sitting in one of the rattan chairs, wearing a sarong-style sundress. Her hair, long, loose and dark, flowed over her bare brown shoulders, her slender legs, emerging from the brightly coloured silk, were crossed so that her gold high-heeled mule hung away from the delicate arch of her foot. Between the gold leather straps Lilli could see the vivid red varnish on her toenails. Her mother was, she thought, the most beautiful woman in the world, and she longed with all her five-year-old heart to be like her. Sometimes she crept into her mother's room and stole the bottle of scarlet enamel, painting her own nails with careful precision, then sliding some of Magdalene's jangling bracelets on to her wrists, pretending she was grown up and every bit as beautiful as Magdalene herself. Now, however, she had eyes only for the man, and she looked at him as she answered her mother.

'We came back. Patsy had a headache.'

'Really! I shall have to have words with her!'

Magdalene sounded annoyed and Lilli leaped to her nurse's defence.

'She couldn't help it. You mustn't be cross with her, Mama.'

'No, you mustn't be cross, Magdalene. It doesn't suit you.' There was a slightly sarcastic note in the drawling voice but Lilli was too young – and too entranced – to recognise it.

'Go and play in the garden, Lilli,' Magdalene said.

Lilli's face fell.

'Do I have to?'

'Let her stay. She's not doing any harm.' The man stretched out a lean brown hand and rumpled her hair.

She ran over to sit on the veranda step, drawing her knees up beneth the gathered skirt of her dress, gazing enraptured at him as he and her mother talked, content simply to be in his presence.

It was an enchantment that was to continue through all the years and she felt it now, strongly as ever, as she remembered the way it had been.

'Coffee, madam?' the air hostess asked. Lilli opened her eyes, surprised almost to see the glossy figure hovering at her elbow. For the last few minutes her mother, dead these last fifteen years, had been far more real to her. Her mother – and, of course, Jorge. Always Jorge. Lilli gave a small shake of her head.

'No, thank you.'

Then she closed her eyes again, continuing her voyage to the distant past.

Jorge had spent a great deal of time on Madrepora that summer and the winter that followed it. Lilli was not clear about why he had entered their lives so suddenly but she knew that he was some kind of business associate of her father's. Often they would disappear together into the room at the villa her father used as a study and sometimes they would drive off together in her father's car – the only one on Madrepora – headed, she thought, for the south-east side of the island where the locals lived in a shanty town of tin huts and corrugated-iron shacks. But one day when she watched the car from the top of the rise at the edge of the estate she saw it turn north, not south, before it was lost to sight behind the thick band of lush green woodland. Lilli had no idea where they could be going. She had no idea what lay on that corner of the island, for though Madrepora covered in all only five square miles she had never been there.

When Jorge came to Madrepora he flew in, piloting his own light aircraft and landing on the tiny airstrip which had been constructed on the flat coastal plane. This made him appear even more glamorous in Lilli's eyes. He did not stay at either her father's villa or the hotel, but in one of the handful of private villas on the island, a pretty pastel-pink house with wood-shingled roof set on one of the wooded slopes and reached by stone steps flanked by sweet-smelling hibiscus and oleander. The house always reminded Lilli of the tale of Hansel and Gretel – and not only because the walls looked as if they were made of sugar icing and the fretwork of white marzipan. She thought that Fernando Sanchez, who owned it, and whom she was supposed to call 'Uncle Fernando', was a sort of man-equivalent of the wicked witch. Fernando was tall and slim as a whippet except for a beer gut which overhung the waistband of his trousers. He had a hook nose and a shock of prematurely white hair and his skin was like a polished walnut. But it was the livid scar on his throat that Lilli could never tear her eyes away from, the puckered flesh falling into a discoloured crater which both fascinated and repelled her, and his voice was a kind of urgent husky whisper with a rasping edge to it.

Fernando had been shot in the throat, her father had explained, and he was lucky to be alive. The bullet had severed the vocal cords, passing downwards at an angle and lodging in his shoulder.

Lilli had shuddered.

'Did it happen in the war, Daddy?' she asked. She knew her own father had been in the war.

'I expect so, yes,' Otto had replied vaguely, and it was only many years later that Lilli had realised that could not be true.

But though she felt sorry for Fernando Lilli could not bring herself to like him and was always glad when 'the gingerbread house' was shut up and Fernando went home to South America.

'Why does Jorge stay there?' she asked her mother one day. 'Why couldn't he stay here with us? It would be much more sensible.'

Magdalene's scarlet lips had twisted with amusement.

'What do you mean – sensible?'

'He wouldn't have to walk all the way over here to see Daddy. He could have the room next to mine and our cook could get his breakfast.'

Magdalene had pretended to consider this.

'Yes, but Jorge has his own cook. She would be very upset if Jorge didn't want her to get his breakfast any more.'

'She's not *Jorge's* cook,' Lilli objected. 'She's Uncle Fernando's.'

'But Lilli, that comes to the same thing.' Lilli looked puzzled and Magdalene went on: 'Uncle Fernando is Jorge's father. Didn't you know that?'

'No,' Lilli replied, shocked. She could hardly believe that a monster like Uncle Fernando could be anyone's father, much less Jorge's.

'Uncle Fernando is your father's business partner,' Magdalene explained. 'You know that. Well, Jorge works for him. Sometimes Uncle Fernando is not well enough to do all the things that people have to when they have a business to run, so Jorge is doing them for him.'

Lilli's heart lifted. It sounded as if Jorge would be spending quite a lot of time on Madrepora. She wondered what Magdalene would say if she were to tell her she planned to marry Jorge, but decided to hug the secret to herself for a little longer. Instead she asked the question she had asked many times before. She always enjoyed listening to the answer and now it had special significance for her.

'Tell me how you came to meet Daddy.'

Magdalene tossed her black hair a little impatiently.

'Oh Lilli, you've heard the story so often you must know it by heart.'

'Tell me again – please!'

'Your father's family were coffee importers back home in Germany. Their coffee was drunk in all the finest coffee houses in Europe, from Berlin to Vienna. But they suffered very badly in the war. Their family home was bombed and their business destroyed. Your father came to South America to make a fresh start. My father – your grandfather – helped him. They knew one another because of the coffee trade, but Grandfather Vicente had entered politics so he was able to arrange for your father to get the necessary papers. When he came to Venezuela we met and fell in love. He was much older than me, of course, nearly forty years old, and I was only seventeen. But that did not matter to us and my father was very happy that I was to marry his old friend.'

A small smile curved Lilli's mouth. That was the very best part of the story – that Daddy had been much older than Mama and that Grandfather Vicente had been pleased because Otto was his old friend. It would be the same for her and Jorge, she thought. It had happened to Mama and Daddy, why not her too?

'Tell me about how you came to Madrepora,' she insisted.

'There's nothing to tell. Grandfather Vicente arranged for Daddy to lease the island from the government and later we bought it. We came here and opened the hotel and Daddy was able to go into business with Grandfather Vicente and Uncle Fernando.'

Lilli did not ask what the business was – that, she thought, was boring.

'What about Jorge? Did you know Jorge then?'

A faint wash of colour tinged Magdalene's cheeks.

'I have always known Jorge, ever since we were children.'

She should have guessed then, Lilli thought, recalling now with startling clarity across the years the look on her mother's face when she had said it. But Lilli had only been a little girl. To her, Mama and Daddy were an item, an indivisible unit. It had not occurred to her then, or later, that Magdalene and Jorge had ever been more than friends who had played together as children because of the close relationship between their families.

Those were the really idyllic days, Lilli thought, remembering, the days when she had taken love and happiness and security for granted. The days before Mama died.

It must have been about a year after she had first set eyes on Jorge, Lilli supposed, and the horror of that night had never left her.

She had been awakened, she remembered, by some sort of commotion – voices raised, not in anger, but in agitation, and the awful sound of someone wailing. Lilli's heart had begun to pound both from fear and from being shocked out of a deep sleep. She knew instinctively that something terrible had happened. She

273

gathered her courage, fought her way through the entrapping folds of the mosquito netting and padded to the door. The voices were coming from downstairs. Lilli crept down, holding tight to the wooden banisters and peeping through. She could see her father in the salon but his hands were covering his face and he did not see her.

'Daddy!' she called in a frightened voice. 'Daddy – what is it?'

He seemed not to hear her but suddenly Patsy was there in the doorway. She was wearing her dressing gown and from the look of her Lilli knew that it was she who had been wailing.

'Patsy!' Lilli cried. 'Patsy – what's happening?' She ran down the stairs but Patsy was there blocking her way.

'No, Miss Lilli, you don't want to go down there.'

'I do! I want Mama . . .'

'Come on, Miss Lilli, you come with me. That's no place for you down there. I'll take you back to bed.'

For once in her life Lilli totally ignored her nurse. She ducked beneath Patsy's outstretched arm and ran towards the salon.

'Daddy . . .'

She dived through the doorway, then stopped dead in her tracks. Magdalene was lying on the floor, half hidden by the rattan sofa. One scarlet-tipped hand was flung out, her scarlet silk dress spread around her like a broken butterfly. And there was blood running in a scarlet stream across the tiled floor.

'Mama!' Lilli tried to say, but no words would come and she stood transfixed. Then Patsy reached her, turning her face into the voluminous skirt of her dressing gown, keening in distress.

'I told you not to come down here, Miss Lilli! I told you, didn't I?'

She scooped Lilli up into her arms and carried her back upstairs where she pushed the mosquito nets aside and sat down on the bed, still holding Lilli, rocking her to and fro and weeping noisily.

Lilli let her do it. She was in total shock. The world had gone black. Black – and scarlet. There was nothing but Patsy's bosom, smothering her, no sound now but the awful weeping and the ringing in her own ears.

The next morning her father had come to her room. He seemed to have aged beyond recognition. He sat down beside her on the bed, taking her hands in his, and his voice, when he spoke, was low and almost totally lacking in emotion.

'Lilli,' he said, 'you have to be brave. We all have to be brave. I have some terrible news for you.'

Lilli said nothing. She wanted to clap her hands over her ears so as not to hear what he had to say. She already knew in her heart what it was but words would make it real, extinguish any last hope that what had happened last night had been no more than a nightmare. But she simply sat, staring at him, feeling her world crumble around her.

'Lilli, your mother is dead,' he said. And she knew there was no more room for hope.

Magdalene's remains had been returned to Venezuela for interment and gradually, very gradually, life on Madrepora had resumed a pattern. Patsy had become Lilli's surrogate mother, and though she still cried sometimes in the night for Magdalene, Lilli's childish resilience overcame her grief. But somehow Daddy had never been quite the same again. His temper was shorter and the stern side of him came to the fore more often. Lilli knew how to get around him, though. She practised all her feminine wiles on him, and he doted on her.

Shortly after Magdalene's death Jorge had disappeared from the island and it was Fabio, his brother, who came to stay in the gingerbread house. Lilli asked her father the reason for this, but he merely said: 'Jorge is busy elsewhere,' and did not elaborate. After a while Lilli had accepted the change as she accepted everything else, and though she never quite forgot Jorge, he ceased to be the centre of her universe.

It was not until years later, when she was sixteen years old, that Jorge had come back into her life and it had all begun again.

Now, flying home to Madrepora, Lilli wondered if this hiatus would be any different to the last. The parting four years ago had seemed to be final and, though her heart had been breaking, she had been determined that never again would she allow him to dominate her life and manipulate her emotions.

But for all that she could not be certain that it would be so. She was not at all sure that she would be able to trust herself to keep the vow she had made the day she had left. Jorge was her weakness, he always had been and Lilli was very much afraid he always would be.

If he was there and he wanted her, would she be able to resist?

Lilli hoped very much he would not be there.

20

GUY DE SAVIGNY stood in the transit lounge at Barbados International Airport watching the flow of passengers who had just arrived from New York. Most had the appearance of holidaymakers, dressed in jogging suits or casual wear, carrying the parkas they had needed in wintry New York and struggling with suitcases, holdalls and cameras. A few, already suitably attired for the Caribbean sunshine in brightly coloured short-sleeved shirts, were, he guessed, locals returning from a trip abroad. But so far he had seen no one remotely resembling the passenger he was waiting for. She would be a woman alone, about his own age, he imagined, and probably instantly recognisable as a German with the fair hair and blue eyes of a typical Aryan.

The rush thinned to a trickle. Guy fiddled with his sunglasses, beginning to wonder if Otto's daughter had been on the flight after all and feeling a fatalistic disappointment creeping in to take the place of anticipation. He'd thought a chance like this was too good to be true – lucky breaks like this didn't often come his way. Perhaps Fräulein Lilli Brandt had missed the flight or changed her plans too late for them to stop him leaving. But the jumbo must have already taken off from New York before he left Madrepora so there would have been no reason for Frau Brandt not to have called the airstrip and cancelled the taxi – unless of course she had, and Manuel had taken the call and forgotten to tell him.

Manuel had been busy this morning with one of his freight runs for Jorge Sanchez. Maybe it had slipped his mind – or, more likely, he'd taken malicious pleasure in letting Guy make the trip, knowing it would turn out to be a fool's errand. Manuel had seemed annoyed that Guy had taken the booking from Frau Brandt the previous afternoon, though he had no one to blame but himself for forcing Guy to answer the telephone. But Manuel seemed to look upon anything connected with the Brandts or Jorge Sanchez as his own personal responsibility – which of course it usually was – and Guy found himself wondering, as he had done at the time, why Frau Brandt should have asked him to meet her stepdaughter. Since Jorge generally flew the family in his private plane or got Manuel to cover for him, that would have seemed the most likely arrangement in this case too.

Guy sighed, on the point of turning away, when a young woman caught his eye, stirring his interest for quite a different reason. Slim, dark, probably of Spanish South American descent, dressed simply but strikingly in a lemon-yellow trouser suit and carrying only an Yves St Laurent purse and an expensive-looking Italian leather tote bag. One step behind her a local porter lumbered along with a suitcase – also labelled with the YSL logo. He was grinning with pleasure, yet somehow, following behind her like that, he resembled nothing so much as a native bearer on an expedition. If he had suddenly shifted the suitcase on to his head Guy would not have been surprised.

What a beauty! Guy thought – and still failed to make the connection. It was only when she came towards him, smiling faintly, that he realised the truth.

'Air Perpetua?' she said in a low, sweet voice. 'I am Lilli Brandt. I think you are taking me to Madrepora.'

The moment she had stepped off the plane Lilli had smelled the Caribbean. No – even before that. The warm scented air had come rushing in as soon as the doors were thrown open and a wave of emotion had engulfed her, conjuring up not the traumas of her last months on the island but all the other, happier days. As she breathed in the perfume of the islands Lilli forgot that her father was dying, forgot Jorge, forgot everything except that she was home. Or almost home. This was where she belonged. For the moment nothing else mattered.

The euphoria lasted as she collected her luggage and went with her as the pilot who had come to meet her escorted her across the apron to where the Twin Otter in the blue-and-gold livery of Air Perpetua stood parked and waiting. He was a stranger to her, dark and strikingly good-looking in his black trousers and white uniform shirt with the captain's insignia gleaming on the epaulettes, but she liked him instantly, an easy rapport which reflected her new happy mood. He settled her into the seat immediately behind his and stowed her luggage whilst she waited, bursting with a new impatience. 'The longest mile is the last mile home.'. The words of the old song came into her mind and the departure checks and clearance seemed to her to take forever. Then they were airborne, skimming out over the sparkling blue and silver of the sea, skimming with a careless ease the airliner that had brought her from New York had lacked, rising and falling gently on the air currents so that she felt as if she might be riding on the back of a seabird rather than flying in a man-made machine.

'Have you been here long?' Lilli asked.

He half turned his head, looking at her quizzically, and Lilli laughed at her own foolishness. Of course he couldn't hear what she said – he was wearing a headset and only the voices of the radio controllers would be clear to him. She waved a hand apologetically in front of her face, indicating that she understood, and settled back, but a moment later she noticed him fumbling under the control panel, plugging contacts into sockets, and with a grin he passed a headset similar to his own back to her.

'Oh – thanks,' Lilli mouthed.

She had worn a headset before – flying with Jorge – but that was a long time ago and it took her a minute to two to get it on, tucking her long dark hair behind her ears so that the muffs fitted snugly and twisting the mouthpiece into position.

'Thanks,' she said. 'I forgot you couldn't hear me. All I said was – have you been here long?'

'No – I'm a new boy. Less than three weeks.' The microphone added extra resonance to his already deep voice.

'I thought I hadn't seen you before. Do you like it here?'

'Sun, sea and deserted beaches? How could I not like it! This is your home, I take it?'

'I was born here, yes. I live in New York now.'

'Some difference!'

'You could say. It's real winter there.'

'I was in England just three weeks ago. It's pretty cold there too. I'm not surprised you wanted to come home for some sunshine.'

'Oh – it's not that,' Lilli said, and broke off as a small sharp barb of reality pricked at the bubble of euphoria.

'What do you do in New York?' he asked, unaware of her sudden discomfort.

'I'm in publishing. Public relations. It can be quite good fun but very tiring. All those business lunches and campagne receptions.'

'Tough!' he said with a laugh.

'Yes, I know,' Lillie said ruefully. 'I'm spoiled.'

'I'm sure you're not. That's the trouble with jobs like yours and mine. They seem very glamorous to everyone but the person doing them. The reality can be very different.'

'That's it,' she said. 'That's it exactly. They don't see me dead tired, wanting nothing but a quiet evening with my feet up in front of the television and a cup of cocoa to drink.'

'But we put up with it.'

'Yes,' she laughed. 'We put up with it.'

The crackle of the radio ended their conversation and Lilli realised that the pilot was busy now with preparations to land. She turned to look out of the window and with a little lurch of excitement saw Madrepora almost immediately beneath them, a tiny speck of land in the blue of the sea taking shape as the plane descended and overflew. So many times before Lilli had seen it, yet the sight never failed to thrill her – the wooded hillsides and white sandy beaches, the hotel and marina, well stocked with yachts, the corrugated tin roofs of the shacks that comprised the shanty town where Josie and the other locals lived, the half-dozen houses dotted amongst the trees, and the villa, with its manicured lawns and swimming pool. Her father's villa. Her home. Once again Lilli's stomach twisted with an emotion that was part pleasure, part pain. Then the plane was skimming in low, too low to see anything but the tiny airstrip and the trees that lined the ridge to the east. She braced herself, slightly nervous as always at landing, but the plane touched down sweetly, wheels almost kissing tarmac, and slowed to a gentle taxi.

'Well done,' Lilli said. 'I'm told this is a very difficult strip to land on.'

'What I'm trained to do,' he said lightly.

She took off the headset, passing it back to him, and unbuckled her seatbelt, stretching comfortably and smoothing her cool-wool lemon trousers over her knees.

Home. Home! In spite of everything it felt so good.

And then she looked out across the grassy apron and saw it, and instantly her happy mood was dissipated. A small white aeroplane gleaming in the sun. Jorge's aeroplane. So – he was here. Lilli felt her heart begin to pound uncomfortably, sending echoes through each and every pulse point.

The pilot was running expertly through his shut-down checks, opening the hatch to let some air into the cabin, climbing out, helping her down. The panic was tightening her throat and she wanted, suddenly, to cling to this pleasant, attractive, efficient man who seemed oddly to be the last bastion of stability before she had to face all kinds of problems and emotional traumas.

'Thank you,' she said. 'That was wonderful. You must come over for drinks sometime.'

'I'd like that,' he said but she could see he was surprised. The daughter of the house inviting the taxi driver for drinks – unheard of!

'I meant it,' she said. 'That's not just a pleasantry. Only I don't know your name.'

'Guy de Savigny.'

'Do I call you Captain de Savigny or Guy?'

'Guy will do nicely.'

The exchange had made her feel better. She felt she had an ally. She was almost calm again as he unloaded her luggage, watched her father's driver collect it and stow it in the Mercedes which stood waiting at the edge of the airstrip.

'Thanks again,' she said.

And then she looked out to sea. The sun had begun to dip and quite suddenly the sky and water, clear and blue only minutes ago, were streaked with scarlet, and again Lilli's heart began to pound. Scarlet. She hated scarlet. It resurrected memories she wanted only to forget. Memories before Jorge and yet all bound up with him. Even safe in New York the colour could turn her spine to water. Here in the Caribbean the significance was magnified so that it coloured her every emotion with foreboding and the chill of fear.

She turned back and saw that Guy was striding away towards the little hut that comprised the airstrip office. With the scarlet sea still staining her vision Lilli felt totally bereft.

In his small white-roofed office overlooking the airstrip, some two to three hundred yards from the hut that was the headquarters of Air Perpetua, Jorge Sanchez was entertaining Enrique Garcia, the carabinier responsible for Madrepora.

The office was no bigger than the one that housed Air Perpetua but it was far better appointed. Though Jorge conducted most of his business from his house, set high amongst the trees, he also needed a base within easy reach of the airstrip and the marina, and since he had begun to spend more and more time on the island he had made it a priority to equip the office with all the trappings necessary for his comfort. Jorge was used to luxury; raised in a family of wealthy landowners he had grown up not simply expecting the best but spurning anything that fell short of those standards. He drank too much – the slightly raddled look of his dark swarthy face bore witness to that – but he drank only the finest wines and spirits. He smoked only hand-rolled cigars, dark and slim. His shirts were handmade, his suits and the bleached cotton jodphurs he so often wore were tailored by the most expensive establishment in Caracas. Anything less offended his natural arrogance, for it narrowed the great divide which separated his kind – the Venezuelan meritocracy – from the masses, the labourers, the servants and the unemployed who occupied the hillside shanty towns and begged in the streets.

It was also important, Jorge believed, to impress business associates – and Enrique Garcia was numbered amongst those. An officer of the law he might be; his goodwill was vital to ensure the smooth running of Jorge's enterprises. Whenever Garcia called at Madrepora Jorge entertained him with lavish hospitality, greeting him as an old friend and spending as much time as was necessary to create a cordial atmosphere and make the customary handing over of the sweetener more of an arrangement between friends and less of what it really was – a bribe to ensure that the report that went back to Garcia's superiors made no mention of Jorge's business dealings.

Jorge did not like Garcia – he liked very few of those who were in his pay – but he was careful not to let his disdain show. He had spent the last hour yarning with Garcia and plying him with planter's punch, watching the intermittent activity on the airstrip whilst pretending to be utterly absorbed in Garcia's rambling account of how he had caught out the owner of a seventy-five-foot yacht who had been contravening regulations in the marina on one of the islands under his control. Jorge hoped that no one here on Madrepora would be foolish enough to do anything to draw attention to 'the Firm's' activities whilst Garcia was actually on the island. Garcia might be aware there were illegal goings-on; not to parade them under his nose was one of the rules of the game.

'It cost him a lost of money,' Garcia said gleefully. 'But then, he can afford it. That yacht was the latest thing. Brand new, global-positioning system, every mod con, oh, he could afford it.'

Jorge nodded, concealing his dislike. Garcia had grown rich on the backs of just those whose activities he was employed to police, but that did not stop him from being fat, stupid and uncouth. Jorge hoped he had had enough planter's punch to make him fall in the harbour when he tried to go back aboard his launch. A wetting was no more than he deserved – so long as he didn't drown. It would not suit Jorge's purpose to have to cultivate a new carabinier who might be more scrupulous and less amenable to his inducements.

'Another drink?' he asked pleasantly.

Garcia belched loudly, patted his chest with a pudgy hand and swung his chair up on to its back legs.

'Don't mind if I do.'

Jorge rose, a tall, strongly built man with a casual raddled elegance, and crossed to the drinks cabinet. As he was refilling Garcia's glass he heard the purr of twin engines almost overhead and descending; a light aircraft on final approach. He took his own glass over to the window, thrown wide open to the cooling breeze off the sea, and watched it come into view – as he had expected it was the Twin Otter in the livery of Air Perpetua, being flown, no doubt, by the new pilot.

Jorge's eyes narrowed, watching it descend and touch down whilst Garcia burbled on. The new pilot was an expert flier, not a doubt of it, the way he had landed on the tiny difficult strip was proof of that, but all the same Jorge was beginning to have serious doubts about him.

'He asks too many questions,' Manuel, the senior pilot, whom he trusted implicitly, had said. 'I think you should keep an eye on him.'

Jorge intended to do just that. He didn't like people who asked too many questions, especially before they had demonstrated their credentials. It smacked of a troublemaker at best and a snooper – perhaps a professional snooper – at worst, and the last thing he wanted was a professional snooper disturbing the smooth running of his operations. He hadn't engaged the new pilot himself, he'd been too busy with other, more important matters, and he'd left what had seemed like a routine appointment to his brother Fabio. Dammit, couldn't the fool get anything right? Had he unwittingly engaged someone who would be a danger to them? Well if he had, the new pilot would come to a sticky end, just as anyone who tried to interfere or get too clever did.

The Twin Otter had come to a stop, the hatches were open and the new pilot was emerging. Jorge eyed him up critically, wondering idly who the passenger was this time. A guest for the hotel, he imagined. They flew in from South America like a flock of wild geese – ageing Germans with the sort of war records that had turned South America and its immediate surrounds into a prison as surely as if they had been brought before the courts at Nuremberg and sentenced to a life behind bars for the rest of their days. But they did not concern him. The hotel was simply a sideline. Running it had been Otto's responsibility – let him be the one to look after his compatriots – and now that he was no longer able to do it, overall management would pass to Fabio. Unless he could persuade his father to close it down. There had always been a measure of dissent within the Firm regarding the hotel – Jorge felt it posed an unnecessary security risk, whilst Fernando, his father, believed it provided a useful cover blind. At present Fernando had his way. He was still head of the Firm. But Otto's illness had reminded Jorge of his own father's mortality. One day in the not-too-distant future, control would pass to him and then he would do as he thought fit.

A smile of satisfaction curved his cruel mouth, then froze. A young woman in a lemon trouser suit was emerging from the Twin Otter, her dark hair blowing in the stiff breeze off the sea.

Lilli.

Though it was four years now since he had seen her, he knew instantly that it was she.

Lilli – the living image of her mother at the same age, slender, graceful, beautiful beyond belief, but with all the freshness of youth that he had seen fade in Magdalene as the passage of the years took their toll.

Lilli. After what had happened he had not expected her to return to Madrepora even again, yet now he realised he should have known that if anything could bring her back it was Otto's illness. Lilli adored her father, worshipped him almost. No disillusion, no heartbreak, could change that. They must have let her know that Otto was dying and she had come back to make her peace with him before it was too late.

Jorge's smile broadened. Somewhere on the periphery of his thoughts he could hear Garcia still burbling on, becoming increasingly garrulous as the planter's punch loosened his tongue, but it had ceased to annoy him much now, a mere pinprick of inconvenience no more or less irritating than the flies buzzing against the hot windowpane.

Lilli was back and the game would recommence. Magdalene had been his and Lilli had been his – and she would be again. Jorge felt the stirring of excitement, the rush of adrenaline in his veins and the first tiny trickle of sweat at the nape of his neck. He moistened his lips, dry from the planter's punch, and followed Lilli's progress across the airstrip towards the waiting car, unaware that he was watching her.

Lilli was back – and he wanted her as much as ever, wanted her with a hunger as sharp as his hunger for all the good things of life, no – sharper. Lilli could not be bought as he bought them, she had to be won, and that made the prize all the richer. But it would not deter him. If anything it only made him the more determined.

Jorge wanted Lilli more than he wanted anything. And Jorge was a man who always got what he wanted.

21

THE VILLA WAS sleeping in the somnolent heat of the late afternoon. The sun might be dropping now, a ball of fire, into the sea, but the residue remained, radiating in waves from the white stone pathway and imprisoning the perfume of the bougain-villaea and frangipani that lined it on either side.

Lilli felt it burning through the soles of her shoes and longed to exchange them for a pair of rubber-soled flipflops, longed, too, to get out of the cool-wool trousers and into a loose cotton sundress. But the discomfort her unsuitable attire was causing her was nothing compared to the tightness in her throat, the hammering of her heart. She was home and in a few moments she would see her father. It was what she wanted more than anything, her whole reason for being here, and yet now that the meeting was imminent she shrank from it. The circumstances of their parting were very immediate now, the awkwardness exacerbated by the years of estrangement. But it was not only that which made her dread seeing him. It was knowing that very soon she would be face to face with the reality of his illness, seeing with her own eyes, rather than with her imagination, the ravages it had inflicted on him. Then perhaps there would be no room left for even the smallest nugget of hope, nothing but the need to accept somehow the finality of the situation and the knowledge that inevitably she was about to lose him forever.

The local boy carrying her suitcase was a step or two behind her. Lilli glanced around at him, at the grinning dark-skinned face growing serious as he approached the villa, which somehow seemed to project the aura of impending death into the brightness of the afternoon like a deep invisible shadow, and took a hold on herself. She must not let him see she was afraid. She was Lilli Brandt, daughter of a former officer of the German army, granddaughter of Vicente Cordoba, who had been a politician and landowner. In her blood was mixed the aristocratic heritage of two civilisations. She owed it to them to hide her weakness. She owed it to herself.

She walked up the shallow steps and pushed the door, which stood ajar, fully open.

'Hello!' she called. 'I'm here!'

Her voice, firm and level, hung in the air like the heat of the day. And then, suddenly, the beaded curtain which led to the kitchen was brushed aside and Patsy was there, arms outstretched, a smile of welcome which wavered between laughter and tears enveloping her mobile brown face.

'Miss Lilli! Oh, Miss Lilli! Praise the Lord – it's you!'

'Patsy!' Lilli hugged her, feeling the ample breasts squash like overripe melons against her own firm body, smelling the indefinable scent of warm brown flesh that whisked her senses back across the years to childhood. 'It's so good to see you!'

'And you, Miss Lilli! Oh, I'se so glad, so glad!'

The tears had begun to flow now, rolling down Patsy's face as she held Lilli tightly.

'Lilli.' The voice with the faint German accent was brisk and slightly disapproving. 'So, you've arrived safely.'

Lilli gave Patsy one last hug and turned to where Ingrid stood, implacable as ever.

'Hello, Ingrid.' She kissed her briefly on both cheeks with none of the warmth she had put into her greeting for Patsy, who still hovered, wiping the tears from her face with the corner of her apron.

'Thank you, Patsy, that will be all,' Ingrid said, dismissing her. And to the boy who stood uncertainly in the doorway: 'Take Miss Lilli's case upstairs, please, Cammy. You know which room.'

'My old room?' Lilli was suddenly horribly afraid that Ingrid might have made changes during her absence – she wouldn't put it past her.

'Of course,' Ingrid replied briskly. 'Well, Lilli, I expect you are dying for a shower and a change of clothes.'

'I am – but not before I've seen Daddy. Where is he?'

'He's in the salon.' Ingrid raised a cautionary hand to stop Lilli, who had already started in that direction. 'But I should warn you first – he really is very ill. Please don't say or do anything to upset him.'

'Of course not!' Lilli replied sharply. 'As if I would!'

'It will be a shock . . .'

Lilli ignored her, brushing past and hurrying into the salon. Then, as she saw him, her step faltered momentarily. For all her apprehension she had thought she was ready for anything but nothing could have prepared her for the shocking change in his appearance.

Otto was propped up by cushions in his recliner and fully dressed in a silk shirt of saxe blue and a pair of fawn linen slacks, but even sitting as he was his clothes hung on him and it seemed to Lilli that he had shrunk to a mere shadow of his former self. The once strong and handsome face was wasted and drawn with pain, his scar standing out livid and angry against the pallor of his skin.

Lilli froze with horror, then the love and concern were rushing in and she ran to him, throwing her arms around him and kissing his cheek, which felt cold beneath her lips.

'Daddy – oh, Daddy!'

'Lilli – *liebchen*!' His voice broke.

For a few moments emotion overcame them, then Lilli dropped to the floor beside his chair, sitting back on her heels and holding his hands in hers.

'You're a fine one, Daddy!'

'I know,' he said ruefully. 'I make a terrible patient. Ask Ingrid.' He stretched out his hand to his wife, who had followed Lilli into the salon, but she hung back, respecting Lilli's need for privacy with her father.

'It hasn't stopped you enjoying your drink, I see,' Lilli said, nodding towards the glass at his elbow and trying to sound light-hearted.

'No, I can still keep a drink down, thank God!' He sighed. 'Oh Lilli, what have I come to? I always thought I'd die with my boots on. I never expected it to be like this.'

'Don't talk like that, Daddy. You're not going to die!'

'Oh yes I am, Lilli.' He said it quite philosophically and she could not bring herself to argue. Any thoughts of trying to persuade him to take some treatment had fled from her mind; it was obvious at first glance that it was much too late for that.

'So – did you have a good flight?' he asked.

'Fine – yes.' It all seemed terribly inconsequential, but at least it covered the awkwardness.

'How did you manage to get time off from your job at such short notice?'

'I had some holiday leave due to me and I just told them I was taking it. Someone can cover for me. It's not a problem.'

'Good. Good. And the air taxi met you in Barbados?'

'Yes. A new pilot. He seemed nice.'

'That's all right then. I didn't want you to . . .' He broke off. There was so much he needed to say to her but it was too soon, and besides, he felt very tired.

'Daddy,' she said, reading his mind, 'if you're worried about Jorge, please don't be. That was all over a long time ago. I'm older and wiser now.'

The shadows around his eyes darkened.

'Does that make a difference?'

'Yes,' Lilli said firmly. 'I was just a child then. I didn't know . . . what I know now.'

'Lilli.' His fingers, almost clawlike now that so much flesh had dropped off them, fastened around her hand. 'You still don't know everything. We need to talk . . .'

The agitation in his voice alarmed Lilli. It also goaded Ingrid into action.

'But not now, Otto,' she said, 'Lilli needs a bath and the chance to change into something cooler, and you need to rest.'

'For heaven's sake, woman, I do nothing *but* rest! It doesn't do me any good.'

'You've already overextended yourself today,' Ingrid said firmly, refusing to rise to his bait. 'You've been worrying yourself about Lilli – don't deny it, because I know you have. Well, she's here now, safe and sound. No plane crashes, no hijackers, no delays and no Jorge. You can have another drink and relax. There will be plenty of time tomorrow for all the heart-to-hearts you have in mind.'

'Ingrid is right, Daddy.' Lilli kissed his hands and released them, standing up. 'I'm here for two weeks at least and if necessary I shall stay longer. So you see, we have all the time in the world.'

Even as she said it she knew it was not the truth. Their time together might be very limited indeed. But another day could hardly make that much difference.

'I'll see you at dinner – before, if I'm ready and you're not resting. Dinner is still at eight, is it?'

'Of course. Nothing changes here.' But the overtones in his voice told Lilli that he was not only referring to the time of the evening meal.

She smiled at him, hiding all her emotions behind a carefully contrived mask of normality.

'Just take care of yourself. No wild parties whilst you're out of my sight!'

Otto returned her smile wearily. Every little movement had become such an enormous effort.

'I give you my word on that, *liebchen*.'

When Gárcia had left, returning to his launch which was moored in the marina, Jorge crossed the airstrip to the hut that housed Air Perpetua. He had hoped the new pilot might still be there, but he had already left. Manuel, however, was in the office, leafing through papers. He looked up, grinning, as Jorge entered.

'Everything going smoothly?' Jorge asked abruptly.

' 'Y-up. No problems.'

'Good.' Jorge picked up a form, glanced at it, put it down again. 'The new pilot did the taxi run, I see.'

' 'Y-up.' Manuel's grin broadened. He knew who the passenger had been and what it meant to Jorge, but he made no comment. What Jorge got up to with the old man's daughter, or anyone else for that matter, was no concern of his, though it amused him sometimes to watch Jorge's womanising in the way it might have amused any voyeur, and he admired – and envied – his many conquests. Jorge still had a way with the ladies that Manuel could not possibly hope to emulate, although he was ten years his junior. Jorge played them like a big-game hunter going in for the kill and they stood no more chance with him than a lame lion caught in the sights of a high-powered rifle. Well, good luck to him!

'How's the new pilot been?' Jorge asked. 'Any more peculiar questions?'

'Nope. But then I haven't seen him much today. He was flying the old man's daughter and I . . .'

'Yes,' Jorge said, cutting him off. 'I know what you were doing. Just keep an eye on him for me, would you, Manuel? Let me know at once if you think there's anything I ought to know.'

' 'Y-up. Will do.'

'I'm off now. I've wasted enough time today with that fool Garcia. I'm going home.'

But he wasn't going home – or at least, if he did, he had no intention of staying there. He was going to pay a visit to the villa and renew his acquaintance with Lilli. And both he and Manuel, who missed practically nothing, knew it.

'Otto – do you have to tell her everything about the Sanchez family and your business dealings?' Ingrid asked.

Lilli had gone upstairs and Ingrid could hear the grumblings in the somewhat unpredictable plumbing that indicated she was showering or taking a bath.

Otto shifted his tired gaze to her face and she winced at his obvious exhaustion.

'Yes, Ingrid, I believe I do. I don't want her finding out when I'm gone and no longer able to explain. And besides, it's best she knows for her own safety. Lilli is headstrong and you know what Jorge and the others are like if they think they are threatened. She has to know they'll stop at nothing . . .'

Ingrid nodded, resigned. Perhaps he was right. And at least it might mean that when Lilli left Madrepora next time she would never return again. Ingrid hoped with all her heart that it may be so – and not only for the reasons Otto had in mind. Seeing Lilli again had been every bit as bad as she had feared it would be. Lilli – so frighteningly like Magdalene – had reminded her once again too sharply for comfort of the woman who had stolen the best years of Otto's life from her.

A knot of bitterness rose in Ingrid's throat at the thought of it. All the long years of the war she had waited for him at home in Germany, praying for his safety. She had seen her own home destroyed by bombing, as well as his, and had told herself she must be brave. The houses were only bricks and mortar. As long as Otto was safe she could bear it. Each night she had slept with his engagement ring under her pillow as a talisman, longing for the day when at last the war would be over and he would return and put a ring on her finger which she would never need to take off again – the ring that would make her his wife.

But everything had gone wrong. Instead of emerging victorious, Germany had been humbled and Otto had not returned home in triumph but fled to South America. Even then she had waited impatiently for him to send for her, but the call had never come. Eventually the numbing news had reached her. Otto had met someone else – a Venezuelan girl, daughter of the man who had arranged his escape – and had fallen in love with her. Ingrid had been devastated. She couldn't believe Otto could do this to her, not after all they had been to one another. The day she heard he had married she thought of killing herself. But then a healing anger had begun to take the place of grief and a fierce hatred burned in her for the woman who had stolen the man she loved. She might be young and beautiful, Ingrid had thought, she might have bewitched him, alone in an alien country, but that didn't mean she would offer him lasting happiness. One day he would tire of her and when he did Ingrid would be waiting.

It had not worked out quite that way, of course. As the months became years Ingrid grew tired of her wasted life. She met a young doctor, and though to her he would never be Otto she decided to accept his offer of marriage. Ironically when she heard of Magdalene's death she felt nothing more than a sense of regret for what might have been. She was happy enough with her marriage and if Otto was alone again, well, so what? He'd got his comeuppance.

It was almost ten years before she thought seriously about Otto again. Her husband had been killed in an accident on the autobahn and whilst packing to move to a smaller house she had found her engagement ring and, with a hint of nostalgia to add flavour, it had all come rushing back. Suddenly Ingrid was desperate to see Otto again, as if a single day more without him was too much after all the wasted years. She wrote to him and he replied, inviting her to Madrepora. She went, as full of hopes and dreams as she had been as a girl, and when she set eyes on him again she knew without a doubt that she had never stopped loving him.

They were married and Ingrid had never gone home to Germany again. In the end all she had ever wanted was miraculously hers. There was only one thorn in her flesh, one person with the power to prick the bubble of her happiness. That someone was Lilli.

Lilli was the image of her mother, everyone said, and Ingrid felt sure that when Otto looked at her he saw Magdalene. Ingrid hated the way he spoiled Lilli, as if he was treating her to the love he could no longer lavish on Magdalene. And she was fiercely jealous not only of the closeness of their relationship but also of Lilli's youth and vivacity which seemed to mock her own lost youth, a constant reminder of the woman who had stolen what should have been the best years of her life.

To her shame, because she knew the grief it caused Otto, she could only be glad when Lilli went away to New York. At last she had felt she had Otto to herself without the ghosts of the past. But those halcyon days had been all too brief. Cruel fate had intervened. Soon she would lose Otto again, finally. And now Lilli was back, throwing her beautiful shadow over what little time they had left together.

Ingrid went to Otto now, standing behind his chair and placing her hands proprietorially on his shoulders where the bones jutted through the soft silk of his shirt.

'She'll be all right,' she said, comforting him with her lips and wishing that she could share Otto's intense love for his daughter. 'She is young and strong. It won't happen again.'

'I hope to God you are right,' Otto said, and they both knew that they were not only speaking of Lilli's involvement with Jorge but of other things, even harder to bear, that should by now be lost in the more distant past but which were too horrendous ever to die.

Guy de Savigny ate dinner alone – a simple meal of fish and mangos prepared for him by the maid. Then he piled the dishes in the sink, opened a fresh can of lager and took it out on to the veranda.

The moon had risen over the palm trees so big and bright that the night was almost as light as day and the still-hot air hummed with the music of a million mosquitoes and the rasp of crickets in the grass beneath the veranda.

Guy dragged a chair round to face the garden and sprawled into it, propping his feet up on the veranda rail. He should, he thought, write some letters home, but he couldn't be bothered. His mind was too busy with thinking about the events of the day.

He could still hardly believe his luck in meeting Otto's daughter

– and getting on so well with her. She might not have meant it, of course, when she extended the invitation for drinks at the villa. She might simply have been being polite. But whether she had meant it or not she had said it and it was an opening Guy did not intend to let slip by. A chance to get into the villa was exactly what he'd been waiting for. He wanted to see for himself the treasures Bill had told him about. Then he would know more or less for certain whether Otto Brandt was in reality Otto von Rheinhardt.

It was a heaven-sent opportunity – and the girl was a cracker, too. An unexpected bonus. Not at all what he had expected of the daughter of an elderly Nazi war criminal.

Guy experienced an unexpected twinge of regret. Under other circumstances he might well have been interested. He thought of her again, seeing her vivacious good looks, hearing her voice, and even imagining how she would feel in his arms. A pity. It wasn't often a girl attracted him as she had. But there it was – she *was* the German's daughter and if he turned out to be Otto von Rheinhardt that would be the end of it. She wouldn't want any more to do with him after he turned her father in to the authorities, and he wouldn't want anything more to do with the flesh and blood of the monster who had murdered his family and stolen their treasures.

For just a moment Guy found himself almost hoping that the German was not Otto von Rheinhardt. Then he caught himself up sharply. He wanted von Rheinhardt. He had wanted him for a very long time, and he wanted his family's heirlooms back where they belonged.

He had no intention of letting a pretty face and a pair of long legs stop him now.

Dinner was over at the villa. Patsy had cleared away and Lilli, Ingrid and Otto sat in the salon talking of inconsequential things.

Otto had eaten very little, picking at the food which had been placed on a tray on his lap, and Lilli watched him in distress. She had tried to imagine how awful it would be to see him so ill but the reality was much, much worse. If he had not always been such a strong man it would have been easier to bear, she thought. As it was, the contrast was heartbreaking, the iron will still there locked inside the failing body. Tears pricked her eyes. She looked away and saw a tall figure silhouetted between the veranda shutters. She gasped, startled, and at the same moment Ingrid spoke, her voice raised slightly in a note of indignation.

'Jorge! What a surprise!'

'Is it?' It was the same amused drawl Lilli remembered so well, the voice she had heard in her dreams.

He came into the salon, moving with the lazy grace of a big cat. The light from the candelabra etched the lines on his face into sharp relief so that he looked older, more debauched, more dangerous than ever. But he still had the power to stir her senses into unwelcome response.

'I heard Lilli was here,' he said. 'I dropped by to see her.'

'You shouldn't have.' Otto was sitting forward in his chair, his anger and dismay lending him some of the strength his illness had taken away. 'Lilli doesn't want to see you. You must know that.'

'It's all right, Daddy. Don't worry on my account.' Lilli slipped from her chair to stand behind his, her hands resting lightly on his shoulders. 'I'm flattered that you should have taken the trouble, Jorge, but as my father said, you shouldn't have. I really don't want to see you.'

Jorge shrugged, apparently unconcerned.

'I'm sorry about that, Lilli,' he said in the same throwaway drawl. 'I thought that you and I meant something to one another. And in any case with things as they are it may well be unavoidable.'

'What do you mean?'

He glanced in Otto's direction.

'Obviously things are going to change around here. There will be new arrangements to discuss.'

The cruelty of the remark took Lilli's breath away but Ingrid was on her feet in a moment, facing him furiously.

'How dare you, Jorge!' she demanded. 'How dare you come bursting in here uninvited and upsetting Otto in this way!'

Jorge half smiled but his face remained curiously expressionless.

'Facts have to be faced sooner or later, whether you like it or not.'

'But this is not the time or the place. I think you had better leave, Jorge.'

Jorge shrugged elegantly.

'As you wish. This is your home – for the present. I am only sorry you choose to be so inhospitable to an old friend and business partner. But – so be it. I'll talk to you alone, Lilli, in the very near future.'

'Can't you understand, Jorge, that I have nothing to say to you?' Lilli was furious at his arrogance and total lack of consideration for her father, furious too at herself for ever having allowed him to gain such a hold over her emotions and her life. 'Ingrid spoke for me, too. I've come back to Madrepora because my father is ill. That is the only reason. And I would be grateful if you would leave him – and me – alone.'

Jorge laughed deep in his throat, a laugh coarsened by too many late nights and too many cigars.

'My darling Lilli, you are more beautiful than ever – especially when you are angry. All that fire – irresistible! I shall look forward to doing business with you.'

He turned, moving out of the circle of light by the candelabra, an actor who knew he had delivered the perfect exit line and did not wish to spoil it by further dialogue. Before Lilli could retaliate the darkness had swallowed him.

'That pig – who does he think he is!' Ingrid blazed. Lilli did not think she could ever remember seeing her stepmother, usually calm and composed to a fault, so out of control. 'He has no respect for anything or anyone. One of these days someone will do to him what they did to his father – blow a hole right through him – and it will be no more than he deserves.'

'Ingrid . . . don't, please.' Otto's voice was strained and beneath her hands Lilli could feel the tension in the rigid line of his shoulders. 'Just leave it, huh? Don't let him spoil Lilli's first night home.'

'He has already done that.'

'No, he hasn't.' Now that Jorge had gone Lilli felt weak and shaky but she was determined, for her father's sake, not to show how upset she was. 'I'm angry that he should say such things but at least I've seen him now, and I have to admit I was dreading that. Now – well, it's done, isn't it? The worst is over.'

'Lilli.' Otto reached up, taking her hand and pulling her around to his side. 'I don't think it is over. You heard what he said. He wants to talk to you – alone.'

'I won't *be* alone with him. End of story.'

'*Liebchen*, it's not as simple as that. You know what Jorge is like. He'll engineer it one way or another. For one thing he won't let you go so easily. It's not his style. For another . . . well, you heard what he said.'

He broke off, strength ebbing from his voice.

Lilli dropped to her knees beside his chair. 'Daddy, what did he mean by those things?'

'Not now, Lilli!' Ingrid said sharply. 'Your father is very tired. I won't have him upset any more tonight.'

'It's all right,' Otto said. 'We've been through all this, Ingrid. Lilli has to know the truth about Madrepora – and about Jorge and the others.'

'But not tonight. It's too much for you, Otto. There's always tomorrow. And now I am going to call Basil and get him to put you to bed.' She spoke briskly, her tone almost schoolmarmish, and as she swept out of the salon in search of Basil Otto raised his hands helplessly before letting them fall back on to his knees, shaking his head at Lilli in an attempt at wry humour.

'You see what it's come to, Lilli? Otto von Rheinhardt having to do as a woman tells him!' His words were slightly slurred by tiredness and the effect of the drugs he had been forced to take earlier, and Lilli looked up at him, puzzled.

'What did you say?'

'I said Ingrid bosses me about shamelessly.'

'No – not that. You said Otto von something – well, it wasn't Brandt, anyway.'

'Did I?' Furious with himself for the slip of the tongue Otto was grateful for once that he could use the excuse of the drugs to retreat into vagueness. 'Oh, it's an old family name. I used it as a boy. Haven't even thought of it for years . . .'

'Oh Daddy!' Lilli's face softened with love and pity. 'I was going to ask you again whilst Ingrid is out of the room what on earth is going on here, but I see she was right. You're in no fit state to talk tonight. Well, I shall still be here tomorrow. You can tell me then all you want me to know.'

'Yes, Lilli, yes. I must confess I don't feel up to it . . .'

The door opened and Ingrid sailed back into the salon, followed closely by the faithful Basil.

'Here he is, Otto. Now you get a good night's sleep and I'll look after Lilli,' she said.

'Yes, yes. Very well. Good night then, *liebchen*. And – in spite of everything – it is good to have you home.'

He touched her cheek and Lilli stood aside, anguished, watching Basil ease him out of the chair and help him across the room.

'I had no idea he was this ill,' she said to Ingrid when he was out of earshot. 'It's dreadful! You should have let me know sooner.'

'I told you – he didn't want it.' Ingrid poured herself a fresh coffee. Her face was smooth and oddly untroubled. 'And now that Jorge has been here causing trouble I should think you can see why.'

Lilli felt a dart of guilt, knowing that her own past indiscretions were at least partly to blame for what had happened here tonight. But only partly. There had been something else, something she did not understand.

'What is it Daddy wants to tell me?' she asked.

For a moment Ingrid was silent and Lilli could see her weighing the odds, deciding whether or not to speak. Then she shook her head.

'No, Lilli, it has to come from him. When he's strong enough. It's not my place – it has nothing to do with me at all.'

'But you are his wife. You must know what it's all about.'

'I know, yes, but it's still not my business. It has to do with arrangements that were in place long before I came to Madrepora and things which concern only you and him.'

'And supposing he isn't strong enough, or lucid enough, tomorrow or the next day? Supposing he's never able to tell me?'

'Then in that case I will do it for him. But he must have the opportunity first.' She spoke decisively and Lilli knew it would be useless to press her further.

'Ingrid,' she said. 'Would you mind very much if I went to bed too? I'm very tired myself. It's been a long day.'

She did not add that she did not want to have to sit here making small talk with her father's wife, that she did not feel comfortable in her presence and wanted, more than anything, to be alone with her thoughts.

'Of course I don't mind,' Ingrid replied. 'I'm beginning to get used to spending my evenings alone, which is probably just as well since it is all I have to look forward to.'

Lilli could think of nothing to say. But she crossed the room and kissed her stepmother on the cheek with more warmth than usual. Ingrid had at least brought Otto some happiness and companionship in the last years of his life. For this alone Lilli knew she would be eternally grateful.

Her old room was unchanged. Lilli undressed by the light of the moon which shone brightly through the unshuttered windows and climbed into the four-poster bed, rearranging the folds of mosquito netting which fell from the canopy to provide a cool white haven.

As a child she had loved this bed which might have come straight out of the pages of a book of fairytales. To her it had been in turn an enchanted castle, a remote island, a pirate ship. Here all the innocent world of a lonely child had been hers, allowing her to dream and pretend and play-act to her heart's content. But here too she had cried bitter tears – for her mother, and, years later, for Jorge who had manipulated and deceived her, and now, with her emotions churning, it was these sadder memories that were the more real to her.

Lilli drew the fine lawn sheet up to her breasts, letting her arms lie on top of it, and closed her eyes. But sleep refused to come, as it had refused to come every night since she had received Josie's letter, and the scene that had been enacted downstairs earlier began to play itself out again, over and over, like a ciné film being run and rerun.

Why had Jorge had to come here tonight? she asked herself, a spark of anger driving sleep even further away. Why couldn't he have left her alone for just a little longer? But that wasn't Jorge's way. He had to gain what he considered to be the advantage, playing his favourite game of interchanging brutal cruelty with intoxicating flattery until his victim was no more than a marionette in the hands of an experienced puppet master. Jorge went all out for what he wanted – and he wanted her. No – not quite true. He didn't want her – he wanted the idea of her. To possess and discard as he chose in the service of his lust and self-esteem. She knew it, hated him for it and yet still felt herself drawn irresistibly to him just as she always had been.

She had known all those years ago that what she was doing was wrong, and had been unable to care. But she had not known then

what she knew now. She had been very young, very impression-
able, very romantic. She couldn't blame herself too much. What
she was most afraid of was that even now, older and wiser, she
would still be unable to resist and would allow it all to begin again.

Jorge was her destiny. That was what she had told herself when
she was sixteen years old and it had been music to her ears. She had
had no idea of what had gone before and what was to follow. And
if she had, would it . . . could it . . . have been different? Lilli did
not know. She only knew that now, lying in her old bed with
Jorge's presence, despicable yet still undeniably magnetic, all
around her, she was as much his plaything now as she had been
then.

22

SHE HAD BEEN sixteen years old when it had begun, and she had been a pupil at the Convent School of Our Blessed Lady in Caracas for almost eight years.

At first, rebellious and homesick, she had hated the school. Then, gradually, things had improved. She had learned that the nuns were ready to forgive almost anything of a girl as quick and clever as she, and her wicked sense of humour made her popular with the other pupils. Lilli, who had so often been lonely, discovered the pleasure of companionship and even love of a sort.

Her name was Rosina, she was bookish and serious – all the things Lilli was not – and for two whole terms they spent their leisure time walking in the school grounds, their arms about each other's waists, sharing their secrets. Once or twice they even kissed and touched one another but the contact gave Lilli no pleasure. For her it spoiled the purity of their friendship, awakening in her feelings not only of guilt but also of disappointment – an emotion which made no sense since she had expected nothing in the first place. She had begun to avoid Rosina, who followed her like a puppy-dog which has been kicked by its master. But there were other friends to take Rosina's place, friends to laugh with and get into scrapes with, and Lilli forgot the vague yearnings and became her old happy-go-lucky self.

Much as she enjoyed school, however, she loved the long holidays when she returned home to Madrepora even more, and the summer when she was sixteen was no exception. Her heart was light with pleasurable anticipation as the little plane her father had sent for her skimmed across the blue sea dotted with tiny islands. But oddly there was no thought in her mind of Jorge. She had scarcely seen him in the last ten years. Instead it was Uncle Fernando and Fabio, Jorge's brother, who stayed at the gingerbread house and did business with her father. Lilli had once asked Otto the reason for the change, but he had merely shrugged: 'Jorge is busy elsewhere,' and if his eyes had shadowed when he said it Lilli had not noticed. After a while she had ceased to wonder, though she had never quite forgotten him.

At first, when she jumped down from her little air taxi on to the sunsoaked landing strip and saw the tall, dark-haired man dressed in white checking out a light aircraft where it was parked up on the grass, she did not recognise him. Then he looked up, saw her and waved, and her heart lurched. It was Jorge!

Instantly all the half-forgotten dreams were there, resurfacing as if it had been only yesterday that she had cherished them. Only now they were tempered with the realisation of just how silly her childish adulation had been, and the teenage Lilli was overwhelmed by embarrassment both for her five-year-old self and for the way she was feeling now, just seeing him again. She waved back and he crossed the grass towards her.

'Lilli! It is Lilli, isn't it? I'd never have known you except that your father told me you were expected home today. You've grown up!'

His dark eyes were moving over her, appraising her, and not bothering to hide the fact that he liked what he saw.

'I should hope I have grown up, since the last time I saw you I was only about five years old!' she said with a little laugh.

'You were beautiful then,' he said, 'but you are even more beautiful now.'

Lilli flushed with pleasure. She brushed her hair away from her face, tucking it behind her ear and holding it there. The sun glinted on the gold bangles which had once been her mother's and which she now wore whenever she was not in school uniform.

'Is that your aeroplane?' she asked.

'The Beech? Yes.'

'Beech?'

'Short for Beechcraft Baron. It's my newest baby. You like it?'

'It looks wonderful.' And so it did, a sleek white bird gleaming against the deep blue sky and the emerald grass.

'I am just leaving for Florida but I shall be coming back in a few days' time and when I do I will take you flying. Would you like that?'

'Oh yes!'

'Good.' He caught her hand and raised it to his lips, kissing her fingers with an extravagant gesture that was pure South American, whilst his eyes, deep and full of meaning, sought hers. Then he released her hand, smiled at her, and turned, walking back across the grass to where his aeroplane was parked.

Lilli watched him go, thrilling with excitement. No one had ever talked to her like that before, no one had kissed her hand or looked at her with that searching, meaningful gaze.

The deliciously tingly feeling of standing on the brink of something new and wonderful remained with her as the car whisked her back to the villa, making her homecoming even more special than usual and making up for the fact that she no longer had her father to herself.

The previous year Otto had married again and the intrusive presence of his new wife, Ingrid, whom, he told her, he had known many years ago in Germany, was the one small cloud that had hung over Lilli's pleasure in returning to Madrepora. She had tried hard to like Ingrid for her father's sake. He must have been lonely since her mother's death, she knew, and she tried to be glad that now, whilst she was away at school, he was no longer alone. But for all that she could not help resenting Ingrid, however unreasonably, for taking her mother's place. And when Lilli had noticed Ingrid wearing a brooch which had once belonged to Magdalene her resentment had deepened. From that day on Lilli had begun wearing Magdalene's bracelets, a small defiant gesture in an effort to reincarnate the spirit of the mother she could scarcely remember.

Now, however, Lilli was too happy to allow anything, or anyone, to spoil her homecoming.

'I saw Jorge at the airstrip,' she said that evening as they relaxed in the salon, cold drinks at their elbows, whilst the overhead fans cooled the room where the heat of the day still lingered.

The soft twilight masked the slight stiffening of Otto's jaw.

'Ah – Jorge. Yes.'

'I thought Fabio ran things here nowadays.'

'Fabio is weak,' Otto said. 'Besides, he has begun to drink too much – a family failing, I'm afraid. All the Sanchez family drink too much, but Fabio can't handle it.'

'And Jorge, of course, can,' Ingrid said. Her tone was silky smooth as ever but Lilli could not mistake the underlying sarcasm and she experienced a flash of the old dislike.

'It was very nice to see him again anyway. It reminded me of the old days when Mama was alive,' she said, glancing slyly at Ingrid and feeling a spark of satisfaction at the twin spots of colour that appeared in her cheeks.

'Those days are over, Lilli,' Otto said sharply.

It was Lilli's turn to flush with guilt at her childish attempt to hurt Ingrid.

'They were good days though, weren't they?' she said defiantly.

'They were a long time ago,' Otto replied firmly. 'Now, tell me, what have they been teaching you at school this term?'

The conversation continued but the happy mood of the evening had been fractured and Lilli was not quite sure how or why it had happened.

Jorge returned to Madrepora a few days later. Lilli met him and her father coming out of the room Otto used as an office.

'It's our little princess!' Jorge said, looking at her in a way which made her pulses quicken. 'You are a very lucky man, Otto, to have such a beautiful daughter.'

'Yes, I know,' Otto said, but there was a tightness in his voice.

'I have promised to take her flying,' Jorge said, his eyes meeting hers. 'Shall we say tomorrow at four, Lilli?'

Otto's face darkened.

'I'm not sure about that.'

'Oh please, Daddy!' Lilli begged. 'Jorge will take good care of me, won't you, Jorge?'

'Of course.'

After a moment Otto relented.

'Very well, Lilli, since your heart is set on it,' he said with a sigh. 'Just as long as she is back before dark, Jorge.'

Jorge smiled and said nothing.

Lilli had expected a short pleasure trip, but to her amazement Jorge flew her to St Vincent, skimming over the sparkling blue water with a skill that excited her. Lilli had always loved flying, especially in the little air taxis, but sitting beside Jorge in the front of his Beechcraft Baron was a whole new experience. They were close enough for his arm to brush hers occasionally and the scent of his aftershave, fanned towards her by the air-conditioning, excited her.

'I hope you are hungry,' he said when they landed on St Vincent. 'I have booked a table at a restaurant. But not just yet. We have time to explore first.'

'You mean – dinner?' Lilli asked with a tinge of alarm. 'But I promised Daddy I'd be back . . .'

'You'll be back – just a little later than you thought. Don't worry about it.'

Lilli did not argue. A sort of madness had taken hold of her. She knew her father would be furious but she no longer cared. Nothing mattered except being with Jorge.

A hire car was awaiting them at the airfield.

'Have you ever been to St Vincent before?' Jorge asked, swinging the car on to the Leeward Highway which ran north-wards up the west coast of the island so that the brown sandy bays were to one side of them and the hilly interior and tropical rain forest to the other.

Lilli shook her head.

'Daddy has always been too busy to take me.'

'Do you know why I like St Vincent?' Jorge asked. 'Because of the volcano. It's more than sixty years now since it erupted, but one day it will erupt again.' His black eyes were glittering.

'You like danger, don't you?' Lilli asked.

'To experience danger is to know you are alive,' Jorge replied. 'Yes, I like that. And so do you, my little princess. I can sense it.'

Lilli said nothing. She had never thought of it like that but now that he said it she felt he had discovered something deep within her which no one else in her charmed, well-protected life had ever touched on.

A few miles north of Chateaubelair the road ended. Jorge stopped the car where they could look down over Petit Bordel Bay.

'I will bring you here another day when we have more time,' he said. 'Then we will take a boat to the Falls of Baleimo. They plunge down from a volcanic hill. Fire and water, Lilli – that, too, is exciting.'

He reached for her hand, curling his fingers around it, and as he did so he also touched her soft inner thigh. Lilli gasped softly. It was as if the excitement of the flight and Jorge's nearness had already sensitised every bit of her and his touch was like a high-voltage electric current, sparking each tiny nerve ending to life. His eyes never leaving hers he moved his fingers in a gentle stroking motion and the thrills of awareness grew sharper. She had never known so much delight was possible from such a little touch, and she sat motionless, hardly daring to breathe.

He kissed her, then drew back, looking at her.

'You are so beautiful, Lilli, and I have waited for you for so long.'

Happiness burst in her. It seemed that all her dreams were coming true.

Jorge had booked a table in a restaurant at the water's edge; while the sun sank in a ball of red fire into the deepening blue of the ocean they ate shellfish and chicken Caribbean style and drank champagne. To Lilli it was ambrosia. Jorge drank little – 'I have to get you home safely,' he said. 'And who needs wine? I am drunk on you, Lilli.'

They flew back through the velvet blackness of the night and the stars were reflected in the dark water beneath them. It was only when they landed on the tiny airstrip that Lilli felt a qualm of apprehension. Her father was going to be furious!

Otto *was* furious.

'Where have you been, Lilli?' he demanded. 'I thought I told you to be back before dark!'

'We've been to St Vincent. And how can you tell me I should be back by dark? I'm not a child any more.'

'No, but you are still far too young to be God-knows-where with Jorge. He is not a suitable companion for you.'

'I'm sorry, Daddy,' she said, anxious not to spoil things with arguments and recriminations. 'Don't be angry, please. I'm back now, aren't I?'

He shook his head sadly, thinking that Lilli was far too much like her mother for her own good. Magdalene had always been able to wind him around her little finger too.

'All right, we'll forget it now. But I don't want you seeing him again,' he said. 'In any case, he is going to Florida again tomorrow and I doubt if he will be back before you return to school.'

Lilli was dumbfounded. Jorge had said nothing about going

back to Florida. All the magic had gone out of the day and Lilli felt her heart would break.

'Lilli, your cousin has telephoned,' Sister Concepta said. 'He is coming to take you out for tea tomorrow.'

Lilli stared at the nun in bewilderment. She did not have a cousin, much less one who was likely to turn up at her school and take her out for tea. There must be some mistake.

'My cousin?' she said blankly.

'Your cousin, Jorge Sanchez. What is the matter with you, child? Why are you looking like that? Don't you want to go?'

Sister Concepta was the one looking bewildered now. The girls were generally only too delighted when a relative came to release them temporarily from the rigours of the convent school.

'Oh – *Jorge*!' Lilli exclaimed, amazed and delighted. 'Oh yes, Sister. Yes, of course I want to go!' she said swiftly and not even the knowledge of how angry her father would be if he should ever find out about this could spoil the magic of the moment.

He came next day to collect her, driving into the white-walled courtyard of the convent in a scarlet Porsche. Lillie saw him arrive from the window of the dormitory from which she had been watching with barely concealed impatience.

'He's here!' she cried, jumping up from the window seat and tidying her hair back into the band which restrained it.

'That's your *cousin*?' Angel Gomez, currently her best friend, rushed over to peer through the window at the tall, slightly raddled man all in white who was climbing out of the Porsche.

Lilli smiled with pride and excitement. She had been aching to confide in Angel but some instinct had prevented her. Angel might be her best friend but she was also a gossip, and Lilli had been very afraid that if she told Angel the truth it would be common knowledge in the convent before she could so much as draw breath and the outing would be put in jeopardy. Now, however, she could no longer contain herself.

'He's not my cousin,' she said smugly.

'I should think not!' Angel snorted. 'He's old! Your uncle, more like.'

Lilli shot her a look of hatred. Angel could be so obtuse

sometimes! Why couldn't she see that age had nothing whatever to do with it?

'You're just jealous because I'm going out and you're not – and your father's car is just a boring old Mercedes.'

She grabbed her purse and ran downstairs, almost falling over in her eagerness before she remembered herself and slowed to the sort of pace more suited to the sophisticated young lady Jorge thought she had become.

Jorge was in Sister Concepta's office and if he had not impressed Angel he had clearly won over the nun. Her small round face was pink with pleasure and the incessant fluttering of her hands betrayed her nervousness.

'Ah – Lilli – your cousin is here,' she twittered unnecessarily when Lilli tapped at the half-open door, and Jorge gave Lilli a conspiratorial wink.

'Now be careful, Lilli, that your behaviour does nothing to bring disgrace on the school.'

'Yes, Sister.'

'And make sure you are back in time for the six o'clock Vespers.'

'You need not worry, I shall look after her, Sister,' Jorge assured her.

Sister Concepta's cheeks grew even more pink.

'Oh, I'm sure you will, Señor. I didn't mean to imply . . . but rules are rules. We have to have them for the girls' own good.'

'Very sensible,' Jorge said solemnly.

As she climbed into the Porsche beside him Lilli could restrain her giggles no longer.

'Jorge – you are wicked! She's such a stickler for her rules and regulations. If she knew the truth she'd have a stroke!'

'She won't know, will she, so long as you are discreet.'

He smiled at her, his teeth very white beneath the dark sweep of his moustache, and her heart turned over.

'Where are we going?'

'It doesn't matter, does it? All that matters to me, anyway, is that I am with my princess.'

'Daddy would be furious, too, if he knew. He forbade me to see you again after you took me to St Vincent. But you weren't around anyway. Why did you go off like that?'

Jorge shrugged.

'I had business to attend to in Florida.'

'What sort of business?'

'Oh, this and that. We don't want to waste precious time talking about something so boring, do we?'

His face had darkened slightly, the suggestion of a scowl, and Lilli felt a moment's dismay. She must not spoil this afternoon by behaving like a spoilt child. But a few moments later his hand snaked over from the gearstick to cover hers and excitement burst in her like a Roman candle, showering her with sparks of brightness which left her aglow even when the first incandescence had died.

They left the convent behind and drove to a rise overlooking the city. They talked, Lilli chattering, Jorge listening mostly with an amused smile, sitting in the hot dry grass that bordered the road. He held her hand and Lilli was afraid to move in case she broke the spell even when her fingers began to turn numb with pins and needles.

There was a wild orchid growing nearby; Jorge reached out and picked it, twining it in her hair, and she thought that this – *this* – was perfect happiness, the heaven the nuns talked about come down to earth.

'My little Lilli,' he said. He kissed her gently, sucking at her lips as if he were drawing the sweetness from them like nectar from a flower.

She longed for him to hold her close, longed to wind her arms around his neck where the hair grew thick and dark, press her body to his, but she dared not. Instead she sat quite still, savouring the moment, remembering it with all her senses so as to be able to take it out and examine it later when the dormitory lights were out and the other girls asleep.

When it was time for them to go back she felt a moment's panic, conscious that time was slipping away from her.

'You will come and see me again, won't you?' she asked.

'Of course. But not too often. The nuns might become suspicious.'

'Yes. Yes, they might – they're so stuffy!' But she was feeling sorry for them, poor deprived souls whose vows prevented them from ever experiencing what she had begun to experience.

He left her in the courtyard just as the bell began to toll for

Vespers. She watched his scarlet Porsche disappear in a cloud of white dust and ran back inside for the evening service. And as she knelt in the soft candlelight in the Lady Chapel she offered twin prayers. One was of thanksgiving – 'Never forget to thank Our Lady for Her blessings,' the nuns always said. The other was a heartfelt plea.

'Let Jorge come again soon. And let him love me as I love him.'

Jorge came twice more to take her out before she went home for Christmas and each time it was the same. He whispered endearments, he kissed her, but never attempted to progress beyond this.

It was because he respected her, Lilli told herself, torn between wanting more and being half afraid of what would happen in the event.

She was also worried about her father's reaction when he saw her and Jorge together, but to her intense disappointment Jorge was not on Madrepora that Christmas and she spent the entire holiday fretting miserably.

'Where were you, Jorge?' she asked when next he came to the school to take her out.

'In Florida.'

'Florida *again*? I thought you'd be on Madrepora.'

'What is this, the Spanish Inquisition?' he asked sourly.

He did not come again for more than six weeks and Lilli was in torment. Perhaps, she thought, it was because he still thought of her as a child that he treated her this way. Perhaps he, too, wanted more, but was unwilling to force her, as he thought, into something she might not be ready for. Well, next time he kissed her – if he ever kissed her again! – she would have to try to put that right.

When the occasion arose her throat grew dry from nervousness. They were parked up in the hills overlooking Caracas, the lights far beneath them like twinkling stars in the soft darkness which had fallen with tropical swiftness. His arm was around her shoulders, her head lying against his broad chest. As she felt his lips in her hair a small shudder ran through her and grabbing hold of her courage she took his hand and, trembling slightly, moved it to her breast. From the moment it lay there it felt so good she forgot to be afraid, feeling his fingers moving gently but firmly against the soft flesh. Then, quickly, decisively, he removed it.

'No, Lilli,' he said.

A terrible feeling of rejection swamped her. She wanted to cry with shame and disappointment.

'No, princess,' he said again. 'This is not the time or the place. I don't want to start something I can't finish.'

'But . . .' You *can* finish, she wanted to say, but she dared not.

'I told you, I can wait for you. Our first time must be perfect. I love you too much for it to be otherwise.'

Her heart swelled with joy. And for the time being Lilli was content again.

As the summer wore on, however, she began to worry. Would Jorge be on Madrepora for the vacation or would he be in Florida again? She summoned up the courage to ask him.

'I shall be there,' he said simply.

'Then . . . we shall be able to see one another?'

'We shall have to be careful. Your father would not approve. But we'll find a way. Just keep quiet and leave it to me.' He smiled, that very white smile she loved so much.

All through that vacation Jorge was on Madrepora and for the first time in her life Lilli neglected her favourite haunts, neglected Josie, neglected everything to spend every waking moment in the secluded cove where she knew Jorge could find her whenever he had time to spend with her. He had become the breath of life to her; it was as if her world had shrunk to hold nothing but him and when they were not together she was only half alive. She thought of nothing but him, cared for nothing and no one but him. She developed a craftiness and a deceitfulness she had not known she was capable of to prevent her father from discovering how she spent her days, and pretended it was no worse than slipping off to meet Josie behind his back.

Sometimes it was perfect. They swam together in the clear sea, lying side by side on the hot sand to dry afterwards, their limbs barely touching, and Lilli marvelled at the beauty of Jorge's body, still taut and lithe, awakening a hunger in her unlike anything she had ever known before. He took her to Johnny Shovelnose's bar on the south side of the island which had always been forbidden to her and which was frequented by locals, buying her drinks she had never tasted before, like planter's punch and gin slings, and whispering endearments to her. And one day he suggested she should come back to his house.

The moment he said it Lilli knew what he meant. Her heart began to pound.

'You mean . . . now?'

'In a few minutes, yes. Don't you want to?'

'Oh yes . . . yes . . .' It was what she had been waiting for for so long; now the moment had come she felt the beginnings of panic.

'Don't look so scared, little one. There's nothing to be afraid of. You don't think I'll hurt you, do you?'

'No . . . no . . . of course not.'

'Then I will go there and wait for you. Leave it a little while so we are not seen together and then follow me.' He took her hand, kissing her fingers so that her fear turned to trembling anticipation. 'After today, Lilli, you will be mine and I will be yours forever.'

She sat on the beach after he had gone, knees drawn up to her chin, looking at the familiar vista and thinking suddenly that it would be the last time she would see it through the eyes of a child.

After a few minutes she stood up, arranging her wrap around her shoulders to cover her still-wet swimsuit, letting her hands linger for a moment on her hips, exploring the softly curving lines between stomach and thighs and hoping desperately that she would please Jorge. Then she turned slowly, walking back beneath the palm trees towards the gingerbread house. The sun, filtering through the fronds, made her skin glow, but it was nothing compared to the warm moistness that was there between her thighs where the fires of desire had already begun to burn.

She climbed the steps, eager yet moving like someone in a dream.

'Is that you, princess?' Jorge called when he heard her push the door open.

'Yes.'

'Up here.'

She climbed the old colonial-style staircase, her bare feet making no sound. Jorge appeared in the doorway of his bedroom. He had changed into a black silk dressing gown which reached to just below his knees, exposing his thick brown calves.

'Wait, princess, I shall carry you in, just like in all the best movies.'

He swept her off her feet and she wound her arms around his

neck, feeling with heightened sensitivity his thick hair and the smooth satiny silk of his robe.

He had pulled aside the mosquito-netting drapes which surrounded the bed and turned back the covers to reveal black silk sheets. Now he set Lilli down, kissing her forehead, damp with a perspiration that came partly from nervousness and partly from the heat of the day, and gently eased the wrap from her shoulders. He paused to kiss her again, this time on the tip of her nose, before finding the hook of her bikini bra and easing it undone. As it fell away he cupped her breasts with both hands and ran a line of kisses down her throat to her nipples, rising in the circles made by his fingers and thumbs. Lilli's whole body was coming alive with shivers of delight but she stood motionless. After a little while he released her breasts, moving his hands slowly and sensuously down over her midriff and hips until he reached her bikini pants, sliding his thumbs inside and easing them down, lifting each foot in turn until she was free of them then tossing them aside. Then his lips were on her pubic mound, seeking the tender warm places as he parted her soft hair with his mouth, kissing first, then licking and sucking until every nerve deep within her abdomen screamed out in sharp delight.

Only when he was satisfied that she was absolutely ready for him did he straighten, shredding his robe with careless grace, and she caught her breath at the first sight of his naked body, gloriously aroused.

He lifted her again, carrying her to the bed and laying her down gently on the silken sheets. She moaned and writhed a little, wanting him now with a fierceness that made all the other wanting pale into insignificance, on the point of orgasm simply from his kisses, the sight of him and the erotic feel of the sheets beneath her fevered body.

He came to her gently but firmly. She felt a moment's sharp pain, felt the hot rush between her legs where before there had been only moist yearning, and moaned deep in her throat. Then he was moving in her deeply but slowly and she gave herself up to the wave upon wave of urgent sensuality, not believing it could get better, still better, scarcely able to bear the sensations that were turning her world upside down, yet wanting it to go on forever . . . and ever . . .

The climax came suddenly, catching her in the maelstrom of sharp dizzying delight, then beginning to drop her gently as a giant roller lifts and discards a body-surfer. She wanted to cry out: No, no, it can't be over! It can't stop – please, please! But although Jorge still moved within her, although his rasping breath told her he was approaching a climax of his own, and inexperienced as she was, she knew instinctively that the glory was slipping away. So desperately did she try to hold on to it that she scarcely noticed Jorge's grasp or his fingers biting into her arms as he reached his own orgasm. Only in retrospect did she realise it was over for him too as he rolled away from her, breathing heavily, and lay beside her, one arm still lying possessively across her body.

For long moments neither spoke. Then Jorge shifted slightly so that his hand once more cupped her breast and turned his face into her neck.

'And now, my little princess, you are mine. Wasn't it worth waiting for?'

'Yes.' She couldn't think of anything else to say; she was drained, exhausted, but happy.

After a while, he reached for her again. She felt his body stirring against her thigh and let the delight begin once more, gentler, less urgent, yet equally exhilarating.

And then, suddenly, an alien sound caught her attention, breaking the spell, bringing her sharply back to pulsing, fearful reality. A door banging in the house downstairs, a voice, loud and angry, calling out.

Otto's voice!

'It's Daddy!' Lilli gasped, horrified.

Jorge was on his feet in an instant, moving with the grace of a big cat, reaching for his trousers which were draped over the back of a cane chair.

'Stay here. I'll see what he wants.'

He thrust his feet into lizard-skin sneakers and left the room. Lilli sat up, reaching for her bikini and pulling it on in trembling haste. She was suddenly overcome with terror that her father might come bursting into the room and find her naked in Jorge's bed. But at the same time she was angry, suddenly, with the need for subterfuge.

I am going to go downstairs and tell him! Lilli thought with a burst of impetuosity. We are in love – we have nothing to be ashamed of. He'll have to know sooner or later – it might as well be now! She flounced out of the bedroom.

The two men were in the living room at the foot of the stairs. As she descended them she heard her father's voice.

'Where is Lilli?'

'How should I know?'

'Cammy saw you on the beach together – and it's not the first time. I won't have it, do you understand?'

Lilli hesitated, frightened by the intensity of feeling in her father's tone. She had heard him angry many times before but this was more than anger. Jorge, however, merely laughed.

'Really? And what are you going to do about it, my friend?'

'You'll leave me no choice. I shall tell her the truth about you and Magdalene. Do you suppose she would want anything more to do with you then?'

Lilli froze, clinging on to the wooden newel post.

'Lilli is besotted with me,' she heard Jorge say, and his choice of phrase shocked her still further. 'Nothing you could say will change that. But you would do well, my friend, to remember your position here. Make an enemy of me and you could lose everything – including your freedom.'

'You bloody bastard!' Otto's voice was almost bestial in his fury; Lilli had a sudden vision of him grabbing Jorge by the throat, of the two men she loved fighting like animals. The vision stirred her to action.

'Stop it! Stop it, both of you!' she screamed, running into the room.

They turned towards her, startled. An angry red flush stained Jorge's darkly handsome face whilst Otto's features were distorted with fury.

'So you *are* here, you little fool!'

Lilli slipped between them, taking Jorge's arm and facing her father defiantly.

'Daddy, listen – I'm sorry if you don't like it, but it's something you are going to have to get used to. I love Jorge and he loves me.'

Otto swore, an ugly guttural sound.

'Oh Lilli, Lilli, you don't love him! You only think you do. And he certainly does not love you. If you knew the truth . . .'

His words, echoing what she had overheard earlier, frightened her.

'What are you talking about? Not that anything you say could make any difference . . .'

'Lilli . . .' Otto broke off, gesticulating helplessly, and in the silence Jorge laughed unpleasantly.

'Well go on, Otto – tell her!'

Otto opened his mouth, closed it again. Lilli could not remember ever having seen him so upset . . . except, perhaps, when her mother had died. He looked old suddenly, his face so drained of blood that it was almost as white as his hair, and she saw that his hands were shaking.

'What is it, Daddy,' she said quietly. 'You can't stop now.'

'No, Otto, you can't.' Jorge's tone was jeering. He moved away from Lilli, reaching for a packet of panatellas and a chunky onyx lighter which lay on a side table. 'All right, if you won't tell her, I will.'

He lit the cigar, drawing on it lazily.

'Your mother and I were lovers, Lilli. From the time we were younger than you are now. Is that so terrible?'

Lilli gazed at him in sheer disbelief.

'You . . . and my mother?' The words were wrung from her, as primitive emotions she could scarcely recognise welled up inside her. 'I don't believe it!'

'Oh, it's true. But it was all over a long time ago. So now you know.'

Lilli stared at him in horror. As yet she could scarcely take it in. She only knew that everything in her world had changed – and Jorge had changed most of all. The man she loved had disappeared; in his place was a cold gloating individual, a monster behind a familiar handsome mask, not so much unreal as obscene.

Suddenly, in spite of the twirling ceiling fans, the heat of the room was stifling and Lilli felt a wave of nausea rise in her throat. She had to get out – get away from both of them. Pressing her hand against her mouth she turned and fled, ignoring her father's anguished plea to her to stop.

Blindly she ran down the stone steps between the fragrant frangipani bushes, running, running, as if she could somehow leave the confusion and shock and pain behind her, but knowing she could not. The soft breeze whipped her hair around her face, she raised a hand to hold it back and ran on. Down to the beach, where the soft sand slowed her footsteps, filling her sandals, dragging her down, and the soft lap of the waves was drowned by the roaring in her ears.

Jorge and her mother. It couldn't be true! Yet at the same time she knew it was. Why hadn't she guessed? Why hadn't she put two and two together long ago?

Images were filling her mind now, images from the distant past as real as if she were seeing them all again for the first time. Jorge and her mother on the veranda; her mother's voice: 'Lilli – why don't you run off and play?' Jorge looking at her mother with just the same intensity with which he looked at her; her mother sparkling with *joie de vivre* – a *joie de vivre* that was absent when Jorge was not there. And another image, even more painful – her mother lying on the floor of the villa in a haze of scarlet. For a long while now she had suspected that Magdalene's death had not been natural – that she had in fact killed herself. Now, remembering how Jorge had disappeared shortly afterwards, she found herself wondering if he had had anything to do with it – and not wanting to know the answer.

'Oh God, oh God!' Lilli sobbed. She sank to the sand in the shade of a palm tree, drawing her knees up and burying her face in them. 'Oh Jorge . . . oh Mama – no, no, no!'

The sun was beginning to drop towards the sea in a ball of fire before could bring herself to go home.

Ingrid was on the veranda sipping a long, cool pink gin. Her smooth round face was bland as ever but her blue eyes flashed her displeasure.

'Where have you been, Lilli? Your father has been very worried about you. I have seldom seen him so upset.'

'Perhaps he's not the only one,' Lilli said sullenly. She was in no mood to take criticism from her father's wife.

'Lilli.' Otto appeared in the doorway. His face was drawn, the scar down his cheek standing out in livid relief. 'Thank God. I didn't know where you were. I thought . . .'

'That I might have done what Mama did?' Her voice was tight, quite unlike her usual light musical tone. She saw the shock come into his eyes. 'That's what happened, isn't it, Daddy? Mama killed herself, didn't she? She and Jorge were having an affair and something went wrong and so she killed herself.'

'Lilli – I think we need to talk.'

He glanced uncomfortably at Ingrid. She remained where she was, sipping her drink in stony silence.

'I don't want to talk!' Lilli said. But she did. Little as she wanted to hear the truth there were things she had to know. She just did not see why she should make it easy for him.

Another glance at Ingrid. Then Otto said: 'Let's go to my study, Lilli.'

'Dinner will be ready in a minute,' Ingrid said testily.

'Damn dinner! I'm not hungry anyway – and I doubt if Lilli is.'

As much to annoy Ingrid as to please her father, Lilli followed him to the study. She did not know why she was so angry with him – it wasn't his fault if her mother had had an affair with Jorge, and she supposed he must have suffered then as she was suffering now. But then again some of the blame must attach to him. If he had made her mother happy she would not have needed Jorge . . . would she? And in any case it was he who had destroyed her illusions. In that moment she hated him for that alone, hated the whole world . . .

In the study Otto motioned her to a chair.

'Sit down, Lilli.'

'I don't want to sit down.' She crossed to the window, looking out at the familiar garden, now subtly altered like everything else in her world.

And the Lord God planted a tree in the Garden of Eden. And all was beauty and the man and woman loved one another. And then the serpent came and the blindfolds were torn from their eyes and in the midst of beauty there was ugliness and pain, jealousy and shame . . .

'Well, I do want to sit down.' Otto had a glass in his hand containing a generous measure of cognac. He tossed it back, set the glass on the table and sat down facing her.

'I am sorry you had to find out like this, Lilli,' he said. 'I suppose I should have told you a long time ago but I hoped you would never need to know. I tried to warn you about Jorge . . .'

'No!' she snapped. 'No, you didn't! You told me he wasn't suitable, but that was all!'

'And nor is he, for a great many reasons, most of which we need not go into now. The most important thing is that you realise that where women are concerned Jorge has no scruples at all. He has broken more hearts that I could count. He certainly broke your mother's twice over.'

'Twice over?' In spite of herself he had Lilli's full attention now.

He replenished his glass from the crystal decanter which stood on his desk.

'You've heard the story before, Lilli, about how I came to South America when Germany was defeated in the war. How I went into business with your grandfather and his old friend Fernando Sanchez. And how I met your mother. I fell in love with her, Lilli, the minute I set eyes on her. She was the most beautiful girl I had ever seen.' His voice had become soft, dreamy; even through the haze of her own pain Lilli knew he was reliving the days before she had been born.

'She was also very unhappy,' he went on, sipping his cognac. 'She had been involved in a relationship with Jorge stretching back almost to the days when they were children together, but he had treated her very badly. That is Jorge's way, you see – he likes to be surrounded by beautiful women, likes to have them crazy about him, but he gives nothing of himself. What Jorge wants, he takes. He is a ruthless womaniser – as well as being a very dangerous man.'

'I don't know what you mean – dangerous,' Lilli said, twisting the bangles round her wrist. 'I know he used to be a racing driver and he rides and flies and things, but that doesn't mean he's dangerous.' She stopped, biting her lip and wondering why she was still defending Jorge.

'I'm not talking about his hobbies, I am talking about something quite different. You may think you know Jorge, Lilli, but you don't. You don't really know him at all.'

'I know I love him.' In spite of everything it was no more than the truth.

Otto sighed.

'No you don't, Lilli. You are too young to know about love. He fascinates you – that's his way. He draws you into his web like a spider with a fly. But you don't love him. At least, I hope to God you don't, because if you do he'll hurt you as surely as he hurt your mother, and I won't allow that to happen.'

Lilli pushed the bangles up her wrist and released them with an impatient little flick.

'You were telling me about Jorge and my mother.'

'Yes.' Otto ran a hand over his chin, buried his face in it for a moment and then continued: 'I knew how your mother felt about Jorge. I knew he had hurt her badly. But I thought I could make her forget him. I asked her to marry me and she agreed. We came here – to Madrepora – and for a while at least I thought I had succeeded. I knew she didn't feel the same way about me as she had about him but I accepted that. I tried to be patient. I gave her everything she asked for and she seemed content. You were born, and for a little while she settled down to being a wife and mother. But I hadn't realised the hold he still had over her. When Fernando became unwell Jorge took over this end of the operation. And when he came back into her life it all began again. Jorge couldn't accept that she was married to me now, he had to prove to himself he could still take her if that was what he wanted. And that is precisely what he did.'

'You mean they became lovers again?'

'Yes, right under my nose. And, fool that I was, I let it happen.'

'Why, Daddy? Why did you let it happen?'

Otto gesticulated impatiently.

'Does that matter, Lilli? The fact is he wound her round his little finger all over again. He didn't really want her, of course. Gratification is all Jorge ever wants. When he told her it was over and he was leaving her she was distraught. She couldn't face losing him a second time. She was . . .' he paused, his voice breaking, '. . . pregnant with his child, and when she told him he snapped his fingers and told her to get rid of it.'

Lilli began twisting the bangles again, an agitated compulsive movement. She had thought things were bad enough, she had not realised they could get worse.

'And so she killed herself,' she said softly.

Otto swallowed hard. 'Your mother shot herself, here in this room. So you see, Lilli, I couldn't stand by and see Jorge use you as he used her. I'm sorry, *liebling*, but there it is. It's better that you should know what a swine he is than end up like your mother.'

Lilli nodded. Part of her wanted to run to him, throw her arms around him and tell him she was sorry she had resurrected all the painful past, but her own pain was too acute, her emotions too confused.

The door swung open. Ingrid stood there, her face impassive as ever, but when she spoke there was irritation in her voice.

'Have you finished your tête-à-tête? Dinner has been ready for a long while. Do we have to let Jorge spoil good food as well as everything else?'

Lilli glared at her with loathing. Did Ingrid make Otto happy? She hoped so, but she couldn't imagine it.

'I'm sorry, Ingrid, but I am really not hungry,' she said, pushing past her. Then she ran upstairs to her room, threw herself down on the bed and wept until she had no tears left.

Next day Jorge left for Florida again and at the end of the vacation Lilli returned to school. For a while, thinking of what her father had told her, she was very frightened that she too might be pregnant. But to her immense relief she was not.

Lilli buried herself in her studies, and when the time came for her to leave school she knew she could not bear to return to Madrepora. A friend of a friend worked for a small publishing house in New York, and Lilli had secured herself a job as a public relations assistant with them. Just once she went back to Madrepora, to collect her things and say goodbye to her father. Relations were strained between them; she knew nothing could ever be the same again. When she left she had promised herself it would be forever.

But of course she had been fooling herself. Now she was back and Jorge was here and Lilli was very afraid that the whole horrible cycle was about to begin all over again. Could she resist him any more than her mother had? With all her heart she hoped so, but she really could not be sure.

23

GUY DE SAVIGNY sat on the veranda of his house watching the pineapple palms shivering gently in the warm Caribbean breeze and thinking about Lilli Brandt.

He could scarcely believe the luck which had presented him with an opportunity to meet one of the members of the family of the elusive German whom he was now almost certain was Otto von Rheinhardt, and also an invitation which, if it materialised, would give him access to the villa and the chance to see for himself the treasures Bill had described. But that was not the only reason he was thinking about Lilli. In fact, since the previous afternoon when he had flown her in he had thought of little else.

He couldn't for the life of him imagine why she kept popping into his thoughts no matter how often he pushed her away, and he found the invasion oddly disturbing. She was a very pretty girl, of course, but he had known plenty of girls just as pretty and their faces had not haunted him as hers did now, distracting him so that it was an effort to concentrate on what had become for these last weeks almost an obsession.

He was on Madrepora for a very specific reason, he reminded himself, and that reason was finding and flushing out the Nazi who had murdered his father and stolen his heritage. There would be other Lillis, there was only one Otto von Rheinhardt – and he wanted him far more than he wanted a pretty girl with a soft voice and a smile to break your heart. He wanted him for his father and his grandfather, for his uncle, and all the others who had suffered at his hands, and if this German was indeed von Rheinhardt then the time left to Guy to bring him to justice might be very short. Rumour had it that Otto Brandt was dying and the realisation of it fired Guy with renewed fervour. Perhaps nature was about to take its course and rid the world of a monster, but he didn't see why it should be easy for him. He hadn't made it easy on the others, those whose deaths he had ordered. They would have given a great deal for the luxury of dying in their beds, no doubt. And he hadn't cared either for the families and friends left behind. Why, then, should he expect mercy now?

But for all his determined heart-hardening Guy could not help thinking again of Lilli and the pain it would cause her, and he experienced another pang of something like regret.

And the sins of the fathers shall be visited upon the children, he thought, unusually philosophical, and this mood too was new enough to him to cause him surprise. He grinned wryly and shifted in his seat, propping his feat on the veranda rail and easing himself into a more comfortable position.

As he did so a movement on the road which wound around the valley immediately beneath his veranda caught his eye. The truck used for ferrying supplies from the airstrip to the villa and hotel was moving slowly along the road. As he watched, it disappeared behind the thick fringe of jacaranda and magnolia, jolting back into view some distance along. Guy's eyes narrowed, watching its erratic progress. He had never seen a vehicle on that road before – not that there were many vehicles on Madrepora, only Otto and Jorge's cars and a few motorcycles that sounded like sewing machines on wheels – and he found himself wondering where the truck was going. To the shanty town on the south-east corner? Perhaps, though he could not imagine why it should be. But before it disappeared completely from sight he was almost sure the truck turned north and his curiosity grew.

As far as he was aware there was nothing on that corner of the island. From his little map it looked wild, with only the merest stretch of beach bordered by the closest thing to a cliff that existed on Madrepora, and flying in he had never noticed anything to make him revise that view. For that reason he had never bothered to explore it. Now, with the day stretching before him – the time off he was due in lieu of having worked yesterday – he wondered if it might be worth a visit, if only to familiarise himself with the lay-out of the island.

He went into the house, changed his linen slacks for a pair of Bermuda shorts and got out the bicycle which he used for getting to and from the airstrip. It was an old-fashioned upright machine, *circa* 1950, he guessed, with a big wicker basket on the front, and in the three weeks he had been here he had grown quite attached to it. Until he had come here it had been years since he had ridden a bicycle, and then it had been a bright-green sports model which had been his pride and joy, but there was something curiously relaxing about pedalling sedately along on the old Hercules, especially at this time of day before the sun had reached its zenith and the breeze coming off the sea cooled the fragrant air.

Guy freewheeled down the slope from his house, then rode steadily north-east, following the route the truck had taken. For a while the sea was hidden from view by the tall scarlet-leafed crotons and sweet-scented frangipani that lined the road, then suddenly it appeared beneath him again, periwinkle blue merging to soft dark grey on the horizon and white-flecked where it broke over the occasional boulder or reef. The road began to slope down again then, curving gently around the rise at this, the island's most elevated corner, and heading indirectly towards the sea.

Again Guy wondered why the truck should have been headed for this remote spot. It had not passed him coming back and he was fairly sure that the track he was on would come to a dead end when it reached the sea. Then, as he rounded a curve, his suspicion was confirmed. The truck was there below him, parked on a narrow strip of beach, pebblier and rougher than the smooth white sand of the beaches on the south and west of the island. The driver, a local, judging by his dark skin and brightly coloured singlet and shorts, was standing beside it, and to Guy's astonishment he appeared to be unloading something on to a trolley manned by another local.

Guy stopped, leaning the bicycle over so that his foot balanced him on the rough dirt track whilst he remained sitting on the saddle, shading his eyes against the sun which reflected from the water to make bright prisms on his Raybans. The packages were large, square and white; three easily stacked the trolley high and the local manhandling it manoeuvred it round on its little wheels and disappeared from Guy's view behind the overhanging crotons. After a moment a similar trolley appeared, wheeled by yet another local. It, too, was loaded, and went the way of the first.

Fascinated, Guy watched. He could not imagine where the packages were being taken unless it was to some kind of cave beneath the overhanging rock, and he wished he dared cycle on down the path to find out if he was right. But intuition was warning him very strongly not to proceed down the path to the cove. Everything about this operation smacked of secrecy and even with his scanty knowledge of the Caribbean Guy could hazard a pretty good guess at what those packages contained. If he was right, then a great deal of money was at stake here, and those who stood to gain from it would not take kindly to an outsider discovering what they were up to. Perhaps, he thought, he would come back when the place was deserted and have a closer look. For now, he was going to let discretion be the better part of valour.

He let the bicycle fall a little closer to the ground and swung his leg over the saddle to dismount. He'd have to push the bicycle for a bit – he certainly wasn't going to struggle to ride back up the incline in this heat. He stood for a moment longer, leaning on the handlebars and watching the operation below him.

He had thought the locals were too engrossed in what they were doing to notice his presence. But as he stood there he heard the sound of an aircraft approaching and the man on the beach heard it too. He looked up suddenly, his eyes searching the sky and in so doing raking the cliff above him.

Guy cursed silently as he realised that the worker could not have failed to see him standing there and watching.

Lilli was having breakfast in the salon when Ingrid came in.

'You are up early, Lilli. I thought you'd want a lie-in after your journey.'

'I've been up for ages.' Lilli swallowed a chunk of ripe mango, relishing the taste and thinking that nowhere on earth did the fruit taste as good as it did here on the island where it was grown.

When she had eventually fallen asleep she had slept soundly for the first time since receiving Josie's letter, exhaustion finally getting the better of her, but she had woken early and been unable to doze off again. At last, giving up the struggle, she had dressed and walked through the grounds as the sun rose, shedding the first warm rays on the hibiscus and frangipani and gaining strength with a swiftness which equalled the suddenness of the tropical sunsets. When she had returned to the villa one of the maids had made her breakfast and eating it in the familiar surroundings she had felt her own strength returning, and with it her resolve to refuse to allow Jorge to upset her any more. She had been dismayed when he had turned up last night uninvited, but at least that first meeting was over now and she had told him in no uncertain terms that she wanted nothing more to do with him. Perhaps one telling would be enough for him; she doubted it, but at least now she had outfaced him once she could do the same again if the need arose. The knowledge gave her courage for what lay ahead.

'How is Daddy?' she asked.

Ingrid did not answer for a moment, continuing to ladle fresh fruit salad from a deep bowl on the dresser.

'He didn't have a very good night,' she said, carrying her dish to the table and sitting down opposite Lilli. 'My honest opinion, for what it's worth, is that he is failing fast.'

Lilli swallowed hard at the lump that rose in her throat. It was no more than she had been able to see for herself, but hearing Ingrid put it so baldly made it all the more real.

'How can you be so calm about it, Ingrid?'

'There's no point being anything else. Getting hysterical is not going to change anything. Besides, it's not my way.' Ingrid smiled, almost apologetically. 'Sometimes, Lilli, I think it might be easier for me if it was. Perhaps you and I would understand one another better.'

'Why should we? I'm not a hysterical person either.'

'Not hysterical, no, but your emotions are there on the surface for everyone to see. I think you mistrust me because mine are not. Sometimes I think you doubt I have them at all.'

Lilli flushed faintly. What Ingrid had said was marginally too close to the truth for comfort.

'Just because I don't show my feelings doesn't mean I don't have any,' Ingrid continued, toying with her piece of mango, but eating nothing. 'I know it wasn't easy for you to have me invade your world. I tried to tell you I knew how you felt but you were never willing to listen to me. Perhaps you don't want to listen now, but with your father close to death I think it is important, for his sake if nothing else, that you should at least try.'

Lilli's mouth set in a hard line. Irrationally she was resentful of the conversation which seemed to her to be shutting her father out, almost as if he were dead already.

'Why does it matter in the least what I think about you?' she asked.

Ingrid leaned forward. Her spoon chinked as she set it down in the dish, elbows on the table, eyes seeking Lilli's.

'Because I love your father and he loves me. We loved one another long ago, before he met your mother, before you were born. We go back a very long way, and that sort of bond is very special. I helped him to be happy again.'

The unspoken rider hung in the air between them – 'I helped him to get over your mother who had betrayed him with Jorge.' Lilli felt a spurt of anger. She didn't need this. She had come to see her father one last time, not to be dragged into this sort of heart-to-heart with a woman she would never be able to like, no matter how good the reasons why she should. It didn't work that way, human emotions were capricious, and they did not respond to reason. And besides, knowingly or unknowingly, Ingrid was pouring salt into wounds that were already too raw for comfort.

'Daddy has us both here,' she said. 'I think that is all that really matters to him.'

Ingrid moved forward as if she was on the point of saying something more, then her lips closed in a tight inverted smile and she sighed.

'Very well, Lilli, if that's the way you want it. I wish it could be different since very soon all we will have left of him will be one another.'

Lilli rose swiftly, refilling her dish with mango and pineapple, though she was no longer hungry, to give herself a chance to hide the sudden uprush of bitter emotion.

'Is Daddy getting up today?' she asked steadily after a moment.

'He'll want to.' Ingrid, too, was making an effort at normality; the confidences of a few moments ago might never have been. 'I'm not sure, though, if he will be well enough – for a while, at any rate. Sometimes he regains a little strength as the day goes by.'

'Is he awake?'

'Oh, he's awake.' Ingrid did not add that she thought Otto had scarcely slept all night.

'I'll go and see him then.' Lilli pushed back the dish, untouched, and left the salon.

Otto was lying propped up against the pillows. Basil had raised the mosquito netting and tied it aside so Lilli had a clear view of him as soon as she entered the room, and Otto managed to raise a weak smile of greeting.

She crossed to the bed, bending over to kiss him.

'How do you feel today?'

'As well, I expect, as I am ever going to feel again.'

'Don't say that! I won't allow it!'

'My dear child, we have to face the truth!' He raised his hand, indicating she should take it. 'Oh Lilli, Lilli, I wanted to spare you all this. You shouldn't have come.'

'I came because I wanted to. I'm here with you – that's as it should be.' She squeezed his hand. 'There's no more to be said on that subject – right?'

He sighed.

'I suppose not. I'm an old man now who can't even argue with his own little girl. But now that you are here there are other things that need to be said. Things I can no longer keep from you under the circumstances.'

His face had grown very serious – even allowing for the pain that racked his once handsome features she saw it, and felt a qualm of apprehension. He had said something of the kind last night, now again it was almost the first thing on his mind.

'What things, Daddy? What's it all about?'

'About me and Fernando and Jorge. About Madrepora itself.'

'Madrepora!'

'Yes.' His fingers tightened around hers. 'I'd like you to leave now, Lilli, and go back to New York, but I don't suppose you will. Which is why I have to tell you. You must leave as soon as I am dead. And you must not come back again.'

She stared at him in disbelief.

'Why? This is my home!'

'No, *liebling*, it *was* your home – whilst I still retained control here. Already the power has passed to Jorge. When I am gone – and Fernando too – Jorge will be omnipotent. I don't want you to be tainted or put at risk.'

'Daddy, you heard me tell Jorge last night to get out of my life. You must believe I meant it.'

'I'm afraid, my darling, it is not that simple. As Jorge himself pointed out, when I am gone new arrangements will have to be made concerning the business. I think he may try to involve you and that is the last thing I want.'

A puzzled frown creased her forehead. Was Otto rambling because of his illness or the drugs that controlled the pain? She decided to humour him.

'I know absolutely nothing about running a hotel and less about the export of bananas and batique cloth wear. Jorge knows that.'

A harsh sound, halfway between a sigh and a mirthless laugh, escaped Otto's dry lips and his fingers tightened on hers.

'You don't understand, Lilli. That is not the business.'

So — he was wandering. Lilli's heart sank.

'Yes, Daddy, it is,' she said gently. 'That and your rare stamps. You have managed all these things for more than twenty years now. You have just forgotten, that's all.'

'No!' There was fire suddenly in the tired voice. She looked at him sharply. His eyes were blazing in his wasted face; he did not look — or sound — like a man who was wandering. Lilli felt a sharp qualm of misgiving.

'What are you talking about, Daddy?'

'The batique cloth wear, the bananas, the stamps, they are just a cover, Lilli, a front for the *real* business. The whole of Madrepora as you see it is a sham, *liebling*. I established them all, together with Grandfather Vicente and Uncle Fernando, for quite a different reason.'

Her head was spinning.

'I don't understand. A different reason? What different reason?'

'Cocaine.' He said it so softly, on a mere breath, that at first she scarcely heard, let alone comprehended, and he repeated it, more loudly, his eyes holding hers so that there could be no mistake. 'Cocaine, Lilli. That is the real business of Madrepora.'

For a full half-minute she stared at him. Her mouth had fallen open, her eyes gone blank with surprise.

'Cocaine. You mean . . . *drugs?*'

'Of course. Madrepora is a staging post for the Cordoba/Sanchez cartel. It's conveniently placed for both South America, where the coca is grown, and the marketplace in Miami.' A brief smile touched his lips. 'I'm afraid, *liebling*, that the hotel and the local exports would never keep us in the style to which you have always been accustomed. Cocaine is big business. There is a great deal of money in it, more money than you could ever imagine, and the further down the line of distribution you go, the greater the profits. We realised that years ago, long before many of the other drug barons. Our operation was far more sophisticated than theirs in the early years – whilst they were still exporting hydrochloride or even cocaine base, we saw the value of cutting closer to home – and taking the profits that the others were allowing to slip through their fingers. Madrepora was set up as a base for that purpose. The stuff arrives here in kilo packages of pure cocaine, we cut it with lactose to make twice that amount, then ship it on to Miami, where Jorge's trading company cuts it again before passing it on to the retailer.'

Lilli shook her head like a sleeper emerging from a dream.

'All that happens here – on Madrepora? But where? How?'

'We have laboratories in undersea tunnels on the north-east corner of the island. There are miles of them – the perfect place. No one but a local would know about them and we have always ensured that no one but authorised personnel goes there.'

'That's why you forbade me . . .'

'I didn't want you to know about it, Lilli. I thought it safer that way. Now I have come to the conclusion that it's safer that you *should* know.'

'Why?'

'Firstly because of Jorge. You have to know the sort of man he is – totally, utterly ruthless. Drug-trafficking does that to people – there is so much at stake. In Jorge's case, of course, he was already a bad lot. That is most likely why he has made such a success of the business your grandfather and his father started.'

'But Daddy, I've already told you – I've finished with Jorge!'

'You say that now, *liebchen*. I'm not so sure it's the whole truth. In any case, it's no longer just Jorge that makes the whole business so dangerous. Things are beginning to get very nasty in the world of drug-trafficking. The other operators are waking up to the fact that the really big money is to be made when it comes to distribution. They are all starting to want to set up wholesale networks in the United States, just like ours. But greed is a hard master. No one wants to share territories. Already they are beginning to fight for them. Soon there will be all-out war.'

'I don't understand . . .'

'And thank God you don't, Lilli. Murder, massacre, gang warfare on a scale not seen since Chicago in the twenties and thirties, that's what I am talking about.'

'But surely here on Madrepora . . .'

'Nowhere will be safe if they decide to challenge our supremacy. Certainly you would not be safe. You are my daughter, heiress to my share of the empire. If you were also Jorge's woman that risk would double and treble and quadruple over and over again just like the value of the coca leaves.' He leaned forward, turning his hand on hers so that his fingers gripped her wrist. 'Your future is taken care of, Lilli. You have no need to worry about that. The money I've made over the years is safe in a Swiss bank account – you'll find all the papers in my desk. Go to my lawyer in Berne. He will arrange for it to be made over to you, and I promise you'll never want for anything again. But you must leave Madrepora and never come back. If you stay here the same thing will happen to you as happened to your mother. And I can't bear the thought of that.'

Lilli's head was spinning. She could scarcely believe what she was hearing – that all her life she had been surrounded by the intrigue and intricacies of a drug-trafficking cartel and never for one moment suspected it. Nothing in her world was as she had thought it to be and in her shock and confusion she did not even stop to wonder what Otto meant when he said that she would die as her mother had died. Only one thing stood out starkly above all the others. Her father was dying and she could no longer escape the fact. He had accepted it, calmly and philosophically, and he was setting his affairs in order as best he could whilst some lucidity and strength was spared to him. And, even now, caring for her as he always had done, making her welfare his first priority, even if that meant telling her things about his lifestyle which in the past he had preferred to keep secret.

'Oh Daddy!' she whispered.

Again his fingers tightened on her wrist.

'Promise me, Lilli. You will go, straight away, if not sooner . . .'

'I don't know . . .' For all his insistence she was reluctant to make a deathbed promise she was not sure she could keep. 'I know I've been away for a long time now, but everything that means anything to me is here. All my memories . . . everything.'

'Memories go with you wherever you are. And you can take whatever personal things you want. They wouldn't be interested in those. And your treasures, of course, we mustn't forget those. Lilli's triptych and all the other things.'

Suddenly her mind was winging back across the years to another conversation, less final than this one, yet no less frightening to the child she had once been. 'I have to go away, Lilli. Remember these treasures are worth a king's ransom. One day you will love them as I do. And if hard times should ever come . . .' Obviously, valuable as they were, the treasures were worth only a fraction of what he was now able to leave to her, but then they had been her insurance for the future as well as a part of her world, the artefacts that could be counted as currency as well as valued for their beauty and because he loved them. She remembered how afraid she had been that day at his seriousness, how she had wanted to cling to him in case he, like her mother, should disappear for ever. But that cloud had quickly passed. Childlike, she had rushed on with her life and everything had been all right. Her father had gone away – perhaps on some business trip to do with the drug-trafficking, she now realised – but he had come back. This time there would be no happy ending. Tears stung her eyes and she turned her head so that he would not see them.

'Perhaps you should get them shipped now, Lilli,' he said. 'Send them to New York whilst you still can. I'd like to think they were safe for you to enjoy. They have given me so much pleasure over the years.'

'I'll see what I can do, Daddy,' she said, but she was thinking: Begin to strip the house before he has even drawn his last breath? I couldn't do that!

'Good, good.' His fingers were going lax on her wrist now, the effort of this long and tiring conversation which had cost him so much taking its toll. 'I'm going to have to rest now, Lilli. Perhaps you would ask Basil to come in.'

He sank back against the pillows, eyes half closed, face gaunt but peaceful. He seemed to have forgotten that he had failed to extract that final promise from her, or perhaps, with exhaustion overcoming him, he had taken refuge in the fact that he had done what he could. He had, at long last, told her the truth about

Madrepora. Now all that was left was to convince her of the dangers that threatened her here.

Otto, who had once ordered the death of other men's children without so much as flinching, Otto, whose dealings in narcotics over these past years had helped to bring about the death and destruction of many more, was suffused – obsessed even – with the desire to protect his own daughter. It had become a religion with him now. It was all that was left to him.

The telephone on Jorge Sanchez's desk shrilled its usual stuttering alarm.

Jorge swore, stretching over the sheaf of papers spread out before him to reach it. The papers were documents relating to his Miami company – Caribbean Trading – and doctoring them took up a great deal of his time and attention – a job he did meticulously in spite of the fact that officials and policemen like Garcia at both ends of the operation were in his pay. One never knew when some new high-flier might appear and take an interest. Such a nuisance could always be dealt with, of course. Overzealous customs officers and their like had been known to disappear, just as, in Miami, less-than-loyal colleagues or rival dealers were likely to be found hogtied, riddled with bullets and stuffed in garbage bags or cardboard boxes, but here on Madrepora it was preferable not to have to resort to such extremes. Generally speaking, neatly prepared logs and ledgers and a good working relationship with officials and carabinieri made such violence unnecessary, and although Jorge was far from squeamish in such matters he preferred it when things ran smoothly.

Annoyed though he was at the interruption, Jorge's tone was silky smooth as ever as he answered the telephone.

'Jorge Sanchez.'

'It's me – Pedro Somoza.'

Somoza was the overman in charge of the labourers who transported the pure cocaine to the laboratories for cutting and supervised its shipping once it had been dealt with.

'Somoza. What can I do for you? No problem with this morning's consignment, I hope?'

'No, that came in as arranged. But someone was watching.'

The man's voice was guttural and jerky and Jorge sighed

mentally. Somoza was an inveterate cocaine-user himself and the drug sometimes made him paranoid. If he got any worse he would have to be replaced. A pity, since he was good at his job, but there it was.

'Someone watching,' he repeated, somewhat cynically. 'Watching what?'

'When we were unloading the truck. He was up on the cliffs. I can't be sure but I think it was that new pilot.'

Jorge stiffened, his lips tightening around his cigar.

'Who saw him – you?'

'No, the truck driver. He reported it to me. I thought you should be told.'

'Yes, thank you, Somoza. You did right. Keep your eyes skinned and let me know if anything else suspicious occurs. There'll be an extra something in your pay packet if you do.'

'Understood, boss.'

Jorge replaced the receiver, his eyes narrowing thoughtfully. Perhaps this time Somoza wasn't just being paranoid. He was the second person in as many days to mention the new pilot's interest in things that should not concern him, and Jorge did not care for the implication. Could it be that Guy de Savigny was working for another of the cartels that were springing up and trying to encroach on their territory – or was even an agent for the Drug Encorcement Agency? Well, if so, he would be dealt with – and fast. Jorge had no intention of letting anything – or anyone – interfere with the smooth running of his organisation.

He leaned forward, grinding the cigar butt out in the ashtray and smiling faintly as he contemplated grinding out Guy de Savigny just as ruthlessly and efficiently.

Ingrid was in the salon when Lilli came back downstairs – hovering, Lilli thought, and wondered if Ingrid had guessed that Otto had been talking to her about the matters which were weighing so heavily upon his mind.

'You were with your father a long time,' she said non-committally, but her eyes were sharp, her expression guarded, and Lilli thought that she was right – Ingrid had known.

'He's asking for Basil. Do you know where he is?'

'In the kitchen, I believe. It's all right, I'll tell him.'

She left the room and Lilli heard her calling for Basil. Lilli stood uncertainly, chewing on a fingernail and feeling as if the whole of her body was churning along with her chaotic thoughts and emotions. A moment later Ingrid was back and this time she went straight to the point.

'Your father has talked to you then.'

'Yes.' Lilli had thought she could not bring herself to speak of what had passed between them, but quite suddenly, she could no longer bear not to. 'You knew, I suppose, Ingrid, what he had to tell me?'

Ingrid nodded.

'I knew, yes, but as I said before, it wasn't my place to say anything. I've been here a comparatively short time and I'm only on the periphery of what goes on. It really has nothing to do with me at all.'

Lilli opened her mouth to speak; closed it again. If it had not been for Ingrid's matter-of-fact confirmation of what her father had told her she would have been tempted even now to put it down to a fiction of a fevered drug-distorted imagination. Madrepora, island paradise, centre of a huge illicit operation. Madrepora, her beloved Madrepora, even more flawed than she had realised and her father a drug-trafficker and international criminal. It hurt – or it would hurt when the numbness began to wear off. But worst of all, at this moment, was the fact that Ingrid had known what she did not about Otto and about Madrepora. Lilli felt the betrayal like a knife thrust in her stomach and wrapped her arms around herself as if by doing so she could somehow ease the pain.

'I can hardly believe it,' she said. 'My father mixed up in something like this! It's terrible – terrible!'

Ingrid's face remained impassive.

'Don't *you* think so?' Lilli flared. 'How can you be so calm about it, Ingrid?'

'My dear, it has been going on for a very long time.' Ingrid took a step towards her, extended a comforting hand which Lilli avoided with a quick impatient gesture.

'That doesn't make it right. I've seen the harm drugs can do. I've lived in the States for four years, remember.'

'We are talking about cocaine here, Lilli, not heroin. You're half South American, you should know better than I that coca has been part of your culture for centuries.'

Lilli tightened her arms around her midriff. It was true, she knew, that the natives of the Andes had chewed the dried leaf since prehistoric times. She knew too that the Incas had regarded the plant as divine, adorning their temples of the sun with solid gold coca leaves, allowing only those with coca in their mouths to approach the altars, promising their followers that if coca was the last thing a man tasted on this earth then his place in heaven was assured. She knew that even today coca was the talisman placed under the cornerstone of new houses, the gift given by Peruvian Indians to the parents of a bride. But knowing made no difference to the instinctive revulsion that filled her when she thought of the lives wrecked in the modern world by the curse of drugs. She thought of the young men and women so obsessed by the need for their next fix that nothing else mattered, blank staring eyes, ravaged bodies, suicides during nightmare trips, horrific murders, all manner of drug-related crimes, and shuddered. Her father – her beloved father – was contributing towards all that. Surely he must know, just as she did, the terrible harm he was doing? Her mind circled wildly, seeking to excuse him.

'It's all their doing, I suppose – Fernando and Jorge. They have forced him to be a part of it. What did they threaten him with if he didn't co-operate? The loss of his home, I suppose. Bastards! But why did he give in to them? Why didn't he go home to Germany?'

'His home there had been destroyed,' Ingrid said. She did not add the other things she knew, that after the war Otto had been a hunted man, a war criminal rather than simply an officer of the German army who had served the Fatherland from a sense of patriotism, nor that Otto had been a willing partner in an enterprise which had made him rich beyond his wildest dreams. There was no point in upsetting Lilli any more, no point in completely destroying her illusions about the man they both adored and whom Ingrid was willing to accept for what he was because he was, to her, her dearest love, whatever he had done. But she could not resist a dig all the same at Magdalene, the woman who had stolen the best years of Otto's life from her and whom Lilli so closely resembled.

'There was your mother to consider, of course,' she said, her face still smooth, only her eyes, hard and blue, revealing the malice in her heart. 'She was Vicente Cordoba's daughter, remember – and Vicente Cordoba was as guilty as any of them.'

Lilli blinked. Grandfather Vicente had died when she was a child but she remembered him clearly as a distinguished old gentleman and respected member of the community.

'Grandfather Vicente was a politician!' she objected.

The corners of Ingrid's mouth lifted in a humourless smile which, for all her efforts to conceal her true feelings, closely resembled a sneer.

'Yes, he was, but he was also as corrupt as they come. How do you think your father came to be allowed to acquire Madrepora and no questions asked? How do you think drug-traffickers manage to carry on their business if they don't have at least some of the most influential of those in authority on their side? Vicente Cordoba had a finger in more crooked pies than you could care to name, and Magdalene – your mother – was his daughter. Your father, more fool he, worshipped her. She would never have cut herself off from her father or left this part of the world and he would never have left her.'

Lilli's confusion and shock began to turn to resentment and anger to hear her mother spoken of in this way.

'You can't blame my mother for this. She died when I was five years old!'

Ingrid's mouth hardened.

'Yes, she did. And have you ever asked yourself how she died?'

'I know how she died!' Lilli snapped, unable to take any more of Ingrid's smug inside knowledge. 'That is something I do know. Daddy told me long ago. She died because of Jorge.'

An expression that might almost have been satisfaction flittered across Ingrid's face.

'In that case, my dear, you must also know why your father is so anxious that the same thing should not happen to you.'

'He need not worry on that score,' Lilli retorted. 'I might have been involved with Jorge once, but I have no intention of killing myself because of him.'

For a brief moment Ingrid looked uncertain. The indecision was there, written all over her smooth face, but Lilli was too upset to notice it.

'I see,' she said after a moment. 'Perhaps your father has not told you quite everything, Lilli. I hope he will. Then perhaps you will realise just why he wants you to leave Madrepora and never return. Oh – don't look like that. I'm quite sure you will be well taken care of wherever you decide to make your life. Your father has made certain of that. I only hope I am as well provided for, but if not, well, I suppose I have had more than I might once have ever dared hope for – some time with your father. It hasn't been enough. It could never be that, and it has been curtailed most cruelly. But for all that, I must be grateful for what little I was allowed.'

Her blue eyes were suddenly full of tears. She half smiled, raised a hand to urge Lilli to say no more, turned and left the salon.

Lilli stood for a moment looking after her, a germ of pity sparking momentarily. She did not like Ingrid, but her anguish at the prospect of losing him was very real. It would have touched a heart harder than Lilli's, and Lilli, raw and bleeding herself, could not help but be affected by it.

What would Ingrid do after Otto's death? she wondered. Had Otto told her, too, to leave Madrepora, or did he consider it would be safe enough for her to remain? Lilli couldn't imagine that she would stay on though. With Otto gone there would be nothing left for her here and she had family at home in Germany. As for the remark she had made about being provided for, what had she meant by that? Had Otto told her, as he had told Lilli, about the fortune stashed away for her in a Swiss bank account? Was none of it to go to Ingrid, his wife?

As far as I am concerned she can have it all! Lilli thought. If it came from drug-trafficking I don't want a penny of it! I'd sooner starve!

But it wouldn't come to that. She had her job in New York which paid enough for her to get by on – and she had the treasures.

Lilli let her eye run around the salon over the items her father had always referred to as her 'treasures' – the silver candlesticks, the little Louis XIV clock, the bronze statuette of Ceres, the triptych, and a fierce determination filled her. They were the only things she would take with her when she left the island, the only things untainted by her father's revelations. They had been his before all this tawdry criminality began, they were the things he loved most. Tears pricked her eyes as she thought of the loving way he handled them, the way his eyes lingered on them, enjoying their beauty, even in the midst of a conversation. As long as she had the treasures the rest of it mattered not a jot. They would be her insurance just as they had been his, comforting in the unspoken guarantee that any one of them would, at auction, fetch enough to see her through the most dire need.

But she could not imagine ever parting with a single one of them. They meant far too much to her. Lilli crossed to the triptych, gazing at its glowing colours until the tears in her eyes blurred the beautiful images, and longing for the innocence of long-gone happier times to somehow reach out across the years and ease her present pain.

24

FROM THE TIME she had been a little girl, when something was troubling her Lilli went to the beach. In those days, of course, the problems had been childish ones and the moments of anxiety and depression which accompanied them as unexpected as a summer storm and as brief. Many times Lilli had cried her frustrations and woes into the silky-soft sand, and the breeze from the sea had dried her tears. It was impossible, she had thought then, to be unhappy for very long with the sound of the ocean beating in her ears like some great pulse which shared its life force with her, with the sun warming her skin and the perfume of the island entering her very soul with every breath. She had gone there when her mother had died and thought she heard the low, lilting voice in the whispering palms: 'Don't be sad, little one. I'm here. I'm always here.' The only time she had not sought refuge on the beach was after the terrible débâcle of her father discovering her with Jorge – the memory of being there with him had been too recent and too painful. But now Lilli changed into a swimsuit and matching overskirt and escaped from the villa where the walls, heavy with unwelcome revelations and impending death, seemed to be closing in on her.

As she followed the path to the beach she felt a moment's guilt for her selfish desire to be alone. Perhaps she should have remained at the villa in case her father wanted her – but he was sleeping, she knew. Certainly she should, if she was going anywhere, be going to see Josie, her friend, without whose letter she would not be here now. Josie would know she had arrived on Madrepora and would be expecting her – Lilli could imagine her sitting at the door of her shack, the baby on her knee, watching the track and expecting to see Lilli come walking down it. But close as the two girls remained, Lilli could not face talking to Josie just now. Her need for solitude

339

and the comfort of the beach from which, if her father had his way, she would soon be exiled, was too great.

At the edge of the sand Lilli slipped off her deck shoes and carried them until she reached a shady corner beneath a tall swaying palm. Then she tossed them down and sat down beside them, spreading her knees beneath the bright print of her skirt and staring out over the creamy breakers to the distant horizon where sea met sky in a soft haze of perfect azure.

The first shock of her father's revelations was beginning to dull now – how quickly the human mind can come to accept the unacceptable! – and so many things which had puzzled her without causing her a moment's real consternation were falling into place like the pieces of a jigsaw.

Why, she wondered, had she never really questioned Jorge and Uncle Fernando's frequent visits to the island? Why had she never stopped to realise that the legitimate exports of batique cloth wear and bananas and her father's dabbling in the trading of rare stamps could not possibly keep them in the lifestyle which she had come to take for granted? And why had she, Lilli the rebel, obeyed her father when he had forbidden her to go to the north-east corner of the island? Was it because she had known instinctively that to do so would be to break the spell of her Garden of Eden; that to visit that one forbidden place would be the equivalent of tasting the forbidden fruit?

But the blinkers had been taken from her eyes now and Lilli could see the forms of all those she loved exposed in their nakedness. Not only Jorge and Uncle Fernando, but also Daddy and Grandfather Vicente; Ingrid, who was prepared to make excuses for any evil provided it meant she could be with the man she loved; even Mama . . .

As Lilli thought of her a frown creased her forehead and she lifted a hand to smooth it out. What had Ingrid meant when she had said Lilli did not know everything about her death? Hadn't she seen her with her own eyes lying on the floor of the salon in a pool of blood? And hadn't Daddy told her that her mother had taken her own life because of the way Jorge had treated her?

The memory was just one pain amongst so many yet sharp enough to inflict its own particular agony. Oh Mama, why, why? Lilli's heart cried, but all the while she knew. Jorge was as much a danger as any drug. However one might despise him one was still addicted to him. Loathing him, loathing oneself for the weakness, it made no difference. Jorge raised his hand and beckoned and those who were enslaved by him thought: Just one last time – just one! Let me taste his lips and feel his arms and love his body once more and then I will leave him forever. Except that one never did. Her mother had not had the strength to do it and for all her good intentions Lilli was terrified that if he put her to the test she would not have the strength either.

Sadness washed over her like the waves of the ocean and she felt old suddenly, as old as the palms, as old as the island itself. The beach shouldn't do this to her! It was her refuge, here she should have been able to lose herself. But she couldn't. Past, present and future seemed all to have become one and she was trapped, unable to escape her destiny, hurt and afraid.

She turned her head slightly looking along the beach and realised with a prickle of annoyance that she was no longer alone. A figure had emerged from the trees – a man wearing shorts and a yellow shirt. Lilli stared almost accusingly and as the man came closer she recognised the pilot who had flown her in yesterday – was it really only yesterday? Then, she had warmed to him, felt almost that he might become a friend and ally, now she saw him only as a stranger encroaching on her private world of pain.

'Well hello,' he said, stopping a few yards away from her, one hand thrust into the pocket of his shorts, the other hooked around a rolled-up bathing towel. 'I didn't expect to meet you here.'

Lilli glanced at him; glanced away again.

'I come here when I want to be alone,' she said pointedly.

'Oh – I'm sorry. Is this beach private?'

'The whole island is private – apart from the hotel, that is.'

'I didn't realise.' He pulled a face. 'A little difficult, really, for those of us who have to work here. But I dare say if you happen to own an island it's your right to decide who goes where.'

With some surprise Lilli noticed the hauteur in his voice, quite different to yesterday's open friendliness, and realised too, with a prickle of guilt, that it was the natural response of a supremely self-assured man to her own hostility.

'I'll leave you in peace then,' he said, half turning away.

'No!' Lilli said quickly. 'You don't have to go. I'm sorry, I didn't mean to be rude. It's just that . . . I really do want to be alone. I've got an awful lot on my mind.'

Behind his sunglasses an eyebrow quirked.

'You're worried about your father. I quite understand.'

No, you don't! she wanted to say. Instead she nodded mutely.

'I am worried about him, yes. He's . . . very ill.'

'I'd heard. I'm sorry. What exactly is the trouble?'

Lilli stared at her feet, emerging, as if dismembered, from the tent of her skirt.

'He has cancer. Didn't you know? I thought it was common knowledge amongst the workers.'

'Well I'm not really one of the workers.' His tone was amused, but again Lilli was all too aware of how patronising she must have sounded. Was this what stress did to you — turned you into everything you most hated? Or had this other self been there all the time, just waiting for the chance to come to the surface. Lilli Brandt, spoilt little rich girl, the daughter and granddaughter of drug-traffickers — Christ!

The lump was there in her throat again. She swallowed hard at it, wishing on the one hand that he would go so that she could cry again, and on the other, suddenly, perversely, that he would stay.

Somehow she managed to turn the choking sound of threatening tears into a small harsh laugh.

'I'm saying all the wrong things, aren't I? I'm not usually like this, honestly . . .'

'Don't worry about it,' he said easily. 'I know you're not like that. At least, you weren't yesterday. In fact when I flew you in I thought how much I liked you. You even asked me over for drinks, remember?' He managed to say it lightly, giving no indication of how important that particular invitation was to him.

Lilli smiled wanly.

'Oh yes, I did, didn't I? I don't know that that is going to be possible. My father is a great deal more ill than I realised.' She broke off, biting her lip, wondering if he might take this as yet another snub. Upset as she was, little as she wanted to be bothered to talk to anyone at this moment, yet somehow she was terribly anxious not to offend him or have him think badly of her. 'Look, won't you please sit down?' she said, then flushed, aware that even this overture had, in her present mood, come out sounding more like a command than an invitation.

He was looking at her with that same wry directness; she knew it, even though his eyes were hidden behind his sunglasses.

'Are you sure you really mean that?'

'Yes, I'm sure. You make the place look untidy standing there,' she said in an attempt at humour.

'All right. As long as you promise to tell me if I overstay my welcome.'

'Don't worry, I will.'

He threw his towel down, then dropped to the sand beside her.

'I take it your father's illness is the reason you came home.'

'Yes. I would have come ages ago if I'd known, but I didn't. Daddy didn't want me to know, so Ingrid didn't write me.'

'Ingrid. Your sister?'

'Stepmother.'

'*Wicked* stepmother?'

'That,' Lilli said, 'is not a question I am prepared to answer.'

He smiled. It was the first time today he had heard any levity in her tone. But he couldn't afford to let up. An opportunity to talk to Lilli might not come again in a hurry.

'They are Germans, are they?'

'Yes.'

'I thought so from the name, though I've never met your father. You don't look German though.'

'My mother was Venezuelan. She died . . .' The cloud was back, shadowing the sun.

'That explains it. How did your father meet her?'

'He came here after the war. It was terrible for them too you know. His family home was destroyed in the bombing . . . everything. There was nothing left for him there.'

'So he came here with nothing.'

'I suppose so.' Her brow furrowed; cleared again. 'He knew my grandfather, Vicente Cordoba, because his family had been in the coffee-importing business before the war. Grandfather Vicente helped him make a new life and he fell in love with Vicente's daughter Magdalene – my mother.'

'I see. It must have been very difficult for him.'

'Yes.' Again, the shadow. She did not want to talk about her family. Not now, not knowing what she now knew about them. 'I think,' Lilli said, 'that I would like to go for a swim.'

'And so you want me to go now.'

'Not necessarily. Stay if you like. I really didn't mean to be rude about the private beach.'

She stood up and unbuttoned the cotton skirt, half expecting him to say he would swim too, but he did not. She dropped it on to the sand and ran towards the sea without a backward glance, a slim, dark-skinned girl in a bright bathing costume who looked, suddenly, almost carefree, but who felt, in spite of all appearances to the contrary, a hundred years old.

The water was warm; it scarcely shocked her sunbathed skin. She ran through the breakers without pausing, then leaned forward, letting the water envelop her. Oh bliss! How she had ached to feel the soothing warm seas of home as she had shivered in New York! She swam away from the beach then turned on her back, spreading her arms wide and letting her body rise and fall with the waves. Above her the sky was blue and wide, a heaven quite separate from the imperfect world beneath, yet *there*, only just out of reach.

The motion of the sea and that blue, blue sky, each microscopic atom which composed it shimmering in the afternoon sun so that it seemed almost opaque, lulled Lilli into a state which was almost trance-like. Her body was totally relaxed for the first time that day – for the first time, perhaps, waking or sleeping, for many days – and by the same token her mind was blank. Lilli gazed at the sky and thought how wonderful it would be to be a part of it, and then that thought was gone too, as though it had been drawn from her by the spiralling heat of the afternoon, and she was quite, quite empty. No – not empty, except as a vacuum is empty. Just a stillness, a quiet place within herself that she never wanted to leave again . . .

The waves rocked Lilli gently and in that same unthinking way she knew she would stay here, just *stay* here, until the sea and the sky took her into their own.

Guy lay back full length on the sand, the end of the towel, which he had formed into a pillow, fanned out across his face to protect it from the fierce glare of the sun.

He could have gone in for a swim with Lilli – the thought of the water which, in the shallows, was tepid as a warm bath, was a tempting one, and who knew? a frolic in the waves might have helped the relationship along. But then again it might not. She was very . . . fragile . . . at the moment and obviously needed her space. Guy did not want to encroach upon it too fast. If he did he was fairly sure she would back off entirely, just as she had done earlier when she had as good as told him to get lost. Under the towel, Guy winced. That had been a nasty moment and he had realised there and then that he was going to have to tread very carefully. The girl was in the midst of an emotional unheaval and couldn't be rushed. Under normal circumstances, all well and good. Guy had won over difficult women before and often more for the thrill of the chase than because he really wanted to catch them. But this was different. He had a reason for wanting to gain Lilli's confidence, and time was running out for him.

Not for the first time Guy cursed the fate that had given von Rheinhardt cancer just when he had caught up with him. If it *was* von Rheinhardt, he reminded himself; that was something he could not yet be absolutely sure about. And if he didn't make headway with Lilli pretty soon, perhaps he never would know. Well, it was up to him to play it right and not mess up this opportunity which had presented itself. Forcing his company on Lilli was certainly not the right way.

A light aircraft droned overhead. Guy shifted the towel and squinted up, more from habit than anything else. The aircraft was a mere speck in the blue – it had nothing whatever to do with Madrepora – but it reminded him all the same of the incident which had taken place this morning and he wondered again about the truck unloading in the most remote part of the island. Very odd. But whatever its reason for being there he couldn't imagine it had any bearing on his self-appointed mission, and after a few moments' idle speculation he let it slide to the back of his mind.

The sun beating down on his body and the towel covering his face was making him drowsy now, his line of thought becoming muddly whilst giving him the illusion that he was somehow making perfect sense, and he dozed, believing himself to be still awake. It was only when a sandfly alighted on his bare arm and the irritating tickle returned him to awareness that he realised he had actually been asleep.

He flicked the sandfly away, folded the towel back from his face and felt with unerring instinct the passage of time. Then, with a slight jar of consternation, it occurred to him that he was alone. Had Lilli returned from her swim and left the beach without waking him? If so, he had let a golden opportunity slip through his fingers. But no, her skirt and deck shoes were still there on the sand beside him.

Guy stood up, rubbing his eyes, which were slightly bleary from sweat and sleep, and looked towards the sea. From the palms which framed it where it met the beach the water stretched deep blue and unbroken towards the horizon – no boat on it today, no sea birds, and – as far as he could tell – no Lilli. Guy experienced the first qualm of concern. Where the hell was she? She couldn't be snorkelling, she hadn't had any equipment with her. He would have expected her to be in the shallows, sitting perhaps with her legs outstretched while the breakers ran over them in lacy ripples, but she wasn't there and she wasn't swimming either.

For God's sake don't be so stupid! he chided himself as his concern grew. This is a girl who was raised in the islands and has swum in that sea since she was a child! She must know every bay, every cove, every tide. She'll have simply swum around the headland to another beach where she can be alone. But the anxiety was too strong to be quelled by reason. Guy got to his feet, shading his eyes and scouring the sea. Idiot, she's run out on you, that's all. She's not there, she's simply not there . . .

And then he saw something way, way out. At first he thought it was a sea bird riding the waves, then he thought it might be a piece of flotsam from a passing ship. And then, for no reason he could explain, he became convinced it was Lilli.

Guy's heart came into his mouth with a jolt, his lazy limbs suddenly suffused with adrenaline. Lilli – if indeed it was Lilli – was not moving, except with the gentle swell of the ocean. From this distance it appeared that she was quite still, quite . . . lifeless. Guy hesitated for only a moment, still disbelieving his eyes and instincts, then he kicked off his shoes, pulled off his shorts to the swimming trunks he was wearing beneath them, and ran towards the sea. He plunged into the breakers, striking out strongly, not stopping to wonder what the hell she was doing or the reasonableness or otherwise of his own actions, thinking now of nothing but reaching the distant floating body. Once he stopped, his arms aching from the effort, treading water whilst he fixed her position, which seemed to be as distant as ever, and glancing back with some unease at the now equally distant shore. Then he swam on, cutting a powerful crawl through the calm warm water. Painfully slowly, it seemed to him, he drew closer, closer.

It *was* Lilli. He could see the vivid pink of her swimsuit contrasting with the blue of the sea. He called to her but there was no response and a mouthful of salt water made him cough. Closer, closer, and still she made no movement. For a gut-lurching moment he thought she was dead, just lying there on the swell with her face upturned to the full force of the sun and her hair floating out behind her like a lost mermaid.

'Lilli!'

No reply. He grabbed her wrist, limp and fragile.

'Lilli!'

Her head snapped over, her eyes wide and startled.

'No!' she almost sobbed.

Unbalanced from her floating position, a wave broke over her face, filling her mouth and nose with water. She coughed, gasped, struggled to free her wrist from his grasp, pulling them both under. He let her go and she began to swim away from him, further out to sea, but the water in her lungs was making her choke and she floundered wildly.

In that moment Guy knew he had to act quickly. He did not know what she was playing at, but he did know that this was no time to ask questions. Were there sharks in these waters? Guy had no intention of hanging around to find out and in any case they were much too far from the shore for safety. If he didn't do something, and quickly, Lilli was going to drown, and so, perhaps, was he.

Long ago, in his youth, Guy had taken a bronze medallion in life-saving. Its validity had long since lapsed; he had never used it or practised it since. Now, with desperation the master, he found the rudiments coming back without him even having to think about them. Before he really knew what he was doing he had swum around Lilli, ducking through the water and grasping her in such a way that her flailing arms could not reach him and pull them both under. Then he began swimming strongly back towards the beach towing her behind him.

If it had seemed a long way out before he had reached her, the return swim seemed even longer. Glancing warily over his shoulder he felt he was making no impression on it at all. But at least Lilli was not struggling now. She lay in the water as motionless as she had been when he had first seen her, only now his hand supported her chin and her legs trailed limply behind her.

At last, just when he thought they would never make it, they were in shallow water. Guy stood up, wading through the breakers, dragging Lilli by the arms and collapsing, exhausted, on to the sand. She lay there, still making no attempt to move. He roused himself once more, wondering if she had swallowed too much water and needed resuscitation, but as he leaned over her she turned her head away from him so that her cheek rested on the sand, and he realised that the drops of water running down her face were no longer sea water but tears.

'Are you all right?' he asked sharply.

'Why didn't you leave me?' Her voice was low and he had to bend close to make out the words. 'Why didn't you leave me there?'

'What are you talking about?' he asked, angry suddenly. 'You were miles out, just drifting out to sea. What the hell's the matter with you?'

'I wanted to stay there,' she whispered in the same soft voice, dreamlike almost. 'It was so beautiful!'

'It was downright dangerous!'

'You should have left me,' she repeated, and the tears rolled faster.

Her hair, heavy with sea water, lay spread out around her like so much seaweed, her cheeks and nose glowed dull fiery red from exposure to the sun. The line of her neck and shoulder was endearingly vulnerable and suddenly he was not angry any more. Puzzled, yes, frustrated, almost, by the strange dreamy acquiescence, but not angry, and a fierce new emotion that was almost desire was pulsing new life into his tired body.

'If I hadn't brought you in you would have died,' he said roughly. 'Is that what you wanted?'

For a moment she did not reply. He could almost feel her thinking it over. Then she said: 'Yes. Yes, I think that's what I wanted. I suppose that was very stupid of me.'

'Very stupid,' he said firmly. 'Christ, I knew you were upset, but nothing is that bad, Lilli.'

She lay unmoving, the tears running in silent rivers down her cheeks.

'I think,' he said, 'that I should get you home.'

She moved then, sitting up, turning to look directly at him.

'I'm really sorry to have put you to so much trouble.' Her tone was oddly formal, like a child apologising for a misdemeanour.

'No trouble. I'm just glad I was here. I hope you'll be glad, too, when you are feeling better.'

'You don't understand.' She wrapped her arms around herself as if she was cold suddenly in spite of the heat of the sun. 'It wasn't that I wanted to die – not really. I just didn't want to go on living.'

'There's a difference?'

'Of course there is! I just couldn't face it any more . . .'

'You're right,' he said. 'I don't understand. But then I haven't had to watch my father die. I never had that privilege.' For a brief moment anger was flaring again. I believe that your father, the man for whom you are now grieving, ordered my father's death, he wanted to say, but he knew this was neither the time nor the place. 'Plenty of people do have to go through what you are going through, though – most people, in fact – and they don't try to drown themselves. It's hard, I know, but you will get over it.'

She threw back her head, eyes closed, and began to laugh.

'Lilli!' he said sharply.

'If only you knew! If only it was just that . . .' She stopped laughing abruptly, shook her head. 'I promise you, Guy, there is a great deal more I want to escape from than simply the slow torture of watching my father die.'

He felt the skin at the back of his neck begin to prickle.

'Like what?'

She shook her head again.

'Oh no, you don't want to hear my troubles and I don't want to talk about them.'

As she spoke the last words her voice was harsh, staccato –

because of emotion, he thought at first, then realised the reason was that her teeth had begun to chatter.

'I really think I should get you home.' He walked up the beach to where they had left their clothes, pulled on his shorts over the swimming trunks which were already almost dry, and picked up her skirt and deck shoes, carrying them to where she still sat, unmoving, except for the tremors that were shivering through her body and the arms which were clasped tightly around her knees.

'Come on,' he ordered.

She stood up obediently, taking the skirt from him and winding it around her waist. But her fingers were shaking too much to fasten the buttons and he had to do it for her, very aware, suddenly, of her beautiful body and his proximity to it, and trying not to show it. She pushed her feet into her shoes and he put his arm around her, willing himself to see it simply as an act of friendly protection, fighting against the emotions stirring his body at the feel of her firm cool flesh.

At the track she stopped, looking at him.

'You don't have to come home with me. I'll be all right now.'

And suddenly there was another dimension to what he was doing, the reason for his being here driving like cold sharp steel into the soft underbelly of his concern and desire for her.

'I'd rather make sure of that,' he said, tightening his arm around her waist and urging her on.

She did not protest again and they walked in silence, Guy wondering how he could actually get inside the villa. Once he had seen her to her door he would have no excuse for going further, but this was the best chance he had had – perhaps the best chance he would ever have – and he had no intention of failing to capitalise on it. But as they neared the villa Lilli made it easy for him.

'You've been very kind. Can I offer you a drink or something before you go?'

She said it stiffly, formally, and he had no way of knowing the inner turmoil she was experiencing, her near-panic at the thought of having to go back and face up to all the things she had thought for a little while, out there in the ocean, she had left forever. With him beside her the shadows receded a little, became less immediate. When he had gone there would be no buffer left between her and the realities she had wanted to escape. She was also horribly certain that Jorge would come calling again. He wasn't one to be put off by the reception he had received last night; it would only make him all the more determined. And if her father was right, he had more reason than she had previously realised to continue to be around. Lilli shrank from the thought of seeing him again, feeling less able than ever to cope with the emotions he aroused in her and terribly afraid that even loathing him as she did she would be unable to summon up the will to resist him.

Guy looked at her and saw a depth of feeling within her luminous dark eyes which belied the coolness of her tone, without for one moment understanding what had engendered those feelings.

'Thanks,' he said, matching her coolness, though for him the hidden emotion was elation. 'I could use a drink, yes.'

The villa was drowsing in the heat of the afternoon. As Lilli led Guy along the path to the hibiscus-covered veranda nothing stirred.

He could feel her tension mounting now, an almost tangible thing, but at least she had stopped shaking.

'Come in,' she said.

A chair that looked as if it might have been made up for an invalid stood just at the point where room became veranda, but no one was sitting in it and the salon beyond appeared equally empty.

'I don't know where they all are,' Lilli said uncertainly. 'Resting, perhaps. What would you like to drink?'

'What are you offering?'

'Pretty well anything. There's freshly made lemonade but I expect you'd like something stronger.'

'Actually, yes. I know it's not *de rigueur* out here, but would you have any cognac?'

'Yes, I'm sure we have . . .' She disappeared into the dim salon and he hesitated on the veranda, oddly reluctant, now that the moment had come, to abuse her hospitality as he had planned to do.

She reappeared a moment later with bottle and glass.

'What about this? I don't know much about brandy. Daddy usually decants it but . . .' She handed him the bottle for his inspection and suddenly the tiny hairs on the back of his neck were prickling again; not just prickling, standing on end.

The bottle she had presented him with was a distinctive green glass against which the label stood out, utterly familiar to his eyes.

Château de Savigny.

He took the bottle from her, turning it between his hands, feeling the filmy covering of dust around the neck. *Old* Château de Savigny. Very old. Twenty – thirty – forty years old. He knew it in his bones.

'Where did he get this?' he asked, barely able to contain the rising excitement.

'I don't know. He's had it in his cellar for years, I think. He had it brought up just the other day. Isn't it . . . don't you like it?'

'Yes, it's fine.' He tried to sound noncommittal. She obviously hadn't made the connection between his name and the name on the bottle – hadn't even noticed, probably, and he didn't want to draw her attention to it.

'Will you pour your own?' Lilli said. 'I'm still a bit shaky. I'm going to get myself some lemonade. I'll be back in a minute.'

'I think you could do with something stronger than lemonade yourself,' he suggested.

'I'll probably put a vodka in it. Help yourself to ice – it's in a bucket on the bar.'

He smiled briefly, imagining his grandfather's outrage at the suggestion that someone might even consider ice in his precious cognac. Was it the habit out here, or didn't Lilli know any better? But the invitation to help himself to ice had given him the excuse he needed to enter the salon. With the bottle bearing his name still in his hand, Guy went in.

At first, after the bright sunlight outside, he could not see anything beyond vague shapes and shadows. He blinked hard, willing his eyes to become used to the dim light. He had a few minutes, no more, to try to discover if the treasures Bill had told him about resembled those stolen from the Château de Savigny. He was now virtually certain that they would, but virtually certain was not good enough.

He saw the candlesticks first, gleaming dully on the dresser. He picked one up, weighing it speculatively in his hand. Solid, heavy, very, very like the candlesticks his grandfather had described. The small bronze statuette sat between them. Excitement formed a tight knot in his stomach. These things were his family heirlooms, he was sure of it. But proving it would be a different matter. He looked around hastily. His eyes were adjusting now and he realised that, as Bill had said, the salon was indeed full of treasures. A Louis XIV clock, a candlesnuffer, a small rosewood box inlaid with ivory, all beautiful, all valuable, none so totally unique as to be indisputably de Savigny property, unless of course the very fact that they were here collectively could be taken as proof.

And then he saw it, hanging on the wall in a position where what light there was made the colours glow like fire. The triptych. He crossed the room with long hurried strides and knew beyond doubt that this was the triptych which had once graced the walls of his family home. From the photographs his grandfather had shown him it was clearly recognisable – the scenes from the life of the Maid of Orleans had never, to his knowledge, been repeated. He gazed at it, mesmerised both by its beauty and by the sense of history it generated. His history – his family's history – a continuity of heritage passed from generation to generation. It was, for Guy, perhaps the most moving moment he had ever lived through, and also the most unexpected. He had been brought up with antiques through his mother's shop and none of them had ever affected him in this way. But then never before had he been brought face to face with something which had been owned, not just by his grandfather, but by his grandfather's grandfather.

'Oh, you're looking at my triptych!'

He had not heard Lilli come back into the room. He turned now and saw her standing in the doorway, a glass of lemonade in her hand. She had slipped on an oversized cotton shirt, and the effect was to make her look more vulnerable than ever.

'*Your* triptych?'

She laughed.

'That's what Daddy always called it. I've always loved it, you see, ever since I was a little girl.'

'It's beautiful. But then you have a lot of beautiful things here. Your father must be quite a collector.'

'Oh, I wouldn't call him a collector, exactly. At least, I've never known him to *collect*. These things have always been around – as long as I can remember. I think he must have brought them with him when he came here.'

'From Germany? But I thought you said his home was destroyed.'

'It was. But the treasures were probably stored for safekeeping when the bombing began. And I intend to go on taking very good care of them. After all, soon they may be all I have left.'

He looked at her quickly, and she gave a small nervous laugh.

'Enough of that. You've suffered enough of my neuroses for one day. Did you find the ice?'

'No, I don't want any, thank you.'

But he did want his brandy. Oh God, did he want his brandy! Guy sipped it gratefully, knowing that to treat very fine, very old de Savigny cognac as medicinal was close to heresy, and not caring one jot.

'Your father . . . ?' he said questioningly.

'He's resting. I just looked in on him and he is asleep.'

'Ah.' So he wasn't going to get to see Otto today. 'Thanks for the drink, anyway.'

'Thanks for saving my life. I was very stupid. I'm sorry.' She looked small and utterly adorable standing there in her oversized shirt, clasping her glass of freshly made lemonade between both hands.

Guy's stomach lurched unexpectedly, but he hardened his heart.

'Perhaps you'd let me buy *you* a drink sometime?' he said, half expecting her to refuse.

Instead she nodded.

'That would be nice. I'd like that.'

'Tonight?' he suggested.

'No, not tonight. Quite honestly I don't think I'd feel up to it. Tomorrow, perhaps?'

'Fine. There's a bar on the other side of the island . . .'

'Johnny Shovelnose's.'

'Yes. Perhaps it's not quite your style, but . . .'

'Johnny Shovelnose's is fine. I love it – though Daddy would have a fit if he knew I was there. Look, don't bother to pick me up, I'll call for you. Your house is on the way, isn't it?'

'Yes, but . . .'

'If I get totally tiddly you can see me home again. Will that satisfy your male pride?'

He shook his head, laughing. Lilli seemed to have recovered all the easy charm he had noted when he flew her in; it was difficult now to realise that this girl and the tortured soul he had rescued from the sea were one and the same.

'I'll see you tomorrow evening then. Unless an unexpected job comes up. If it does I'll let you know.'

He finished his drink, set down the glass and turned towards the veranda. As he looked back into the room he was aware of two things: Lilli, looking so beautiful it tore at his heartstrings, and the triptych, glowing so that it seemed the flames of the fire were rising once again around the figure tied to the stake. The hair of that woman was fair and shorn short like a boy's, not long and dark, yet to Guy it seemed that for a moment, by some trick of the light, the features of the saint burning at the stake seemed to resemble Lilli's.

Guy sat on the veranda of his house, staring into the softly humming darkness, a glass at his elbow.

He had drunk a great deal since he had got back from the villa but he was completely sober and the alcohol had done nothing to lift the strange mood that had settled upon him.

He should feel elated, he told himself. He now had the proof he needed to bring von Rheinhardt to justice – if he lived long enough for that – and to reclaim the family's stolen inheritance. But it was not elation he was feeling, but confusion – a confusion of emotion unlike anything he had ever experienced before. And he knew that the reason was Lilli.

He wanted justice for his family – had wanted it with all his heart – and still felt he owed it to them to try and right some of the wrongs that had been perpetrated against them more than thirty years ago. But in carrying out his mission he would destroy Lilli. The knowledge tore at him, the vision of her beautiful yet tormented face rising before him in the darkness, the sound of her voice, low and husky: 'It wasn't that I wanted to die . . . I just didn't want to go on living', whispering at him with the crickets in the murmuring night.

He could do without these complications, he thought bad-temperedly. He must put them to one side and concentrate on doing what he had come here to do. But it wasn't that easy. Oh no, it wasn't that easy at all.

With a protracted sigh, Guy reached for the bottle and refilled his glass.

25

NEXT MORNING LILLI kept her promise to herself and went to visit Josie. Otto had had a rather larger dose of drugs than usual the previous evening and was still sleeping, so she had no need to explain where she was going. He would be less than pleased if he knew she was visiting her old friend, but she wanted to see her, and in any case, after what had happened yesterday she did not think it was a very good idea to be alone.

Lilli could still scarcely believe what she had done – or almost done. Never in all her life had she even contemplated suicide, and now the memory of the strange lethargic trance which had almost destroyed her was frightening as well as inexplicable. If it hadn't been for Guy she would be dead by now, simple and horrific as that, and she wasn't sure she would ever quite be able to trust herself again.

The shack where Josie lived with her husband Abel was close to the edge of the shanty town, and Lilli was glad of it. It was not the most pleasant place on the island, with its sprawling cluster of corrugated-iron shacks and the not entirely agreeable aroma of spices and sweat, imperfect sewage arrangements and people living in too-close proximity which hung over it. Once upon a time Lilli had made up her mind that one day she would see to it that living conditions for the locals were improved, now she realised with a sinking heart that that day would never come.

Josie had been doing her washing in a tin tub outside her shack and was spreading the clothes out to dry in the sun when she saw Lilli coming down the track. She dropped the laundry into the basket, scooped up Winston and ran to meet Lilli, a beaming smile lighting up her pretty round face.

'Lilli! Lilli! I can't believe it! You came home! Abel said he heard you was coming, but I thought he'd been on the rum again!'

The two girls hugged one another, little Winston squeezed tightly between them.

'Of course I came,' Lilli said. 'The minute I got your letter. I'm so glad you wrote to me, Josie.'

'Well, I thought you should know, though Abel didn't think I was doing right to interfere.'

'You weren't interfering. I'd never have forgiven myself if I'd been too late.'

'How is he?' Josie asked, her dark face growing serious.

'Very poorly indeed. But let's not talk about Daddy. Let's talk about you. Tell me all your news.'

'Well, as you can see I'm going to have another chile – very soon!' Josie patted the huge bulge beneath her brightly coloured dress, smiling again. 'It's due in just a couple of weeks, Lilli, and I hoped you might talk to your father about it for me. I want my baby to be born here, but you know the rules . . .'

Lilli grimaced. She knew the rules about locals having to leave Madrepora to give birth to prevent a new generation being able to claim that they were native Madreporans. It seemed to her to be very unfair and very unnecessary but she wasn't sure there was anything she could do about it.

'I don't think Daddy is up to making a decision about something like that, Josie,' she said apologetically. 'I'll try to talk to him about it if I get the chance but I can't promise anything. All I can suggest is that you try to produce early and take everybody unawares.'

Josie laughed.

'I'd certainly like to do that, Lilli – for my sake as well as the little one's. I'm real uncomfortable now. This is going to be one big chile.'

The two girls sat for a while in the sun chatting, but for the first time in her life Lilli felt a distance between them and it saddened her. They had been so close once; now their lives were running on quite different tracks. But for all that Josie had so little, Lilli envied her. What did money and possessions mean? They had brought her nothing but heartache and disillusion, whilst Josie was utterly content with the man she loved, an adorable child and another one on the way. Lilli ached inwardly, longing for the same unquestioning contentment.

'Now you,' Josie said when she had imparted all her news. 'Tell me about New York.'

'There's nothing much to tell.' How could she explain such a totally different world to a girl who had never left the islands? 'I go to work, I come home to my apartment . . .'

'Your own apartment?'

'Yes.'

'Imagine – an apartment all to yourself!' Josie said, impressed. 'No boyfriends?'

'No one important.'

Josie flicked away a fly which was bothering Winston.

'Have you seen Jorge?' she asked, not looking at Lilli.

'Yes.'

'And . . . ?'

'Josie, it's all over between Jorge and me. You know that.'

'Do I? I didn't think it would ever be over between you and Jorge,' Josie said truthfully.

Lilli hesitated.

'Do you . . . have you ever heard anything about Jorge's business interests?' she asked haltingly. 'What he does on Madrepora and when he goes to Florida, for instance?'

Josie shook her head.

'There must be talk in the village,' Lilli persisted.

Josie's face had gone shut in.

'I don't listen to talk, Lilli. It's safest to know nothing.'

And she refused to be drawn any further on the subject.

'Well, I'd better go home I suppose,' Lilli said at last. 'Daddy might be awake and wondering where I am. I'm going out tonight, too. To Johnny Shovelnose's bar.'

Josie's eyes grew round.

'Who you goin' there with?'

'The new pilot with the air taxi service. He's called Guy de Savigny.'

'You just be careful, Lilli. Jorge won't like you seeing someone else.'

'It's none of Jorge's business,' Lilli said tartly.

But as she walked away from the heat and smells of the shanty town she thought about it a little anxiously. Josie was right. If Jorge knew she was seeing someone else he *wouldn't* like it. But

359

she had to let him see he no longer had a hold over her. And in any case, she rather thought that terrifying as Jorge could be, Guy de Savigny was more than capable of looking after himself.

Johnny Shovelnose's bar stood on the very edge of the ocean within easy reach of both the marina and the hotel. The thatched roof covered the central bar area and provided shade for the tall stools which were drawn up to it on all four sides, whilst smaller thatched umbrellas covered tables that were dotted about the surrounding area right down to the beach itself.

The bar was perhaps the liveliest spot on Madrepora. Sometimes there was music – a small steel band or an itinerant guitarist, and always Johnny Shovelnose was on hand to regale customers with his extraordinary stories of the island. For those who wanted to eat as well as drink there was the famous roti – deep-fried rolls of dough pastry filled with cubes of chicken and potato and wrapped in greaseproof paper. In the jolly, informal atmosphere locals rubbed shoulders with visitors to the hotel and as the night wore on the music invariably grew louder and the conversation more raucous.

In the old days the bar had attracted Lilli as a flame attracts a moth. Sometimes, as a child, she had crept out of the house late at night and watched the frivolities from the cover of the palm trees which surrounded the bar area on the landward side; later she had been daring enough to go there with Josie and sit on one of the tall stools, hoping that no one would risk Otto's wrath by telling him about it. And of course she had been there with Jorge . . . Tonight, however, the bright oasis of light and music held little allure for her, setting her already taut nerves jangling.

'Have you been here before?' she asked Guy as he brought her drink – a long cool Pimms – over to the small table where she was waiting for him.

'Once or twice,' he admitted.

'On your own or with the other pilots?'

'What other pilots? There's only Manuel and he doesn't seem to want to be friendly.'

'No, he is a bit of a loner.'

She didn't add that he was also one of Jorge's henchmen. She did not want to think about Jorge, let alone talk about him, though knowing what she now did, she could not help wondering if Manuel was mixed up in some way with Jorge's illicit activities and if that was one of the reasons for his standoffishness. The drugs had to be ferried in and out and Jorge couldn't possibly do it all himself – if indeed he did any of it. He was the Mr Fix-it, she imagined; the actual drug-running would be done by yacht and plane, with someone else taking the risks such an operation would involve.

She glanced at Guy. Was it possible he was in the pay of the cartel? She didn't think so – it was almost unimaginable that he should be mixed up in something like that, but how could one tell? She would never have dreamed her father and Grandfather Vicente could be drug-traffickers either. How wrong could one be?

'How is your father today?' Guy asked, settling back in the white plastic chair and stretching his legs. He was, Lilli noted, wearing cotton chinos in a shade of pearly grey with a bright-yellow polo shirt, and she was glad he had not opted for white. White reminded her too sharply of Jorge.

'He was a little better this afternoon,' she said. 'It's difficult to tell with him, though. He's a fighter. He hides the way he's feeling if it's at all possible – he hates to be fussed over. But then, I expect you've noticed that.'

'I've never met your father.' He took a pull of his drink, then added conversationally: 'I wish I had. He's quite a character, I imagine.'

Lilli nodded.

'Yes, he is. He has always seemed to me to be the epitome of power and strength. It's very hard to see him the way he is now.'

'Doesn't he have any yearning to go home and see Germany again before he dies?'

'He's never said so. I told you – his home was destroyed in the war and his family killed, or so I imagine. None of them have ever come to visit and certainly he has never talked of having anyone left in Germany.' She broke off, biting her lip, and wondering for the first time just why she knew so little of her paternal roots.

'He must have fought in the war, I imagine,' Guy said.

'Oh yes, of course. He was a general.' She was aware suddenly

of the slight tautness of his features and felt a rush of embarrassment. 'He was an army man, though,' she added swiftly. 'Not SS
or Gestapo or anything like that.'

'A general. Ah! Where did he fight then? The Russian front? The
desert, with Rommel?'

'I think he was in France for most of the war.' A slight pink flush
was spreading from the area of her cheeks that had taken the brunt
of yesterday's sun. 'Not really fighting at all – more, well,
administration.'

'It's a small world then. Actually my family is French.' He said it
lightly, coversationally, but he was watching her closely.

'Of course – your name – I never thought!' she said, a little too
quickly, but he could see there was no recognition, simply that
edge of awkwardness that was only natural in a girl whose
German blood made her vulnerable to inescapable guilt for what
her countrymen had done. She was obviously totally in the dark
regarding the origin of her father's treasures.

'His family were in the coffee trade, I think you said?' he said,
changing tack.

'Yes. They were importers on a huge scale.' She was relieved to
be on a less emotive subject. 'Their coffee was drunk in the best
coffee houses in Vienna, Daddy always said.'

'Brandt. I don't know that I've ever heard of a firm of coffee
importers of that name.'

'Well you wouldn't have, would you?' Lilli said ingenuously.
'Since they were all dead and their business destroyed before you
were even born.'

'Not before I was born.' He smiled at her look of surprise. 'I
think I may be a little older than I look, Lilli. Not everyone is as
young as you, you know.'

She felt foolish suddenly. She had not really thought about
Guy's age, simply placed him on a par with herself as we often do
with those we feel comfortably at ease with. Now she looked at
him more closely, noticed the small crow's-feet at the corners of
his eyes and the way his hair was receding slightly at the temples.
He was, of course, older than she was – he had to be. But
compared with Jorge he looked very young.

Guy drained his glass. 'Another drink?'

'Oh, I don't know. I've still got some left . . .'

'Not a lot though. I'll get you another one. Don't look so worried. Pimms won't hurt you – if you want the same again, that is.'

'Yes, all right. Thank you.'

He took her glass and walked back towards the bar. She sat watching him, watching the easy sway of his shoulders, the lithe athletic way he moved, and liking what she saw. Strange how it was possible to feel so comfortable with someone one scarcely knew when some people inspired only awkwardness even if one had known them all one's life. And it had been like that from the very first, she realised, remembering the rapport they had struck up when he had flown her in. Guy de Savigny. She savoured the name and decided she liked that too. Strong, simple, yet far from ordinary. Very like the man himself.

'Well, well, Lilli! What are you doing here?'

Shocked, she jerked her head up, jarring a tendon in her neck as she did so, recognising those sultry dark tones instantly and feeling herself beginning to tremble.

Jorge.

He was standing at the edge of the circle of light, a white-clothed figure against the dark mass of the palm trees. He was smoking a cigar and though his voice sounded amused she could see he was scowling.

'I didn't realise you still frequented Johnny Shovelnose's dive,' he said, coming towards her and placing one hand carelessly on the back of her chair.

'I don't,' she said, 'but I think I have a perfect right to do so if I wish.'

His hand moved from her chair to her shoulder.

'Why are you fighting me, sweetheart?'

Her eyes blazed up into his.

'You know perfectly well why! It's over, Jorge. It has been over a very long time now.'

'But you came back.'

'Because my father is dying.' She shrugged her shoulder, attempting to dislodge his hand. 'Leave me alone, Jorge.'

But his fingers still bit into her flesh.

'Is that what you really want, Lilli? I don't think so.'

'It is what I want! And I should tell you, Jorge, I'm not here alone. I'm with someone.' To her relief she saw Guy making his way back towards the table. 'He's here now. Please go!'

'What's the rush? I'd rather like to meet the man who is taking my place . . . Wait a minute. It's my new pilot, isn't it?'

Guy had reached the table now, standing with the drinks still in his hand, looking somewhat sternly at the man whose hand lay so proprietorially on Lilli's shoulder.

'It *is* my new pilot,' Jorge drawled. He extended one hand, leaving the other on Lilli's shoulder. 'Perhaps I should introduce myself. Jorge Sanchez.'

Guy set the drinks down, completely in control of himself, and took the extended hand.

'Guy de Savigny. Yes, I'm the new pilot. I'm only surprised we haven't met before.'

'I'm a very busy man, de Savigny. I hope you are too, since it's my operation you are working for. But not too busy to entertain Lilli, I see.'

'I do have to have some time off,' Guy said easily. 'I met Lilli when I flew her in two days ago.'

'Ah, so you scarcely know her yet. I expect she enjoyed the flight. Lilli loves flying, don't you, darling? Amongst other things. We must get together sometime and I can tell you all Lilli's little likes and dislikes. It could save you some time, couldn't it? Such a help, knowing a lady's fetishes.'

'That is very kind of you but I don't think it will be necessary,' Guy said smoothly. 'Were you intending to join us? If so, perhaps I could get you a drink.' His tone was courteous yet pointed and Lilli grasped the opportunity it presented her.

'Jorge was just leaving, weren't you, Jorge?' She shrugged her shoulder again, more decisively, and this time Jorge released his hold on it.

'Unfortunately, yes. But I expect we shall meet again, de Savigny. When perhaps both of us will be ready for a longer conversation.'

He turned, walking towards the bar. Guy looked at Lilli. She was visibly shaken and when she lifted her glass, draining what was left in it in one quick swallow, he saw that her hand was trembling.

'So that was Jorge Sanchez,' he said reflectively. 'Not the most agreeable person I've had the pleasure of meeting.'

Lilli said nothing.

'Are you all right?' he asked. 'He upset you, didn't he?'

She nodded, not looking at him.

'Jorge always upsets me. Stupid of me, really, to let him.'

'Would you like to go home?'

'No!' She said it quickly, without thinking, the instinctive response wrenched from the turmoil within her. No, she didn't want to go home, to the oppressive atmosphere of a house where a man lay dying and she would have to make small talk with Ingrid. She didn't want to be alone with nothing to do but dwell again on the revelations that had turned what was left of her world upside down. And she did not want to leave this man who was somehow a buffer between her and Jorge, whose strength and niceness and lack of involvement with the whole bloody mess made her feel safer than she had felt at any time since she had returned to Madrepora. But neither did she want to remain here. The atmosphere of conviviality was stifling, adopting psychedelic proportions, blowing her mind and setting her nerves on edge. And besides, Jorge was still here, somewhere close by. She did not think he would bother her again tonight but she would be happier to put some distance between them.

'I don't want to go home, but could we . . . we couldn't go back to your house, I suppose?'

'Well, yes – if you like.'

She got up quickly, leaving her fresh Pimms untouched, and waiting while he tossed back his own drink. The tension was there in every line of her body, in the way she held her purse, tucked tightly beneath her arm, and in her hands folded around her waist as if to protect herself from some unseen evil. Instinctively he placed an arm around her shoulder and felt a small tremor run through her before she leaned against him, seeking support.

They walked, not talking, until they reached his house.

'God knows what sort of a mess it's in,' he said, opening the door. 'I'm not the world's tidiest.'

But the house was, of course, immaculate, thanks to the maid who had been in to wash up the dishes from the meal she had prepared for him earlier and had spared time to rearrange furniture, books and discarded clothing whilst she was about it. Guy switched on some lights, strategically placed table lamps which illuminated the soft darkness with a gentle glow, and opened the doors of an old-fashioned sideboard.

'I can't offer you Pimms, I'm afraid, but I do have rum or cognac.'

'No gin?'

'Sorry, no. Oh – wait a minute, I do have some champagne. It was in the fridge when I took over the house – left by the previous occupant, I imagine. But I don't suppose they'll be back for it.'

'Champagne would be very nice.'

He opened the bottle and set out two glasses.

'I suppose I might as well join you. I'm not a champagne man, really, but it would be a pity to let it go to waste.'

She sipped the champagne – a good one, whoever had left it there had expensive tastes – and began to feel some of the tension leaving her.

'I'm really sorry,' she said. 'You must think I'm a total neurotic.'

'No, I don't think that.'

'Oh come on, you must do! First yesterday, then tonight . . . I don't normally behave like this, honestly!'

'I'm sure you don't. You are under a lot of strain '

She nodded.

'I am, actually. Far more than you know. I feel very . . . alone.'

'You don't have to.'

She looked up quickly.

'Don't have to – what?'

'Feel alone. Oh, I know I'm more or less a stranger to you, but if I can be any help, well, you know where I am.'

'Oh Guy, thank you!' Whether it was the champagne chasing the Pimms on a virtually empty stomach, since she had been unable to eat properly for days, or whether it was the gentleness of his tone, Lilli could not be sure, but suddenly her eyes filled with tears.

Ashamed, she turned her head away. What the hell was the matter with her? She hardly ever cried and when she did it was in private. Now she seemed totally incapable of controlling any of her emotions any more.

She bent her head, fighting back those treacherous tears, and he came up behind her, taking her gently by the elbows and holding her so that the rigid line of her back rested against his chest. For a few moments she could think of nothing but the effort not to break down completely, then, slowly yet surely, she began to be aware of him. His hands felt good on her arms, his touch firm and supportive, and the tiny nerve endings around her shoulders and spine had begun to tingle slightly, as if responding to an unseen magnet.

The sundress she was wearing was halter-necked; above the ruched waist her back was bare. She felt the slightly rough cotton of his polo shirt rasp against her skin and instantly new areas became sensitised. She stood motionless, savouring the sensation and enjoying, without even realising it, the fact that briefly at least, something was obliterating all those chaotic and depressing thoughts from which she had begun to think there was no escape.

The nearness of him felt so good, a comfort and a promise magically combined. Lilli thought she would be content to stay there forever, losing herself and her problems in this swimmy, dreamlike trance that was not unlike, in some ways, the one she had experienced floating in the arms of the sea. But the sea had lulled her further and further inside herself, sapped not only her will but her very consciousness, whilst there was an urgent restlessness buried somewhere within this soporific state, a restlessness which was an almost unrecognised desire. Just when she thought she could stay there, unmoving, for ever, it was not enough for his touch to be confined to her upper arms and back. The rest of her body was aching to feel it too.

She turned towards him, the champagne glass still in her hand, and buried her face in his neck. It smelled faintly of soap and the salt which was carried on the sea breeze. His arms were around her now and a warmth began to suffuse her body, punctuated by the tiny sharp shivers emanating from the deepest parts of her and the tingling in her veins. She pressed against him, giving herself up to a barely recognised need, believing she sought only refuge yet responding to those deep primal urges he had stirred in her, and he held her close, allowing her to discover for herself that she wanted more, more . . . Only when she raised her head did she realise his mouth had been in her hair and suddenly she wanted to taste it. His face was close to hers, strong lines of cheek and chin almost touching her own. She tilted her head further back and saw his eyes, dark and burning with a reflection of her own desire, and then his lips were on hers, kissing her, gently at first, then more deeply and urgently.

After a moment he released her, looking down at her tenderly, taking a strand of her hair and twisting it back behind her ear, and a part of her cried out for him to kiss her again whilst another part stood back and marvelled at the warmth and excitement she was feeling. She had known desire before, with Jorge, but never this wonderful sense of . . . rightness.

She withdrew the glass of champagne she was still holding from behind his back and sipped it, the bubbles tickling where his mouth had touched.

'Well,' he said, 'if that's what champagne can do, perhaps I should drink it more often.'

His tone was light, teasing, but with underlying depths. She laughed, a little tremulously.

'Perhaps I should too.'

They were looking at one another as if seeing the other for the first time, and drinking in what they saw. Lilli thought that the world had come suddenly, miraculously, right – nothing mattered at that moment but being here with Guy.

And then the telephone began to ring.

The spell shattered. Lilli's first thought was for her father, that he was worse, had suffered some kind of crisis, and this must be Ingrid ringing to tell her to come home. It couldn't be, of course – how would Ingrid know she was here? But she couldn't dismiss the fear all the same and she stood frozen in an agony of waiting as Guy went to answer it, trying to hear what he was saying but learning nothing from the monosyllabic conversation.

After a few minutes he was back.

'Sorry about that. My timing never was very good.'

'Was it . . . ? It wasn't anything to do with me?'

He looked surprised.

'No. Just work, that's all. It was Manuel – a job I have to do tomorrow.'

'Oh.' An initial flood of relief, but the sharp anxiety of a few moments ago left echoes she could not ignore. Suddenly Lilli, who had not wanted to go home, could not wait to be there to satisfy herself that her father truly was all right and the telephone call had not been some sort of portent.

'I think perhaps I should go,' she said.

'Have your champagne first,' he suggested, 'otherwise anyone wanting to track down Lilli would be able to find her by following the trail of half-finished drinks.'

She laughed, but even to her own ears it sounded hollow. Her happy mood had gone, fragmented by the harsh urgency of the telephone bell.

'I'll see you home,' he said.

They walked with his arm about her shoulders and outside the villa he kissed her again, but this time her heart was not in it.

'I'm sorry, I really do have to make sure he's all right. It's the reason I'm here, after all.'

'You want me to come in with you?'

'No. No, I'll be all right now. Thank you for the evening.'

She laid her hand on his arm, her fingers caressing the bare skin for a moment, and then she was gone, running towards the veranda.

He looked after her and saw that someone was sitting there, propped up on a lounger, looking out over the gardens. A man. Otto? He heard Lilli's voice, speaking to him, heard the low answering growl, and strained his eyes in the dark. Then a light on the veranda went on and he saw him quite clearly for an instant – a drawn, once-handsome face beneath a head of cropped white hair, and a scar, livid still, running the length of his cheek.

In that moment Guy's last remaining doubts melted away and he knew he had found Otto von Rheinhardt. But the only coherent thought in his brain was to marvel that a man like that had managed to father a daughter like Lilli. And to wonder what the hell he was going to do about it.

'Daddy?' Lilli said. 'What are you doing still up? I thought you'd be in bed by now.'

'Why? Are you trying to get rid of me, Lilli?'

'You know I'm not!' She dropped to her knees beside his chair, taking his hand, wanting to share with him some of the warmth and happiness she had experienced earlier.

'Did you have a good time? Is the new pilot nice?' he asked.

'Yes, he is. Very nice.

'Good. That's all right then. I couldn't help worrying about you. I do worry about you, you know.'

'Yes, I know you do, but you mustn't. I'll be all right.'

'Yes, I think you will, Lilli. Just as long as you remember what I told you.'

'Hush, Daddy, I don't want to talk about it now.'

'Very well. Very well.'

They sat together in the murmuring dark, close once more. For tonight, at any rate, the threats within the shadows had receded and Lilli felt at peace.

26

THE GLOW WAS still with her when she woke. The morning sunshine was streaming in between the half-open shutters, bathing the room with bands of golden light, and for a moment Lilli could not remember why it was that she felt so happy. Then memory returned, the memory of closeness and safety and vibrant anticipation all rolled into one, and she lay hugging herself and imagining it was Guy's arms that held her, his hands on the curve of her hips through the clinging silk of her nightdress.

It was not possible, Lilli thought, that she should actually feel this way about someone other than Jorge. But she did, she did, and it was wonderful! In spite of everything the realisation was making her light-headed, light-hearted. Whatever she had to face, with Guy there she could do it. Jorge had been exorcised. He had no power over her any more, and Lilli soared on the wings of freedom.

When would she see Guy again? They had made no plans, but she would see him, she was quite certain of it. Not today perhaps –he had to work, didn't he? – and perhaps not tonight. But tomorrow, or the next day . . . Lilli felt the excitement sparkle inside her. She couldn't wait! She couldn't bear to wait! But she had to, and whilst she did she would spend every moment she could with her father, sharing some of this new-found happiness, and letting him know that nothing of what he had told her made the slightest difference to their relationship.

She did not approve, could never approve, of what he had done, but she did not blame him. He had had no choice, she was certain of that. It was all Uncle Fernando and Jorge's doing. They had forced him into it. And she would do all she could to ensure that the repercussions did not blight his last days on this earth.

Lilli pushed aside the sheets and the mosquito net and climbed out of bed, stretching luxuriously. For the first time since she had received Josie's letter she felt rested, relieved of a burden. She still had to come to terms with the imminent loss of her father, but this morning she felt strong enough even to deal with that.

Little did she know what a short respite had been granted to her.

Lilli had just showered and washed her hair when she heard some kind of commotion going on downstairs.

It was mid-morning; she had eaten a lazy breakfast and sat drinking coffee on the veranda before bothering to get dressed. Now, as she turned off the tap, she caught Ingrid's voice, raised in anger. She twisted a towel round her wet hair and opened the bathroom door.

'You're not welcome here! I thought we'd made that clear!'

Unusual enough to hear Ingrid so totally out of control; the words themselves made Lilli freeze. There was only one person Ingrid would order out of the house in that tone – Jorge.

Then, as she heard the low drawl of a man's voice replying, she knew she had been right. It was Jorge.

Lilli began to tremble with anger. How dare he come here again bothering her father – and her! Why couldn't he leave them alone? She grabbed her towelling robe from the hook on the door and pulled it on, fastening the tie tightly around her waist. She had no intention of skulking upstairs out of Jorge's way now – she had got him out of her system, hadn't she? She would go down and add her voice to Ingrid's, try to make Jorge see once and for all that she would not stand for him pestering her father when he was so ill.

She flounced down the stairs, barefooted. In the hall she met Ingrid, whose usually serene features were blanched with fury.

'Jorge is here. The bastard!'

'I know. I heard.'

'I told him to go but he insisted on talking to your father – alone. And Otto has gone along with it. He asked me to leave the room. He won't have you in there!' she warned as Lilli tried to pass her.

'Oh yes he will!' Lilli snapped. 'I'd like to see either of them try to stop me!'

She marched towards the room her father used as a study and threw open the door.

Otto was sitting in the huge leather secretary's chair behind his desk, the vastness of it emphasising his frail and wasted frame.

Jorge was sprawling elegantly against one of the bookcases which lined one wall from floor to ceiling, hands in the pockets of white linen jodphurs, booted ankles carelessly crossed.

'Ah Lilli!' he drawled. 'Do come in.'

The remark fuelled her anger. How dare he invite her into her own father's study as if it belonged to him! But before she could retaliate Jorge continued lazily: 'It was you I came to see, in any case.'

'Won't you understand, Jorge, that I don't want to see you!' she flared.

He shrugged.

'What you want or don't want, my dear, has nothing to do with it.'

'It has everything to do with it! We're through, Jorge. And now . . .'

'Lilli.' Otto's voice was weak, yet somehow it still retained echoes of authority. '*Liebchen*, please. This time you must listen to what he has to say.'

'I don't have to listen to anything! Daddy, you know . . .'

'Lilli, please! My God, when you lose your temper you are more like your mother than ever! But you must control yourself for a moment and hear Jorge out. What he has to say is important. It's about the man you were with last night – the new pilot.'

'Guy? What about him? Oh, you don't like me seeing someone else, I suppose, Jorge. Well, that's too bad. It really is none of your business who I see.'

'That's where you're wrong, Lilli.' Jorge drew a cigar from a packet in the breast pocket of his shirt and placed it between his lips, feeling for his lighter. 'I'm afraid it is very much my business when the man in question has very doubtful motives for making your acquaintance.'

'His motives are perfectly straightforward. He likes my company. Is that so hard to believe?'

The lighter flared; Jorge pulled on his cigar and the tip glowed, filling the room with sweet pungent smoke.

'Oh Lilli, always the innocent. Perhaps if you were to explain things to her, Otto, she might understand.'

'Understand what?'

'*Liebchen*, you remember I told you about the business here?' Otto's tone was tender and regretful. 'Our illicit business?'

'The drug-trafficking, you mean. What has that to do with Guy?'

Otto stretched out his hand to her. She ignored it and he sighed.

'Lilli – Jorge has reason to believe that this man may be an agent for the Drugs Enforcement Agency. He thinks he has come here to investigate our enterprises.'

Lilli's mouth dropped open.

'Guy? But that's ridiculous! What on earth makes you think that?'

'He has been acting very suspiciously,' Jorge said. He was smiling but it was not a pleasant smile. 'He has been asking too many questions about things which don't concern him. He was seen poking about near our laboratories, spying on a truck which was unloading a shipment. And now, judging by what I saw last night, he is trying to worm his way into your confidence. Any one of those things is enough to make me wonder about him, taken all together I think they paint a pretty damning picture.'

'I don't believe it. I won't believe it! You're jealous, Jorge. You don't like me seeing someone else and this is your way of trying to stop me. Well, it won't work!'

'Lilli, you must listen!' Otto said urgently, struggling to pull himself into a more upright position. 'What Jorge is saying makes sense. We know nothing at all about this man. He was taken on by Fabio on the recommendation of the former pilot, but for all we know he could have been working for the DEA too. They are beginning to be worried about the stuff that is getting into the USA – Jorge will tell you that they have been sniffing around trading companies like the one he runs in Miami. It's possible they have traced it back here through his connection with the island and put in an agent to get hard evidence.'

Lilli tossed her head defiantly.

'And you really expect me to be upset about that? When I've seen the harm drugs can do? I'm sorry, Daddy, but I can't condone what's been going on here. I don't want to see you upset, but as for the rest of them . . .' She threw Jorge a look of pure hatred. 'If your nasty little empire falls to pieces, Jorge, it's no more than you deserve.'

'That, my dear, is a very ill-advised attitude.' Jorge was still smiling but the muscles of his face seemed to have turned to alabaster and his eyes, behind the curling cigar smoke, were cold and hard. 'I should warn you, I think, to reconsider the stance you are taking on this – unless of course you want to end up like your mother.'

Lilli's chin jerked up.

'What has my mother to do with this?'

Jorge shrugged.

'You don't know? Perhaps you father should enlighten you. But I don't want to go into that just now. Suffice it to say I would like to be assured of your support in this matter and leave it at that. Oh – and please don't mention to your friend the pilot that I have my eye on him. I don't want him to be warned off just yet. And for you to give him any hint of this would be most unwise, both in your interests and those of your father.' He leaned forward, stubbing out his half-smoked cigar in the crystal ashtray on Otto's desk. 'I'll go now. But please think over what I have said and try to look at it sensibly.'

He turned for the door but as he passed Lilli he coolly and deliberately placed a hand on the nape of her neck and bent to kiss her. Cheeks flaming, she tried to pull away and he laughed.

'Oh Lilli, Lilli, you are so young and beautiful. What a terrible waste it would be if anything should happen to you!'

Then he was gone, calling a goodbye to Ingrid in a sick parody of a friendly social visit.

As the door closed after him Lilli looked at her father. He had slumped in his chair again and the beaten look of him, which had been inflicted not only by the disease that was ravaging him but also by the humiliation of his fierce pride, tore at her heart. She could kill Jorge for doing this to him! But however painful, there were questions that had to be answered.

'What did Jorge mean, Daddy?' she asked.

Otto raised a now-frail hand, plucking at his lips with fingers grown skeletal and nails neatly manicured but a fraction too long.

'He was warning you to be careful in what you say to this pilot fellow – and probably asking you, in a roundabout way, to report back to him with any suspicions of your own.'

'No,' Lilli said, 'I'm not talking about that. What did he mean about Mama? You told me that she killed herself because of Jorge. That was bad enough, for goodness' sake, but since I've been back there have been several mentions of Mama's death and the implication that I don't know the whole truth about it. Don't you think it's time I did?'

Otto sighed deeply.

'I hoped you would never need to know the whole truth. I didn't know it myself until quite recently – since I became ill, in fact, and Jorge came back from Miami to take over again. It's a terrible thing, Lilli, and I wanted to keep it from you if I could, but I think you are right. The time for secrecy is over. Your mother didn't kill herself. She was murdered.'

Lilli froze. A band of steel seemed to be tightening around her chest, making breathing difficult.

'But you said she shot herself!'

'She was shot, yes, but it wasn't suicide as we thought. She died because she had become a threat to Jorge.'

'You mean – Jorge killed her?'

'Not personally. That isn't Jorge's way. But he put a contract on her – hired someone to do the job for him. As you know, he and your mother were having an affair, but he was beginning to tire of her. She was no longer as young and beautiful as she had been and Jorge only likes women who are young and beautiful. Then she became pregnant and tried to press him into going away with her. He refused – told her to get rid of the baby. He wanted no more to do with her. She became desperate and tried to blackmail him into doing what she wanted, threatened to expose the cartel to the authorities. In doing so she signed her own death warrant.'

'Oh my God!' Lilli whispered.

'He couldn't risk her doing what she was threatening, you see. He made sure he was safely out of the way in Miami and the man he had paid to do the job came to the island, shot your mother and arranged things so that it looked like suicide. Then he slipped away again, back to whatever cesspool he had come from.' He paused, his eyes brilliant in his wasted face. 'Now do you understand, my darling, why I am so afraid for you? You have the same fire, the same disregard for danger, that she had. I don't want you to die as she died.'

Lilli shook her head from side to side. 'No – no! I can't believe it! It isn't true!'

'You must believe it. Please, *liebling*, you must. You heard what

Jorge said – he was threatening you too. He's a dangerous man, Lilli – I've always known that but until a few months ago I didn't realise just how dangerous. Perhaps he is a little crazy too. I don't know. But I do know that he will stop at nothing to protect his empire here. Stand in his way and he will crush you are surely as he crushed my lovely Magdalene.'

Lilli wrapped her arms around herself, rocking in an agony of revulsion. The realisation that she had made love with her own mother's murderer was so horrendous she did not know how to bear it.

'Lilli . . . please . . .' Otto murmured in distress. 'Don't take it like this, *liebchen*. It all happened a long time ago.'

'No, no . . . it didn't,' Lilli sobbed. 'I loved him, Daddy. I loved him and all the time he . . .' She broke off, burying her face in her hands for long minutes. When she raised it again her cheeks were wet with tears. 'Why did you have to get mixed up with him, Daddy? Didn't you realise how evil he was?'

'I told you, Lilli, I didn't know he had had your mother killed.'

'But you knew she had died because of him. And you knew about the drugs. Why did you stay here? Why didn't you go home?'

'I couldn't do that.'

'Why not? The war was long over.'

'I couldn't. Let's just leave it at that. And in any case, I had you to think of. I wanted you to have everything, my darling – a comfortable home, a good education, money to buy pretty clothes . . . you were – you are! – the most important thing in the world to me.'

'Oh Daddy! Can't you see that if I'd known what was paying for all those things I wouldn't have wanted them? And if I'd known about Jorge . . .'

The sickness rose again in her throat. Otto stretched out a hand to her but she could not take it. In that moment it seemed to her that he, too, was tainted. She saw the pain in his eyes yet still drew away, into herself, not wanting to hurt him, yet unable, for the moment, to understand or forgive.

'I have to be alone for a little while, Daddy.'

'Lilli, please . . .'

'You should be somewhere more comfortable. I'll get Basil.' Her voice, curiously controlled, sounded to her own ears to be coming from a long way off.

Ignoring the plea in his haunted blue eyes she left the room.

For what seemed like hours Lilli stood at her window, looking out over the sun-soaked gardens which seemed to her to be edged with the blackness which filled her.

If only she could get away, leave the island now, this minute, and fly back to New York! She might have felt in exile there, but at least life had some sort of normality and reason, at least she could bury herself in her work and begin to rebuild her life. In New York everything that surrounded her had been gained through her own efforts and she was a person in her own right, not the daughter and granddaughter of drug-traffickers, whose mother had been murdered by her lover. But even as the thought crossed her mind she knew she could not leave just yet. In spite of everything Otto was still her father and she still loved him. Whilst she could not even begin to condone what he had done, nothing could alter that fact. And she believed him when he said he had cared for nothing but her. The bond between them was too strong to be denied. She couldn't leave him now, when the end was so close.

Lilli shivered. Somehow she must find the strength to go back downstairs and tell him that she understood. It wasn't true – she did not understand, and she knew it would be a long while, if ever, before she did. But time was a luxury that was not on her side. If she delayed it might be too late. Her father might die thinking she despised him and if that happened Lilli knew she would never forgive herself.

A light aircraft droned overhead. Lilli saw it, a silver speck in the blue, catching the sunlight, and suddenly she was thinking not of her father but of Guy and remembering the things Jorge had said about him.

In all that had followed, Jorge's denouncement of Guy as an agent of the Drugs Enforcement Agency had been driven from her mind. Now, suddenly, it was there once more and with a sick heart Lilli realised that she believed what Jorge had said. The evidence was all too damning – and not only that evidence which Jorge had outlined. Lilli found herself remembering all too clearly Guy's questions to her – about her father and her mother, about the island itself – and the tiny sharp edge that had been there in his eyes when he had asked them.

Yes, dammit, she believed Jorge – she didn't want to, but she did – and the realisation was yet another betrayal. She had liked Guy so much and she had trusted him. He had seemed to her to be a rock to which she could cling in the shifting sands of her world. But it had been an illusion. What she had seen as strength had been steely determination to do a job, his seeming concern for her and the pretence that he found her attractive had been nothing but a means to an end. Guy had used her and she, fool that she was, had fallen for it.

How dare he! she thought, anger flashing through the haze of wretchedness. Yet somehow it was no surprise that he should. In the last days she had learned that nothing was as it seemed, no one was quite the person she thought them. Why should Guy be any different?

When he left the villa Jorge Sanchez went straight to his office and telephoned his brother Fabio in Venezuela.

'I'm not sure, but I think we may have trouble here. You know the new pilot you took on? I think he may work for the DEA.'

'Holy shit!'

'Exactly. How the hell could you have been so careless, Fabio? I warned you the authorities had been sniffing around the office in Miami.'

'I thought you said you'd bought them off!' Fabio blustered.

'Yeah, sure, I thought I had. It's not difficult, God knows, the greedy pigs will close their eyes to anything if you make it worth their while. But once in a while you come up against one who can't be bought – or who takes your money and double-crosses you. You've got to be ready for it, Fabio. I should have thought you'd been in this game long enough to know that. But you're still a stupid jerk, aren't you? You still foul up every damn thing you touch.'

There was a slight pause, then Fabio said sourly: 'Can't you buy him off too?'

'Why the hell should I? It's time someone was taught a lesson here. I shall have him dealt with. I just wanted you to know.'

'Dealt with? A hit man?'

'I haven't decided yet. But in his line of business it shouldn't present too many difficulties.'

Fabio laughed, a high-pitched whinny.

'True. Well, I'll start watching the obituaries.'

'Do that.'

Jorge replaced the receiver, running his hand over the beginnings of stubble on his chin and thinking about the new pilot.

Bastard! Coming here to undermine the operation, and thinking he could get away with it! And seducing Lilli into the bargain. If he hadn't done that Jorge might well have offered him money to buy his silence. As it was . . .

Jorge smiled unpleasantly.

As it was, the bastard was going to get more than he bargained for. And Jorge was going to enjoy every minute of it.

Guy put the Twin Otter down on the runway at Hewanorra International safely but with something less than his usual perfect touch, and realised that his mind was far from being completely on what he was doing. He taxied to the apron, locked up the aircraft and went into the airport building to complete the formalities, resentful of the fact that simply doing his job was preventing him from giving proper thought to the problems that were worrying away at the back of his mind. Only when he had dealt with the necessary documentation and got himself a cup of coffee could he allow them back to the surface, and when he did he felt much as he had felt as a novice pilot caught in thick and unexpected low cloud.

What the hell was he going to do?

His plan, when he had come to Madrepora, had been straight-forward and clear-cut. Find out for certain if Otto Brandt was in reality Otto von Rheinhardt, recover the family heirlooms and bring the war criminal to justice. But somewhere along the line his priorities had changed. And the reason for that was Lilli.

He had known instinctively from the moment he had met her that she was going to cause him problems, but he'd thought he could handle it. She might be beautiful, she might appear sweet-natured and pleasant company, but she was Otto's daughter, and as such she couldn't escape the legacy of what he had done any more than she could avoid carrying his genes in her body. It was unfortunate for her, but there it was. He couldn't let sympathy for an apparent innocent stand in the way of the justice he intended to secure for his family.

But last night he had held her in his arms and everything had changed. The cold desire for revenge had been replaced by feelings so powerful that no amount of determination could conquer them. He had wanted her physically, more than he could ever remember wanting any woman, but it was more than that. When he'd seen Jorge Sanchez standing beside her with his hand on her shoulder he had wanted to hit him, hard, right in the middle of his handsome debauched face. When he had realised how upset Lilli was he had wanted to kill him. And it had come to him in a flash that what he intended to do would hurt Lilli far more than anything that arrogant South American bastard had done.

I can't put her through all that, he had thought, sitting late into the night with a glass of his favourite whisky at his elbow and one eye on the clock – 'Eight hours between bottle and throttle' was the rule pilots lived by. I can't destroy all her illusions that way. What good would it do? Otto would be unlikely to live to face trial and the heirlooms were just inanimate objects. Whatever their intrinsic value, whatever their sentimental worth, they counted for nothing compared with the feelings of another human being, especially one who meant as much to him as Lilli. But it wasn't easy, all the same, to give up on something which had become an obsession. And if he did give up, what then? Should he stay in Madrepora, continue to do the job he had taken for such ulterior motives and see how things developed with Lilli? It was what his heart was urging him to do but he couldn't see that that could have a satisfactory outcome either. How could they ever have a close and loving relationship when so many secrets lay between them, secrets that would destroy her if she learned about them? He couldn't bring himself to tell her, but he couldn't see how he could ever be truly close to her if he did not. The dilemma was real and insoluble. Guy could not see any way out and it was tearing him apart.

And of course in all probability Lilli would return to New York when her father died. If she did the affair would end before it had properly begun and Guy would be able to put it all behind him and get on with his life.

That, he thought ruefully, would be the best solution for all concerned. And he realised that, best solution or not, it offered him no comfort whatsoever.

As soon as he was back on Madrepora Guy telephoned Lilli. None of his heart-searching had resolved anything. He simply wanted to hear her voice; see her again.

The telephone was answered by a voice he recognised as belonging to a local servant – the elderly woman who acted as housekeeeer, he imagined. But her tone, when he asked for Lilli, was forbidding.

'Who is this?'

'Guy de Savigny.'

'Oh.' She seemed to relent a little. 'I'll tell her.'

He waited, drumming his fingers on the desk. A few minutes later she was back.

'I'm sorry, Miss Lilli does not want to speak to you.'

He was startled, so totally taken aback that for a moment words deserted him, and before he could recover himself the telephone had been replaced, cutting off contact.

Guy stood holding the receiver, still too surprised to feel anything but disbelief.

Why didn't Lilli want to speak to him? Why had the servant been so rude – no excuses, no pretence that Lilli was unavailable even, nothing but this blunt rejection. After the warmth they had shared the previous evening it didn't make sense.

'Well,' Guy said aloud, 'I suppose that takes care of that!'

Tomorrow he would hand in his notice and when he had worked it out he would leave Madrepora, go back to England and look for a job there. Perhaps it was for the best.

But he knew, all the same, that he would not find it as easy to put Lilli out of his mind as she apparently had to cut him out of her life.

27

'DADDY, I'M GOING out for a little while,' Lilli said.

A guarded look shadowed Otto's eyes. He worried about Lilli almost all the time; couldn't bear to have her out of his sight, especially since the terrible scene the other night when he had told her the truth about her mother's death and thought that as a result he had lost her. She had come to see him later, putting her arms around him and promising that no matter what, she would always love him, but somehow her assurances had not totally comforted him. There was still a distance between them, a lack of understanding if not blame, and that alienation, however she might try to hide it, had frightened him badly. He loved Lilli so much; to lose her love and respect was the one nightmare left to him. Besides worrying that some harm might befall her, of course. That anxiety was still as real as ever, knowing as he did just how ruthless and dangerous Jorge could be.

'Where are you going, *liebchen*?' he asked now.

'Oh . . . just out.'

His mouth tightened.

'You are going to see that pilot, aren't you? His plane flew over a few minutes ago, didn't it? I saw you looking at it.'

Colour flooded Lilli's cheeks. She had not realised how transparent she was.

'It might not have been him. It's too dark to see properly.'

'But it sounded like the Twin Otter, and who else would it be flying into Madrepora at this time of night? Apart from Jorge, that is, and he is already here.'

'Well, yes,' Lilli admitted, cornered. 'I did think it was Guy's plane, and I thought that if I went down to the airstrip I could speak to him there.'

'And why do you want to speak to him?'

'Oh – I just want to, that's all.'

She could not explain to him the way she felt. For two days she had mooned about the villa, trying to hide her misery and trying to tell herself that if Guy was a DEA agent who had used her to further his investigations he really was not worth wasting a moment's sleep over. But it hadn't worked. She still felt as wretched as ever. Then, slowly, insidiously, she had found herself beginning to doubt what she had been told. The denial was born of her natural resilience, a refusal to believe, deep down, that the very special magic and the feelings of comfort and safety which she had experienced with Guy had existed only in her imagination.

'Jorge is evil,' she said now, voicing at least one of the arguments she had put to herself during those days of heart-searching. 'He'd say anything if he thought it suited his purpose. I just don't want to condemn Guy without a hearing, that's all.'

'I wish you wouldn't go. Jorge wouldn't like it.'

'Why should Jorge know? There won't be anyone at the airstrip but Guy.' She dropped a kiss on his forehead. 'I promise I won't be long. And don't worry!'

He sighed, shaking his head. She was wilful and stubborn – Magdalene all over again.

'Be careful, *liebchen*.'

'I will.'

Then she was gone, and it seemed that some of the brightness and warmth from the room had gone with her.

He felt tired and old suddenly, sitting there alone in the shadows. Ingrid had gone to bed early, pleading a headache, and he had no company to come between him and his thoughts.

Not that company had done much to stop him thinking these last few days. When the pain was not so bad that it wiped everything else from his mind, he had become very introspective. He thought of Lilli and what would become of her when he was gone; he thought of Vicente and Fernando and Jorge and the business they had run between them which had enabled him to amass a wealth such as he had never dreamed of; he thought of the women he had loved – Magdalene, who had never really been his, though she had married him and borne his beloved child, and Ingrid, whose devotion to him had survived even his rejection of her. But most of all he thought of days long past when he had been a general in an occupied country, fighting a war for his Führer, and those times seemed almost more real to him than any of his other memories.

Why this should be he could not imagine, he only knew it was so. The château where he had spent so much of his time was clear in his memory; he had only to close his eyes to see it again – the sunlight on the old stones, the tall cypress trees swaying gently, the hillsides where the vines grew in neat rows for all the world as if they too were an army of soldiers. The people were real to him, too – the old Baron, the tutor who was not what he seemed, the daughter-in-law of the house and her child . . . what was his name . . . Guy? Guy! What a coincidence that that name should occur in his life again now, the name of the man Lilli was so transparently in love with. What had become of them? he wondered. Oh, he knew what had become of the subversives who had tried to work against him. They were long since dead – he'd seen to that – and he had not a single moment's regret for what he had done. War was war – he had never either given or received mercy. They couldn't expect that – and for the most part they had not deserved it. God alone knew, there had been those amongst their number ready to betray their own, the son of the old Baron among them, though afterwards he had had a change of heart and paid the price.

Otto's mind wandered on, remembering what had happened after the showdown that night, almost thirty years ago, when information he had received from the Baron's son – Charles, wasn't it? – had enabled him to catch the band of Resistance workers red-handed. That night had been one of the greatest successes of his career. But then had come the unfortunate incident with the attempt on the life of his old friend, Heydrich, who had taken over a cottage in the area for his recreation. Otto had been furious to think that such a thing could be attempted right under his nose. He had taken hostages and had them shot by way of example to the rest of the community of what they could expect if they did not toe the line, and for some reason that fool Charles had insisted that his life should be taken in place of one of the hostages. Otto had argued with him but to no avail. The man was determined to die – driven crazy by guilt over his betrayal of his own wife, no doubt. In the end Otto had lost patience and snapped at him: 'Very well, if you want, that's what you shall have.'

He had watched the executions in the village square and felt nothing but anger. Any regret was confined to his disappointment that these people did not have the sense to know when they were beaten and accept Nazi rule with good grace.

But things had changed from that day on. He was no longer welcomed at the château, and his exclusion had hurt and infuriated him. He had thought the Baron and his elder son, at least, understood his position and sympathised with it. Now he was treated like a leper, and he hated them for it.

He hated them even more, of course, when the war began to swing the way of the Allies. But he had had his revenge. When he had discovered that the younger son, Christian, was secretly working against him he had no hesitation in signing his death warrant, and he had evicted the family from the château and taken it for his headquarters. It had been a good feeling, presiding over the table where once he had been a guest, sleeping in the bed which had belonged to the head of the house for generations. But even that had not lasted and when he had finally been forced to accept that defeat of the Fatherland was inevitable he had begun to make his plans. All the treasures of the château which were manageable enough to transport he had had packed and shipped, sending them ahead to the safekeeping of the man he knew would offer him refuge, his old friend Vicente Cordoba in South America. When he had finally fled into exile he had found them waiting for him.

He glanced at them now, gracing the room in which he lay dying – the candlesticks, the little bronze of Ceres, the triptych. Over the years he had enjoyed them, both for their aesthetic beauty and for the satisfaction which came from knowing that he had, in his own way, won that particular battle. The Baron and his family might have had their home and their country returned to them but the treasures were, and would remain, his. Soon now he would have no further use for them. But Lilli loved them. They would pass to her and to her children, indisputable proof that in this, at least, he, Otto von Rheinhardt, had triumphed.

Otto smiled, his lips curving with some satisfaction in his wasted face.

The telephone had begun to ring, the bell shrilling harshly in the guest house, but he scarcely heard it. Patsy or Basil would answer it. He was too lost in his memories to even wonder who might be calling at this time of night.

'Otto — telephone for you!'

Otto came out of his reverie to see Ingrid standing in the doorway. She was wearing a dressing gown of heavy ivory satin and an expression of extreme displeasure.

'Ingrid — I thought you were in bed!' he said, rousing himself.

'I was. I don't know where Basil and Patsy are that they didn't hear it ringing. What do they think we pay them for?'

'They are outside, I expect, in the garden. Who is it on the telephone?'

'Jorge. I told him I wouldn't have him upsetting you but he was quite insistent he should speak to you. Told me in no uncertain terms that business is business where the two of you are concerned.'

'He's right, I suppose. Is he still hanging on?'

'I suppose so.'

'Then I'd better speak to him.' With an effort Otto levered himself up from his chair and Ingrid rushed to help him, lending her arm for support and placing his cane in his free hand so that he could help to balance his frail frame.

'Where is Basil? He should be here when you need him!'

'Oh stop fussing, woman!'

They made it to the study and Otto levered himself heavily into his chair, picking up the telephone receiver from the desk where it lay awaiting his attention.

'Hello?'

'Otto — it's me — Jorge.'

'Yes, I know it is. What do you want?'

'I won't keep you long. I just wanted to let you know that I am having our DEA friend taken care of.'

'What do you mean?'

'Precisely what I say. I didn't want to take any chances with him — he's been asking too many questions. I have arranged to have him disposed of.'

'You mean — shot?'

'Not exactly. I felt like being inventive.' Jorge laughed. 'Our friend is going to be blown up by a letter bomb — or, to be more precise, a box-file bomb. I sent him on a job which should mean him returning to the airstrip when it is deserted, apart from him, of course. Whilst he has been gone my man has booby-trapped the box file he will be certain to open to complete the necessary documentation on his flight. It will possibly mean that our little office will be destroyed, of course, but it's time we had a better headquarters for Air Perpetua. It isn't good for our image, that shack, so we shall be killing two birds with one stone, as you might say. Our DEA man will do the demolition work for us the moment he opens that box file.'

For a moment Otto could not speak.

'I thought I should let you know in case you heard the explosion and wondered what was going on. And in any case I wanted to set your mind at rest about the agent. He won't be bothering us – or Lilli – any more.' Jorge was quite unable to keep the triumph out of his voice.

'And this is due to happen tonight?' Otto asked. His eyes were wild in his sunken face, his bony fingers held the receiver in a vice-like grip.

'That's right,' Jorge confirmed. 'Any time now. I think I heard the Twin Otter overhead a little while ago. Well, I'll let you get to your bed now, Otto. Sleep well.' And he was gone.

Otto sat for a moment transfixed with horror. When the pilot opened the box file the bomb would go off. But it wasn't only the pilot who would be there when the explosion ripped apart the shed housing Air Perpetua. Lilli was on her way to the airstrip to talk to him. She could be there, taking the full force of the explosion with him. She might escape it, of course. The pilot might have opened the box file and detonated the bomb before she arrived. But it hadn't happened yet, and it would have taken Lilli only ten minutes or so to reach the airstrip. How long was it since she had left? He didn't know . . . he couldn't be sure . . .

Beads of sweat stood out on Otto's face as he thought of what was almost certainly going to happen. Lilli was going to die just as her mother had died before her, because of the drug-smuggling, because of Jorge.

With the thought Otto suddenly found some of the strength he thought had gone forever. He slammed down the receiver and yanked open the drawer of his desk. At the back lay his service revolver. He pulled it out and struggled to his feet.

'Where is my car?' he demanded.

'Otto?' Ingrid was at his side, confused, concerned.

He pushed past her, ignoring her.

'Where are the keys?'

'Where they always are . . . Otto, what are you doing?'

Still he ignored her. He stumbled past her, the man who had scarcely walked unaided for weeks past, and out of the villa, grabbing his car keys from their hook as he went.

The car was on the drive outside. Though it was some time now since Otto had used it he had instructed Basil to drive it regularly to keep it in tune. He levered himself into the driver's seat and switched on the engine and headlights.

'Otto!' Ingrid screamed, almost beside herself. 'Where are you going?'

'Get out of the way!' He slammed the lever into drive and pressed his foot down hard on the accelerator. The car shot forward as a half-hysterical Ingrid threw herself clear and he turned the wheel in the direction of the airstrip. The headlamps cut a broad path of brightness through the dark; moths and mosquitos smashed into the windscreen in kamikaze flight. He felt no pain now, was aware of nothing but the all-encompassing sense of urgency. Get to Lilli. Save Lilli. Nothing else mattered.

Otto prayed to a God he had long since stopped believing in that he would be in time.

When Guy had landed on the tiny airstrip he taxied slowly towards the office buildings and commenced his shut-down checks. But tonight, instead of putting the baby to bed as quickly as possible, he found himself lingering over the procedure. Even when he was all through he made no move to get out of the aircraft, but sat holding the yoke between his hands, staring into the soft dark and wondering what the hell was the matter with him.

It wasn't just the unexpected turn of events over the last few days or the way his priorities had changed that was bemusing him, it was the change in himself that was throwing him into a state of utter confusion. He had always been such a decisive character before – the ability to think quickly and clearly, select a course of action and act upon it, was one of the things that made him a good pilot. Waffling, as he called it, annoyed him. It was a total waste of time. Yet here he was doing the very same thing himself. And for what reason? He had made up his mind to terminate his contract and return to England for all the reasons he had enumerated, and he knew, deep down, that it was the only course he could take. But he had put off actually doing anything about it and in odd moments, whenever his mind was not actively occupied with something else, he found himself going over it all again as if he was still clinging to the hope that this time he might come up with a different answer. It was stupid, he told himself, to go on tossing it round and round, stupid and unproductive. There wasn't another answer and he might as well accept it. But he couldn't. And he knew the reason was that he could not bear the thought of never seeing Lilli again.

To Guy, this in itself was deeply unsettling. He'd never felt this way about a woman before, and being at the mercy of his emotions was an experience he wasn't sure he cared for. Yet another reason to go – and go quickly, especially since she was refusing to speak to him for some reason he could not fathom. But still he delayed the moment of final decision – and despised himself for what he saw as his own weakness.

Guy sighed, reaching for his soft leather pilot bag, and began packing his equipment away in it. Then he tidied the cabin, locked the plane and tied it down, and walked back across to the little office building, somehow summoning up the energy to move at his usual brisk pace.

The office was in darkness. Guy turned on the lights, dumped his pilot bag on the desk and went to the shelf to fetch the box file in which the tech. log was kept. Funny – it wasn't there. Somebody must have moved it. Guy suppressed a feeling of irritation. He liked everything in his working life to be methodical and tidy and expected his colleagues to behave with the same professional efficiency. He cast his eye around the office and spotted the dark-grey box on a lower shelf, laid flat instead of stacked upright as it usually was, beside a pile of flight magazines.

He fetched it, set it on the desk and opened his flight bag, extracting the clipboard bearing the details he needed to make up the flight log. He sorted them, made a few quick calculations and reached for the box file, pulling it closer. As he did so a sound from behind him made him turn, and he saw a slim figure, dressed in floaty cream cheesecloth, in the doorway.

'Lilli!' he said, pleasure as well as surprise in his tone. 'What are you doing here?'

A slight flush of colour rose in her cheeks and she raised a hand to push her hair back behind her ear, a self-conscious gesture which betrayed her nervousness.

'I heard the plane go over. I guessed you'd be here.'

'A fair assumption.' He said it with throwaway sarcasm to cover the fact that he too felt self-conscious. Something else he was not used to! He guessed it was because she had occupied his thoughts so exclusively these last days; now, face to face with her, it was as though he was afraid she might realise it. 'I didn't think you wanted to speak to me though. That was the message I was given the other evening.'

Her colour deepened.

'I know. I'm sorry . . . I shouldn't have done that. That's really why I'm here now – to apologise.'

'That's all right. Apology accepted. You had some problem with your father, did you?'

'Not exactly. I guess I got things out of proportion again. Could we . . . do you think we could forget what happened and just . . . well, take up where we left off?'

He could see what it was costing her and he was melting inside. But he still couldn't understand why she seemed to behave so irrationally. She was upset about her father's terminal decline, obviously, but even so, surely there was no need to be quite so neurotic. And the fact that she had come to apologise for cutting him dead could make no difference to his decision to leave Madrepora. The basic problems were still unchanged. It simply meant he would have to tell her himself instead of leaving her to find out from someone else.

'I'm not sure that will be possible,' he said. 'I might not be here for much longer.'

Her face fell.

'What do you mean?'

'I'm probably going back to England.'

'When? Why?'

'I'm not sure when – I haven't actually told Manuel yet that I want to terminate my contract. As to why – I came here for a specific reason – something I had to do. Now it's done there's no reason for me to stay.'

The colour left her cheeks, then returned again to burn dully, not from embarrassment now but from shocked disbelief that not only had Jorge been right about him but also that he should admit it so freely.

'So it's true then,' she said dully. 'You did come here to spy on my father.'

It was Guy's turn to experience shock. How did she know what he had been doing?

'I haven't been spying on anybody,' he said evenly. 'There were some facts I wanted to establish, that's all.'

'And in order to establish them you made use of me!' Lilli's eyes were blazing with anger as well as unshed tears. 'How could you do that?'

'Lilli, I didn't . . .' But a thought had occurred to him. If Lilli knew about her father and about the treasures, then there was really no need for him to leave at all! Perhaps there was still something to be salvaged from this whole mess.

'Lilli, I promise I haven't used you,' he said.

'I trusted you, Guy. I really trusted you.' Her eyes were glittering. 'How could you do it?'

'I had my reasons and I'd like the chance to explain. Just let me finish up here and we'll go and have a drink and talk about it.'

'Is there anything to talk about?'

'I think so,' he said firmly, reaching for the box file. 'I just have to do the tech. log.'

His hand was on the box file, his eyes on Lilli, when they heard the sound of a car approaching at speed. Startled, he straightened. 'What the hell . . . ?'

The car came to a halt outside with a screech of brakes. And then the door of the hut burst open and Guy found himself face to face with the man he had chased halfway across the world but never now expected to meet.

Gaunt, white-faced, the unmistakable scar etched down his sweat-beaded cheek, he stood there, and though he held on to the door frame for support it seemed to Guy he still retained something of the powerful presence which had once been his.

Otto von Rheinhardt. The monster who had terrorised his family and stolen his inheritance. Otto von Rheinhardt. Lilli's father.

As he flung the door open with a strength born of desperation Otto's fevered brain registered two things.

The first was the box file which he knew contained Jorge's letter bomb, less than two feet away from his beloved Lilli and about to be opened.

The second was the man whose hand lay on the file, and the sight of him was somehow even more of a shock to Otto than the file itself.

In a brief timeless moment it seemed that the years had melted away. He was back in France, scene of the excursions to the past which he had been making mentally these last days, only this time he was looking into the face of the man whose death he had ordered.

Charles de Savigny.

A cry gurgled in his throat and in that second he wondered wildly if he was dead already and this was a ghost come to greet him. Then, as swiftly, the illusion passed and he was totally lucid once more. This was no ghost. It was the pilot Lilli had come to see. But not just any pilot. Guy. Guy de Savigny. The child of the château. Charles' son.

The knowledge was upon him in a flash, the truth illuminated in his fevered brain like a scene made clear suddenly by an explosion of forked lightning.

Guy de Savigny. Would he have recognised the name if he had heard it? He did not know and in any case it did not matter now. This was the man Jorge had denounced as an agent of the DEA. But he was not an agent of the DEA. The reason he was here had nothing whatever to do with drug-trafficking. He had come in search of Otto von Rheinhardt. And he had found him.

Otto gasped again, shock immobilising him momentarily. Then Lilli moved towards him, her lovely face the picture of bewilderment, and that other part of his brain, the part that knew about the bomb in the box file, activated again. The pilot's hand was on the box – one small move and both he and Lilli would be blown to pieces.

'Stay back, Lilli!' Otto ordered.

Collecting what was left of his wasted strength he grabbed the box file before the startled pilot could stop him.

Into the night he stumbled, holding the box in front of him like a sacred offering, forcing his weak legs to a run. He threw the box into the passenger seat of the car, threw himself in after it and slammed the gear lever into drive. The car shot forward and beads of sweat gleamed on Otto's forehead.

He had done it. He had saved Lilli.

But there was no way he could prevent her discovering the truth about him. Guy de Savigny would certainly tell her. Emptiness and despair yawned in Otto as he remembered the distance that had begun to open up between them when he had told her the truth about her mother. That was nothing to the way she would react when she knew the truth about him, particularly if she learned it from the man she was so obviously in love with, son of the man whose death he had ordered.

Lilli would never forgive him – or at least, not in the little time that was left to him. She would despise him – and he could not bear it. To have her look at him and see the accusation in her eyes, to sense her horror at what he had been, what he had done, to feel her revulsion . . . no, he couldn't bear it. Better that he should die . . .

Otto slowed the car, reaching for the box which lay on the seat beside him, and opened the lid.

The resultant explosion shattered the night and turned the car into a ball of flame.

'He died to save me,' Lilli said. She was pale, her eyes red-rimmed from crying, but Guy thought she looked quite beautiful. 'Oh, I know he should never have been mixed up with Uncle Fernando and Jorge and the others. I know drug-trafficking is terribly wrong, but I'm sure he had his reasons. And in the end he was a hero, wasn't he?'

She pressed her hand over her mouth, choking over the words.

'Damn Jorge,' Ingrid said. 'I hope he rots in hell!'

'He will certainly rot in prison,' Guy said.

Since the explosion had rocked the night, killing Otto and totally destroying the car, it had all come out. Lilli, in total shock, might have said nothing, but Ingrid was made of sterner stuff. She knew that Jorge had been responsible for the bomb and she was determined he would not get away with it. Denouncing him to the authorities might mean she would be arrested as an accessory to the drug-trafficking to which Madrepora had been home for years — Ingrid no longer cared. Her life had ended, she felt, with Otto's death, and that death had to be avenged.

Besides, she knew that as long as Jorge was free there might be more blood spilled. He would undoubtedly try again to kill the man he believed to be a DEA agent and she was not prepared to allow that. Enough was enough. A telephone call to the appropriate quarter had alerted the authorities; they had arrived on the island in force. Jorge had fled back to South America but his minions had all been arrested and Ingrid fervently hoped it would be only a matter of time before they caught up with Jorge too. It wouldn't be easy — the basis of the empire in Venezuela was a stronghold and too many of those in power were part of the enterprise. But they'd get him eventually, she was certain of it, and in any case, the chain was broken. Never again would the undersea passages on Madrepora's shores be used for their wicked illicit purpose.

'Guy — I'm so sorry I doubted you,' Lilli said. 'Honestly, so sorry. Do you really have to go?'

Guy looked at her and felt sick at heart. She knew now that he was not a DEA agent, but she did not know the truth about his mission here and Guy knew that he could never tell her. Lilli had suffered enough. She had taken on board the unpalatable facts about her father's life on Madrepora and somehow managed to make excuses for him. She had accepted his death, inevitable yet premature, with a courage that shone from her dark eyes along with her inconsolable grief. He could not do anything to destroy her last precious illusions. Loving her was both a prize and a penance. The price of it was his silence.

'Yes, Lilli, I have to go,' he said, steeling himself.

'Couldn't you stay . . . for me?'

I'm going for you, he wanted to say, and knew he could not.

'What will you do?' he asked, changing the subject.

'I don't know . . . go back to New York, I suppose. Life has to go on, doesn't it?' But her expression was bleak.

'I shall go home to Germany,' Ingrid said.

But neither of them was looking at her. Guy was absorbing the last minutes with Lilli, locking them in his heart for the lonely days he knew lay ahead, she was gazing at him, loving him, blaming herself for all that had happened, and still praying that even at this late stage he might relent and stay.

But why should he? He was a pilot – he had a job to do and there was no longer an Air Perpetua to employ him. Besides, who would stay with a girl whose father was a drug-trafficker, a girl who had mistrusted him, on an island where he had come so close to meeting a violent death at the hands of those who had shared her suspicions?

'At least it was a good way to die,' she said, returning to the subject of her father and comforting herself with the one good thing that had come out of all this. 'It was better, I suppose, than failing day by day. Daddy always said he wanted to die with his boots on. I don't know how he found the strength to do what he did, though.'

'Desperation lends people incredible strength,' Ingrid said. 'He was a hero, Lilli. Be proud of him.'

'Oh, I am – I am!'

And that, thought Guy, was the heart of the matter. There was really nothing else to be said.

28

KATHRYN DE SAVIGNY carried the tray of tea and biscuits into her tiny living room and looked at her son sitting sprawled in front of the roaring fire. There was something different about him, she thought, something she could not put her finger on, and wondering about it was mitigating the fierce relief she felt at seeing him back in England.

'So,' she said quietly, setting down the tray on a low table and pulling it up to her chair so that she could pour. 'I take it the German you went to investigate turned out not to be von Rheinhardt after all.'

For a moment Guy did not reply. He sat staring at the sparks showering up the chimney from the split log and again she felt a qualm of misgiving. What had he learned out there in the Caribbean that had wrought this change in him? Had he, after all, discovered the full truth of what had happened in occupied France after all these years? Then he turned, his eyes, dark and full of secrets, meeting hers.

'Oh, it was von Rheinhardt all right. Without a doubt the same man who was the cause of so much suffering. I've even seen the treasures – the family heirlooms. They are all there in his villa.'

Kathryn frowned.

'Really? Then why . . . ? What changed your mind about handing him over to the authorities?'

'He's dead.' Guy's voice was curiously flat. 'He was already dying when I got there – of cancer.'

'Oh.' Kathryn's eyes went very far away. In spite of herself, in spite of her hatred for von Rheinhardt, she was experiencing a sense of shock. It was difficult to picture the man she had known, strong and cruel, on his deathbed. Destruction was what von

Rheinhardt brought to others. Associating it with him required a total turnaround in conception.

'What about the treasures then?' she said. 'Didn't you try to claim them and bring them back with you?'

'No.'

'But why not? If they really were the family heirlooms. You were so set on getting them back, Guy.'

He sighed, sipped his tea and took a biscuit, twisting it between his fingers but making no attempt to bite into it. 'It's a very long story.'

'And I'm waiting to hear it.' She sat back, curling her feet beneath her. 'I've shut up the shop for the day. There's no hurry.'

'All right,' he said.

And he began to tell her.

Lilli was helping Ingrid sort through her father's possessions ready to vacate the villa and leave Madrepora for ever.

It was a heart-rending task – every item held memories for her and made her want to weep not only for her father but for the happy days of her lost childhood. But it had to be done. Ingrid was going home to Germany and Lilli knew that she would never again live in the villa that had been her home. There was nothing here for her now. Madrepora was to be sold – to a legitimate buyer this time, it was expected, who would develop the hotel and the marina and turn the island into a holiday paradise for those able to afford the luxuries it would be able to offer.

The last weeks had been traumatic ones, lightened only by the birth of Josie's baby – a little girl. With Otto dead and the Sanchez family holed up in Venezuela there had been no one to insist she should leave the island for the birth – in fact Lilli had insisted she should not. And so the child had become the first native-born Madreporan for almost twenty years – and once again Josie had asked Lilli to be godmother, an honour she was reluctant to accept in her present state of depression.

Now, as she helped Ingrid sort through the possessions accumulated by her father in his twenty-five years on Madrepora, the bleakness was there again. Was this all a lifetime amounted to in the end – a houseful of furniture and clothes and bric-à-brac? Valuable though some of it might be, at the same time it was a poor substitute for the wealth of a close-knit family and the love of those dear to you, who asked for nothing but that you should be yourself and give them love in return.

Lilli straightened up from packing her father's books into a crate to be despatched to a bookseller who would be able to separate the rare first editions from the run-of-the-mill volumes and dispose of them accordingly. Already she and Ingrid had sorted Otto's clothes, which would be shared out amongst the servants who wanted them, and arranged for a dealer to acquire the collection of rare stamps. Now the time was coming when they would have to decide between themselves who would have the various household effects. Otto's will had made provision for Ingrid but left the bulk of his estate to Lilli, but Lilli was determined that Ingrid should not be dispossessed. She had, after all, been Otto's wife, and she had been there at the end when he had needed her. Besides, Lilli did not particularly want any of the large items of furniture. She had no room for them in her little apartment in New York. Better that Ingrid should have them shipped to Germany to form the basis of the new home she would be making there.

No, as long as she had one or two personal mementos, and her treasures, Lilli did not very much mind letting Ingrid have everything else. Just as long as Ingrid knew that the treasures were hers and did not try to lay claim to any of them.

Lilli got up, going to the little bronze of Ceres and running her fingers over it lovingly as she had seen her father do so many times, then appraising each and every one of the treasures in turn. She must have them professionally packed, she decided. She couldn't risk them being damaged in transit. She lingered in front of the triptych, seemed to hear her father's voice across the years telling her that it was 'Lilli's triptych', and tears stung her eyes. She turned away, picking up one of the silver candlesticks and turning it idly in her hands whilst she regained control of her emotions. It was cold to the touch, solid and heavy, a perfect piece of silver, wrought in an elaborate design. She upended it, holding it to catch the light and looking for the hallmark. Then, to her surprise, she realised that there was another inscription of some kind engraved on the base.

She carried the candlestick to the window, looking at it more closely, and as she made out the words her forehead creased into a frown.

De Savigny.

I'm imagining things, Lilli thought. It would be too much of a coincidence for Guy's name to be on my candlestick! But no, there was no denying it. The engraving was minute but nevertheless clear.

De Savigny.

The salon door opened and Ingrid came in carrying a box of slides.

'I don't know what you want to do with these, Lilli. They are mostly photographs of you when you were a little girl . . .' She broke off, realising that Lilli was not paying her any attention. 'What's the matter? Are you all right?'

'Ingrid, where did Daddy get these candlesticks?' Lilli asked.

A faint flush coloured Ingrid's ivory cheeks.

'I don't know. He had them long before I married him. Why do you ask?'

'Didn't he ever say where they came from?' Lilli persisted, ignoring Ingrid's question. 'They've been here as long as I can remember, of course, but they couldn't be from his old home in Germany, could they? That was bombed in the war. And they don't look like something he would have picked up in South America. There's no Spanish influence there. In fact, none of the things look German or Spanish. They're more . . . Well, even my triptych is Joan of Arc, isn't it?'

'They are French,' Ingrid said. 'I thought you knew that.'

'I've never really thought about it until now.'

It was true, she never had, or at least, not in any depth. But quite suddenly she was thinking about it very hard indeed, and the thoughts she was having were unwelcome ones. French treasures had been in her father's home ever since he had come here to make a new life after the war. And where had he done most of his service? In France.

'He brought them with him, didn't he?' she said. 'He got them out of France.'

Ingrid's colour was higher now and she looked unusually agitated.

'You mustn't blame him too much, Lilli,' she said, her words tumbling over one another. 'He had to have something to help him start his new life. He had nothing – nothing! His home was destroyed, his family dead, the career that he had worked and lived for in ruins – is it any wonder he needed some things as an insurance for the future? And in any case, he loved them! He had wanted those treasures from the first moment he set eyes on them. He couldn't have borne to leave them behind. That family whose house he lived in had everything – everything.' Her voice was growing harsh now with the bitterness of defeat. 'They didn't have to flee their country and never see it again as he did. Their château was still standing, their lands returned to them . . .'

'You are telling me he stole these things from a French château,' Lilli said. Her voice was cold and level.

'They came from the château, yes. I wouldn't say he *stole* them.'

'Well I *would*!' A tremble crept into Lilli's voice now. 'If they belonged to the family of the château there's no other word to describe what he did. Unless they *gave* them to him, of course.'

'Don't be ridiculous, Lilli.'

'Or sold them to him? Did they do that, did they sell them to him for privileges of some kind under the occupation?'

She was grasping at straws and she knew it. More than anything she wanted Ingrid to say yes, they had come into his possession as a result of a bargain of some kind. But she did not. Far from making excuses, Ingrid seemed to want Lilli simply to accept the truth as she saw it. Perhaps she herself had felt some guilt over the years regarding the treasures which belonged elsewhere and by making Lilli face the truth was in some way sharing the burden of that guilt.

'The family weren't in the château when your father was there,' she said. 'They were living in a cottage on the estate.'

'Why?'

'Your father had to have a headquarters of some kind for his officers. They needed decent billets. They weren't the hoi polloi, you know.'

'So they turned out the family who lived there and then stole their belongings,' Lilli said. She was very cold.

'It was wartime. These things happen in time of war.'

'And should be put right afterwards,' Lilli said. Her heart felt like lead in her chest. Shock after shock, would they never end?

First her father's illness, then the horrible truth about her mother's death and the evil beneath the beauty on the island she loved, now her precious treasures which her father had given to her not hers at all, for they had not been his to give.

'These things must go back to their rightful owners,' she said firmly.

'You're upset, Lilli. Think what you are saying.'

'You think I could keep them now, knowing they were stolen? I shall see they are returned where they belong, each and every one of them.'

'And how will you do that?' Ingrid asked scornfully. 'For one thing you would have to admit that your father took them and bring shame on his memory. For another, how would you know where to return them? I can't remember where he was posted in the war – I only know it was somewhere in the middle of France – and I don't want to remember. You can't begin trying to find out now.'

'I don't need to do any investigating,' Lilli said. 'I know where they come from and to whom they belong.'

'How can you possibly know that?'

Lilli upended the candlestick again, looking at the inscription.

'You know the pilot who came here? The one we thought was investigating the drugs cartel? Well, he wasn't. He was investigating Daddy for quite another reason.'

Ingrid was staring at her blankly.

'Lilli, you have lost your reason. You don't know what you are saying.'

'Oh yes, I do know,' Lilli said. 'His name was Guy de Savigny. Take a look at this, Ingrid.'

She passed the candlestick to Ingrid. For a moment the older woman refused to take it, as if shrinking from contact with confirmation of what Lilli had told her. Then, reluctantly, her fingers closed over the smooth silver, she glanced quickly at the base, then set it down.

'You may be right.'

'I'm sure I am. Anything else would be too much of a coincidence. It's a very unusual name.'

'Yes, it is. So why didn't Otto recognise it . . . ?' She broke off. Perhaps he had never heard it. He had already been too ill to care

402

about such things when Guy was engaged, and certainly when she had booked the air taxi for Lilli she had told him only that the pilot had a French sounding name. But certainly he had reacted strangely to that nugget of information. He had, she remembered, become very distant, lost in a world of his own. At the time she had put it down to the effect of the drugs, now, suddenly, she found herself remembering that those glazed eyes had not only stared into space, but also strayed around each and every one of the treasures, and all the while that slightly puzzled frown had remained.

Could it be that some sixth sense had warned him that the man with the French sounding name was somehow connected with his past?

'But I still don't understand,' Ingrid said slowly. 'If this man is one of the same de Savignys, if he came here looking for your father and his family's treasures, why didn't he say something? Why did he go away again? Obviously, with your father dead he couldn't have brought him to justice, if that was his intention, but I'm surprised he didn't at least try to look for his family's heirlooms. If he had come here and seen them he would presumably have been able to identify them. Why didn't he do that?'

Lilli's hand flew to her mouth. Tiny cracks of light were beginning to illuminate her shock and confusion.

Guy had been here. He had seen the treasures – they had even talked about them – on the afternoon she had almost drowned. But he had said nothing. It could mean only one of two things. Either he had not recognised them – or he *had*, and chosen to say nothing. Why should he do that? Unless . . . Unless . . .

'I really think you should forget all about this, Lilli,' Ingrid was saying. 'Let sleeping dogs lie. Those things are yours now.'

'No,' Lilli said. 'They are not mine and they never have been. I am going to get in touch with Guy de Savigny and clear the matter up once and for all. Please don't try to stop me, Ingrid.'

Looking at her small, determined face, Ingrid realised with a sinking heart that further argument would be a waste of breath.

'So,' Kathryn said when at last Guy finished his story, 'you decided not to reclaim the family heirlooms because you felt sorry for von Rheinhardt's daughter.'

'I suppose you could put it like that.' Guy's tone was hard. Knowing he would never see Lilli again was a constant weight on his heart and the fact that he was still certain he had done the right thing did not help. All very well to tell himself they could never have built a real relationship on a foundation of secrets and lies, even to know with the thinking part of his brain that it was undoubtedly true, he still could not get her out of his mind. His senses all remembered her with a clarity that ached in the night and the hardest thing he had ever had to do was try to forget her and get on with his life.

'I couldn't hurt her any more,' he said. 'I honestly don't think she could have taken it.'

'What a wicked man he was!' Kathryn said. 'Not content with being responsible for God knows how many deaths in the war, he went on to peddle death and misery in the drugs trade. Well, at least he got his just desserts in the end. Except that it was too quick and easy for him. He should have suffered the way he made others suffer.'

'Believe me, he suffered,' Guy said. 'And in the end he saved my life, I hope you realise. The letter bomb in the box file was meant for me.'

Kathryn shuddered at the thought of what might have happened. But still she could not find it in her heart to be magnanimous to the man she hated.

'He didn't do it for you, though. He did it for the girl. If she hadn't been with you he'd have let you be blown up and not lost a moment's sleep over it. I'm sorry, Guy, but you can't expect me to forgive him just because he inadvertently saved your life. If he hadn't been mixed up with such evil and dangerous people it wouldn't have happened at all.'

'But it wasn't Lilli's fault,' Guy flared. 'She can't be blamed for what her father did and I don't want her to suffer any more for it. She adored him. It would have broken her heart to know that besides being a drug-trafficker he was also a butcher. I wanted to leave her some illusions. Surely you can understand that?'

Kathryn was silent for a moment, shocked by his vehemence. He was in love with the girl – that was what had effected the change in him. It was what she had wanted for him for so long – but why, of all the girls in the world, had he had to fall for Otto von Rheinhardt's daughter?

Revulsion filled her, a wash of emotion which owed nothing to logical thought, before, with an effort, she pushed it away.

Who was she to condemn anyone – much less Guy – for falling in love with the wrong person? Wasn't it exactly what she had done – and with dire consequences? At least Guy had had the sense to realise it could never work.

As for his reasons for not telling Lilli the truth about her father, they, too, seemed to echo the deceit she had practised on Guy. She had been desperate to spare him the knowledge of what his father had done too. And in that, at least, it seemed she had succeeded.

'Well at least there won't be a public trial,' she said quietly. 'At least we shall be able to leave the past where it belongs.'

He nodded and they sat in silence for a moment, each lost in their own thoughts.

'What will you do now?' she asked eventually.

He shrugged.

'Start looking for another job, I suppose. But I think I should go to France first and fill Grandpapa in on what has happened.'

'You won't tell him, though, that you know exactly where his family heirlooms are?'

'No,' he said, 'I shan't tell him that.' His face was shadowed and once again Kathryn thought how changed he was in some subtle way. 'I think I should be going, Mum. I'll come and see you again very soon.'

'Please,' she said. The change in him seemed to have extended to mending the cracks which had appeared in their relationship when she had told him about her wartime affair – he had not mentioned it again and neither would she.

'I'm glad things have turned out the way they have,' she said.

He raised an eyebrow. He looked, she thought, very sad.

'I'm glad you are pleased, anyway,' was all he said.

Spring had begun to bless Charente with its first gentle touch. The trees were still bare but the promise was there in the softening of the air and the new green spikes which would soon blossom into early flowers. But the dankness of winter still hung in the vast and lofty rooms of the château, making its presence felt as soon as the pale sun sank in the weak blue sky, and Guillaume still shrank into his heavy tweed suit and warmed himself whenever he could in front of the roaring fires which blazed in the cavernous fireplaces.

'Well, Guy, if I'd been you I think I would have stayed in the Caribbean until the weather was a bit warmer in this part of the world,' he said, stretching his long thin fingers out towards the blaze and rubbing them together to generate extra warmth. 'But then, I suppose at your age you don't feel the cold as I do, with my old bones.'

'No, Grandpapa, I don't suppose I do. Though it's still a bit of a shock to the system to be swimming in a warm sea one day and freezing in a European winter the next.'

'So – you've come to tell me how you got on, no doubt,' Guillaume said, changing the subject. 'Did you find the man your friend told you about? Was it von Rheinhardt?'

'Yes, Grandpapa, it was. But he's dead now.' Guy related the story as he had to Kathryn, but omitting any mention of Lilli or the treasures.

Guillaume, however, was not to be so easily satisfied.

'Did he have our heirlooms, that's what I want to know. I must say I was hoping you might bring them home with you. It would have been so good to see them again – and have them back here where they belong. Of course, it might not have been von Rheinhardt who stole them. There were others. But I always thought it was him.'

'Getting into the villa wasn't easy when he was so ill,' Guy said evasively. His grandfather's obvious longing to have his treasures back was making him feel guilty, but the decision was made now; there could be no going back on it.

'No, I suppose not. A great pity. Though he might not still have the treasures now even if he had them in the first place. He might have sold them years ago, before he made his fortune out of drug-trafficking. I imagine he needed a great deal of money to keep him in the lifestyle he was used to.'

Guy said nothing, and Guillaume went on: 'Talking of identification, there was something I thought of after you came here. I remembered some of the things were engraved with our name. Not all of them, of course. Many of them couldn't be. But some of the silver . . . the candlesticks, for instance . . . had our mark on them. Still, I suppose that's of no use now. Unless we could get in touch with the authorities who are investigating the island, of course,' he added, brightening. 'Perhaps they could get into the villa and see what's there.'

'I doubt they'd be interested,' Guy said swiftly. 'They are drugs enforcement people, not ordinary policemen.'

'Ah well.' Guillaume sighed deeply. 'It's probably all for the best. I never wanted von Rheinhardt to be brought to justice after all this time. Raking up the past would have done more harm than good. But then, I expect you realise that now that you know the full story.'

'Actually, Grandpapa, I think you all made far too much of it. Collaborating in the early days was a very understandable thing to do. I don't think anyone would blame you too much, especially in the light of what happened later,' Guy said.

A faintly puzzled look furrowed Guillaume's brow. He passed his fingers lightly across his bloodless lips.

'And what about the British agent? What do you think people would make of that? You do know about the British agent?'

Guy's face took on a shut-in look.

'The one my mother had an affair with, you mean? Well, yes, I can see that isn't something you, or she, would want to be public knowledge. And I have to admit I was pretty shocked that she could betray my father in that way. But I don't suppose it would exactly make world headline news.'

'Guy.' Guillaume hesitated. 'I'm not sure we are talking about the same thing. In fact, I am not at all sure your mother has told you the whole truth.'

Guy found himself remembering his own earlier suspicions concerning his mother's absence when he had been a child.

'You mean there's more? He wasn't killed and she ran off with him? Christ, no wonder she didn't tell me. She'd know how I'd feel about it, I imagine.'

'It wasn't like that,' Guillaume said slowly. 'I think I am going to have to fill you in on a few points, Guy. I am glad, of course, that you feel such loyalty to your father. But it must not be at the expense of your regard for your mother. No, I won't stand by and see that happen. We didn't always see eye to eye, Kathryn and I, but I admire her all the same for a number of reasons. Not least in the way she has brought you up and made your father an icon in your eyes, in spite of everything.'

'In spite of the fact that she loved another man?'

'No – in spite of what your father did to him.' Guillaume faced his grandson squarely, his mind made up that at last the full truth must be known. 'Your mother had an affair, yes. The rights and wrongs of that could be argued by anyone knowing the way things were at the time, but I am not going to go into that now. Suffice it to say I cannot find it in my heart to blame her too much. But your father blamed her all right. He blamed her so much he betrayed the British agent to the Germans – and very nearly got you, your mother and your Aunt Celestine killed into the bargain. He didn't know, of course, that you would be there that night. But it was unforgivable, what he did, all the same. He wanted to see Paul Curtis captured and killed and he betrayed him to von Rheinhardt. A man who was here risking his neck to help us, and your father let his personal jealousy dictate his actions.'

Guy had turned pale.

'Grandpapa – he couldn't!'

'He did. He admitted it to me himself. The guilt nearly killed him. It did kill him. When he could bear it no more he gave himself up to von Rheinhardt, demanding to take the place of one of the hostages. It was an act of heroism, yes, but he did it because he could no longer live with the knowledge of what he had done.'

Guy was silent, trying to assimilate what he had been told. At last he shook his head.

'But why didn't Mum tell me this? Why did she let me go on thinking . . . ?'

'She wanted you to respect him, Guy. And so you should. We are all human, God knows. None of us is perfect. Why should your father be any different? But it isn't right that you should canonise him and underestimate your mother. She is a remarkable woman.' He was silent for a moment, then he went on: 'You know, of course, that she worked for the Resistance herself, I presume?'

'While she was here – in France?'

'No, afterwards. She worked for a special branch of the SOE, gathering information, making contacts, escorting out those who wanted to go over. I imagine she was perfect for the job, an Englishwoman who could pass as native French. She never came back here, of course, but I gather she came in and out of France on different missions at least six times. And you never knew?'

'No.' So that was the reason she had been away so much when he had been a small child. The story about working for the Ministry in Scotland had been a blind. Had his grandmother, who had looked after him, known the truth? He doubted it.

But why had Kathryn kept her secret all these years? He shook his head, puzzled still, yet with the beginnings of a deep respect stirring in him. She had done this for his father. All this time he had been idolising his father as a hero of the Resistance when in reality he had been little better than von Rheinhardt. No, not true, but all the same . . .

'We are all human,' Guillaume had said. How true that was! Now he, like Lilli, had to make some adjustments to his view of those he loved. The irony was supreme.

'Yes, your mother is a remarkable woman,' Guillaume said again. 'Treasure her, Guy.'

'I do.' But now, knowing what he did, he realised that in the recent past, at least, he had been less than fair to her. He would put that right as soon as possible.

'Oh – I almost forgot,' Guillaume said suddenly. 'A letter came for you, Guy.'

'A letter for me? Here?' He was puzzled but still too preoccupied to give it much thought.

'Yes. With a Caribbean postmark. When we first saw it we thought it must be from you – until we saw that you were the addressee.'

'Strange. Who on earth in the Caribbean would write to me here? Air Perpetua have my home address.'

'Here you are.'

Guillaume crossed to his desk, leafed through the papers stacked there and produced an envelope. Guy took it, looking at it curiously. He did not recognise the writing and could not imagine who the letter could be from.

He took his grandfather's paperknife and slit open the envelope, drawing out the two sheets of paper inside and flicking over the first so as to see the signature at the end.

Then he froze, the blood clamouring at his temples.

Lilli.

'Excuse me, Grandpapa, I think I'd like to read this in private,' he said.

'Of course, Guy, of course.'

But he hardly heard his grandfather's reply. He was already on his way out of the study.

Lilli was standing on the veranda looking out into the soft darkness, drinking in the scents and sounds of the Caribbean night. In two days' time she would be leaving Madrepora for ever and she wanted this much at least to take with her and remember for the rest of her life.

Strange, she thought, how after all the traumatic events, it was only the happy times that were with her now. The villa was empty of all the familiar things which had made it her much-loved home, yet it seemed vibrant with the ghosts of the past, every room echoing with her childish laughter, every corner presenting her with memories. In the salon and the study her father's presence was still very real, not the tortured wraith of the past weeks but the powerful figure he had once been; out here on the veranda her mother's perfume seemed to mingle with the scents of the night. So real did she seem that Lilli felt that if she turned swiftly enough she would see her sitting there in the rattan chair, her scarlet-tipped fingers playing with the stem of a glass as she sipped at a fine champagne, bangles jangling around her slim wrist.

My happiest times were spent here, Lilli thought. Nothing that came afterwards can take that away.

The ache within her grew and spread and Lilli knew that leaving, never to return, would be the hardest thing she had ever done.

She had left before, of course, promising herself she would never come back. But there had been no finality to that leaving. She had known, deep down, all the time, that her father and her home would still be here waiting for her if she changed her mind. This time she had no such consolation. Someone other than her father would own Madrepora. Strangers would move into the villa, impressing their personalities upon the rooms along with their furniture and effects. The old and familiar would be gone forever as if it had never been.

Dear God, I can't bear it! Lilli thought. This place is a part of me and I am a part of it.

Within the villa the telephone began to ring, startlingly loud in the stillness of the night. Lilli frowned, wondering who could be calling. Ingrid, perhaps? She had left for Germany the previous morning. Perhaps she was phoning to say she had arrived home, but Lilli could not imagine it. They were not that close and they had said their goodbyes. Besides, it would be the middle of the night in Germany.

Lilli lifted the receiver, brushing her hair aside to hold it to her ear.

'Hello?'

The line was crackly and not very clear. But for all that the voice at the other end was excitingly familiar.

'Is that you, Lilli? It's Guy.'

The blood rushed to her cheeks, and she was suddenly tinglingly alive.

'Guy! I . . . You got my letter?'

'Yes. I was afraid you might already have left Madrepora. I tried to ring earlier but there was no reply.'

'I've been out.' She did not explain that she had been touring the island, revisiting old haunts, for the last time. 'Where are you?'

'France.'

'France! But it must be the middle of the night there!'

'It's very late, yes. I just kept trying your number. I wanted to speak to you.'

She laughed nervously.

'After what my letter told you I didn't think you'd ever want to speak to me again.'

'It wasn't a surprise to me, Lilli. I already knew. In fact . . . look, it's a long story. When are you due to leave?'

'The day after tomorrow. Why?'

'Don't go,' he said. 'I'm coming back.'

'You're . . . what?'

But the line had gone dead. Lilli stood holding the telephone, staring at it in disbelief. Guy – coming back! Why . . . why?

But in her heart she knew. And the happiness began inside her, the first half-fearful bubbles rising through the well of darkness and quickly exploding in a fountain of joy.

Guy was coming back. At that moment nothing else in the world mattered.

*

'You mean you knew all the time about Daddy and you said nothing,' Lilli said.

'I didn't want to hurt you any more. You'd had all you could take.'

'Oh Guy!' she said softly.

They were in the salon, bare now but for the crates containing the treasures packed and ready for shipping.

He had flown in earlier that day in an Islander which he had hired when he landed at the international airport, and the first awkwardness between them had soon melted, though they had not yet quite regained their previous easy rapport.

'I wanted to leave you something,' he went on. 'And I knew, after the day I came back here with you, just how much these things meant to you.'

'But they are your family's heirlooms!' she said. 'As soon as I realised that I knew I had to return them to you. They had been in your family for generations and that is where they belong – to be there for your children and your children's children.'

He did not speak the thought that was in his mind – the hope that perhaps even yet the treasures would not be lost to Lilli; that his children and grandchildren would be hers also. It was too soon for that. Yet somehow it was as if she shared his unspoken thoughts, for a faint pink colour came into her cheeks.

'I know all about inheritance, you see,' she said. 'I'm just trying to come to terms with leaving mine behind for ever. It's very hard – you don't know how hard. I don't think even I realised how much I loved Madrepora until I faced up to the fact that soon I'll never see it again. And that strangers will be living in our house and taking over all the haunts I thought of as mine.'

He sipped the drink she had made him, regarding her over the rim of the glass and loving every line of her face and body with an intensity he had never believed himself capable of.

'Maybe not strangers,' he said evenly.

She looked up at him, puzzled.

'But Madrepora is to be sold.'

'Yes, I know.' He hesitated, awkward again, not quite knowing how to tell her this. 'I think we may be going to put in an offer to buy it.'

'You . . . Madrepora . . . ?'

'Yes. My grandfather is a very wealthy man, and he rather likes the idea of a Caribbean hideaway. He's suffering at the mercy of a European winter and he thinks the sun would warm his old bones. Personally I doubt he'll ever leave Charente now, even for a holiday – it means every bit as much as Madrepora does to you, and probably more. But it's his way of justifying the idea.'

'I don't know what to say!'

'Madrepora could be a wonderful exclusive holiday island. The hotel could be developed for legitimate guests and a few luxury homes built. What's more, there is a shocking lack of air taxi facilities here now that Air Perpetua has gone – and I always fancied being my own boss.'

'You mean ... you'd come here and operate a charter company?'

'That's exactly what I mean. It would only be a small outfit, of course – I wouldn't want the paperwork to take up so much time that I wouldn't be able to fly myself. Though I suppose I could always employ someone to take care of that side of things. And we shall have to put in someone to run the hotel and perhaps develop the marina. I know nothing whatever about business and my grandfather is too old to want to be bothered with it either, though in his heyday I'm sure he could have organised it single-handed.'

'It's a wonderful idea, Guy!' Her eyes were shining. 'You've no idea what it would mean to me to know that Madrepora was in good hands. I'd love to think of you here.'

He raised his glass, sipped, looking at her speculatively.

'Actually, Lilli, I was rather hoping you might do more than just think of Madrepora. I was hoping perhaps I could persuade you to stay and help me develop it.'

She caught her breath. He could see he had taken her totally by surprise.

'You mean ... work for you?'

'Not for me – with me. We could make quite a team, you and I.' He did not add that he was thinking of more than simply business when he said it.

'Oh Guy, I don't know! I've got a job in New York ... an apartment ...'

His heart sank.

'Well, I suppose if you don't want to ...'

413

'I never said I didn't want to! I just said I don't know! Are you really sure? You are buying the island?'

'Sure as I can be.'

'Can I think about it?'

'Of course.'

She touched her fingers to her lips. They were speaking words that were quite different to what was in her heart. She didn't need time to think – she already knew what she would do. To be able to stay on Madrepora and help bring about all the changes that would transform it into the island paradise she had always believed it to be, and to be with Guy into the bargain? No, it wasn't a decision that needed much thought at all!

She glanced around the room; saw the boxes packed and ready for shipping.

'And the treasures?' she said. 'What will you do with them?'

'Well,' he said slowly, 'I think they should go back to France for the time being. It would mean a great deal to my grandfather to have them back in the château. But one day they will be mine. When they are, I'll think again. Whether to leave them in the family home or whether to bring them back here . . . it will depend on the cirumstances at the time.'

His eyes met hers and without a word being spoken she knew what he meant. She stretched out her hand to him.

'Whatever your decide, Guy. But they are still only objects, however beautiful and however valuable. There are other things that are worth far more.'

He took her hand.

'Yes, there are.'

And without another word being spoken she knew what he meant.

She had been through hell and now miraculously it was all coming right. She couldn't believe it yet, didn't dare believe it, yet knew in her heart that it was so.

The soft Caribbean moonlight slanted in through the slatted windows, illuminating the bare room and the two people with eyes only for one another.

This, Lilli knew, was truly the Eden Inheritance.

"I never said I didn't want to—" "And I don't know if for you really like? You are leaving the—"

"Sure as I can be."

"And I think about it."

"Of course."

[faded paragraph, largely illegible]

He glanced around the room... the boxes packed and ready for shipping.

"And if it means more the rain... what will you do with them?"

"Well, as usual right... I think they should go back to France for the time being. I've told... it mean a... it used to my grandfather, to hang them back in the chateau... but one day they will be mine. When they are, I'll think again... whether to leave them in the family home or whether to bring... back here... I will indeed."

[large faded blank section]

She had been through hell... no matter what, it was all starting right... she couldn't believe... yet, didn't care being upset. She know in her heart that it was...

The son Katharine... means... started in peace... the stored window-dressing... but then it... [illegible]...